LOOKING FOR LUCY

LOOKING FOR LUCY

Julie Houston

An Aria Book

This edition first published in the United Kingdom in 2019 by Aria, an imprint of Head of Zeus Ltd

Copyright © Julie Houston, 2016

A CIP catalogue record for this book is available from the British Library.

ISBN 9781789542271

Typeset by Silicon Chips

Aria
c/o Head of Zeus
First Floor East
5–8 Hardwick Street
London EC1R 4RG

www.ariafiction.com

Prologue

The continuous drone of a large, hysterical bluebottle repeatedly crashing against the glass of the closed window joined forces with the low moans of the girl, until she was unsure which sound was hers and which was that of the insect.

'Come on, love, there's a good girl, push.' The midwife, rotund and sweating slightly in the oppressive heat of the delivery room, urged the girl to work harder. This one was taking forever, she thought in exasperation and, glancing up at the delivery room clock, tutted irritably, wiping the film of sweat from her forehead with the back of her hand. She had a date in a couple of hours and still had to wash her hair and change the sheets on her bed. A frisson of excitement shot through her as she pictured herself naked except for the new scarlet basque she'd treated herself to in anticipation of just this event.

Impatient now, the midwife grabbed the girl's arms in an attempt to heave her up the bed and into a sitting position that might hasten the birth. The girl moaned again, louder this time as a contraction tightened her abdomen and pain coursed through her whole body. As the pain drained away once more, she turned to the midwife, her face flushed with the exertion of the labour.

'I can't do this anymore, Debbie…' The girl grasped the cool metal of the bedhead behind her, her own head thrashing from side to side on the plain white sweat-soaked pillow. 'There's no point, anyway. Is there? Is there…?'

'Now stop that,' the older woman snapped and then, feeling an unexpected wave of pity for the silly young thing, relented and spoke kindly. 'Come on, love, a few more pushes for me and we'll soon be home and dry.'

The girl began to shout, as much in frustration at the ignominy of the position she found herself in as from the tidal wave of pain and fear that was overwhelming her once more. She pressed her chin down onto her chest, grunting with pain as the child's head appeared between her legs. The midwife expertly manoeuvred the baby's crown, positioning the head until, with one final push, the child slithered wetly into her waiting hands.

'One down, one to go.' The midwife was jolly now, secure in the knowledge that she would be in time for her date. 'Come on, sweetie, don't give up now. Just a bit more hard work and you'll be through with all this.'

Fifteen minutes later, accompanied by a commotion from the floor above, the second baby was delivered. Cutting the cord deftly, the midwife wrapped it in a waiting towel and placed it next to its sibling in the double Perspex cot.

'Now don't start getting attached,' Debbie warned as the girl struggled to see the babies. 'Far better if you have nothing to do with them. Honestly, love, it's the only way.'

'But, Debbie, I can't let them go. They're mine. Can't you

say something? Tell them I'll look after them. Tell someone. Whoever it is…?'

'I know, I know,' Debbie soothed, glancing at the clock once more as she interrupted the girl's rising hysteria. 'But you know as well as I do, you have to let them go. Yes? Best to let them go.'

I

When Peter Broadbent asked me, as I served his treacle sponge with custard—freshly made tinned crème anglaise, none of your packet stuff—if I'd ever contemplated being a camp follower, I told him my hairdresser, Charles, was gay and that I'd followed him over the years from salon to salon and did that count? Peter had frowned slightly, his Adam's apple bulging as the hot syrup hit the roof of his mouth, before putting down his spoon and clearing his throat.

'I know you're really busy, Clementine, but I think you might enjoy a day out with me at Roddington Castle next Sunday. If I may quote General Douglas McArthur Thayer: "In my dreams I hear the crash of guns, the rattle of musketry and the strange mournful mutter of the battlefield…"'

'Right. OK.' I looked down at Peter, at the white paper napkin strategically placed across his beige V-neck sweater and wondered what the hell he was talking about. He'd been a Saturday lunchtime regular at The Black Swan in Midhope for the last six months or so, sometimes accompanied by one or more of his two children but more often, as now, on his own. He always liked to sit in the corner, away from the other diners, and would invariably opt for the full carvery roast that we served on Saturdays as well as Sundays, and always followed by the treacle sponge.

'You *do* have Sundays off, don't you?' Peter asked, still concentrating on his pudding rather than on me.

'Well, yes I do. When I took on this job it was on the proviso that I wouldn't have to work on Sundays. Saturdays are bad enough. I have a little girl, you see. I need to spend as much time as I can with her.'

Peter frowned again. 'That's a shame. So you can't come with me?'

'I don't know where you're wanting me to go with you,' I laughed. 'Some sort of poetry society do?'

'Poetry?' Peter looked momentarily shocked, as if I'd suggested pornography. 'Oh, I see what you mean. Because I quoted the General? No, no, Clementine. I'm inviting you to do battle.'

Battle? I did that on a daily basis: every time I looked at my bank statement and knew there wasn't enough to pay the bills that were lurking, a horrible shade of red, behind the clock on the mantelpiece; every time I had to leave Allegra with my mum while I tried to finish the Catering and Hospitality degree course at Midhope University; every time I tried, in vain, to get my life on track.

'To do battle? With what?'

'No, Clementine, not with what. With whom.'

I wanted to giggle. Hard enough to say that empty-mouthed, but with treacle sponge gumming up his molars and mouth, the earnest expression on his rather handsome face appeared comic. With a quick glance round to make sure Godzilla, the duty manager, wasn't watching, I slid into the chair opposite.

'So, *whom* then?'

Peter finished his pudding, leaned across the table towards me and whispered almost conspiratorially, 'Charles the First.'

Right.

'Hasn't he been, erm, *dead* these past few hundred years?' I whispered back. 'Or at least without his head?'

Peter smiled somewhat evilly. 'Absolutely, Clementine. We finally got him. Took a while but eventually his head rolled! You obviously know your history. That's why I think you'd really enjoy being a camp follower.'

'Sorry, Peter, I'm still not with you.'

'I'm a pikeman in the Marquess of Colchester's regiment.' Peter beamed proudly. When he smiled his whole face lit up and I thought for the second time in only a couple of minutes that he really did have a rather nice face. Solid, dependable. Not my type at all, really, I thought hastily. I'd never managed to find a solid, dependable type, which was probably why my life had teetered dangerously from one flaky, *undependable* type to the next. 'We have the Battle of Marston Moor near York next Sunday,' he went on. 'We always need a few more women around, and I would be honoured if you'd accompany me into battle.'

The penny began to drop. 'Ah, you're with one of those re-enactment thingies, are you?'

'Well, a bit more than "*with them*" Clementine. As I say, at the moment I'm a pikeman, but I'm hoping I will soon be promoted to musketeer.' Peter had the same look on his face as Allegra when Izzy, my best friend, took us both to London and Hamleys toyshop as a treat for my daughter's fourth birthday last year. 'You see,' he went on, 'musketeers are armed with a smooth bore matchlock musket—replicas of the actual weapons used in the 1600s—as well as a sword as a secondary weapon.'

'Right. Look, sorry, Peter, it's a wonderful offer for a girl but I'm not sure it's for me. And I'm really going to have to get a move on. They need help in the kitchen.'

Peter's face visibly fell as I looked across towards the kitchen door where I could hear the clattering of metal. If Boleslaw—pronounced *Bolly Slav* and not anything like the grated raw cabbage, carrot and salad cream concoction that was a major staple of every salad served in The Black Swan—the Polish chef, didn't feel he was being helped enough by the lesser mortals in the kitchen, he simply threw the pans across the stainless steel work surfaces and onto the floor until he caught their attention. If he was really that way out, he'd start lobbing potato at the serving staff and the last thing I wanted was an earful of creamed Smash.

As I stood, Peter took my hand. 'Will you think about it, Clementine?' His face flushed slightly. 'I've been thinking a lot about you lately…'

Really? Along with his smooth bore matchlock musket?

'… You must have realised that you're the main reason I come here every week?'

Me? Not the treacle sponge, then?

I needed to get back to the kitchen but he still held onto my hand. It was a nice hand really. Warm—but not sweaty—with short, clean nails. I can't bear men with dirty nails—or long ones. I suddenly remembered a pâtissier chef I used to work with who purposely kept the nails on his little fingers the lengths of talons in order that he could have a good root-around in his ears in between rolling out his pastry and kneading great lumps of sweet dough. I shuddered at the memory, forgetting, for the moment, that Peter still had a hold of my hand. 'So, *will* you think about it, Clementine?' Peter asked once more. 'I mean, if you can get someone to look after your little girl?'

'Look, I really must get back,' I said, glancing once more towards the kitchen door where an argument appeared to be revving up to a full-blown fight. 'I'll let you know next Saturday. OK?'

The remaining hours at The Black Swan seemed interminable and I longed to be home with Allegra, my four-year-old. Now that she'd started school full-time, it was much easier with regards to childcare issues while I was at university. Saturdays, however, were still a problem and I had to depend on my parents to look after her while I tried to earn a bit of money that would help towards the rent of the tiny terraced cottage Allegra and I shared not too far from the actual town centre. I was always broke by the end of the week and I worried constantly about the electricity bill, council tax and other horrors, real and imagined, that lay in wait, ready to jump out at me with an evil cackle like some mentally deranged jack-in-the-box, just as I thought I was in the clear.

At 6 p.m., feet aching and with a headache threatening, I hung up my Black Swan apron and black-feathered swan cap—a uniform that was supposed to give the waiting staff the appearance of graceful swans gliding from table to table but which, in reality, made the majority of us look like malevolent black crows or, worse, like some fat little Disney cartoon character having a bad hair day.

'Hey, Clem-en-teeena, 'owsabout yous and me goes outs for dat dreenk now? Dees over bastards theenk you theenk I'm bahneet yous end yous will says nos to a dreenk wit me.'

'Sorry, Boleslaw, not tonight,' I grinned. 'I have to get home to my little girl.'

'Yous don't know what yous missing,' he said seriously, thrusting his groin in my direction. 'I shows yous a good time, yes? We goes to dees leedle poleesh place I knows end I gives yous all I has? Yes?'

'Nos. I mean no.' I grinned again. 'Sorry, Boleslaw, another time maybe.'

I hurried towards the door, fastening my old mac against the rain that had started to fall and, glancing at my watch, hurried for my bus. My mother wouldn't be at all impressed that I was so late and I could already hear the note of impatience in her voice that would greet me as I let myself into my old childhood home in order to pick up a waiting Allegra.

'You're very late, dear,' my mother said, smiling in an attempt to soften the waspishness in her tone. 'I did say that the Gilberts were coming over for dinner, didn't I? I thought you might have remembered and made that bit more of an effort to get here on time? I've still got a mountain of stuff to do and your father isn't back from the golf club yet.'

'Sorry, but it couldn't be helped,' I said, returning the smile. 'We were really busy and the bus took forever.' Years of practice meant there was no way I was going to snap back at her, much as I would have liked to have. I needed her to help me with Allegra on the days that Izzy wasn't around to take her, and I just couldn't afford to fall out with her as I had so often fallen out with her over the years.

'Hello, my darling,' I said, bending to swing Allegra off the steps as she came racing down them towards me. 'Have you been a good girl for Granny?'

'She's always a good girl for me, aren't you, Allegra?' My mother visibly preened before adding, 'Do you not think it's about time she had a haircut, Clementine? It's getting terribly long and straggly. Rather common, in fact, if you don't mind me saying so.'

I did mind but, clamping my mouth shut on what I really wanted to say, I hurried Allegra into her navy duffle coat and headed for the door.

'Are we going to Auntie Izzy's today?' Allegra asked hopefully as she bounced on my bed the next morning.

I glanced at the little travelling clock on the bedside table, a present many years ago from one of my own aunts. 'Allegra, it's the middle of the night. Either go back to your own bed where you should be, or get in with me. But just go back to sleep.'

'The little hand is pointing to six which means it isn't the middle of the night. It's morning and I want to go to Auntie Izzy's.'

I raised my head from the pillow squinting at her in

surprise. Were four-year-olds able to tell the time? Or was I raising a little genius? I knew nothing at all about children apart from the fact that I had one. Unplanned for, certainly and, at the time, not overly wanted. Now I couldn't imagine my life without her. Having said that, it wasn't easy having a four-year-old when I had no money and no prospect of ever having any until I finished my degree at the end of the academic year and joined the queue of graduates hoping for hotel management work. My problem was that, being a mature student, I'd be that much older than the rest of the bright young things clawing their way to the top through unpaid internships and work experience and, whereas years ago I'd have applied for jobs anywhere, including abroad, now I had to think about Allegra. Not for the first time I wondered at the sanity of my embarking on a three-year degree course when Allegra had been just a baby. But at least the university crèche had been subsidised and I wouldn't have to pay back my student loan—which was racking up at an alarming rate—until I started earning some decent money. Which, when I woke in the middle of the night, heart pounding, I panicked might be never.

Pushing out of my mind all panicky thoughts about the future and how I was going to pay the council tax bill that had landed on my doormat yesterday morning, I took Allegra in my arms and snuggled her down under the covers with me.

'OK, here's the deal: we go back to sleep for an hour and then I might just—only might, mind you—take you round to Auntie Izzy's for lunch.' Which was a bit mean really as Izzy had already invited us round there. 'Deal?'

'Deal.' Allegra headbutted my stomach, closed both eyes

in a theatrical simulation of sleep and sighed heavily. 'Has an hour gone yet?'

We managed another fifteen minutes before Allegra's wriggling and squirming had me at the edge of the bed and I gave up the idea of any further sleep, swivelled my bare feet onto the statically shiny nylon carpet and drew back the curtains onto a dank, miserable, early March morning. Someone, or something, had pulled over my overfull dustbin—the dustbin men, according to a letter I'd received from the council yesterday were refusing to come down our street because of some incident with next-door's pit bull—and empty cans of beans, pasta packets and potato peelings were strategically strewn over my excuse for a garden. Oh shit. That was all I needed. Leaving Allegra still in her pyjamas and dressing gown in front of a DVD and the gas fire, I pulled my mac over my own pyjamas, grabbed my old boots and opened the back door.

'Mummy, it's cold,' Allegra whimpered from the depths of her chair. 'Close the door…'

'Just a minute, Allegra, won't be long.' Armed with rubber gloves and a black bin liner, I spent the next five minutes freezing my tush off, picking up two weeks' of uncollected rubbish while the pit bull hurled itself against the adjoining fence in fury at being unable to get at me. At least it was *my* rubbish: I wasn't picking up what didn't belong to me—although the slug that was hanging tenaciously to the soggy cereal packet, I hadn't been acquainted with previously. I bent to pick up a twisted plastic bag but dropped it in revulsion when I realised it was a condom. Used. At the same time, the broken sash of an upstairs window was perilously shoved up and the woman next door shouted, 'Shut the fuck up, you fucking animal,' before banging it down once more. I looked at the used condom, at the mean little patch of gravel where a dandelion leaf was optimistically reaching for what passed as light in that dark corner of the garden, and burst into tears.

2

'Are you OK?' Izzy stood back from the open front door as she ushered us in and gave Allegra a bear hug while simultaneously peering over her dark hair to look me in the face. 'Have you been crying?' she mouthed, when I shook my head but didn't actually say anything. 'Sid, Allegra's here…' she yelled over her shoulder …'you wanted to show her your new Lego thingy, didn't you? Take her down to the playroom and let her play with it with you.'

A mop of black curly hair appeared round the kitchen door and then the owner of the hair itself. 'Come on, Sid, frame yourself. Take Allegra with you and then Clem and I can have a coffee.'

It always took a few minutes for our respective offspring to shake off their shyness with each other if they hadn't seen each other for a week or two, and it had been a good three weeks since we'd been together.

'Actually, skip the coffee. You look as if you could do with a drink. What's up?' Izzy reached for a bottle of white wine in her huge American fridge-freezer and opened a bag of crisps with her teeth. 'Come on, Clem, knock that back and relax. You look as if you've got a bloody poker up your backside.'

It always made me smile when Izzy, a beautifully spoken, public-school-educated doctor came out with things like that. 'Do you talk to your patients like that when they come in to see you at the surgery?'

'I have been known to in the past,' she said, her face deadpan. 'That's the beauty of working for one's husband— one can get away with murder. Although,' she added, 'the sexual harassment can be a problem. That's better,' she said, as I laughed at the idea of Declan slipping through their adjoining surgery doors for an opportunistic between-patient goosing. 'Come on, what is it?'

'Don't be nice to me,' I sniffed, 'or I really will cry. I'm pre-menstrual, that's all. Everything seems worse than it really is.'

'What's everything? What's happened?'

Tears threatened and I took a big glug of the wine. 'It was the used condom that did it,' I spluttered as the wine went down the wrong way.

'Condom? And used?' Izzy stopped wiping the kitchen table where she'd spilled wine in her overenthusiastic filling of my glass. Her eyes gleamed. 'A man? At last? Four years since you had Allegra and no sex since then. And now a man? And you very sensibly used a condom?'

I laughed at her hopefully raised eyebrows. ''Fraid not. The condom was in my back garden. I picked it up this morning by mistake just as next door's pit bull nearly had me for breakfast.'

'Oh, nice. Who left it there?' Izzy visibly grimaced.

'One of the girls that makes her living round the back of my house, I guess. There's a little gang of them who seem to prefer being outside rather than taking their punters back home with them. I suppose by the time they've actually taken someone back to the flats on Emerald Street where a lot of them live, they can service twice as many and save themselves the money for the gas meter.'

'God, can you imagine anything more awful than having sex for money? Bad enough having sex with one's husband when one's not in the mood, but feigning passion on a cold, wet street with some sleazy punter with bad breath and week-old boxers must really be quite horrific.'

I was torn between thinking there must surely never be a time when one wouldn't want to have sex with the very gorgeous Declan, Izzy's husband, and wondering where Izzy got her information about the girls from the Emerald House flats.

'You seem to know a lot about the johns who pick up the girls,' I said.

Izzy laughed. 'The johns? God, that's a handle I've not heard for years. Do they still call their clients that? I only know as much as anyone *assumes* they know about the sex trade. And Emerald House is on my patch. Gosh—' here she laughed '—that makes me sound like a copper doesn't it—*on my patch*? Anyway, a couple of the girls come to see me when they need their methadone prescription or if they think they've picked up something a bit more worrying than Mr Smith from suburbia who's told his wife he's popping out for a quick one.'

'A quick one being a hand job as opposed to half a pint of Taylor's best?'

It was Izzy's turn to raise her eyebrows. 'You seem to know a bit about it yourself.'

'Only what I see from my backyard.' I smiled.

'Well, if it was up to me,' Izzy said, 'I would totally legalise prostitution. There'd be properly run brothels where the girls are warm, where they are helped with anything like drug addiction and where there are bouncers on the door and regular check-ups by in-house doctors.'

'But the problem with that is that people don't want brothels in their neighbourhood—the price of houses would plummet if an area was known for its great knocking-shop rather than the fabulous grammar school that everyone wants to get their kids into. I mean, look at you two, you moved here because of the schools. You wouldn't have looked at this house twice if there was a busy brothel next door.'

'Absolutely not, I agree. But brothels wouldn't be in the suburbs; they'd be in town with the nightclubs and open-all-hours bars. Just get me into government and it's one of the first things I'd do. In fact, it would form the basis of my maiden speech.' Izzy's eyes lit up with a crusader's fervour as she threw back the contents of her glass of wine and poured herself another.

'I actually think you're missing the point about prostitution. The expensive call girls have *never* been on the streets and I'm sure *they* have regular medical check-ups. No, most of the girls haven't the energy or inclination to organise themselves into a properly run whorehouse. What they want is a quick couple of quid to feed not only their drug habit but for a lot of them, their kids as well. And anyway, you organise legal brothels and I guarantee a lot of the punters will continue to cruise the streets looking to pick up girls. Organised sex in a warm room is too clinical for some men. They want the *illegal* thrill of picking up a dirty little whore, not the sanitised version in some warm room where a receptionist will charge them a fortune on their credit card.' I paused for breath when I realised Izzy was looking at me curiously.

'You *do* know a lot about it, don't you? It really is time you got out of that hellhole you call home and found somewhere decent. You need to think about Allegra.'

I sighed. 'Don't start, Izzy. Don't you think if I could afford more I'd be out of there?'

'But why down in that part of town, so near the centre? Surely there are little cottages you could find at the same rent in a more salubrious area. Maybe out into the countryside a bit?'

'It's very near to college and now Allegra's school. We can walk to both—saves bus fares.'

Izzy looked at me curiously. 'Are you that hard up? Really? Surely your mum and dad will help you out?'

'I wouldn't dream of asking,' I said shortly. 'You know what they're like.' Izzy had met my parents on only a couple of occasions and hadn't warmed to them at all.

Izzy frowned. 'But why are they like this? I don't mean their politics, although I *don't* understand anyone voting how you've said they vote. I mean about helping you and Allegra when you so obviously need it. Surely they can't be happy their only granddaughter is living down on Emerald Street?'

I hesitated. 'One day, Izzy, I'll sit you down with a bottle of wine and tell you it all.'

'Tell me now, Clem.' Izzy poured us both more wine and leaned forward eagerly. 'Come on, trust me, I'm a doctor. Ever since I met you, you've kept this part of yourself to yourself. I know everything about your life since meeting you at that playgroup, but very little before it.'

When I didn't say anything, she patted my hand encouragingly. 'Don't you trust me, Clem?'

I laughed. 'Oh, stop doing your doctor act on me. There's nothing to tell. I'm just a disappointment to my mum and dad. Haven't really turned out as they wanted me to. But then how many kids do?'

'Well, I did,' Izzy said, surprised. 'Went to gym club and pony club, was prefect at school, got all A's at GCSE and A level. Went up to Cambridge. Became a GP like my dad. Married Declan...'

'Are you boasting?'

'No, no not at all,' Izzy said seriously. 'Just trying to get over that I've been very lucky. But maybe that's why I want to get into politics. Maybe I'm filled with zeal to make life better for others.'

'You're too good to be true, you are. I'm not sure how you can side with the unemployed, the families with no money, the down-and-outs when you have no experience whatsoever outside your white, middle-class, educated, *Telegraph*-reading cocoon.'

'That's a bit unfair,' Izzy protested. 'And I read *The Guardian*.' She hesitated as if racking her brain to come up with something that might dispel the myth that she had it all and then went on, '*And* I've been in trouble this week because of what Sid took to Show and Tell... my life isn't all a bowl of cherries, you know.'

I laughed at Izzy's expression. 'Go on, what did he take that was so awful?'

Declan, coming in from where he'd been doing something gardener-ish with a hosepipe and overhearing the dreaded words 'Show and Tell', sniggered and grinned lasciviously at both of us before reaching for a bottled beer from the fridge.

'Well,' said Izzy, 'as you know, all schools have this *dreadful* weekly Show and Tell session, a mind-numbingly boring thirty-minute parade of—well, God, anything. I've got to the stage, having had three kids demanding something different to take every Friday morning, of dreading the very words "Show and Tell". Over the years they must have taken everything conceivable from the usual array of birthday presents to free plastic rubbish from McDonald's Happy Meals to plasticine models, lovingly constructed, but often resembling an oversized phallus rather than the intended space rocket.' Izzy paused for breath, caught Declan's eye and giggled. 'Anyway, we'd all overslept, I knew I had the usual huge Friday list of patients waiting for me—everyone trying to get their bunions and bad backs sorted for the weekend; it's always the same—and Sid was wittering on about Show and sodding Tell. I told him to take the McDonald's plastic yo-yo he'd got the week before—and that was what I assumed he'd taken.'

'And wasn't it?'

'Not quite.' Izzy grimaced, remembering. 'When I went to pick him up from school, Miss Walters, who must be as old as God—you know one of those infant school teachers who've done nothing but terrorise five-year-olds for the last forty years—handed me Sid's Show and Tell offering neatly wrapped in heavy duty brown paper and string. "I think this must be yours, Mrs Stanford," she said, without a hint of humour in her little shark eyes.' Izzy was in her stride now, enjoying my attention. 'I had no idea what it was until she handed it over and it began, all by itself, in its brown paper covering to vibrate... "Why didn't she like it, Mummy?"' Izzy mimicked a tearful Sid. '"It was all pink and rubbery and tickled my hand and looked like a rabbit".'

'Oh my God,' I laughed. 'How embarrassing.'

'I know, it's ridiculous, isn't it? I get men to slap their willies on my examining table, peer at people's piles and women's bits and pieces on a daily basis without hesitation, but, faced with Miss Walters looking at me as if I was some sort of sexual deviant, I was a red-faced gibbering wreck. Anyway, enough about me, Clem. I reckon it's time you went out on a date. You know, get back on your horse as it were.'

'Get back on my horse? You know I'm allergic to horses as well as being terrified of the damned great brutes.'

Izzy got up from the kitchen table and started assembling ingredients for Yorkshire pudding batter. 'Exactly,' she said, warming to her theme as she searched for a cookery book on her shelf. 'You're becoming allergic to men and frightened of them to boot. Oh shit, Clem, how do you make sodding Yorkshire puds?'

Izzy, a notoriously bad cook, was the first to admit to the handle. 'Come here, let me do it,' I said, pushing her out of the way.

'I can't invite you to lunch and then expect you to make it,' Izzy said, handing me the milk with obvious relief.

'You normally do,' I said, smiling and cracking eggs.

'Do I? Well maybe I do. The kids always cheer when I tell them you're coming over. I mean, you are such a brilliant cook.' Izzy took a good slurp from her glass of wine and relaxed. 'Why don't you open your own restaurant? We'd all come and eat there every night.'

'Hang on. I thought you wanted me to find a new man? Now you want me to open some restaurant into the bargain?'

'Oh yes, we were talking men, weren't we? Forget the restaurant, even though you *are* the most brilliant cook I know and people would flock to its doors. Let's find you a husband.'

'I thought you were an emancipated woman who reckons you don't need a husband to get along in life?' I said as Izzy started peeling carrots, taking off huge layers of skin with what appeared to be a blunt knife. 'And use a peeler,' I said, handing her one from the jar of utensils on the black granite, 'you're wasting half of them.'

'I *am* a strong, independent woman,' she said, 'but I also like being married to Declan.'

'Anyone would like being married to Declan,' I said, reaching for the hand whisk hanging from the *batterie de cuisine* above my head.

'Would they?' Izzy asked vaguely. 'Well yes, I suppose they would. Do you want the electric thingy for that?'

I shook my head. 'No, this is better, really.

'So, where were we? Right, a man for you. I'm going to

trawl through a list of all the single men that Declan and I know...'

'Actually,' I said, suddenly a bit cross that Izzy seemed to think I couldn't sort out a man for myself, 'I've got a date for next week.'

'Have you? Who?' Izzy stopped her massacring of a cauliflower and looked across the granite island at me.

Had I? Until this moment I hadn't given Peter Broadbent and his suggestion of a date for next Sunday another thought. 'A very nice man called Peter Broadbent. He comes into the restaurant every week; asked me to go and assassinate King Charles with him.'

'What?' Izzy looked up from her cauliflower, knife in hand.

'He's into one of these reconstruction things. Civil War, I suppose it must be. There's no way I'm going. I only said I had a date to shut you up.'

'Oh, but you must, Clem. You must go.' Izzy waved her knife in my direction, her greying dark hair bouncing as she enthused. 'You must help Cromwell against those rich, vain Cavaliers. They were the forerunners of the Tories, you know.'

'Right. Sorry, history's not my thing. Anyway Sunday is my day for Allegra.' I adjusted the temperature of Izzy's oven as blue smoke began to build up alarmingly inside. 'God, Izzy, are you trying to sacrifice this beef?'

'Never mind the sodding beef. Listen, we'll look after Allegra. We'd planned to go down to Alton Towers for Robbie's eleventh birthday—Allegra can come with us and you can go off with this very nice man and have your first date in years and trounce a few Cavaliers into the bargain.'

'I'd rather come to Alton Towers with you,' I protested. 'Anyway, there won't be room in the car for Allegra.'

'Oh yes there will. It's Declan's parents' birthday treat. We're taking two cars anyway, so just one more little one will fit in nicely. Sorry, no room for you, Clem. You'll have to go off on your date.'

Before I could protest further Emily, Izzy's fifteen-year-old bounced in. 'Thank goodness you're here, Clementine. We might get some decent food for once.' She poked suspiciously at the brownish contents of a Pyrex dish by the sink. 'What in God's name is this, Mum?'

'Trifle,' Izzy said dismissively. 'Once it's got some cream and cherries on it'll be fine.'

'You said that about that meringue thing you made last week. It wasn't.'

'Emily, I have far too much going on in my life to worry about puddings. We have more important things to think about at the moment. Clementine has a hot date next Sunday.'

'Oh, brilliant.' Emily grinned, helping herself to a handful of nuts as I insisted that I wasn't going on any date, hot or otherwise. 'What are you going to wear?' She looked me up and down critically. 'You can't go out with some man in those cords. I've got a great pair of jeans I don't wear anymore. You can borrow them if you like.'

'If they're so great, why don't you wear them anymore?' I didn't know whether to be pleased that Emily reckoned I could get into what must be her size eight jeans, or be offended that my own clothes didn't pass muster.

'I've had them a year and they're a bit out of date now. They'd be great for you though.'

'Hey, hang on. I'm not as old as your mother, you know. I'm young. I'm a student.'

Ellie didn't bat an eyelid. 'No, no, it's a compliment. I know you're nowhere near as old as Mum: God she's ancient. *You're* really pretty and slim. And Mum doesn't care about what she wears—she's only interested in reading and getting to be an MP. And can you persuade her to do something with her hair, Clem? Put some colour on it or something? It's embarrassing having a mother with grey hair.'

'God, the confidence and egotism of youth,' her mother exploded. 'Get back to your homework, girly, or at least go and lay the table.' Izzy turned to where I was now starting a béchamel Parmesan cheese sauce for the leeks that Declan had brought in earlier from the garden. 'Do I look old, Clem?' she sighed, running a hand through her hair. 'And do I mother you? I'm sorry if I do—I don't mean to.'

'Hang on,' I smiled, 'it's *me* making *your* Sunday lunch, not the other way round. And you're what, nearly forty? Ten years older than me? Hardly old enough to be my mother: my big sister more like. And if you do mother me a bit, I'm grateful, you know that.' I began to feel a bit tearful again and turned to the gas hob, giving a good beating to the flour I now spooned into the melting butter.

'I worry about you, Clementine. You hide so much and rarely drop your guard. I can't bear to think of you spending so much time alone down on Emerald Street. Why don't we look for somewhere round here for you?'

'You're mothering me again, Izzy. Allegra and I are fine.

She loves her school and it's dead easy for me to walk to college. Once my course finishes and I begin to earn some money, then of course I'll think again. At the moment I just can't afford anything different—you know that.'

'Fine, fine. I'll get off your case with regards to where you're living—but not about this date. I mean it, Clem. You need to get out and see life.'

I laughed. 'And being a camp follower on a muddy field somewhere with some history nerd I don't really know is seeing life?'

'Camp follower? Is that what they're called? Bloody hell, great stuff. Do it, Clem. Do it.'

I looked over my shoulder to the sitting area of the kitchen where Allegra and Sid had just come up from the playroom and were now intent on jumping off the back of the sofa onto Robbie, Izzy's elder son, who, despite being under attack calmly carried on reading, totally and wonderfully engrossed in the last of the Harry Potter novels. I took in the shabby chintz chair covers with their split piped edges, the excess books that were towering, Pisa-like, from the threadbare Persian rug and the slumbering tabby cat that slept on despite the shrieks and laughter from an overexcited Sid and Allegra. My eyes moved to the French windows and the huge garden beyond where Declan, one booted foot resting on a rusting wheelbarrow, was lighting up a crafty cigar.

And I wanted to cry. Cry with frustration and longing for a family such as this. The family I'd never really had, and which I'd give my all for Allegra and me to have.

3

'So, are we all set then, Clementine?' Peter Broadbent's beaming smile as I opened my front door didn't quite mask his obvious surprise—dismay even—at finding me down on Emerald Street. I'd given him my address the day before when he'd been seemingly overwhelmed with joy when I'd told him, if the offer was still open, I'd like to go with him to his re-enactment thingy.

'All set. My friend Izzy picked Allegra up ten minutes ago so ready when you are.' I felt ridiculously nervous: my first date in four years, letting Allegra go off without me, wondering what the hell I was letting myself in for. Izzy had hung around for a good five minutes hoping to catch a glimpse of 'the pikeman' as she'd dubbed him, until Declan had shouted for her to get a move on, that they'd hit the traffic on the M1 if they didn't get off that minute. I'd reluctantly fastened Allegra into the borrowed car seat, but she was off without a backward glance, eager to be part of Izzy's noisy, busy family once again. I'd felt quite bereft when they'd all gone, leaving me alone on my doorstep on this quiet Sunday morning. It was a beautiful morning, quite spring-like and, as a couple of daffodils nodded their heads optimistically at me from the bottom of the pebbled backyard, I'd berated myself for my lack of enthusiasm at being taken out for the day. It would be a laugh, I told myself; something to tell the other students about for once when, every Monday morning, they dissected every little event, every drink imbibed, every man slept with over the weekend.

'Car's down here,' Peter was saying over his shoulder as I locked my front door. 'I couldn't quite get it down this narrow street so thought it best to leave it up on the main road.' I understood his sentiments once we'd walked the few hundred yards to where his car, a Porsche Cayenne, stood haughtily like some grand dame, between the Khyber Tandoori and John's—*Ring For Attention*—Adult Books shop. It was huge, black and gleaming and, once Peter had opened the door for me and helped me up, the smell of new leather hit me head on.

I was relieved to see he was in mufti—jeans and a soft red cashmere sweater rather than the Roundhead outfit I'd been terrified he might have been wearing as I'd opened my front door to him. In fact, he really did look rather nice. Smelt nice too. As we left the town centre and headed for the motorway and York, I took a sneaky glance at his profile: pleasant clean-shaven jawline, fair, wavy hair just beginning to curl over his ears and, as he turned to me for a second, aware no doubt that I was giving him an appraising once-over, I saw that he had blue eyes. Nothing amazing, nothing to shout out about … but solid, dependable, pleasant.

'So where are your children today?' I asked. 'With your wife?' I assumed, because he was only ever with his two children and never with any sort of wife or partner, that he must be divorced or separated.

'They're with my wife—ex-wife I should say. Sophie, my eldest, is away at school and, even when she's here, is really of an age when she doesn't feel she has to be with her father every Sunday for the obligatory visit to the zoo or McDonald's.'

'Or The Black Swan?' I smiled, recalling the different permutations of one or sometimes both his children who, at different times, had accompanied him to eat at the pub.

'Well, I'm not the best of cooks,' he said ruefully, 'so when they are with me we do tend to eat out quite a lot.'

''And do they never come with you to this...' I was momentarily stumped for words, '... this history thingy?'

Peter winced slightly. 'History thingy? I can see I'm going to have to educate you, Clementine.'

Hmm, bit pompous, I thought, noticing for the first time the receding hairline and the rather hooked nose.

Peter smiled and patted my hand. Oh dear, condescending too.

'Well, in their time, both the children have accompanied me. Max, my eight-year-old still does when he's not playing football at the weekend, but Sophie is no longer interested.' He looked sad for a moment but then smiled. 'But it's always great when someone new wants to come along.'

I didn't like to tell him that my interest level was probably that of, or below, his daughter's: that I was only along for the ride and that I'd have been, at that very moment, screaming from the heights of some death-defying rollercoaster if Izzy hadn't banned me from going with them—'for your own good'—as she'd put it.

'What about your wife? Your ex, I mean?'

'Well yes, Vanessa is very much into it, particularly the mustering and skirmishes. We actually met at the Battle of Naseby.'

Right.

'And now?'

'Now, I'm afraid, she's batting for the other side.'

'Oh you poor thing.' I felt immediately sorry for this man. 'That must be so hard. Bad enough being left for another man, I guess, but another woman… Another *camp* follower, was it?'

'Another woman?' Peter frowned as he pulled out into the fast lane, his upmarket Porsche dominating the other vehicles on the road. 'No, she didn't leave me for another *woman*. Left me for a bastard *Cavalier*…'

Sod 'The Laughing Cavalier,' it was me on the verge of hysterics. I glanced across at Peter. There was no humour whatsoever on his face. 'Right,' I said with a straight face, 'I've got you now.'

'… Yes,' he said gloomily, totally unaware that I was biting the inside of my cheeks to stop the laughter that was threatening to erupt. 'Married Prince Rupert himself.'

Jesus, what was I getting into? We were just passing the York Designer Outlet and I had a sudden insane urge to ask him to pull up at the next junction and jump ship. Six hours trying on stuff in L. K. Bennett and Ralph Lauren—stuff I didn't have the money to buy even at outlet prices—suddenly seemed a much better option than spending

Sunday standing in a muddy field watching men charging at each other with sticks.

'Won't be long now, Clementine.' I could see he was beginning to get a little excited, a bit like an over-eager puppy raring to be off the leash. 'And, I've taken the liberty of bringing some clothes for you. They should fit you—I borrowed them from one of the good wives.'

A good wife? Blimey, this was getting worse. I had sudden visions of Kelly McGillis in that film about the Amish. Mind you, it had Harrison Ford in it as well. Maybe being a good wife wasn't all bad.

'Erm, Peter, I think I'd rather just watch. Seeing as how I've never done this sort of thing before. I'll just watch this time and take it all in.'

His face dropped. 'I was really hoping you'd join in with it all, Clementine.' He was suddenly shy. 'I've told everyone about you, you see. How pretty you are and all that, and… and you see it's the first time I've brought anyone along after, after, well you know, after my divorce.'

He looked so crestfallen I suddenly thought, what the hell. 'That's fine, Peter.' I smiled, 'I'll put my frock and shower cap on and join in.' Peter beamed. He really did have a lovely smile—almost cherubic. 'So, just fill me in a bit about what it's all about and what I'll have to do.'

'Well, this is the first meeting of the annual campaign season. We don't really get together much during the winter months apart from meeting up for a Christmas do in early December.'

'Hang on a minute. I thought your leader cancelled Christmas once he was in power?'

Peter looked slightly uncomfortable for a moment. 'Well, yes, there is that, but we tend to exercise a bit of poetic licence over the Christmas period as it were. So, as you know, I'm a pikeman. The pike is referred to as "The Queen of Arms" and was originally wielded by only the strongest and fittest of men.' I could sense Peter visibly preen, proud, obviously, of his ability with his pole. 'Our main job is to protect the musket from the cavalry.'

Right.

Peter did a sharp turn down a muddy track and the Cayenne bumped along for a couple of hundred yards until he turned once more into a field busy with people erecting tents, or just standing chatting and laughing while children ran around, excitedly greeting long lost friends. As a little girl, I'd been taken on a school trip to the Jorvik museum in York and, while today this configured history of the Civil War was at least seven hundred years on from that Viking village of my school visit, I suddenly felt the same sense of excitement I'd felt as an eight-year-old as we were shown and experienced an age long since gone.

'What do you think?' Peter asked, half anxious, half proud.

I looked at his eager face and smiled. 'Well, it's certainly different,' I said.

Peter relaxed. 'Honestly, Clementine, I promise you, you will have such a good day. Now, I'll just park up and then show you to one of the tents where you can change.'

'So who's this, Peter?' Any enthusiasm I'd mustered earlier

had begun to wane as I stood, dressed in some loose, grey, cast off good wife's dress and mob-cap, shivering in the sneaky March wind that was intent on showing my knickers to a whole load of Roundheads. The early morning's spring sunshine was a distant memory and clouds were gathering ominously. Jesus, what was I doing here when I could be at home with Allegra, curled up together on the sofa watching *Shrek* and eating cheese on toast?

'May I introduce Clementine Douglas?' Peter said proudly to the man who'd spoken. 'Clementine, this is Oliver Cromwell, our leader.'

I didn't know whether to curtsey or howl with laughter. What I really wanted to do was to say, 'Oh for fuck's sake, Peter, enough. Enough already. Take me home, or at least let me get back into the warmth of the car with a good book and a Twix. Pick me up in a couple of hours when you've piked and poled each other senseless.' But I didn't because, well-brought-up girl that I was, I'd had it instilled into me by my mother not only not to avoid saying 'fuck' in polite society but to defer to my betters and elders. And Olly here must have been seventy if he was a day.

'Very pleased to meet you, my dear,' Oliver Cromwell said, taking my now very cold hand and holding it a lot longer than was absolutely necessary. 'You were right, Peter.'

I glanced across at Peter, dressed to kill in jacket, breeches and some sort of woolly tights on his rather shapely legs. His feet were firmly entrenched in sturdy leather boots and a helmet—a *morion*, as he corrected me later—sat atop his fair curls. He reddened slightly at OC's words but, intent on the agenda for the morning's muster that his leader was now explaining, Peter turned his full attention away from me and I never did get to find out what it was that Peter was right about.

'Now, Peter,' Oliver Cromwell was saying as I continued to shiver and long for home, 'the Royalists appear to be having a "capture the flag" exercise, regiment against regiment. Somewhat facile, I always think. So I suggest, as it is the first muster of the season, you round up the pikemen—' here Peter reddened further at the honour bestowed on him by Ollie '—and do a bit of pike block drill.'

'Erm, what do I do?' I asked. 'I'm happy to go back to the car and watch from there.'

'Gosh, no, Clementine.' Peter's eyes scoured the Roundhead crowd anxiously. 'Just give me a second until I can find... Ah, there she is.' He raised his pole and waved enthusiastically, almost decapitating a passing Cavalier into the bargain.

'Oy, watch it, Peter. We've not started yet,' the handsome, ringleted man said, coming to a standstill and dodging as he avoided Peter's pike. Now, he was something else, I thought appreciatively. Dark hair, and blue eyes that held mine for a good few seconds.

'Oh hello, Justin,' Peter said abruptly. 'I'm looking for Brenda. She promised she'd show Clementine the ropes. And there she is.' Peter raised his stick once more and waved as Justin came over to me, drew off his hat with a flourish and whispered, '*Oh my darling, oh my darling oh my darling, Clementine...*'

'How original.' I smiled through clenched teeth. 'I don't think anyone has thought to sing that to me before.'

Justin the Cavalier laughed. 'Welcome anyway.' He replaced his hat before striding away towards his mates who looked to be having a great time 'capturing the flag.' Weren't Cavaliers supposed to whisk themselves away on horseback or was that highwaymen? Was I getting the Laughing Cavalier mixed up with Dick Turpin?

'Come on then, erm… let's get you sorted.' A large beefy woman with an impossibly red face towered over me before taking my elbow. I turned to Peter, about to plead a headache, migraine, imminent swine fever—anything to be allowed back in the car and away from this sodding pantomime.

Peter beamed encouragingly and I had no alternative but to go off with Brenda, following her to where a whole gang of similarly attired women was awaiting her instructions. 'Clarissa, is it?' she asked, breathing heavily as she hurried me along but, before I could put her right, she wiped her brow. 'Phew,' she exhaled, panting now as we made our way through a gaggle of excited children playing with a small dog, 'warm today, isn't it?'

Warm? Was the woman mad? I was frozen.

'Now,' Brenda said importantly, 'I'm the current Good Wife, sometimes called The Matron of the field. The camp followers here get closer to the action than would have been the case in reality.'

'How close?' I asked nervously, looking over to where a small skirmish was already underway between a gang of Cavaliers and a corresponding number of Oliver's lot. The cold morning air was suddenly filled with the rich smell of gunpowder as a plume of black smoke billowed in the bitter east wind like an out of control inkpot.

'Oh, don't worry about the guns,' Brenda said dismissively, 'the men all need to get their tools out and give them a good seeing to after they've kept them under wraps all winter.'

'Oh, that's really funny,' I giggled.

'What is?' Brenda gave me a strange look and then continued without waiting for a reply. 'So, we women play a vital role in ensuring all the men survive the battle. Fighting in woollen clothes and armour can be very dehydrating so we have to be on hand with water. How's your first-aid?'

'Non-existent I'm afraid. I can rub butter on a bump and kiss it better but that's about all.'

'We have to take this seriously, Clara,' she barked. 'We need to be able to spot if someone is in need of assistance or rest. In fact, if necessary, we can overrule an officer. There, what do you think of that?'

'Fabulous,' I enthused. 'Great stuff.'

'It is, isn't it? If we say "off", off they damned well go. No messing.'

God, I didn't think I'd ever dare mess with Beefy Brenda.

The chattering and laughter from the gossiping gang of women camp followers seemed to suddenly quieten. I turned to where the women were now looking, peering round each other to get a glimpse of a tall, regal-looking female astride a handsome white horse. She put me in mind of a much younger Princess Anne. Maybe it was the rather strange hairdo. Or, quite possibly, the horse.

'God, I don't know how she has the nerve,' a very pretty redhead camp follower said in a low voice, yet loud enough for me to hear.

'Vanessa has plenty of nerve,' sniffed a woman who,

I deduced by the same red hair and freckles, must be the younger one's mother.

Vanessa? Was this Peter's ex? I suppose if she'd been promoted to princess by marrying Prince Rupert she had every right to look regal. *And* ride the horse. I am so over the top allergic to horses that just one whiff of a passing horse is enough to make my throat itch and set me off sneezing. And Vanessa wasn't just passing. She was deliberately flaunting the fact that she'd gone over to the enemy. She came right up to me until I could feel the heat from the animal's flanks. I started to sneeze. Bugger, no pockets in this rag of a dress I was wearing. No tissues on me at all. I sniffed, my eyes watering. 'You must be Clementine,' she said. 'Peter has told me all about you.'

Had he? 'Oh hello,' I wheezed, stepping back from the horse. They really are huge brutes close up. 'Sorry, I'm terribly allergic to horses. I need to move away from it.'

Vanessa laughed or possibly sneered—whatever it was I didn't think it was overly pleasant—pulled the horse round and galloped off back towards her own camp, scattering Roundheads as she went.

'Hmph, she hasn't improved by going over to the other side, has she?' the younger redhead sniffed. 'I reckon Peter is well shot of her. I don't know how she could leave him like that. I mean he's lovely, isn't he? And not without a bob or two, I bet, when you look at the car he drives. I'd make a play for him myself if my Jamie wasn't around…' She held up her left hand where a tiny diamond solitaire was almost camouflaged by the mass of freckles on her ring finger.

'Shh,' her mother nudged the girl before they both turned

in my direction while I tried to stem the continuous stream from my nose caused by the horse.

'How long have you known Peter?' A rotund little woman, no more than five feet in height, smiled across at me and pulled a pack of tissues from her leather jerkin.

'Not long at all,' I said, giving my nose a huge blow. God that was better. Nothing worse than not knowing what to do with a runny nose. 'He comes into the pub restaurant where I work and thought I might like to experience this.' I pulled a face. 'Not sure it's me though.'

'Oh, you'll get to love it. I've been with Sir Thomas Grenville's regiment since I was a girl. Met my husband here.' She waved her arm to the pack of children and dogs that seemed to be expanding by the minute. 'And my three kids are among that lot somewhere.'

'I don't really know much about Peter,' I said. 'You'll know more about him than I do.'

'Well, as you probably know, he's been terribly cut up about his wife leaving him. I think—'

What she was thinking, I wasn't allowed to know, because Beefy Brenda suddenly yelled, 'Oy, you lot, stop gossiping. There's men out there dying for us.'

'There's allus a man dying for me, Brenda, love,' one of the older women cackled. 'One glimpse of me petticoat—' she lifted a corner of her brown linen dress '—and they might as well have been knocked on th' 'ead wi a pikestaff.'

Ignoring the laughing women, Brenda suddenly pushed me towards what I can only describe as a sort of yellow cart with two wheels. 'Right, Christine, you grab that end. We're needed.'

The next thing I knew we were running onto the field like maniacs, pulling the water cart behind us. 'Where are we going?' I puffed, realising how terribly unfit I was.

'Man down,' Brenda panted importantly. 'Needs assistance.'

We tugged at the cart, water slopping over its sides as we steered it over uncut winter grass and molehills ancient and modern. A few hundred yards in the distance I could see several men sprawled out over each other. I did hope there wasn't blood. Dodging a pile of dog shit, we made for the casualties: two were Roundheads, the other a Cavalier, his hat and long black wig on the muddy grass beside him.

'Never mind the Royalist,' Brenda barked as I went forward with a cup of water. 'Help our men first.'

I did as I was told, pouring water into cups that, unfortunately, spilled onto the faces of the men on the floor. They were actually laughing, obviously enjoying the attention. I moved over to the Royalist still lying on his back. No one seemed to be coming to his aid. I did hope he wasn't concussed or anything. As I leaned over him, looking for signs of life, a hand snaked out grabbing mine.

'Ah ha, got you now,' he said, as I lost my balance and toppled over onto him.

'Oof, didn't recognise you with your wig off,' I said from the depths of his rough wool jacket, realising suddenly that it was Justin from earlier.

'Do get up, Justin,' a voice said coolly from behind me. 'I'm sure the last thing Clementine wants is a goosing from you on her first attempt as a camp follower.'

Vanessa, hands on hips, was surveying us both from her

vantage point of standing, a little smile playing on her full lips. Now that she was *sans* horse she didn't look a bit like Princess Anne. The strange hairstyle was, I now realised, a wig and, like her new husband's, obviously not very secure. She reached up and pulled it off completely, releasing as she did so a mane of long blonde hair that snaked, river-like, down her back. I bet she'd been practising that, if not for my benefit, certainly all the winter months preparing for her promotion to princess. Peter's ex was actually very attractive in a Viking warrior sort of way—tall, blue-eyed and obviously very sure of herself.

'Is everything all right here?' Peter had come running up from further down the field and was now glaring at Justin, who still had his arms wrapped round me.

'Bit of concussion, I reckon, Peter. Don't seem to be able to quite remember where I am or even who this is.' He gave my leg an experimental squeeze as if by feeling me up he might better recall who I was.

'Oh, for heaven's sake, Justin, get up, you pillock,' Vanessa sighed. 'Leave the poor girl alone.'

'My sentiments exactly,' Peter said, taking my hand and prising me, not too gently, out of the arms of the man who had replaced him in the marital bed. At least I'd been warm down there.

'Come on, Clementine, let's get you something to drink and warm you up,' Peter said. 'You look frozen.' He put his jacket around my shoulders and led me to a tent where people from both sides were gathering, sheltering from the cold wind that now held the promise of rain. 'I'm really sorry about that. You know, with Justin. Typical of the man.'

'It must be very hard for you,' I said as we were served with some sort of warm ale. While beer really isn't my thing, this drink was lovely and I drank it down in one, feeling the heat begin to spread back through my frozen hands and feet. 'Seeing your ex like this, I mean. Having her flaunt her new husband in your face.'

'It was to begin with. I even considered giving all this up, or at least changing regiments; Newcastle is a busy and lively one and I even went up to see what was going on there. But then I thought, why should I be the one to leave? Last season was not easy, I admit. I think—' and here he turned to smile at me '—I hope it might all be a lot easier now.'

We spent the rest of that Sunday mainly socialising. There were a couple more skirmishes where I played my part running onto the field like some lowly actor in an amateur dramatics production—which, I suppose at the end of the day was what it was—but most of the time we were in the large hospitality tent drinking more of the lovely warm ale and eating a shared lunch. I felt a bit guilty that I'd not brought anything but Peter more than made up for it with fabulous Waitrose salads and quiches he dug out from the boot of the car.

Once Beefy Brenda was out of the way in another tent, the rest of the camp followers relaxed somewhat and were very friendly, offering drink and homemade puddings until I was stuffed. There was a real feeling of bonhomie, of people being where they really wanted to be. The children, whose ages ranged from toddlers to teenagers, seemed particularly happy with their lot. There was no whining to go home, no wanting PlayStations or mobile phones: they were simply running around, fresh-faced in the chill wind.

Allegra, I realised, would love all this.

4

I couldn't see Peter when he arrived on my doorstep the following Sunday lunchtime because of the huge bunch of white and pink flowers obscuring his face from view. For one awful moment I thought someone had died—I always associate flowers with death, probably because no one had ever bought me flowers before. I seem to remember a certain Jason Butterworth, at the age of six, thrusting a bunch of wilting dandelions from his sticky paws into mine when we were at junior school but no man since—and particularly the said Jason Butterworth whose thrusting, I also recall, developed into something more overt—had ever thought me worth even a bunch from the petrol station down the road.

I truly hadn't intended seeing Peter again after the Sunday charade, telling him gently, on the way home, that while I'd had a really good time I didn't think it was for me. When he'd asked if he could take me out for dinner during the following week I'd had to say—honestly—that I couldn't leave Allegra, that there was no one to babysit. Which is why he'd suggested meeting me for lunch in between lectures. At this point I'd run out of excuses not to take up his offer and, anyway, I wasn't averse to exchanging my ubiquitous cheese sandwich for something a little more exciting.

I thought, as it's such a beautiful day, we could have a bit of a picnic.

Peter had texted so, instead of the little bistro I'd suggested five minutes from the main campus, I made my way down to the canal area beyond the university sports hall.

Spring appeared to have sprung without my noticing it during the past week—the tabloids had been screaming from their front pages that we were in for the hottest summer on record—and I delighted in the carpet of purple and yellow crocuses that seemed to have shot up overnight. The canal, once part of the Leeds to Liverpool transport system, had been subject to a lottery-funded regeneration, and was now busy this Thursday lunchtime with students as well as office workers from the town determined to cast off their outer layers of clothing as well as the remnants of what had been a particularly cold and miserable winter.

'Cast ne'er a clout and all that.' I smiled as I found Peter, standing over a picnic rug away from the main horde of sun-seeking students, looking round for somewhere to hang his expensive-looking suit jacket.

'Sorry?' He started as I spoke and I took the jacket from him, hanging it on the branch of a willow.

'You know, *Cast ne'er a clout 'til May be out*? My granny used to say that every spring—didn't think we should be without our cardigans until the sunshine was cracking the flags. And never without our vests, even in August…'

'Sorry?' Peter said again. He seemed anxious, distracted. 'What flags?'

'Flagstones? As in 'it was so hot the sun was cracking the flagstones?'

'Right.' Peter kissed my cheek and looked at his watch. 'I'm sorry, I don't have as much time as I thought. I need to be in a meeting in forty minutes.'

'That's fine. I've a lecture this afternoon. It's just so lovely to be out in the sunshine. And what a brilliant idea to come down here.' I looked at the picnic basket that Peter had started to unload onto the upmarket tartan travel rug. 'My goodness, Peter,' I laughed, 'when you said a picnic I thought you meant a sausage roll and a can of coke.' I gazed in wonder, like Mole in *Wind in the Willows*, at the French bread, expensive cheeses, pâtés and olives.

'… *cold-tongue-cold-ham-cold-beef-pickled-onions-salad-french-bread-cress-and-widge-spotted-meat-ginger-beer-lemonade*…' I recited, laughing as I sat down. It felt so good to be outdoors, in the warmth, with the sure knowledge that, for today at least, winter was history.

'Oh, I'm sorry, Clementine. Did you want ginger beer?' Peter began to get to his feet as if about to sprint off to the Co-op down on the ring road.

'Nooo, sit down, you daft thing. I was just remembering that brilliant line when Mole is invited to Rat's picnic on the river…'

When Peter continued to look a little blank, I offered, 'Mole and Rat? As in *The Wind in the Willows*?'

'I guess reading has never been on the top of my agenda,' he apologised, looking a little crestfallen.

'Couldn't live without it myself,' I said cheerfully, spreading the most divine hummus onto French bread. 'God, this is good. I'm starving.'

Peter appeared to relax somewhat, although he did look a little out of place among the denim-and-trainer-clad students in his navy pinstriped suit and red spotted tie. We ate companionably for a while and then, curious, I asked, 'I know you have your own business, Peter, but what is it exactly that you do? Something to do with finance?'

'Sort of. I'm what's fashionably called a hedge fund manager.'

'So people consult you about their hedges?'

Peter didn't smile. 'In a nutshell, I make people's money work for them. All very boring, I'm afraid.' He poured orange juice into a plastic cup before drinking deeply. He didn't appear to want to talk at length on the subject of his business and I didn't probe further. He hesitated slightly and then said, 'Clementine, I'm afraid I'm going to have to get back to the office sooner than I thought. I'm really sorry that I've invited you for lunch and am going to have to go...' He looked at his watch again, agitated once more.

'Oh, that's fine,' I said, my mouth still full of sweet, luscious Medjool dates. 'You get off. I'm more than happy to sit here by myself for another ten minutes.' I reached over for my bag, pulling out the latest Kate Atkinson. 'I've got to a really good bit in this. Just leave me that bag of grapes and I'll be as happy as Larry, although who the hell Larry is I'll never know.' I laughed.

Peter didn't.

'The thing is, Clementine... what I'm trying to say... could we repeat this on Sunday...?'

Oh Jesus, not the bloody camp follower thingy again.

'Erm, well you know what Sundays are like for me. It really is the one day that I keep for Allegra.' No way was I going back for a second helping of Bossy Beefy Brenda.

Peter frowned. 'No, no, I know that, Clementine. That's why I wondered if you'd like to come over to my place for the day.'

'Your place?'

'Yes—there's a garden for your little girl to run around in. As you know, I'm not much of a cook, but I'm sure I can rustle up a steak and salad or something.'

'What about your piking and poling? I thought you'd be off doing that again?'

'Oh no, it's not every weekend by any means.'

'And your children? They wouldn't mind us being there?'

'Sophie is at school and Max will be with his mother. It's been my turn to have him at home during the week and then he'll be back with her from Saturday morning.'

As I say, I seriously had not intended a second date with Peter Broadbent and yet, it appeared, I was about to sign up for a third. What was the alternative? My rented place on Emerald Street with maybe a film at the local fleapit with Allegra if finances stretched that far by the end of the week?

'And you don't mind if I bring Allegra?'

'No, no. That would be wonderful. I'd love to meet her...' Peter hesitated, '... especially if she's anything like you.'

I looked across at him. What a kind man—I wasn't used to such lovely compliments. 'OK,' I smiled, 'that would be lovely but with one proviso.'

Peter looked worried for a split-second and I wondered what he was thinking.

'We'd love to come, as long as you let me do the cooking. It is the one thing I know how to do, you know.'

'Well, of course, of course if that's what you'd like to do.' He beamed, his whole face an open book of delight.

And so here we were, three days later, Peter twinkling at me through the flowers while Allegra looked on in wonder. Not normally a shy child, she wasn't used to men bearing gifts, and hid behind my legs as Peter followed me through into the kitchen while I endeavoured to find some receptacle for the flowers. As I decanted the seemingly never-ending array of blooms—roses, lilies, beautiful creamy tulips and others I wasn't able to name—into various jugs and bottles, Peter bent down to Allegra's level and solemnly held out his hand.

'I think I have something here for you too, Allegra,' he smiled, producing a rather large Easter egg from behind his back.

'Gosh, I don't know how you managed to carry that as well as the flowers,' I laughed, seeing Allegra's eyes light up with lust. 'Now, you have to save that, Allegra. Easter isn't for another two weeks.' I glanced over at Peter who was obviously thoroughly enjoying being the Easter Bunny and Interflora rolled into one. 'Right, I seem to have done as much as I can with these flowers. Allegra, fetch your coat and we'll be off. Oh, what about a car seat for her, Peter? Never having owned a car, I don't have one...'

'No problem. All taken care of. I found Max's old one in

the garage. We don't want any harm to come to this lovely little lady, do we?'

While I totally agreed with Peter's sentiments, I cringed a little at the saccharine-sweet words but Allegra, I could see, was totally won over and trotted out after him as I closed and locked the door behind us. He'd left his car at the top of the street once more and, as we walked up towards it, Peter began to move rather more quickly so that Allegra, who was holding my hand, and I had to break into a little run to keep up.

'Sorry, Clementine,' he puffed, red-cheeked, 'just a bit concerned about leaving the car in this neighbourhood. There were a couple of unsavoury-looking characters lurking around it as I locked up. Chavvy, hoodie types, you know?'

This neighbourhood? Hoodie types?

I was on the point of saying, 'Hey, this is where *I* live, Peter, don't knock it,' when he suddenly broke into a sprint.

'Oy, get your hands off that car,' he shouted, as two young men in their late teens appeared from the other side of the car.

'Hey, man, chill, we was just admiring your wheels. Hey, Clem, how're ya doing? Didn't realise *you* was with this motor?'

I smiled when I saw who was speaking. 'Hey yourself, Yusuf. Yes, this is Peter, my friend, and it's his car. He's taking Allegra and me over to his place for the day.' I turned to Peter who had come to a standstill near the car, getting back his breath. He obviously hadn't been doing enough piking and poling over the winter months and his forehead was glistening with sweat. 'It's fine, Peter, they're only *looking*. Yusuf and Musa here are more likely to guard your car than run off with it.'

Yusuf held out a hand. 'Yous OK, man? Nice motor. I wouldn't leave it round here though—you'll come back one time and the wheels will be gone.'

'Yes,' Peter said, wiping his brow with a neatly folded handkerchief, 'that was what I was worried about.' He ignored Yusuf's outstretched hand. 'OK, are we ready, Allegra? Clementine?'

'Ooh, Mummy, this is lovely,' Allegra said from her child seat behind me as we left the empty grey streets of Midhope town centre behind us and followed the main road out towards the gently rolling countryside of the Pennine foothills. The spring sky was an artist's dream: duck egg blue with just a hint of cirrus cloud high above us.

'We are lucky, darling, aren't we?' I said cheerily, glancing over to where Peter was sitting rather stiffly beside me. He'd said very little, in the five minutes since Yusuf and Musa had saluted us goodbye, apart from a polite, 'Can you manage the seatbelt?' and, 'Are you warm enough?'

'You're very quiet, Peter,' I said gently.

'You must think I'm ridiculous making such a fuss over the car,' he said eventually. 'It's just… it's just I hate to think of you living down there. I mean it's not the most salubrious of areas, is it? And those two—how do you know those two? Are they friends of yours?'

'Yusuf and Musa? Yusuf's dad is my landlord and his sister, Amirah, has babysat for me on a couple of occasions when I've been unable to take Allegra to my parents or to Izzy's.'

'But I don't understand, Clementine,' Peter said, echoing Izzy a couple of weeks earlier, 'surely your parents would prefer you living closer to them, away from the town centre?'

I laughed. 'Peter, you have no idea where my parents live. For all you know, they could live in... in Wigton.' Wigton was even more downmarket than where Allegra and I lived.

Peter looked startled for a moment. 'Wigton? Your parents live in Wigton?'

'No, they don't.' I laughed again. 'But they *could* do. That is really awful of you, Peter, judging people on where they live rather than who they are.'

Peter flushed slightly. 'I do apologise, Clementine. You're right, of course...'

'Yes, I am.'

'But the thing is...' Peter turned to look at Allegra who, fascinated by the landscape from the window, altered now from the grey slate roofs of terraced houses to glorious green fields where cows and sheep were herding their newborn offspring away from danger, was paying no attention to what Peter's thing might be. 'The thing is, Clementine,' he repeated, 'I know you'll think me presumptuous—forward even—and I know we hardly know each other, but I would very much like to know you better...'

I glanced across at him. What did he mean by '*know you*'? As in the biblical sense? I wasn't sure that I could ever fancy him enough to go down *that* route.

'...and, what I'm trying to say is, you've become very important to me in fact.' Peter's already pink face reddened and I felt a sudden affection for him. Here was a lovely, solid, dependable man who, for some reason, had decided to take me on board. I smiled across at him and we continued the journey in a companionable silence.

'Mummy, Mummy, there's a fishpond and a white house on a pole with some white birds in it... and a swing... and the grass goes all the way down to a wall and over the wall there are some horses and...' Allegra grabbed my hand and pulled me excitedly from the kitchen through the French windows and into the garden.

The most beautiful garden I'd ever seen.

I was immediately taken back to one of my favourite childhood books—*The Secret Garden*. Maybe it was the time of year: early spring with all its promise of the warmth to come, or maybe it was the fact that there was an actual gate in the tall, ivy-clad stone wall that ran down one side of the garden to the fields beyond. Allegra and I left Peter, head in the fridge as he searched for ice cubes, and walked, hand in hand, down to the wooden gate. I turned the heavy metal handle and cautiously went through.

'Mummy, look, it's like at the park.' Allegra's eyes widened at the mass of 'daffydowndillies'—I was still in *Secret Garden* mode—dancing in front of us on the grass, and her mouth became a round 'O' as we gazed over the carpet of yellow to the large cream-painted wooden summer house and on to the beautifully laid out tennis court beyond. I found myself having to heave up my own dropped jaw. Blimey, when Peter had said I might like to see where he lived, I had never for one moment imagined anything as beautiful as this.

'What do you think?' Peter had come up behind us with

a glass of juice for Allegra in one hand, and some lovely-looking concoction, sporting fruit and leaves of fresh mint, in the other for me.

'What do I think? Peter, it's the most beautiful garden I've ever been in.' A thrush, its white speckled breast stark against the leafless black of the huge, ancient oak branch on which it sat, began a rendition, seemingly oblivious to the human voices below it.

'I so wanted you to see it, Clementine. What do you think, Allegra? Shall you and I see if we can hit some tennis balls over the net later?' When Allegra carried on just staring, her hand tight in my own, Peter continued, almost anxiously, 'Let me show you the house. I think you'll like the kitchen.'

We walked back up to the house that, with its beautiful mellow-stoned frontage now ahead of us, I could see was even more amazing than the secret garden we'd just left.

'George, get down,' Peter suddenly yelled, as a huge bundle of black raced from the open front door and flung itself at Allegra who immediately reacted by flinging herself onto me with an accompanying scream.

'Oh, God, I'm so sorry, Clementine,' Peter said, as he took hold of the dog's collar and dragged it away from Allegra. 'He is *so* completely harmless; just a very daft, overfriendly puppy.'

Puppy? The beast was huge.

'We're all so used to dogs here that I forget others might not like them,' Peter went on as the puppy sat at his feet with a split-melon grin on its hairy face.

'The thing is,' I said, as I tried to uncurl Allegra's fingers from my own, 'the only dogs that Allegra comes across are the canine mafia that roam, full of themselves, down on

Emerald Street. Plus the fact that we have Dog Corleone himself patrolling his patch at the other side of our fence.' While I didn't want to give Peter any more reason to think I was living in an unsuitable area, I needed to explain Allegra's reaction to George, who was now gazing up adoringly at Peter.

'Gosh, no, I totally understand. Unforgiveable of me to forget about George. I should have warned you.'

'Look, Allegra,' I said, going over to George and stroking his silky ears, 'he's just like Hairy McClary. You know, from Donaldson's Dairy? You love Hairy McClary.'

And George really was Hairy's double. A big, black, curly Labradoodle, he rolled over on to his back, his great pink tongue flopping out of the side of his mouth and his eyes closed in ecstasy as I tickled his tummy.

Peter took Allegra's hand gently. 'You don't have to say hello to him, Allegra, but I know he'd love it if you did.' I watched as Allegra inched towards George's head and, still holding Peter's hand, gingerly patted his dappled tummy.

Allegra had left my side by the time we were back up to the house, and a few minutes later, she and George were running round each other on the lawn. I was amazed; dogs had never featured on her birthday or Christmas wish lists and yet, after her initial shock at being almost knocked over by him, here she was, seemingly unafraid and more than happy to throw his ball over and over again for him.

'I love George, Mummy,' she whispered solemnly into my ear as we followed Peter back into the kitchen.

'He *is* very lovely, isn't he?' I smiled at her rapt expression, realising with a jolt that, apart from when she was with

Izzy's lot, it wasn't an expression I saw too often on my little girl's face.

The same rapt, silly look must have been on my face too once Peter suggested that, if I was still happy to cook lunch for us, I might like to make myself at home in his kitchen. While Allegra went back out into the garden with Peter and the dog, I had a nosey around cupboards and drawers to find the necessary equipment for what I needed to utilise the ingredients that Peter informed me were in his fridge. I felt a bit like I was on *MasterChef*—kept expecting Monica Galetti and Greg Wallace to be peering over my shoulder asking me what I was going to prepare for lunch. I'd already planned what I wanted to make for pudding—meringue discs with passionfruit cream and pistachio praline—and, assuming Peter would not have any of the ingredients needed, had gone overboard at Sainsbury's the day before, wincing when I saw the final amount needed at checkout and praying my card would be able to shoulder the weight. It had—just—and I'd hurried out of there, after my stint at The Black Swan, before both the supermarket and the bank realised I was almost in the red. *Sod it*, I'd thought, *I won't have to pay back my student loan until I'm actually earning enough to be able to pay it back.*

I found the stuff Peter had bought for the main course— some fillet steak and rather limp looking salad. Not overly exciting. What the hell was I going to do with that? I rooted around and found some cheese—Gruyere, a bag of Parmesan and a large lump of cheddar with the beginnings of a beard—and decided I could make a three-cheese soufflé for a starter. A couple of wizened apples in a fruit bowl on the dresser gave me the idea for a Waldorf salad: I just needed walnuts and we'd be in business.

While the contents of Peter's fridge might not have been the most riveting on this planet, what I discovered in his kitchen drawers and cupboards almost blew me away—and all top-quality and virtually unused. I pulled out drawer after drawer, each effortlessly advancing towards me on expensive invisible rollers, and opened cupboard after cupboard, gazing in wonder at the Kai and Wusthof knives; the Heston Blumenthal 'Boss' blender; the top of the range Rosie melon baller and apple corer together with a pair of Rosie fish tweezers still firmly ensconced in their Harvey Nicks packaging and bearing a thirty-pound price tag. Thirty pounds for a pair of tweezers? Blimey, since when did a halibut need its eyebrows plucking? There was a pasta-maker, an extremely expensive ice cream maker and, best of all, a Kenwood Titanium Major food processor. I stroked its cool metallic sides and knew myself guilty of breaking at least one of the Good Lord's commandments. Never mind coveting thy neighbour's wife—it was his Kenny I was after.

I was still stroking his sides somewhat lasciviously when a voice behind me interrupted my dreams of the whisked meringues, soufflés and other such goodies Kenny and I would produce together if he only were mine.

'Hi,' said the voice, 'you look to be far away. Sorry to interrupt you. I'm looking for Peter.'

5

'Oh, hello.' I hastily extended my hand to the stranger who stood now in front of me. 'I'm Clementine. Peter is down in the garden throwing balls to the dog—and my daughter.'

The man, tall, dark-haired and with a lovely smiley face shook my hand. 'Hi, Clementine, we're neighbours of Peter's—just live across the fields. I wanted a word with him *about* the fields actually.'

'Well, I was just about to start cooking, but I'll come down the garden with you. Peter must be fed up of playing with my daughter by now.'

The man walked towards the open French windows that led directly on to the lawn. 'It's OK, don't let me disturb you.' He glanced at the ingredients I'd amassed on the granite worktops. 'You look as if you're going to have fun with this lot. And Peter's here now.'

Peter bustled in, obviously delighted to see the newcomer. 'David, how are you? Don't seem to have seen you for ages.

May I introduce Clementine Douglas, a very good friend of mine? Clementine, this is David Henderson. He and Mandy live just two minutes across the fields.'

David Henderson? Was this *the* David Henderson? The one they called The Richard Branson of the north? The way Peter was acting, hopping up and down, offering coffee, wine, beer, his soul, I guessed this was the great man himself.

'No, really. Thank you but no, Peter. I just walked across to ask if you had any idea what was happening about the fields. They're in an awful mess. Not been looked after at all over the winter months. The dry-stone walling onto my garden has fallen down and I had a whole load of sheep on the lawn the other day.'

'Who do the fields belong to?' I asked, once I'd recovered from being in such hallowed company as David Henderson.

'Chap named Rafe Ahern,' David said, smiling at Allegra, who had followed the dog into the kitchen. Her usually pale cheeks were pink, her eyes shining. 'His family has owned most of the land round here for years but, bit by bit, he's had to sell it off. Both Peter's and my gardens were once part of his estate. His mother lives over at the old manor house still, but trying to get hold of Rafe himself is a bit of a nightmare. He spends a lot of his time in London and Ireland and abroad. And if you go over to the house to find him he's invariably not there and Annabelle, his mother, is so charming she just plies you with drink and you forget why you were there in the first place.' He laughed. 'Oh well, never mind, been nice meeting you, Clementine.'

David headed back towards the open French window and Peter, obviously not wanting to let him go, suddenly said, 'Erm, how about dinner here in a couple of weeks, David? Clementine is an exceptional cook...'

I looked at Peter in horror. I knew I was a good cook, but exceptional? And for the legendary David Henderson?

'...and we'd love to have you here. I'm just in the process of inviting Oliver Cromwell along at some stage too. I think you two would have a lot in common.'

David Henderson looked totally bemused for a couple of seconds and then glanced across at me where I stood, trying not to laugh, and grinned.

'Well, if Clementine is cooking, then we'd be delighted. Mandy is the social secretary; I'll get her to give you a ring sometime, Peter.'

Hmm, bit dismissive, that, but Peter, now encouraged, was in raptures. 'Ooh,' he said, 'that's marvellous. And how about Harriet and Nick Westmoreland? I have met them a couple of times and I know they're very good friends of yours, David...?'

'I'm er... guessing they'd be delighted too. Nick, I'm sure, would love to meet, er, Oliver. I'll leave it all up to you, Peter. Look forward to hearing from you.' David winked at me and patted Allegra on her head before stepping out into the garden with Peter, apparently reluctant to let the great man out of his sight, hot on his heels.

'Mummy, I love George. And I love Peter,' Allegra said solemnly as she nursed another glass of juice while I turned back to the lunch ingredients on the granite. 'I'm really good at tennis now. I think I'd like to be one when I grow up.'

'One what?' I laughed, delighted to feel the happiness radiating from her.

'A tennis lady at Wimbledon. Peter says that's where

ladies who get good go. I don't know where it is but I think that's where I'm going to be when I'm a big lady…'

'Well, better a big lady than a bag lady, sweetie pie,' I smiled, wiping the ring of orange from her top lip.

'… Or a dog lady. I'm very good with dogs too, you know.'

'Well, I'm very pleased to hear it. Why don't you have a look at some of those lovely books on the shelf over there?' I indicated some children's picture books that were arranged neatly on the bottom shelf over in the 'family area' of the kitchen. 'I can see *Farmer Duck* and *Owl Babies*, I said, spying Allegra's favourite stories. 'And then I can get on with cooking lunch.'

'Who do these books belong to?' Allegra asked, as she walked over to the bookshelf. 'Does Peter read them? Does Peter like ducks and owls too?'

'I'm sure he does,' I laughed. 'But those belong to his children.'

'Where are they?' Allegra asked, looking round as if his children were about to manifest themselves in front of her.

'Well, the big girl, darling, is away at school.'

Allegra's eyes widened. 'At school? On Sunday?'

'Well, yes. She goes to boarding school. She lives there.'

'She *lives* at school? Why?'

'Er, well…' I shrugged my shoulders. I couldn't think why anyone would send their children away to school. My own parents had sent me to a second-rate private school that I'd not always enjoyed.

Peter strode back into the kitchen, his face one big smile, and I was able to pass Allegra's question over to him. 'I've just been telling Allegra that your daughter is away at school, Peter. She wants to know why she lives there and not here.'

'Well, Allegra, you see my children's mummy isn't here anymore…'

Allegra looked worried. 'Is she with Jesus?'

'No, with Justin.' Peter said this without a hint of humour and I wanted to giggle. He was obviously still unable to see the funny side of his wife's defection.

'So it's easier for me if she is away at school. And,' he went on almost to himself, 'Vanessa was determined that she should go away to the same school as she'd been to. Head girl, captain of the first-eleven hockey and all that…' He turned back to Allegra and smiled. 'Max is eight and lives with me some of the time and with his mummy the rest of the time. You'd like Max, Allegra.'

Peter walked over to where I was just about to whisk egg whites in Kenny. 'I hope you don't feel I was being presumptuous in assuming that you would help me with this dinner party, Clementine? I do apologise. It was very rude of me. If you'd rather not, I can always cancel…?'

Peter looked so anxious, I didn't have the heart to tell him that yes, I thought he *had* been bloody rude in assuming I'd cook for it. And anyway, I didn't think for one minute it would go ahead. I couldn't see Oliver Cromwell coming all the way from North Yorkshire, and the vibes David Henderson had been sending out didn't look promising for a cosy dinner party chez Broadbent. I supposed he was a bit like someone famous—well, he *was* famous in the same way that Yorkshire flaunted James Martin and Freddie Truman—and was always being sucked up to and invited here, there and everywhere. And to be quite honest, the thought of cooking for a dinner party in such a fabulous kitchen excited the hell out of me. Terrified me, but excited me as well. Wasn't this what I wanted with my life? To cook?

'Clementine, I can truly say that was the most delicious lunch I've ever experienced,' Peter enthused a couple of hours later as he scraped his pudding plate with his spoon in an effort to retrieve the very last morsel of meringue and cream.

'It was a pleasure,' I said. And it was. Any fears of the past, and worries about the future, were totally put to one side once I was stuck into cooking.

'So, why don't you do this professionally?' Peter asked. 'Why go back to university to do a hotel management course when you could have been out there, in London, in Paris for heaven's sake, cooking wonderful food like this?'

I raised my eyebrows towards Allegra who was toying with her pudding. Her little tummy was full from the starter and main course and I suggested she leave the food and go out into the garden again for a while.

'How could I possibly work in restaurants around the world—Midhope even—when the hours are so erratic and I have a child to look after?' I said, once Allegra was out of earshot, outside in the garden with George. 'If I were working in a restaurant I'd not be home until after midnight. I can't do it, much as I'd love to. So, I made the decision, once Allegra was able to go to nursery, that I'd do the next best thing and go for hotel management...' I hesitated, thinking of the future. 'But even then, I assume

I'm going to have to do shift work—that is if I manage to find a job once I've finished in the summer.'

'Yes, I can see that might be a problem,' Peter frowned. He was just about to say something else when the house telephone rang and he excused himself. While he was talking, I cleared the pudding plates, filled the kettle for coffee and went out into the garden to check on Allegra. I found her sitting on a wooden bench, her back towards me, swinging her legs and stroking George, who appeared now to be her new best friend.

'... And if I lived here, with you, George, I'd take you out for walks all the time,' she was saying, unaware that I was behind her. 'And I'd let you sleep on my bed. And I'd be a Wimbledon lady...'

I didn't disturb her, didn't let her know I'd heard what she was saying, but turned around, retracing my steps back to the kitchen. Peter was just coming off the phone, his face an absolute picture.

'Well,' he said, 'that was Mandy Henderson, David's wife, on the phone. She said she had her diary in front of her that minute and, if the offer was still on, they'd love to come for dinner.' Peter looked a bit stunned. 'She's given me a couple of dates and, because the Westmorelands are over there for lunch at the moment, has already mentioned it to them too and checked dates with them.' Peter hesitated. 'Vanessa asked them over loads of times in the past, but they always appeared booked up or busy or something. This is marvellous.' Peter giggled almost girlishly. 'Your amazing cooking must have wafted across the fields, Clementine, and they just can't keep away. Now,' he went on importantly, 'I just need to check with Neville that he and his wife might also be free on those dates.'

'Neville? Who's Neville?' There were so many names being bandied around, I wasn't sure who this Neville was. Was he the Westmoreland man?

'Neville?' Peter almost sucked in his teeth at my apparent lack of respect in not knowing his leader's real name. 'Neville Manning is Oliver Cromwell, Clementine. You remember? You met him?'

'To be fair, Peter, I don't think you introduced him as Neville. He was Oliver Cromwell from the kick-off.'

'Kick-off?' Peter looked puzzled, as if I were suddenly talking about a World Cup football game.

'You know what I mean—from the start of the re-enactment whatsit, the other Sunday. Why do you want to invite him anyway?' From what I recalled of the little man who'd held my hand for longer than was entirely necessary, I couldn't see him having anything in common with David Henderson whom I'd liked enormously from the ten minutes or so of knowing him.

'Oh, I think they will get on really well. Only the other day Neville was asking whether, as my neighbour, I had any connections with David.'

'So you're sort of parading David out to show him off to Oliver Cromwell?'

Peter had the grace to look a little shamefaced. 'No, really, no, Clementine. They are both businessmen and I feel they would enjoy each other's company.'

Or not.

Anyway, nothing to do with me really. I was just the cook.

'So, there will be you and me, Clementine,' Peter ticked

us off on his fingers, 'David and Mandy Henderson, the Westmorelands—I can't quite recall her name, a bit dizzy from what I remember of her—Neville and Hilary Manning of course and… that's it.'

Hmm, I wasn't quite sure if it was going to be a lot of fun. I was only just thirty and all these people seemed a lot older than me. Still, I would really enjoy the cooking and that was the main thing.

'I hope it's going to be fun for you,' Peter said anxiously as we cleared the table and stacked the dishwasher. Blimey, was the man a mind reader? 'Is there anyone *you'd* like to bring along—if you can cope with catering for additional people of course?'

'Actually, would you mind awfully if I ask Izzy and Declan? Allegra and I are always round at their place, so it would be lovely if I could do something for them for once.'

Peter beamed. 'Absolutely. I'd be really delighted to meet them. I'd like to get to know all your friends, all your family.'

I laughed nervously. 'Steady on, Peter, you don't really know *me* yet, so how do you know you'd want to meet my family?'

'I know you have your mum and dad and Allegra. Well, I've met Allegra now and she's as delightful as you. She's lovely, Clementine. And I'm sure your parents are equally pleasant?'

Well, they'd certainly like you, Peter, I thought. 'The first normal boyfriend you've ever had,' I could hear my mum saying. 'And knows David Henderson, too,' she'd tell all her cronies at the golf club. 'Drives a Porsche, you know. And very educated—into history, knows all about Oliver Cromwell and that war he was in…'

'Clementine,' Peter said, his face pink, 'you must know how I feel about you? Surely you know that's why I've been coming into The Black Swan all these months?'

When I didn't say anything, didn't really know *what* to say, Peter put down the red striped tea towel he'd been using to wipe the beautiful stainless steel pans that I'd said were far too good to bung in the dishwasher, and took my hand. 'I've got to say this, Clementine, before I lose my nerve. I've fallen in love with you.'

Oh bugger.

I was just about to say I was very honoured about his having fallen in love with me, but really, this was going nowhere, when Allegra ran in from the garden and, seeing Peter had hold of my hand, grabbed both our spare hands, forming a little circle through which George then forced his way as if playing a canine game of The Farmer wants a Wife. I looked at the three grinning faces, from Allegra's delighted one, to Peter's hopeful one and then to George's hairy one and thought again, *Oh bugger*.

On the way home in the car, seeing that Allegra was asleep, exhausted after her day out, Peter turned to me and said, 'You say I know nothing about you, Clementine. Well, tell me. Tell me about Allegra. Where is her father? Does he still have contact with you both?'

I sighed, glancing over my shoulder to look at four-year-old Allegra. Her dark head had fallen to one side of the car seat and her mouth was open slightly in a little 'O' of tiredness. She'd played with George and run herself ragged in the huge expanse of garden, and the spring sunshine had brought out a smattering of freckles on her usually pale face. I felt a tightness in my chest as I gazed at her. She was the one important thing in my life; she was, quite literally, my life.

'Clementine?'

'Sorry?'

'Look, I don't want to pry, and tell me to shut up and mind my own business if you like, but you did say I knew nothing about you. So, tell me.'

How could I tell this kind, if rather dull, man the circumstances of Allegra's birth?

'Clementine?' Peter probed once more.

'I used to work at La Toque Blanche in Leeds...'

'Goodness, you worked at La Toque Blanche? Peter was impressed. 'I didn't realise you had actually trained as a chef?'

'I hadn't. Haven't. I started as a general dogsbody, washing up, sweeping floors, a *plongeur.*'

'Plongeur?'

'Sorry, Peter, if you read George Orwell's *Down and Out in Paris and London* you'd understand the term.'

When he looked at me blankly, not really understanding, I smiled and said, 'Just take it from me, I was the lowest of the low, the one all the chefs shouted at when things went wrong.' I frowned, remembering how awful it had been to start with—that I'd only taken the job to be with Ariav. 'Then I started being allowed to help with the actual food—you know, weighing ingredients, veg preparation, that sort of thing? And then I began to look forward to going to work. It became not just a means to an end but— and I know this sounds a bit dramatic—suddenly became something I was good at.'

Peter looked puzzled. 'But didn't you realise you liked cooking? Didn't your mum let you make buns and then... and then saw that you were good at it or something?'

'My mum? Make buns?' I laughed. 'All my mum was interested in *making* was her way to the top of the social ladder and pulling Dad up with her. She used to buy all her meals from Marks and Spencer when she was entertaining the golf lot or Dad's office boss and then pass them off as her own. The bin used to be full of M&S packaging pushed down to the bottom so that no one would know it was bought stuff.'

Peter looked a trifle uncomfortable. 'I do have a fondness for the old M&S stuff myself...'

'Fair enough,' I smiled, 'but I bet you don't pass if off as your own?'

'Oh no, no,' Peter said, hastily. 'Never that.'

'I remember once asking could I make Rice Krispie buns for Comic Relief, but she said I'd get chocolate everywhere and make too much mess, and that she couldn't see anything remotely *comical* about turning her kitchen upside down for Johnny Foreigner...'

'You can come over and make Rice Krispie buns in my kitchen any time you want,' Peter said indignantly. 'Any time at all.'

I laughed. 'I think I've moved on a bit since then.'

'You certainly have, Clementine,' Peter said. 'What you produced today was wonderful.' Peter slowed down for traffic lights and then, as we gathered speed once more, asked, 'So, what happened then? Did you just train on the job?'

'In a word, yes. I was there quite a while, learning more

and more and being given more advanced stuff to do. And then one of the main chefs was ill—got meningitis, poor thing—and I just sort of took over. I loved it.' I smiled. 'Eventually, I left because I had Allegra to care for…'

Peter glanced at me from across from the driving seat. 'All by yourself? You had no help?'

'Mum and Dad have been very helpful,' I said carefully. I really didn't want to talk about this, especially with Allegra asleep in the back, so I tried to change the subject. 'So you look after your kids as well without any help?'

'Well, apart from Mrs Atkinson who does my cleaning and looks after Max if I'm not around, yes. Yes I do,' Peter said importantly, pleased that we obviously shared some common ground. 'To be honest I'm finding Sophie, my fifteen-year-old, quite challenging at the moment. I'm really rather relieved when she goes back to school…'

Peter pulled up and parked in the same spot he'd left the car earlier that day. He switched off the engine and took both my hands. 'I very much want to take care of you, Clementine.' His pink complexion and fair curls had me in mind of the cherubs that used to peer down at me from the picture above our heads in the school hall and that thought, together with his earnest expression, made me want to laugh.

'Oh, Peter,' I smiled. 'I've been taking care of myself— and Allegra now—for years. I'm quite used to it.'

'No, but you see, Clementine,' Peter was perspiring slightly in the warm interior of the car, 'I *want* to be there for you. I'm sorry, I'm not very good at this…' He took out his ubiquitous laundered handkerchief and dabbed at his forehead.

'Look, Peter, Allegra and I have had a lovely day. We really have. Let's not rush anything here...' I really didn't know what else to say because we had, in all honesty, had a really super Sunday. Allegra stirred and yawned. 'Come on, sweetie, we're home.' I smiled across at Peter and patted his hand. 'And we'll see Peter—and George—again soon. Really soon, I promise.'

Peter beamed his cherubic smile and jumped out of the car to open my side of the door and to help Allegra out of the car seat before accompanying us both down the street.

Once I'd got Allegra bathed and into bed and given into her—very sleepy—demands for *Paddington* and then tucked her up with Hector elephant—now rechristened George—I spent the next couple of hours of that Sunday evening catching up with the jobs most people have to do at the end of a weekend. I made sure Allegra's uniform, PE kit and book bag were sorted and ready for a quick getaway the next morning. I pottered, ironing a few bits and pieces; re-potting my one and only plant that had been gasping for more accommodation for weeks, and putting off until the last minute when I would have to sit down and get down to an already overdue essay.

What I really wanted to do was curl up on the sofa with a glass of wine and *Poldark* on TV but, in the sure knowledge that an hour with Aidan Turner aka Ross Poldark would not give me the 'A' I needed to pass this particular module, I went to fire up my laptop. Ignoring the huge bunch of flowers that Peter had brought earlier and which were doing a very good job of distracting me from my essay, I silently thanked Izzy, as I did on a daily basis, for her donating her old laptop last Christmas when Declan had given her a fabulous, up to date, Mac computer. God, what would I have done without Izzy and Declan these past few years? They never probed, never really asked about Allegra's father, but had willingly offered help and friendship for which I was eternally grateful then and now.

Cursing, not for the first time, my lack of broadband, I put to one side the research that could only be completed once I was back in the university computer suite and began typing up the notes I'd made earlier in the week. Academic stuff—the essays, the research, the exams—had never really fazed me. Despite the truly awful, second-rate private all-girls school my mother had insisted upon, I came out with a very credible clutch of GCSEs and was then allowed to transfer to the excellent Midhope College to do A levels. I reckoned by that time my mother had given up all hope of moulding me into something she wanted me to be and was probably highly relieved when my father no longer had to fork out the annual school fees. More money, after all, for her to spend in M&S food hall and on her twice weekly blow dry and manicure at Bruno's in the centre of Midhope.

Pushing Peter's flowers out of sight, as well as his declarations of love from my mind, I was soon engrossed in the nuances of the Management of Food and Beverage Operations.

I didn't realise, until I happened to glance up at the wall clock, that it was after midnight. Tired, but pleased with what I'd achieved in the last couple of hours, I pushed back my chair and went to fill the kettle.

The noise of tap water hitting my ancient kettle initially

drowned the cries. I was about to make my way up to Allegra when I realised the sound was coming from outside and not from my daughter's bedroom. The cold night air hit me as I opened my back door and peered into the dark. It may have been a glorious day earlier, but we were still only early April and I shivered, wrapping my cardigan more closely around me.

'Oh, fuck off then, you fucking pansy.' The female voice floated from the alleyway and over my garden fence before breaking down into a mixture of curses and mutterings.

'Shh,' I warned. 'I have a little girl asleep here. Are you OK? Do you need some help?'

'Nah, I'm fine. Just get me breath back and I'll be on me way. Bloody cold out here any road…'

I walked down the path to where the girl was leaning against my garden gate lighting a cigarette and made a quick decision. 'Are you on your own…?'

The girl laughed. 'Well, I am now, love. Hopefully won't be for much longer, though.'

'Look, I've just put the kettle on. Do you want a quick cup of tea to warm yourself up?'

She must have been still in her teens, but the layer of tan foundation together with the thick black rings of kohl around her eyes were unable to mask the lack of life and light in her world-weary eyes.

'A cup of tea? In there?' The girl nodded her bleached-blonde hair towards my back door. 'Why?'

'Well, I thought maybe you'd been on your feet all night…' I stopped, embarrassed.

'Well, I 'ave, but I'm 'oping to get off 'em soon, if you

know what I mean.' She looked up from under her sooty lashes, suddenly suspicious. 'Is there just you in there, 'cos I don't do nowt *perverse*. Don't do nowt like freesomes like some sickos want.'

'Forget it, really. I just wanted to see if you were OK…'

'Well, if yer offering, like, I could do with a cup of tea.'

I led the girl into the kitchen, already regretting my impulsiveness. I had Allegra upstairs, for heaven's sake. Making sure my bag was in sight, I made tea, poured her a mugful and watched as she drank thirstily.

'Is this tea?' she asked suspiciously once she'd surfaced from the mug. 'Tastes a bit different from usual. You haven't put summat in it, have you?'

'Oh sorry, it's Lady Grey. It's the only tea I drink.'

She nodded and continued drinking, even though mine was far too hot to do anything more than sip at.

'So, what happened out there tonight?'

'Oh, he couldn't get it up and was about to go off without paying me. Then he got mad and said I'd called him a fucking fag and no way was he giving me money if I thought he was a fucking fag.'

'And had you?'

'What? Called him a fucking fag? No I certainly hadn't. I said he were a fucking gay twat.'

'Erm, maybe just as bad, do you not think?' I wanted to smile. She was so young, so indignant.

The girl handed me her empty mug, took a mirror from one pocket and an eye pencil from the other and proceeded to add another layer to her already black eyes. 'Right, love, thanks for the tea and all that. Best get going now.'

'Look,' I said, 'there was a reason I asked you in.' My heart was beating uncomfortably and I took a deep breath. 'Can I show you something?'

She looked alarmed for a second and then tittered, 'As long as it's not yer bits and pieces, love. As I said, I'm not into any of that pervy stuff.'

I picked up my bag and took out my wallet and realised the girl probably thought I was about to give her money. From the back pocket of the purse I found what I was looking for and handed the photograph to her.

'Do you know this girl?'

The girl looked at it for several seconds before looking back up at me.

'It's you,' she said, frowning.

'No, it's Lucy,' I replied before taking the photo out of her hands, putting it back in its place in my purse and ushering the girl out of the house.

6

The only way Godzilla at The Black Swan would let me have the Saturday of the dinner party off was if I did a swap with someone else's shift. Luckily Bronwen, another student, was desperate to have the Friday night off for her boyfriend's birthday bash somewhere in town and was more than willing to swap with me. And because my mother realised that I had to do this swap in order to 'free up my Saturday for David Henderson and his colleagues' as I heard her telling one of her golf mafia on the phone, she agreed to have Allegra on the Friday night without applying her usual 'you are putting me out' demeanour on top of her Revlon Cool Beige foundation.

'Erm, Peter, is it OK if a couple of Izzy's friends come along on Saturday?' Peter had been waiting on the doorstep when Allegra and I had arrived home from school on the Thursday evening, eager to collect instructions and a list of the food that I didn't have the time, transport or, let's face it, the money to go shopping for myself.

'Friends of Izzy's?' Peter frowned. 'Who are they? What are they like? I mean, I don't know who they are... I haven't even met Izzy and Declan yet...'

I was quite taken aback. Before I could say anything, Peter went on, '...Will they get on with Neville and David Henderson? They're rather VIP, you know. Neville and David Henderson, I mean.'

I wanted to laugh; he was acting as if I'd told him I'd invited a couple of the *Big Issue* sellers from the town centre when the Queen and Prince Philip were coming to eat. In fact, I nearly did, then thought better of it.

'Apparently Izzy's best friend from years ago is soon to be moving back to Midhope from Essex. Izzy has totally got her dates mixed up and had forgotten that this friend and her husband were staying with them this weekend while they're house-hunting in the area. Mel and Julian, I think Izzy said they were called. And, the problem is, Peter, that if you'd really rather these two didn't come, then Izzy and Declan won't come either. It had totally slipped Izzy's mind they were up for the weekend when she accepted our invitation for dinner.'

'Bit forgetful, is she?' Peter was still put out. 'She will get on with Neville and Hilary, won't she?'

'Oh, Izzy gets on with everyone,' I soothed. 'She's a GP. Meets all sorts—doesn't bat an eyelid.'

Peter frowned again, trying to work out if, in the process of praising my mate, I was also dissing Oliver Cromwell. He smiled suddenly. 'I'm sorry, Clementine. Of course they're welcome. I was just thinking of you.' Peter came up behind me and put both his hands on my shoulders 'As I do all the time. You must know that? And, you see, I really want this to be a special occasion with special people…'

'Oh?' Gosh, he was putting a lot in store by old Chief Roundhead Neville. Ah, maybe this was the build-up to his being promoted? Well, if that was what Peter wanted, I was more than happy to cook my little socks off to help him up the slippery Roundhead pole as it were.

I smiled at Peter, at his anxious face. 'I think I know what you're hoping for, Peter? Why don't you get some champagne while you're out? Just in case?'

Peter beamed. 'Already sorted. Now, if there are two extra do I need to up the food?' He glanced at the list I'd handed over. 'Gosh, Clementine, I don't even know what half this stuff is, never mind how you'd go about cooking it.'

'Just leave that side to me, Peter. It will all be fine. Don't worry.'

'Mummy, when we get to Peter's house will George be there?'

'Of course he will. You know he will.' I smiled at Allegra, who was thoroughly overexcited at the thought of a sleepover at Peter's. She'd already packed her little case with pyjamas, books, dog treats she'd insisted we buy at Mr Shadique's corner shop up the road plus as many dolls as she could reasonably squeeze in.

'And Max as well?' Allegra must have asked this twenty times already so far and it was only 9 a.m. My daughter's love for Peter's dog was nothing compared to the obsession she seemed to have developed for his eight-year-old son.

And I could understand why: Max was a good-looking boy, blond-haired and blue-eyed who, on the couple of occasions we'd met, had been polite and friendly with me and tolerant of a little girl trailing after him wherever he went. He'd even tried to teach Allegra how to play cricket, which, according to Peter, came only second to his son's love of football in general and Manchester United in particular.

'I've told you, darling, I'm sure he's going to be there for some of the time. It depends if his mummy lets him…'

'Peter's here!' Allegra shouted, running into our tiny patch of garden where the already warm May sunshine was intent on brightening even my scrubby patch of lawn. 'And Max is with him too,' she added triumphantly over her shoulder.

Unfortunately Allegra's shouting, accompanied by the sudden opening of my rusting and unoiled garden gate, sent next door's dog into a paroxysm of angry barking and flinging itself against the dividing fence—and Allegra back in screaming.

Max's face as he came into my tiny sitting room was a picture. He'd probably never, in all of his privileged eight years, seen how the other half lived. 'Gosh, do you live here?' he asked, gazing round in wonder at the knackered sofa, the mismatched cushions and the table, laden with ancient computer, papers and files, which acted as my study as well as where we ate.

'Hello, Max. Where's your dad? What's he doing?'

The three of us, Allegra now holding my hand, went back out into the garden where a red-faced Peter was involved in some sort of argument with the dog's heavily tattooed owner.

'There's really no need for that language,' Peter was saying. 'I merely asked if you think it a good idea to let out such an obviously bad-tempered beast into such a small garden and next to where a little girl lives.'

'Well merely fuck off then and mind your own merely fucking business. Don't you come round here so fucking early on a Saturday morning waking us all up with your noise.'

'*My* noise?' Peter was incredulous, momentarily silenced by my neighbour's invective, and I took the opportunity to grab our bags, lock the door and usher Allegra and Max towards the street.

'Come on, Peter,' I soothed, touching his arm and pulling him away from the altercation. 'It's OK, the dog can't get over the fence. Let's go.'

'Yeah, fuck off, *Peter,* or I'll set Cyril on you.'

'Cyril?' Peter looked at me, his eyebrows raised, as he took our things and made sure Max was following. 'Who on earth is Cyril?'

'The *dog,* you wanker,' came from over the fence. 'Named after me granddad Cyril—and he were an evil bastard too.'

'Clementine, I don't see how you can find any of that remotely funny...' Peter said as we walked up to his car.

'No, you're right, Peter. It wasn't—*isn't*—funny living next door to that. It's just the idea of calling a pit bull— or whatever the damned thing is—Cyril. I mean, they're usually called Titan or Caesar or something...'

'I can't believe you continue living down here, Clementine. With Allegra, I mean. It's dangerous. It's just not suitable. It's not fair on her.'

I didn't say anything: I knew Peter was right. I'd initially moved back into my parents' home, out of necessity, when I needed help with Allegra as a tiny baby and was no longer able to work at the restaurant. Once I'd enrolled at the university and been able to put Allegra into its subsidised crèche, things were a lot easier and, a year ago, I'd taken the lease on the house on Emerald Street to be nearer to the centre of town and college. It had seemed the right thing to do at the time. My mother had a good idea why I'd chosen the Emerald Street area of town but, relieved to have a sticky-fingered toddler away from her Capodimonte and symmetrical, forty-five-degree-angled cushions, she'd said very little.

And my father had never said anything.

7

'I've put Allegra in here,' Peter said, opening a door next to the room he'd already allocated to me. 'It's Sophie's old room—when she got to thirteen she insisted she'd outgrown the pink, and Vanessa did up the loft space for her birthday. It was one of the last things she did before she left.'

'What's Sophie now? Fifteen?'

'Nearly sixteen. I've been meaning to do something with this old room of hers, but I've been too busy—never got round to it. It was always Vanessa who sorted the design and décor—that was her job after all.'

'Oh, I didn't realise that was what she did for a living. And does she still?'

'Well, she likes to think she does, but I'm not sure how much she's taking on now. Her widowed mother has Alzheimer's, and Vanessa has her in that really expensive home up near Upper Clawson. Costs an absolute fortune—'

'Mummy, Mummy, look.' Allegra grabbed my hand

and pulled me into what I can only describe as a pink paradise. A bedroom any little girl could only dream of. I remembered seeing a feature on some IT girl—possibly Tamara Ecclestone—in the *OK!* magazine I'd picked up in the dentist's waiting room. It had photograph after photograph of a room not dissimilar to this old room of Peter's daughter's, and I'd felt almost as much pain knowing I could never give my own daughter anything like this as the root canal procedure I'd had to endure ten minutes later.

I was in heaven that Saturday morning. Saint Peter had opened the golden doors to his kitchen and let me in, while the white-bearded God of my Sunday school days felt ever present, smiling and encouraging as my cooking revved up and took off, and canapés, starters and puddings began to rack up in the huge American fridge. I'd be singing 'All Things Bright and Beautiful' in a minute.

Allegra was off outside as if she owned the place, running across the lawn with George at her side, and then settling herself down on the spring grass, making daisy chains and singing the latest ditty she'd learned at school, before festooning both the dog and a plethora of her dollies in garlands of white.

Peter had gone back into town for some reason, dropping Max off at football practice for an hour or so on the way. So engrossed was I in slowly dribbling oil onto an emulsion of eggs and vinegar for mayonnaise that I didn't realise someone had walked in through the French windows until he spoke. I jumped, spilling oil onto the granite work surface.

'Oh sorry, Clementine, I've made you jump,' David Henderson said, patting my arm as he reached for a cloth. 'I was just out walking—it's so glorious out there today—and thought I'd pop in and ask if you had any preference for wine for this evening?'

'Wine? Oh gosh, I'm afraid I've very little knowledge about wine.' I frowned. 'Apart from knowing some is red and some is white. Are you a bit of a wine buff?'

'Well, I do have a wine cellar—most of it inherited from my father when he died. I'm learning all the time and adding to what's already there, but I do find it really interesting. It's becoming a bit of a hobby of mine deciding what goes with what food.' He smiled and I thought what an incredibly attractive man he was. Too old for me—he must have been pushing forty-five—but his dark hair, cut short and greying at the temples, together with those very dark eyes and an almost olive complexion, meant he must have broken some hearts over the years. 'Would you mind giving me some rough idea of what you're cooking?' he asked. 'And then I can go home and get my books and magazines out and annoy Mandy, my wife, who thinks I do it to show off.'

I couldn't imagine this man ever having the need to show off; he carried such an air of calm intelligence that anyone would want to listen to what he was saying without thinking he was boasting about it.

I screwed up my eyes, concentrating on recalling all that I intended to make, ticking off on my fingers as I gave David the lowdown on what I was cooking and, again, feeling as if I was a contestant on *MasterChef*.

David stared at me for a couple of seconds. 'Goodness,

Clementine, where've you learned all this? Are you a chef somewhere?'

I was embarrassed, but then shook myself. I *could* cook. It was the one thing I could do with a fair degree of confidence. 'Used to be,' I said. 'Worked at La Toque Blanche in Leeds for several years. Learned on the job as it were. It's what I love doing…'

It was David's turn to look a bit flustered. 'La Toque Blanche? Wow, I often take Mandy there if it's a special occasion. Golly, I didn't realise you were such a professional. I hope I can sort out the best wines for you. So, where are you cooking now? Somewhere in Midhope or are you still in Leeds?'

'Neither. I'm doing a degree in hotel management at Midhope University. After my little girl came along, working in restaurants with split shifts and all that that entails just wasn't on any longer.' I smiled. 'I miss cooking dreadfully.'

David smiled, showing perfectly white teeth. 'So now you cook *wonderfully*?'

I laughed with him. 'Hopefully. You'll have to tell me after you've eaten, this evening.'

'And Peter? I've met up with him quite a bit recently over the situation we're having with Rafe Ahern and the fields, and he's obviously smitten with you,' David teased.

I could feel myself blush and turned away, opening a couple of drawers to hide my face.

'Oh, I am sorry, Clementine. That was terribly rude of me …'

'Ah, David,' Peter said affably, making a show of looking at his watch as he walked into the kitchen with Max. 'You're a tad early.'

'Just going, Peter. I dropped in to have a word about wine and also on the off chance you might have been in touch with Rafe this week?'

'Nope, 'fraid not. Mind you, I've not actively searched him out—been too busy really.'

David frowned. 'I've tried a couple of times. His sheep have been in the garden again. I'm going to have to get someone to mend the dry-stone walls and send him the bill if he doesn't fix it soon.'

'I think you're a bit of a hit with our Mr Henderson,' Peter said when he came back into the kitchen after seeing David out.

'Nice man,' I said. 'I liked him very much—he's easy to talk to.'

'Mind like a steel trap,' Peter said admiringly. 'Very clever man. Made a fortune over the years. Er, Clementine, I hope you won't take this the wrong way and do tell me if I'm out of order...' He handed me a black and gold expensive looking carrier bag sporting the unmistakable logo of Midhope's most expensive and exclusive dress shop.

Bows and Belles stood out, among the pound shops and charity shops of Midhope's High Street, like a Ferrari in a forecourt of Corsas and Fiats, and was a real magnet for Midhope's as well as neighbouring Leeds and Manchester's wealthy women shoppers. I'd once, in a fit of temper over something my mother had said, spent an hour when I should have been in a food hygiene lecture, trying on the most expensive of their dresses and then slunk out, overcome with guilt at wasting the very pleasant owner's time as well as utterly despondent that I would never be able to own such beautiful things.

'Oh, Peter...' I took out the beautifully designed and tailored black gabardine dress. 'I can't accept this...'

His face fell. 'Don't you like it? I can always go straight back and change it if it's not you or if it's not your size...'

'Not like it? No, no, it's not that. It's absolutely beautiful...' I stroked the soft material and, avoiding looking at the price tag, placed it back in its carrier.

What was that old film with Demi Moore and Robert Redford when she's in some casino and he offers to buy her the ridiculously expensive little black dress that, like me, she'd been trying on for the sheer hell of it? She'd shoved it back at him saying something like: 'The dress is for sale— I'm not.' Robert Redford, if I remember rightly, had taken the rejection with aplomb; Peter, I could see was upset. He took my hand, looking at me anxiously. 'Clementine, you're doing all this cooking for me. Please let this be a sort of payment for that. Look, I'll go and hang it up in your room and then you can see what you think.'

'Mummy, you look like a princess.' Allegra gazed open-mouthed as I went into the little snug where she'd just come from upstairs to join Max in watching some early Saturday evening television. I'd put Allegra in the bath while I showered, and she was now squeaky clean after a day playing in the garden, already snugly ensconced in the chair she seemed to have made her own, her slippered feet resting on George's black woolly head.

'I thought princesses wore pink and silver, not black,' I

laughed. Izzy had lent me a pair of black high heels to go with the simple red and black shift dress I'd found in the Oxfam shop and which I'd planned to wear before Peter presented me with the ravishing dress that had now taken its place. My scruples, it seemed, were not in Demi Moore's class, but I justified accepting and wearing of the dress by telling myself that Demi Moore had just been swanning around, gambling in some casino, while I had spent the previous seven hours or so cooking as if my life depended upon it.

'Oh my God.' Izzy, for once at a loss for words, suddenly appeared at the door of the snug. She said nothing for a few seconds but just stared at me. 'Been looking for you all over. Wow, you scrub up well.'

I laughed and kissed Allegra, taking Izzy's arm and leading her into the sitting room where I could hear voices. 'Oh my God, Clem,' she said once again as she stood gazing at the sumptuous décor of Peter's sitting room. Vanessa, it appeared, had been going through a more flamboyant period just before she upped and left Peter for her Cavalier. As with Sophie's new loft bedroom, at which I'd had a sneaky gander before getting changed, Vanessa had obviously decided it was time to get rid of the old rag-rolled walls, which according to Peter had been her stock in trade. 'You stood still at your peril when we first moved here,' Peter had said without a glimmer of humour. 'Sit down and relax and you risked being rag-rolled into submission along with everything else.'

'Oh my God, Clem,' Izzy now whispered, for a third time and indicating with a nod of her head the man pouring wine for the two women in front of him. 'I had the impression

Peter was fair-haired—you didn't tell me he was so dark and bloody gorgeous.'

I grinned at her. 'He isn't—dark I mean. That's David Henderson. Close your mouth, Izzy—you're showing your fillings—and I'll introduce you to him.'

'Hang on, I've lost Mel and Julian. We've actually been here ten minutes—Allegra was waiting and took us straight up to her room as soon as we walked through the front door. I think Mel's still up there or got lost in all these rooms. Allegra's in heaven, isn't she?'

I nodded. 'Bit worrying, really. Not reality, as you well know…' I broke off as Peter walked in with Declan and a fair, curly-haired and very smiley man who I didn't know.

'Ah, Clementine. I found these two looking for a dinner party. I believe we have one planned this evening?' Peter chortled. 'And you must be Izzy?' He took Izzy's hand and squeezed it between his own, rather white, palms. 'I've heard lots about you.'

'All good, I hope?' Izzy appeared momentarily at a loss as to what to say next as Peter continued to hold her hand.

Declan came over and gave me a kiss. 'Hi, sweetheart.' He looked me over appraisingly. 'You look absolutely fabulous, Clem. Something obviously agrees with you out here in the sticks.'

'I'm rather hoping it might be me, Dec.' Peter chortled once more as Declan winced slightly. He hated having his name shortened to Dec—said it made him want to add 'chair', sing '… the halls with Christmas holly' or look around for his mate Ant.

'Clem, this is Julian Naylor.'

The smiley-faced man came over and gave me a kiss too.

'This is so kind of you both inviting us along this evening. We've brought lots of goodies with us. Mel and I love France—we actually got engaged in Cannes—and we've just returned from another trip and brought back lots of stinky cheese.' He proffered the Monoprix bag and laughed. 'Just in case you were thinking the pong was my feet...'

'Oh wow, fabulous stuff,' I said, peering into the bag and recognising some of the cheeses we used to have on offer at La Toque Blanche. 'You obviously know your *fromages*.'

'*Mais, bien sur*,' Peter giggled, joining in the conversation before recoiling slightly as the cheese odour hit the room. 'Now, do come over and meet the Hendersons and I'll take this bag into the kitchen.'

The two women chatting over by the window and drinking wine were obviously Mandy Henderson and Harriet Westmoreland. The taller of the two blonde women turned as we made to join them, appraising me immediately with her amazing, almost navy blue, eyes. She was stunning: long blonde hair falling to lightly tanned shoulders and an elfin face beautifully but very subtly made up to show off the incredible eyes, high cheekbones and full mouth.

'Hi, you must be Clementine,' the other woman said, coming forward to give me a hug. 'It's so lovely being invited over when Peter hardly knows us. This house is ravishing, isn't it? And is this your little girl?' The woman drew breath for just a few seconds to bend down and shake hands with Allegra who was, very importantly and with great seriousness, helping Max to hand round the canapés I'd made earlier that day.

'Sorry, Clementine,' David Henderson came over and kissed both my cheeks. 'You don't know Mandy, my wife.

And this is Harriet Westmoreland and...' He paused, looking over his shoulder. 'This is Nick, Harriet's husband.'

Nick Westmoreland smiled, unable to say anything for a moment, proffering his hand as he attempted to finish what was in his mouth.

'Gosh, has Peter got outside caterers in?' he finally managed. 'These canapés are to die for.'

'All Clementine's work,' David said, almost paternally. 'I was a witness to her actually making them this morning. I think we are being party to the birth of a huge new culinary talent. I should get her autograph now, Nick—it will be worth something in a few years.'

'That is incredibly kind.' I laughed, embarrassed at the attention as all eyes turned on me while enthusiastic hands reached for more of the canapés, eager to verify David Henderson's sanctioning of my cooking. 'Wait until the end of the meal,' I pleaded. 'You might change your mind by then. Is there anything anybody can't eat? Oh gosh, no one is vegetarian, are they?' I cursed myself for not establishing this simple fact earlier.

'Pork pies—can't bear them,' Harriet shuddered.

'And tha's a born and bred Yorkshire lass?' Declan laughed, affecting a broad Yorkshire accent.

'Oh, I used to *adore* them—plenty of mushy peas and mint sauce—until my sister Di and I raided my mum's cupboard for jelly cubes when we were kids.' Harriet giggled. 'We couldn't find any but found a bag of jelly. Very strange colour it was—we assumed it was a new brand and made a whole bowlful of the stuff and hid it in our toy cupboard to wait for it to set. I can still remember that first huge spoonful I crammed into my mouth.'

'Oh my God, it wasn't…?'

'It was. Aspic jelly. That disgusting stuff they put into pork pies that sits looking accusingly at you on your plate once you've discarded it because it's so revolting.'

'You're right,' Mandy Henderson shuddered delicately. '*Quite* revolting.'

Harriet laughed, filled up her glass and went on, 'But that's not all. For you non-Yorkshire folk—' she looked around almost accusingly at her husband, Nick, David Henderson, Declan and the Naylors '—the local word for a pork pie is a "growler". Unfortunately, the term "growler" has a quite different connotation for those born and bred in certain parts of Southern Ireland.' Harriet paused for effect. 'A growler, to the Irish, is, erm, how do I put this delicately, is a woman's pride and joy…'

Izzy chortled. 'Her bits and pieces?'

'Exactly. So when I told Lilian, our sixty-five-year-old Southern-Irish nanny, that Nick had rung from India, where he'd been working for the past two weeks eating endless curry, to say that all he could think of was coming home and getting his mouth round a "growler" she said, in that wonderful Irish lilt of hers, "To be sure, dear, your man will be after what's his when he gets home…".'

Ribald laughter filled the room. I liked this woman, Harriet. I wanted her to like me and be my friend. I looked across at Peter, who was looking a little worried. I saw him glance across at David Henderson and, when the great man guffawed along with the others, relax somewhat.

'If you want to torture Julian, give him beetroot,' a voice from behind me said. I turned to see a slim, sassily dressed brunette of around my height with beautiful brown eyes.

'Hi, everyone, I'm Mel. Sorry, I was waylaid in Allegra's bedroom having a little play with Barbie's horse and her Action Man.'

'Ooh you're joking,' Izzy said. 'I love beetroot.'

'You love the *effects* of beetroot on your digestive system,' Declan grinned.

'Too much information, Declan.' Izzy glared at Declan but then tutted and laughed as she said, 'I'm such a hypochondriac I spend my life looking down the loo to see if everything is as it should be. I always forget when I've had beetroot the day before and, for a split-second, think this is it—this is what I've been terrified of seeing. When I realise it's the effects of the beetroot, and that I'm not actually at death's door, that I am going to live to see my children grow up, the sense of relief is so great I'm on a huge high for the rest of the day. Who needs cocaine when you've got beetroot?'

Everyone laughed apart from Peter who looked slightly confused, if not offended; I wasn't sure if it was the thought of Izzy peering down her loo on a daily basis or the mention of drugs that had thrown him.

'But how can you be a doctor if you are such a hypochondriac?' Harriet giggled.

'It's *because* I'm a doctor,' Izzy said, almost sadly. 'I come home with a new debilitating illness every evening after my stint at the surgery. Right, let's move on. Where's your leader, Peter?'

'My leader?'

Izzy knocked back her glass of white and happily accepted the top-up that David Henderson offered. 'I thought Clem said Thomas was coming?'

'Thomas?' Peter looked worried once more and glanced my way. Was this someone else I'd invited and not told him about?

'Thomas, you know, what's he called? Thomas *Cromwell*. Clem said Thomas Cromwell was coming.'

'Bit too early in history, that one, Izzy,' David Henderson laughed as his wife raised her eyes in a gesture of disbelief.

'*Oliver* Cromwell I think you mean, Izzy...?' Mandy said somewhat condescendingly.

'Don't let Izzy fool you,' I smiled across at Mandy. 'She knows her history better than anyone. She's just teasing Peter. Which, Izzy, is extremely naughty of you since you've only just met him.'

'Oh!' She laughed, stroking Peter's arm, 'I only tease people I like. And to be honest, what with watching Mantel's *Wolf Hall* on TV recently, added to the fact that this *rather* delicious SB is going down *rather* too well, I did get my Olivers mixed up with my Thomases.'

'Actually, Peter, we do need to be eating fairly soon,' I said. 'Where *are* Neville and Hilary, do you think? They're terribly late.'

'I know, I know,' Peter frowned. 'I am a little concerned. They are coming all the way from Harrogate and I'd really rather not start without them.'

'Dad?' Max came into the sitting room trailing Allegra and George in his wake. 'Oliver Cromwell's here.'

8

Peter had insisted on laying the huge table in the dining room himself and, according to Max, had spent half the previous evening deliberating and dithering as to who should sit next to whom. Max was such a sweetie and hadn't needed much persuading to help carry dishes to the table. I'd tied a blue checked tea towel around his waist for effect and he grinned widely at me as we crossed and re-crossed paths from the kitchen to where the guests were passing the basket of bread I'd made earlier that day.

'Is this bread from that new artisan bakery up in the village?' David was asking as I finally took my place at one end of the table where Peter had obviously thought I should be. 'Charges an absolute fortune for a small loaf but it's so good there's always a queue outside ready to pay.'

'Clementine made it,' Peter said proudly, smiling down at me from his end, where he'd seated himself between who I assumed he thought were the most two important females: Mandy Henderson and Hilary Manning.

'Well, it's certainly better than the Mother's Pride white sliced I had for my lunch,' Neville Manning said, patting my knee for what seemed the fiftieth time.

'Neville Manning, I've never once given you sliced bread, white or otherwise,' his wife scolded him, her already broken-veined cheeks turning pinker as she spoke. 'What will people think?'

'Can't beat a white sliced loaf every now and again.' David Henderson smiled at Hilary as Mandy gave him a pained look of disbelief. 'Especially toasted with Nutella or peanut butter.'

There was a lovely hum of conversation as people 'oohed' and 'aahed' over my starter and, as they cleared their plates with gusto, I started to relax. Peter caught my eye and mouthed, 'Well done, darling.'

Darling? Gosh I'd been promoted. Olly, catching the endearment, patted my knee once more and I shifted my legs out of the way of his clammy hand, unfortunately rubbing my right one against David Henderson's left. I hastily centred myself and offered the breadbasket once more.

'Clementine, I don't think I've ever tasted such wonderful food,' Mel said as she put her knife and fork together. 'Julian and I try to get over to France as often as we can and that wouldn't have been out of place in a top French restaurant. What exactly was it?'

'Crab with burned butter and potato mousseline,' I smiled. 'I'm glad you enjoyed it.'

'I'm really looking forward to coming back to live up north if we're going to find food like this,' Mel said. 'Apart from the fact it will take longer to get over to France—that will be one big disadvantage,' she added ruefully.

'Don't admit to burning the butter, Clem,' Izzy leaned across David and whispered theatrically. 'Mine didn't taste burned at all—in fact it was quite delicious.' She pronounced it 'wash quite delishush.'

'Don't give her any more wine, for heaven's sake, or she'll be under the table,' I said with a grin.

'Give her another and she'll be under the host,' Mel said. 'You always could knock it back, Izzy.'

'It's all scurrilous lies, young man,' Izzy sniffed, downing her drink.

'Right, on your feet, doctor,' I said. 'You can come and help me clear plates.'

'So,' Izzy said as she started to load the dishwasher in what can only be described as a haphazard manner. 'This is all wonderful, Clem. The most beautiful house I've ever seen, a man who is obviously mad about you and, best of all, Allegra looking rosier than I've ever seen her.'

I looked up from putting the final touches to the pan-fried stuffed lamb cutlets. 'Rosier? What do you mean, *rosier*?'

'Well, she's usually such a pale little thing, isn't she? The countryside is obviously doing her good; she's bouncy, happy… *shiny*.'

'If you weren't my friend, I'd probably be hugely offended at that,' I said. 'In fact, I *am* offended. Are you telling me she's usually, flat, unhappy… *dull*?'

'Oh, don't go all uppity on me, Clem. All I'm saying is, I've never seen her so full of it all. It's probably the dog—buy her a dog when you get home.' Izzy scraped a plate, missing the bin with its contents.

'Oh, now you're being ridiculous,' I said crossly. 'Shh, Max is on his way to help.'

Max came into the kitchen, followed by his father. 'Darling,' Peter said, as Izzy raised her eyebrows and grinned at me behind Peter's pink-shirted back, 'that was so delicious. You are such a clever girl. I could see Hilary and Neville were *most* impressed. Now, what can Max and I do to help? What can we take in?'

'I really like doing this,' Max whispered to me as I loaded him up with a huge bowl of Ottolenghi salad. 'I think I might be a waiter when I leave school.'

'Good gracious, I hope not,' Peter said, seriously. 'I haven't forked out all this money for your education for you to end up *waiting* on people.'

'Like I do at The Black Swan, you mean?' I said. It was my turn for raised eyebrows.

Peter's cheeks reddened. 'Well, no, *darling*... I mean, you, well... you're just doing it until you finish university aren't you...?'

I smiled at him. There was no point getting cross with him. I don't suppose I'd want Allegra waiting on tables for a living. 'Right,' I said, patting Peter's arm, 'are we all ready for the second course?'

When we arrived back in the dining room I saw that Allegra was firmly ensconced on Mel Naylor's lap, explaining how she loved George, but was really very frightened of the big scary dog living next door to her at 'my other house'. Golly, I realised with a jolt, she'd very quickly become awfully proprietorial over Peter's house and George.

'Allegra, I really think it's time you were in bed.' I smiled as Max, Peter and I passed round dishes and offered salad and the deliciously creamy gratin potatoes that, I thanked God, had cooked to perfection.

'My daughters were always tucked up in bed *before* any guests arrived,' Hilary Manning said, her accompanying smile not quite reaching her eyes. 'Youngsters get to *hear* such things from adult conversation, don't you think?'

'Oh, if I had a gorgeous little girl like this, she'd be with me all the time,' Mel laughed, stroking Allegra's dark hair. 'She really is the image of you, Clem, isn't she? There's no mistaking whose daughter she is. Anyway, I reckon the French and the Italians have got it right, letting their kids out to restaurants with them and introducing them to wine at an early age.'

'Totally agree with you,' Izzy and Harriet Westmoreland said simultaneously.

'As long as they're well behaved and no school in the morning,' Harriet went on. 'Teaches them how to be sociable and how to behave in grownup company. Mind you, if they start whining and interrupting conversation, I'm the first to cart them off out of sight.'

'Do let Allegra stay up a bit longer,' Peter pleaded.

I was surprised: I'd have thought, particularly as Mrs Cromwell had spoken, Peter would have wanted the children out of the way.

'Just a bit longer then,' I smiled. 'But Allegra, get down and let Mel eat now. Do you have children of your own?' I asked Mel as Allegra slid down and trotted off with George.

'No, I'm afraid not,' Mel smiled. 'But I'm stepmother to Penelope from Julian's first marriage, and I have four nieces who I spoil whenever I can.'

'Well, once you're up here, next month, you can come and spoil my lot whenever you want,' Izzy grinned, before rolling her eyes with theatrical delight as she swallowed her first bite of lamb cutlet with its accompanying white bean puree.

With two courses produced, I felt I could relax. I took a huge glug of the red wine that David had brought and poured, catching his eye as I did so.

'Steady,' he smiled. 'What do you think of it?'

'Gosh, that is *delicious*,' I smiled back, savouring the taste. 'What is it?'

'It's a Sans Soufre from a northern Rhone producer called Thierry Allemand,' David said.

'He's been saving it for years,' Mandy Henderson tutted. 'Thank goodness it's finally seen the light of day.'

David looked slightly embarrassed. 'Well, I just thought anyone who has been a chef at La Toque Blanche must be going to produce food worthy of it…'

'Hear, hear, David,' Olly Cromwell smirked, knocking back an almost full glass of the stuff before simultaneously kneading my knee as if it were the bread dough I'd made earlier that day, while holding out his hand to David for a top-up. Olly, looking more than ever like Mr Mainwaring in *Dad's Army*, polished his glasses on his napkin before leaning behind me to talk to David on my other side.

The wine began to reach into every corner of my body and, relaxed, I leaned forward, surveying the guests around the table, listening in to snippets of their conversations:

'… and Rafe Ahern is so full of himself round here. In fact, there's only one head bigger than his and that's Birkenhead…'

'… I only asked him how many acres he had. The look he gave me I might as well have asked him how much money he had in the bank…'

'… the cricket? England's always expecting… No wonder they call her the Mother Country over in Australia…'

'… and Kit is only seventeen and already wanting to go off to all-night parties in Leeds…'

'… so why does everyone call you *Mouse*, Mel…?'

'… and he said he couldn't make it as something had come up and I thought, "yes, his cock most likely…"'

'… vvery poorly connected, I believe…'

'… voh so are we… vour internet is forever crashing…'

'… and I was telling my eldest daughter, Libby, that I would just love to see the Terracotta Army and she said, wasn't that the posh pudding we had last week…?'

'… so, this piece of string goes into a pub and the landlord says, "Out, we don't serve string in here." So the string goes out and rubs and rubs at his head and then goes back in and asks for a pint. "Aren't you that piece of string I refused to serve earlier?" asks the landlord. "No," says the string, "I'm afraid not…"'

'… I don't get that…'

'… and do you think I could interest you in joining the Regiment, David…?'

I realised I was actually very tired. I could see through the glass doors leading into the snug that Allegra was supine, half asleep, her pyjama-d legs over one arm of the chair she appeared to have made her own, her dark plaits hanging over the other and mingling with George's black curls below, until it was impossible to say where one started and the other ended. I knew I should stir myself, get her to bed and then go organise the pudding and cheese.

Peter appeared to be fully engrossed in conversation with both Mandy Henderson and Mrs Cromwell but, obviously realising I was looking across the table at him, glanced up and smiled at me. He did have a rather handsome face, I thought tipsily. I'd never been attracted to fair-haired men—had always gone for the dark haired and dark eyed type, preferably with an emergence of dark stubble on their jaw—but Peter, blond-haired, clean-shaven and pink cheeked was growing on me. Or was it simply the rose-coloured wine having its effect?

'I need to get Allegra to bed,' I mouthed across at him. 'Give me ten minutes and then I'll sort pudding.'

Looking rather flustered, Peter suddenly shot out of his seat, telling me to stay where I was. Assuming he was going to bring in the cheese board to which I'd already added the lovely French cheeses Julian had donated earlier—Mandy Henderson and Mel had just had a conversation about enjoying the cheese board before pudding as is the mode in France—I began to clear the plates.

When Peter reappeared a few minutes later, he was carrying a tray of full champagne flutes rather than the cheese board I was expecting. Looking somewhat ill at ease, he stood at the head of the table and, with the help of Max and Allegra—who was now very much awake—passed his guests a glass each. As Peter cleared his throat and asked for their attention, I glanced across at Olly Cromwell. Surely he should be making the speech to promote Peter to Musketeer and not Peter himself.

Peter cleared his throat again, and his rather prominent Adam's apple bobbed up and down reminding me of the first time I'd seen him eating the scalding treacle sponge in The Black Swan.

'Ladies and gentlemen, I'd like you to raise your glass to Clementine, our wonderful and talented cook.'

'To Clementine.' Glasses were raised, their contents drunk and then returned to the snowy linen tablecloth.

'As many of you know,' Peter went on, 'I have known Clementine for quite a while now. I have come to think a lot of her and of her beautiful daughter, Allegra…' He paused and smiled at Allegra who giggled self-consciously before hiding her face in my shoulder. 'In fact, erm…' Peter cleared his throat and reached for his water, taking a sip with shaking hands. His Adam's apple bobbed and he replaced his water glass with his champagne glass. 'I'd like you all to know how much they have both come to mean to me and… and… erm… and…'

And what?

'… and Max, and hope that you will join with me in hoping… praying…' More Adam's apple bobbing… 'that she, Clementine, I mean… erm… will…'

Will what?

'… erm… will make me the happiest man in the… in the… erm… in …

The world?

'… the world, by agreeing to become my… my… er…

Cook?

'… my, erm…'

What?

'… my wife.'

Fuck!

There was a stunned silence from those around the table as all eyes turned from Peter to me. All I could think of were those dreadful radio, or worse, TV programmes, usually on Valentine's Day, when some pillock corners his intended in front of zillions of listeners and proposes. I'd always yelled at the radio, 'Don't do it. Don't do it! You don't have to accept just because you're on national radio.' I looked across at Max who, standing by his father's side, appeared to be holding his breath; at Izzy whose mouth was one big 'O' of shock; at David Henderson whose face was impassive and across to Peter himself who stood, red-faced and hopeful.

Finally, I looked down at Allegra. One of the ribbons on her plaits had come undone, she had a smudge of chocolate on her right cheek and her huge brown eyes were holding mine with such hope I had to smile. Or cry.

'Well then,' I said, and it was as if someone else, not me, was speaking. 'Well then, thank you, Peter and yes, that would be lovely. Pudding anyone?'

9

SARAH

Poppy Rabbitt kicked her foot impatiently against the broken netting of the netball-court door while simultaneously making a futile attempt to pull down her too-small pleated gym skirt over her school regulation navy knickers. Thank God she had only one more term to go before she could leave this dump of a school and move on to the local sixth-form college. Despite her father's insistent ranting that she continue at the girls-only private school to do A levels, she knew it was all hot air on his part and he would be more than relieved at not having to fork out the fees for the next two years. Even with the reduced fees he'd negotiated with Mrs Appleby, the current headmistress, in return for his ecclesiastical presence on the governing body, as well as his taking of assembly every Friday morning, the termly bill hung over the Reverend Roger Rabbitt like a bad smell.

Where the hell was her mother? All the other girls had been picked up in over-the-top, four-wheel-drive monsters by young mothers with hair as long, blonde and shiny as that of their sixteen-year-old daughters. Polly scowled crossly and looked at her phone once more. Serve her mother right if she was propositioned by that sleazy old gardener who made no attempt to avert his rheumy-eyed gaze from the girls' bouncing chests as he regularly mowed the grass perilously near the goal end of court.

Why hadn't Kit Westmoreland texted her like he'd promised after she'd shared her bottle of Co-op vodka with him at Tamsin's cousin's party in Leeds last weekend? Poppy had noticed him as soon as he'd walked into the room—well, you couldn't miss him really, he was so gorgeous. Dark blond hair and the most wonderful brown eyes she'd ever seen. She'd always gone for dark hair and blue eyes in the past, but the contrasting combination of blond hair and dark eyes plus the rugby physique, obvious under Kit Westmoreland's black T-shirt, had totally turned her head. Literally. Unfortunately, other heads, including bloody Gabbie Ferrier's, queen bee of the lower sixth, had also swivelled when Kit and his rugby mates had walked en masse into the kitchen looking for booze. All the other girls, particularly those who, like Poppy herself, had come along with Tamsin from school and knew of Gabbie and her gang's reputation, stood back while the older girls, like so many exotically attired birds of prey moved in, taking first pickings, before leaving what was left to the lesser mortals in the fifth form.

Poppy scowled again. Bad enough standing here, freezing her tush off in this ridiculous games kit while waiting for her mother who was *never* on time, but knowing that Kit Westmoreland had chatted her up—and yes, snogged her long and hard too—just to drink her vodka was humiliation indeed. And it was bloody Easter, which meant her father would be in a foul mood for the next few days as he grappled with his sermon for the big day on Sunday. He'd been like a bear with a sore head ever since last Sunday's morning service when, after a telling off from the archbishop and in an ensuing effort to bolster his ever-decreasing flock, he'd purposely opened his arms to the inmates of all the rest homes in the locality. He'd ushered them in, helping with wheelchairs and walking sticks and generally acting so out of character, that the usual steadfast if dwindling congregation had wondered if he'd taken to drink. Unfortunately his sermon, urging the younger and fitter members of his brethren to help and visit the elderly at the end of their years, had rendered the older ones to turn in bewilderment and the younger members to giggle when, with a flourish he'd pressed his CD button and, to the introductory notes of Gerry and the Pacemakers' 'You'll Never Walk Alone', had smiled beatifically at his ancient guests and said gently, 'You'll never walk again.'

'… Darling, I'm here. Yoo-hoo, Poppy, over here, sweetheart.'

Why in God's name was her mother so loud and—what was the word she'd used in creative writing that very morning that had sent old Ma Draper into spasms of delight? Effusive. That was it. *Effusive*. She was so bloody *effusive*. And what on earth had she done to the car this time? The ancient lime-green Ford Focus—Kermit to all that knew it—that should have been put out to pasture years ago was trailing what sounded like a cacophony of tin cans in its wake.

'Oh hell, Poppy, your father will kill me,' Sarah Rabbitt sighed through the open window as Poppy tried, but failed, to open the car's front passenger door. 'Give it a good pull. That's it. I've just mounted another sodding bollard. Can you believe it?'

Poppy could. Bollard-mounting appeared to be her mother's raison d'être lately: this had to be the third one this year.

'I missed the turning to Mr Davison's house—I was trying to deliver some parish leaflets your father forgot to give him last Sunday—but knew all I had to do was a U-turn at the next street to get back on to the main road. So... are you hungry, darling? I think there's half a Kit Kat in here somewhere... I indicated, turned right to go round the bollocking bollard and hit something. I honestly couldn't think what it was; I knew I couldn't have hit the bollard like I did last time because it was *there*, intact to my right...' Sarah paused and said vaguely, 'Try the glove compartment, darling, I think there's the remains of a Mars Bar in there if you can't find the Kit Kat... but the car wouldn't move. Wouldn't go back or forwards. I realised I was rocking on something, a bit like being on a see-saw...' Sarah smiled across at her younger daughter as Poppy finally extracted the remaining finger of a Twix from the car's console and proceeded to denude it of its wrapping. '... And then this *very* nice young man roars up on his bike and says, "Someone's nicked the other bollard, love. You're stuck on its plinth...".'

Poppy took a surreptitious glance at her phone. Still nothing from Kit Westmoreland. Five days now and not a word.

'… So I said, "what shall I do? I can't sit here like an extra from the bloody *Italian Job*".' Sarah giggled, crashing the Focus's ancient gearbox as she slowed down for the lights ahead. 'Anyway, luckily for me, there was a minibus full of rugby players just arriving back at the boys' grammar school on Arthurs Avenue and they came over and bodily lifted me off the plinth. How kind was that? No damage done at all to the car.'

'No damage?' Poppy looked up from her phone and across at Sarah. 'Mum, half your exhaust pipe is trailing behind us. We'll probably set on fire soon with all the sparks it's creating.'

'Oh, I can soon tie that back up with a piece of string once we get home. Your father will never know. And don't you go telling him, either.'

'I don't know why you're so frightened of him,' Poppy said dismissively. 'Kermit's your car and Dad's supposed to be a man of God. Turning the other cheek and all that when you prang the car yet again.'

'Oh, don't be so silly, darling.' For a split-second Sarah wavered, before smiling brightly. 'What a thing to say; frightened of your father, you daft thing. Oh, look, Jenny's arrived. I didn't think she was leaving Birmingham until this evening.' Sarah jumped out of the car, oblivious to the recalcitrant exhaust pipe now lying prostrate in full view of the rectory windows, bounded up the steps to the huge oak front door and went to find her elder daughter.

Poppy wasn't listening. She was too busy texting, hitting wrong keys in her excitement to tell Tamsin that Kit Westmoreland had just left a message asking to meet up with her in Leeds the following weekend.

The enthusiasm Sarah had shown for Jennifer's arrival was largely for Poppy's benefit, and as she crossed the rectory hall noticing, where usually she didn't, that the heavy oak chest of drawers was long overdue for a good dusting, Sarah's heart sank even further as she realised Rosemary was also in attendance. The strident tones of the Rev Roger's large, raw-boned harridan of a sister who had, down the years, delighted in terrifying myriad girls in her role as head of games at some large comprehensive in Liverpool, could be heard holding forth from behind the closed doors of Roger's inner sanctum. Rosemary, it appeared, had arrived a day earlier than expected for the Easter break and, in typical egotistical Rosemary fashion, had failed to inform them of her unexpected and, from Sarah's point of view, not overly welcome arrival.

Rosemary was not, Sarah imagined, the sort of games mistress on whom adolescent girls developed a crush. She was far more likely to be on a par with the virago of Sarah's own school days who had kept a precise note in a green record book of the girls' menstrual cycles. Any girl pleading 'time of the month, Miss Dennison,' in the hope of being excused the humiliating ritual of the communal shower and its accompanying cheap pink soap was met with a finger down the register and a raised eyebrow. But then, Sarah supposed as she hovered, picking dead leaves from the drooping spider plant—anything to put off going into the sitting room for a couple more minutes—nowadays, what with student rights and all young girls' use of Tampax from day one of menstruation, as opposed to the horror of creaking sanitary towels and a garter belt, that excuse was out of the window anyway.

For a second, Sarah considered going straight down to the beautifully sunny kitchen at the other end of the rectory and trying out the chocolate cake recipe that had been kicking around in her head for the last couple of days. The chillies she was going to add to the 80 per cent chocolate were ripening nicely to a deep red on the kitchen's south facing window sill, and she longed to avoid both her elder daughter and sister-in-law and take herself off to the place where she could immerse herself in the one thing at which she knew she was any good: cooking.

The Reverend Roger, very good-looking in his youth, was, in his mid-fifties, still thought a handsome man with his full head of thick, strawberry-blond hair and rather unusual almond-shaped green eyes. The ensuing years had, however, proved something of a disappointment to this servant of God and, apart from a stint in Cheltenham and latterly in the leafier suburbs of Harrogate, he appeared to be stuck on the outskirts of north Leeds for the duration. It hadn't helped when, with the release of the Disney cartoon, *Who Killed Roger Rabbit* in the early Nineties, he was now universally hailed as Roger Rabbit rather than the Reverend Roger which, as well as being pleasingly alliterative had, he'd always thought, a rather dignified ring befitting an up and coming clergyman. He railed constantly about 'that damned film' and blamed it for his lack of promotion to bishop; a bishop called Roger Rabbit would, after all, surely be a laughing stock among the down to earth Yorkshire folk who, as well as calling a spade a spade, now had the gleeful right to call a vicar Roger Rabbit.

'Why, in God's name, are you skulking out here?' Reverend Roger said, frowning as he flung open the sitting room door, narrowly missing colliding with his wife. 'Jennifer's here. And Rosemary as well. Do you think we could have some tea?' Roger's green eyes narrowed slightly as he caught sight of Sarah's pale wrist protruding from her grey ethnic-looking sweater as she reached to pull more dead foliage from the plant above her. Why did she have to dress like some aging hippy? he thought irritably, before saying quietly, 'Do pull down your sleeves, Sarah, or those bruises will become a talking point.'

Pouring tea and handing round the deliciously crumbling scones she'd made earlier that day, Sarah acknowledged, not for the first time, that she felt a stranger in her own home. Rosemary, hogging the sofa while tutting over that morning's *Daily Telegraph*, appeared more at ease as a guest than Sarah did as the lady of the house. She was, she knew, nervous both of her sister-in-law and—much, much more sadly—of her own daughter, Jennifer. She must remember to call her that and not the Jenny she'd always been until her appointment, at the age of just twenty-nine, as deputy headmistress at one of Birmingham's most prodigious private girls' grammar schools. Jenny—Jennifer—was, apart from their respectively held political views, a clone of her Aunt Rosemary with whom she was now discussing the merits or otherwise of the current Secretary of State for Education.

'Pompous little squirt,' Rosemary was saying, spraying crumbs onto the newspaper as she spoke. 'What do *you* think, Sarah? Hope you're going to vote the right way next month?' Rosemary lowered the paper, simultaneously shoving the remains of her scone into her cavernous mouth and peering over her glasses at her sister-in-law.

Sarah had absolutely no idea who was in charge of education at present, and her only reason for visiting the polls at all was guilt at letting down Emily Wilding Davidson who'd thrown herself under the king's horse all those years ago fighting for votes for women, if she didn't. She knew she should take more of an interest so as to be able to give an opinion at times such as this but, once she'd sorted the day-to-day running of this mausoleum of a house with its ancient bathrooms and stained glass windows that Roger demanded she kept polished 'to let in God's good light' and then met Roger's demands as his unofficial secretary and gofer on church errands, all she wanted to do was escape to the sanctuary of her kitchen.

Sarah smiled vaguely, hoping that would suffice, and luckily it did. Rosemary had bullied her sister-in-law for years, but particularly since that awful day, ten years ago, when Roger had let slip where he and Sarah had met. These days Sarah no longer rose to the bait and Rosemary tended to leave her alone preferring, instead, to take part in a much more equal-sided argument with her elder niece on the shortcomings of private education. Sarah sighed, wishing once again that Jamie was here to back her up, but her nineteen-year-old son was taking a gap year in France, working as a plongeur in the kitchens of a Michelin-starred restaurant before supposedly going up to Durham

University to study law in September. Sarah knew he was in his element out there in Provence and was already dreading the ensuing arguments when Roger learned Jamie was seriously contemplating throwing his university place away and staying on in France in order to learn even more about French cuisine.

Sarah gathered up the tea things onto a tray and made her excuses. She needn't have bothered: Roger had already left to practise his Sunday sermon on 'Family values', Poppy she hadn't seen since she'd gone up to her room straight from school and Jenny and Rosemary were still in heated discussion—this time both in agreement—over the issue of competitive sports in schools.

Solace was waiting in her kitchen and, as she made her way down the long corridor leading to the more modern part of the house Sarah wondered, not for the first time, how on earth she had ended up here, living this life.

10

Peter and I decided we'd get married in the July, just a couple of months after the dinner party where, right there at the table, after shocking everyone including me with his proposal of marriage, he'd slipped a huge diamond onto the ring finger of my left hand. Although at first Peter had wanted a big do with a marquee on the lawn, he finally agreed with me that, because of his children and, more importantly the speed with which we were going to tie the knot, a simple ceremony at the local register office with Izzy and Declan as witnesses would be preferable. I'd also had a—not pleasant—vision of a whole load of guests turning up in their re-enactment gear and even having to start my new life as Mrs Broadbent dressed as a seventeenth-century wench, stepping through a piking pole guard of honour. This was another thing to discuss with Peter; I would have to firmly tell him that my agreeing to marry him did not mean I was agreeing to fight the Cavaliers every Sunday.

Once or twice a year, maybe. And only then if the sun was out and I could take a book with me if I got fed up.

I still hadn't met Peter's fifteen-year-old daughter, Sophie, in my new role as stepmother-to-be. I'd been acquainted with her, of course, on the numerous occasions he'd brought both his children into The Black Swan when I was serving on a Saturday—Sophie had always, without exception, gone for the Caesar salad—but apparently she wasn't at all happy at her father 'making a fool of himself with some waitress dressed in black feathers'.

'Did Peter tell you she'd said that?' Izzy had asked, surprised. 'I think he should have kept that to himself.'

'No,' I'd replied, somewhat ruefully, 'Max told me. But Max said it was because she doesn't really like anyone except herself, and it was all OK because *he* really liked me. *And* my food. So that was all that mattered.'

Izzy had had plenty more to say on the whole subject of my forthcoming nuptials. She'd rung me constantly on the Sunday after the dinner party but, still at Peter's house and coming to terms with what I'd done, I'd ignored her calls, finally turning off my phone until Peter took Allegra and me back home on the Sunday evening.

'But why don't you just stay here with me? Now?' he'd asked. 'You don't ever have to go back to that dump you call home.'

I'd winced slightly at his referring to my home as a dump, but had to concede that, in all reality, that's what it was. I needed space—and time—to think about what I'd done in accepting a proposal of marriage from a man whom I didn't love. And why I'd done it. So, on the Sunday after the dinner party, once we'd cleared up, tidied the kitchen and taken the children and George for a walk and eaten a late lunch, I told Peter I needed to get Allegra home. When Peter saw that I was really determined to go home, he kissed my cheek and said I was right and that he had to get Max back to his mother's anyway.

'Will you tell Vanessa about us?' I asked as I loaded Allegra into the backseat of the car alongside Max.

'Yes of course. Why wouldn't I? I shall take great delight in telling her that you've agreed to be my wife.' Peter kissed the top of my head. 'She knows I'm going over there now with Max. There are quite a few things I need to sort out with her.'

'Oh? What like?'

'Nothing for you to worry about,' Peter said, almost grandly. 'I shall be taking care of you and Allegra from now on.'

'Oh, so you're finally answering your phone are you?' Izzy sounded exasperated. 'I've been ringing you all day.'

'I didn't realise,' I lied.

'Are you at home?'

'Yes.'

'Alone?'

'Yes.'

'Do you want me to come over?'

'Why should I want that?'

'Clementine, you've just become engaged to a man I know you don't love… No, no, hear me out,' she went on as I started to speak. 'Listen, Clem, you don't have to do this… Oh, this is no good. I'm coming over. I'll bring Jim.'

'Jim? Who the hell's J—?'

'Gin, Clem, *gin*. Now, don't argue, I'm on my way.'

Allegra, after the excitement of the weekend, was already drooping and irritable and made little objection to the idea of an early bath and a boiled egg and soldiers eaten in front of a DVD. I'd just got her settled, in clean nightdress and dressing gown, in front of *Toy Story* which she must have seen umpteen times but of which she never tired, when Izzy arrived brandishing a giant Toblerone.

'Sorry, someone appears to have drunk the gin. Can't think who,' Izzy added, dropping a kiss on Allegra's dark hair that, still damp from the bath, was framing her face in curls. 'Anyway, the chocolate's from Declan. He thought we might need it.'

'You're making it sound as if I've committed some terrible crime,' I said stoutly as I broke off huge chunks of Toblerone. 'Come on, let's go into the kitchen where little ears can't hear if I'm going to have a telling off.' An awful anxiety had enveloped me and I knew Izzy was only going to confirm what I already knew: that I was marrying Peter, not because I loved him but for what he could offer me.

'Clementine,' Izzy said, coming over to me and giving me a bear hug. 'Look, I know why you've agreed to marry Peter but you know you don't *have* to. Declan and I can help you move—help you look for somewhere better than this.' She glanced around at the kitchen, at the 1960s blue laminated cupboard doors, at the freestanding two-hob cooker under which an ancient copy of *Yellow Pages* kept it on an even keel and then down at the pebble-decorated lino, split and scuffed in too many places.

I was suddenly tired, tired of people who thought they knew better than me how I should be living my life. 'Izzy, what would you do for your children? Anything? Everything? Die for them? Yes of course you would.' I put down the chunk of Toblerone I was about to eat. I didn't need chocolate to get me on a roll—I was already on one. 'You have no idea, Izzy, with your white, middle-class GP life; with your lovely Declan and no money worries; with your three gorgeous children all on the right road to success in their schools and beyond...' I knew I was gabbling, that what I was thinking was coming out in a torrent and not totally coherent. 'Well, I want *my* gorgeous child on that right road too. And, as you can see—' I waved my arms around the kitchen, taking in what Izzy herself had surveyed a few seconds earlier '—I'm not even under starter's orders yet.'

'Clem, you are doing an amazing job with Allegra. She's beautiful, happy, incredibly bright—far more with it than any of my three were at her age. You are a strong woman, for heaven's sake. We're not living in the Fifties where a woman needed a man—and, let's be honest here, not the brightest specimen on the planet—'

'Just stop there, this minute. How dare you?' It was like a red mist coming down and I'd had enough of Izzy's condescension. Did she think a bar of Toblerone—albeit giant—could persuade me that the decision I'd made last night was pants? 'Do you really think, Izzy, that I don't know what Peter is? That, OK, he doesn't read *The Guardian*; that... that he doesn't know anything about Mole in *The*

Wind in the Willows; that he likes…likes dressing up in funny clothes and brandishing a pikestaff? But don't tell me that he's not overly bright. He's worked damned hard with his business and must have some sort of financial head on him to have achieved all that you saw last night. And there's Max. I happen to really like his little boy—I shall be more than happy to become his stepmother. And the best thing about all this, Izzy? Do you want to know what the very best thing about all this is? That for some reason he fell in love with *me*, with *me* even though I'm a single mother, broke and living on Emerald Street with a four-year-old…'

'Oh, for God's sake, Clementine, you are a *totally* beautiful and talented girl and there is no reason why anyone shouldn't fall in love with you. And there's no reason why you should marry a man you don't love!'

'Yes there is,' I almost spat. 'There is one very good reason why: Allegra. Peter will be able to give her all the things I can't. He loves us both—I truly believe that. He's a good man, and Allegra is a different girl since Peter and Max—and of course George—came into her life. I'm doing this for her and nothing you say will make me change my mind. So, you either help me with all this or you… or you can leave now. I mean it, Izzy.'

Izzy didn't say anything for a while. 'OK, OK,' she finally said. 'Let's eat chocolate and you can tell me all your wedding plans. If you truly feel this is the best thing for you both then I give you my blessing.'

'Your blessing? Don't be so bloody pompous, Izzy. You're not my dad, you're my friend, and I want you to be pleased for me, be there for me. Look, I know Peter is a bit, well, *different*, but Allegra will have a proper family with a dad, a big sister, a big brother and a fabulous home. She won't have to be the kid who is dropped off first and picked up last from after-school club every day because her mum is having to work all the hours God sends just to keep her head above water. And do you know what, Izzy? Over the past few months I've come to realise there are two things I'm jolly good at. One is cooking and the other is being a mum—'

'Absolutely,' Izzy interrupted. 'You are a bloody good mum which is why I don't understand why you feel you need a man to help you with Allegra. You are more than capable of bringing her up yourself.'

'I never let myself think about having any more children because I reckoned it might be years before I met anyone and then I'd be too old, but I know I really, really want children—'

'You're thirty, not ninety,' Izzy exploded. 'You've years left before you have to start thinking it's too late to have more babies.'

'No, I haven't. If I'd not met Peter I might be years trying to find that special someone with whom I'd like to have children.'

'Exactly. I'm sorry, Clem, but Peter *isn't* that *special someone*. You know he isn't. Is it fair marrying him for what he can provide for you? Does he know you don't love him—? Izzy came to a sudden stop as Allegra came into the kitchen yawning and trailing Hector, her pink elephant.

I smiled across at Izzy as my daughter popped her thumb into her mouth and climbed onto my knee, burying her head into my chest. 'This is what it's all about, Izzy, this is the only thing that matters…'

★

So, here I was, gazing round, for almost the last time, at my home for the past year. The Artexed walls, resembling nothing more than grubby Christmas-cake icing on which I'd snagged numerous pairs of black tights before heading, late, for The Black Swan, were looking particularly drab now that I'd taken down posters and the myriad pictures Allegra had brought back from nursery and, latterly, from school. Once I'd taken out yet more black plastic bags to the dustbins, I went upstairs to check on Allegra who was fast asleep in the smaller of the two bedrooms. It was a beautifully warm evening at the beginning of July and, although we'd had the longest day a week or so earlier, the days were still long with no hint, yet, of the nights closing in. Around ten, once I heard the expected knock on my front door, I grabbed a sweater, slung it over my shoulders and went downstairs.

'Allegra knows you're babysitting,' I said to Amirah as I followed her into the kitchen. 'She thinks I'm off to the cinema with Izzy, so if she wakes up—which she very rarely does—just tell her I'll be back very soon once the film is over. Right,' I said, looking over towards Yusuf and Musa who were waiting by the open front door, 'shall we go?'

11

'So, where do you think we should look?' I asked. 'I've been up and down Emerald Street loads of times in the past few months but not seen anything of her.' As always, as we headed right into the centre of Midhope's main red-light area, I felt the usual frisson of hope and fear. Hope that Lucy would suddenly manifest herself before my eyes and fear as to her reaction if she did.

Yusuf said nothing, but carried on walking, occasionally taking my arm, steering me round a broken pavement, pulling me back from the otherwise quiet road when a car went by. We eventually turned onto the wider road that led to the 1960s tower block of flats: the infamous, incongruously named Emerald House. This was no jewel in the local authority's crown; more a thorn in its side—a dumping ground for Midhope's down-and-outs. Condemned at least five years ago by the then new Tory-led council in a deal with Tesco to clear the area and build a mammoth supermarket and sports centre, the flats lived on, housing the down and out, drug dealers and, latterly, asylum seekers from Iraq, Libya and now Syria.

Instead of going in at the double doors of the flats at ground level as I'd expected, Yusuf took my elbow and shook his head slightly, walking past and heading towards a street beyond. A row of mean Victorian terraced houses, very much like my own, stretched on either side of the street, grey and drab apart from an unexpected couple of hanging baskets, a shiny letter box and knocker, a newly painted yellow door standing out primrose-like in a field of green and brown sludge.

Yusuf stopped a quarter of the way down the street and Musa touched my elbow, silently indicating I should follow them down the narrow passage that led to the house at the back of the terrace. We were obviously expected, because the brightly painted, pillar-box-red door which opened onto the neat patch of garden was ajar and welcoming.

'Come on in, all of you,' a disembodied voice floated down the flagged path. 'I've got the kettle on. Is it warm enough to sit outside in the garden, do you think?'

Musa pushed me from behind and all three of us went through the red door that led directly into the tiny kitchen. A motherly looking woman, at a glance I calculated to be around sixty, was reaching into one of the cupboards for a tin.

'I know I shouldn't.' She grinned as she opened the tin, taking a long, almost lascivious look before taking out a chocolate biscuit. 'But they're M&S and, quite frankly, I'm totally addicted to anything that comes out of their food hall. Bloody expensive, all of it, but, at my age, I reckon I deserve it...' She stopped suddenly as she turned her full attention onto me rather than the biscuits she was lovingly and proudly decanting onto a plate. 'Jesus,' she said, 'you're the spit of her.'

She said nothing more but handed the tray of tea things to Musa and indicated to Yusuf that he should bring one of the chairs from the kitchen in order that all four of us could be seated around the tiny table outside. She poured Yusuf a mug of brackish-looking tea and frowned slightly. 'Does your dad know you're hanging around down here on Emerald Street?'

'I do actually live round here, you know,' Yusuf laughed.

She snorted disparagingly. 'Don't give me that, Yusuf, you're up in the posh bit. Your dad's my landlord and wouldn't be too happy with you coming down on a social visit. I know what your dad and his brother think of us lot actually living down here on this side of the river. Why aren't you studying, any road? I thought you were set on becoming a lawyer?'

'That's what my dad wants, rather than me. Anyway, I've finished for the summer and promised Clem I'd bring her down to meet you.' Yusuf turned to me and smiled. 'I told you, last time I was collecting rents for my dad, Sheena and I started chatting and she said to bring you down. She does know who Lucy is, don't you, Sheena? I mean, now that you've seen Clementine, is Lucy who you thought she was?'

My heart started pounding uncomfortably in my chest. 'Is she OK, Sheena? Do you know where she is now?'

'Well, love, that's why I suggested Yusuf bring you down. When he said Lucy, I said to him I don't think any of the girls are called Lucy. You have to remember that most of the girls change their name, usually to something rather more exotic. Tracy becomes Brigitte one night and Genevieve or Lulu the next.' She laughed. 'I don't know what it is with the French names, but we've all been there, love. I mean, I was born Margaret and I've ended up as Sheena. If you hadn't come down, I wouldn't have known who the hell he was talking about. I have to say, love, you're looking a lot better than Lucy did last time I saw her.'

'When was that? When did you see her last?'

Sheena dunked the remains of her biscuit and ate the soggy result in one mouthful, washing it down with a large mouthful of strong tea. She shook her head as she swallowed. 'Not for a while now, love. I bet it's a year at least. I know several of them moved over to, er, Manchester, I think it was. The special constables like to move the girls on. There's a big push to try and clean up the streets every now and again—usually around election time—and those with no real ties leave for a while and try other cities. Mind you, that's the younger ones. Most of the girls have children to get back to and are stuck around here.'

I realised I'd been holding my breath, tensing every muscle as Sheena spoke. I breathed out slowly, trying to calm the beat of my heart. 'Has she definitely left the area, Sheena? I've been living around here for nearly a year now and in that time I thought I saw her in the distance a couple of times. The last time I saw her was over two years ago when she was clean. She came to my parents' house for a fleeting visit and I really thought she was going to be all right that time… She promised me she'd come off the stuff…'

Sheena looked across at me. 'Sorry, love, but she's certainly been using again since then *and* working the streets. So, how come you're obviously very all right and your sister—your twin—isn't? Where are your parents? Have they been looking for her too?'

'It's complicated—' I began, but Sheena interrupted me.

'It always is, love. And believe me there's nothing I haven't seen or heard.' She leaned forward and said, almost proudly, 'If Helen Rytka hadn't gone off with that bastard Yorkshire Ripper, taken him into yon wood yard… you know where I mean? Well, it could well have been *me* he finished off that night. Helen had only just moved from Bradford with her twin—yes, she had a twin too, you know. And *they* didn't stick together either.'

'Sheena, I really don't think Clementine wants to hear this.' Yusuf looked uncomfortable. 'You said you might be able to help, we thought you might be able to tell us where Lucy is living.'

'I've been to Emerald House,' I said. 'Several times over the past few months. But no one seems to know of her. Or at least they're not telling me if they do.'

Musa, usually very much the quieter of my two escorts, was obviously fascinated by Sheena's claim that she'd only narrowly missed becoming one of the Yorkshire Ripper's victims. 'You must have been very young to have been out on the streets when the Ripper was about. I was reading an article about him in the *Yorkshire Post* the other day; it's years ago, isn't it?'

Sheena's possible escape from the Ripper's clutches was obviously her party piece and, after pouring more tea for herself—the three of us hadn't really touched ours—she launched.

'Well, to you it'd seem like years ago, history I reckon, but to us that went through it all it seems like yesterday.

I'd only been at it a couple of weeks—me dad had hit me mum again, you see and he were allus drunk. I knew he'd be coming after me next so I left and went to find one of me cousins down in town. Any road, she put me up in her bedsit for a few nights—let me sleep on her floor—and it were only then I realised she were making her money on the streets. Bloody naïve, I was. After a couple of days, she said I'd either have to go back home or I could try going out with her on the street, which I did. Quite a few of the girls had moved over to Midhope from Bradford and Leeds because of the Ripper, and the Rytka twins were a bit like me: they were fairly new to the game.'

Musa was fully engaged with Sheena's story, his eyes wide, his mouth slightly open, but Yusuf was indicating with little movements of his head that we should be off. I shook my head slightly; if Sheena was going to be on my side I didn't want to offend her when she was so obviously relishing the retelling of the tale she must have told hundreds of times over the years.

'Anyhow, one night, it were a Tuesday in January back in 1978, me and Lisa—that's me cousin—and Helen and Rita Rytka were out for the start of the night. It were bloody cold I can tell you. All the girls were a bit spooked because the Ripper had struck in Leeds the month before, and so we tried to stick together, work in pairs as much as we could. Some of the girls from Bradford and Leeds had come up with a plan: they worked in pairs and one would take down the car number that the other were going off in and then once they returned the piece of paper would be ripped up in front of the driver. Lisa and me thought this were a right good idea, like, and we did it too.' Sheena dipped another biscuit, sucked at it and cackled. 'Eh, love, you should have seen some of them johns' faces when they saw us tekking down their number plate—probably thought we was going to blackmail 'em or summat. Anyway, there wasn't much doing that night so the twins moved down towards the timber yard end of the street arranging to rendezvous—' Sheena pronounced it rendy vooz '—back at the public lavs. They've gone now, those, so you won't really know where I mean. Lisa and me were going to go with Helen and Rita and try our luck down there too, but then a couple of cars stopped for us and they went off by themselves. That's when the bastard had Helen—killed her with his bloody 'ammer and dumped her body in yon timber yard. And do you know, Rita were so frightened of the cops she didn't go and tell 'em that Helen were missing for three days. Three bloody days, knowing your twin hadn't come back…'

I felt sick. I had to get out of there, get some fresh air. Get back to Allegra who at that very moment was being tainted by my stubbornness in moving us into Emerald Street. I stood up, swaying a little, knocking into Sheena's table. The teacups rattled and I clutched at the table for support.

'I think we'll be off, Sheena.' Yusuf got up from his chair. 'Thanks for seeing us. If you see or hear anything about Lucy could you let me know? You've got my phone number.'

Sheena put her hand on my arm. 'I'm sorry, love. I shouldn't have gone on about the Rytka twins and the Ripper, especially as you're a twin yourself. I suppose I were just telling you about what it used to be like round here. It's all different these days, I don't know all of the girls like I used to. There's quite a few from Europe, you know, Poland and Romania and I think there's even a couple of

Russian girls out there too. Some don't even speak English.' She cackled again. 'Mind you, I don't suppose a chat on what's going on in the world is what the punters are after.' Sheena paused and then said, 'And you wouldn't believe this but some of them are students at the university, trying to make their grants go a bit further I suppose. I reckon they think it's a bit glamorous, a bit of fun; think that they can make a bit of cash on the side and then go back to who they were. It dunt work like that though—once you start it becomes addictive, especially if you've got a habit to feed.' She looked across at me and raised her eyebrows. 'Everyone seems to be at it.'

I sat down again, the rising panic that had made me want to get out of the garden and Sheena's company beginning to subside.

'So how do you know these two, Clementine?' Sheena stood and walked over to the tiny patch of garden where pots of herbs were taking in the last of the evening light. She pulled a weed from the oregano, crumbled rosemary between her fingers and sniffed before moving over to the coriander where she pinched compound umbels of tiny purplish flowers from the abundant pot.

'We're all at Midhope University together,' I said, soothed by the loving way this woman was tending her herbs. 'We're on different courses—I'm doing Hotel Management— and Yusuf's dad is my landlord too. Amirah, his sister, is babysitting my little girl at the moment.'

Sheena turned from where she was dividing a clump of lavender and gave me an appraising stare. 'And you live round here with a little girl? Not the best place for her, is it?'

'No, you're right,' I said, staring back. 'It's not. In fact I'm in the process of packing up. I'm getting married in a couple of weeks and taking my daughter to live in Westenbury.'

Sheena whistled. 'Westenbury? Well that's certainly a better spot for you both to be. Look, love, I'm sorry I upset you talking about the bloody Ripper and all that. I'm allus here—if you want to come down again at any time, feel free. I did have a bit of an idea about moving myself—I were hoping for a little council flat just out of town but, you know, I've been here so long now, it's home. I still have me regulars, can't let them down even though they're getting on a bit like me. And, if I do hear anything about your sister, I'll let Yusuf here know and he can get in touch with you.'

It was almost ten-thirty by the time the three of us retraced our steps back towards Emerald Street. The street workers were out in ones and twos, plugged into their iPhones, talking on mobiles or to each other. Most stood alone, skimpily dressed or wearing strange combinations of high boots with backless dresses or tiny skirts. I scrutinised each one, desperate to see my own features reflected back at me from just one of them.

Lucy wasn't there.

'You're right to get Allegra out of this area,' Amirah said, as she picked up the textbooks she'd been reading and walked with me down the path to where Yusuf was impatiently waiting at the gate. Cyril, next door's dog, was doing its usual flinging against the fence trick, barking as it did so and I could see she was relieved once she was away from it.

I went to check on Allegra. She had flung off her covers in the warmth of the July evening and her cheeks were flushed as she slept. A moth was bashing itself against the night-light on the little table by Allegra's bed and as I watched it, I felt, for the first time since I'd accepted Peter's proposal, I'd made the right decision about where our lives were heading. I didn't love Peter—I wasn't even going to pretend to myself that I did—but I'd had enough of our life down here on Emerald Street. Even if Peter hadn't come into my life, I told myself, I'd have spent the summer break from college looking for somewhere more suitable for us to live.

I kissed my daughter's warm cheek. She stirred and muttered, 'My dog, George,' before turning and settling back into a deep sleep once more.

'We're moving to the country, my darling,' I whispered. 'You deserve better than this.'

12

'Taxi's here,' Peter shouted up the stairs. 'Are you ready?'

'Mummy, you look lovely. Why can't I come with you on your hen night? I'm a hen too, aren't I?' Allegra was having a bit of a sulk, traipsing round the bedroom in my new high heels and refusing to take them off. 'Look, these fit me really well,' she said, pushing her feet to the very end of the open toes so that, if one ignored the huge amount of space at the other end, they did indeed appear to be a perfect fit.

'Come on, Allegra, Izzy is waiting for me and Peter is taking you and Max to the cinema. He's ready to go as well, so give me my shoes, go and find your trainers and then we can all get off.'

'But I want to come with *you*,' she whined. 'Sophie is coming with us too…'

'Well, that's lovely, darling. You'll have a lovely time all together. I think Peter said something about an ice cream once you get there…'

'But, Mummy, I don't like Sophie. She's a big lady, she's not a little girl like me. She's bossy.'

I knew just where Allegra was coming from re Sophie, but now was not the time to be analysing either Allegra's or my relationship with Peter's fifteen-year-old daughter. I had to push the not overly pleasant thoughts of my soon-to-be stepdaughter from my head for later.

The irritable honking of the taxi's horn in the drive had me gathering up my bag and phone in one hand and Allegra in the other. 'Come on, come downstairs and say hello to Auntie Izzy and then I can get off.'

Trailing her feet, Allegra followed me outside into the early evening sunshine where, through the open taxi window, Izzy was wafting her arms, obviously trying to find some cooler air as well as impatiently shouting at me to get in. Swallows were swooping over the newly mown garden and the smell of honeysuckle and lavender had me almost swooning. The two weeks that Allegra and I had been living at 'Cocky's Crest' had coincided with the longest heatwave, apparently, this century. I thanked Peter, God and anyone else listening that Peter had fallen in love with me and we were now living out here in this heavenly house surrounded by glorious countryside.

I breathed in the warm scented air, relieved to see that Allegra was now running off with Max and George—like characters in an Enid Blyton story, I smiled to myself—and got into the back of the taxi with Izzy.

'What are you grinning at?' Izzy asked, 'Is it *Cocky* or his *crest* that's put the big smile on your face?'

'Bloody stupid name for a house,' I laughed. 'Something to do with an Australian cockatoo, I think. Apparently

Vanessa spent some time out there and it was her idea to call the house that.'

'And have you?'

'Have I what?

'You *know*.' Izzy patted my leg and raised her eyebrows suggestively very much in the manner of Les Dawson. 'Had a cock or two?'

I tutted as the taxi driver grinned at me through his mirror. 'Oh, God, have you been drinking already?'

'Might have. Declan opened a bottle and we drank your health even though you weren't there. The thought was there though, so I do hope you appreciate it.'

I peered over her shoulder and then squinted down at the floor of the cab. 'Well at least you haven't brought pink cowboy hats or veils with 'Learner' emblazoned on them.'

'They're actually silver *and* pink,' Izzy said, 'and all safely in the boot. This very kind taxi man said I could put them in there so they wouldn't crease.'

'Oh, you *are* joking. Please say you're joking. I can't see Mandy Henderson wearing a silver and pink cowboy hat.'

'Ah, but *you* couldn't see her actually wanting to come with us in the first place.' Izzy grinned. 'But Harriet said it was actually Mandy herself who asked if you were having a hen do. Hat couldn't say no and she sort of invited herself along. She and Hat and Grace go back a long way. They were all at school together apparently.'

'So have you met this Grace woman yet?' I asked. It seemed a bit weird having a hen do at all but with women I didn't really know, it was even stranger.

'No, but if she's anything like Harriet she'll be great fun. You did like Harriet, didn't you?'

'Very much. Yes, I really did.'

'Well, you weren't overly helpful in providing hens of your own,' Izzy said, slightly crossly. 'You've lived in Midhope all your life and yet you turned down all my suggestions as to whom you could invite…'

Still in a total panic about my having accepted Peter in the first place, the idea of a hen do was anathema to me when Izzy first mooted the idea, and I'd tried every which way to tell Izzy I didn't want any fuss. Apart from saying, 'Izzy, I don't *want* a fucking hen do,' there seemed little alternative but to go ahead with her plans.

'OK, so who do you want there?' she'd probed, once I'd accepted she was like a runaway train and it was going to go ahead regardless of what *I* wanted, or even whether I'd actually turn up. 'Friends from school?'

'I've lost touch with them all.'

'*All* of them?'

'Yep.'

'Friends from university?'

'Izzy, they're all nineteen. Remember, I'm a mature student…'

'Well, a couple of nineteen-year-olds would be fun. Remind us what we used to be like…'

'Nope.'

'No?'

'No,' I'd said firmly.

Izzy had racked her brains for a while. 'Staff from the Black Swan?'

'Godzilla and Borislaw?'

'No, maybe not.' I'd kept Izzy and Declan entertained over many a curry and Sunday lunch at their place with stories from the Black Swan kitchen, and Izzy had sadly shaken her head in agreement. 'Shall I ask your mother?' Izzy had finally asked in desperation.

'Please don't,' I'd replied, shortly.

'Well then,' Izzy had said cheerfully, 'up to me to provide the hens myself.'

And so she had.

'I thought we were having a hen do, not going shopping,' I said as Izzy led the way into the Trinity Centre in Leeds.

'Have patience, all will be revealed.' She grinned as we walked past the Apple Store and Victoria's Secret and took the lift up to the sixth floor. A bouncer on the door of Angelica gave us the once over and then, unsmiling, let us through onto a wraparound, planted terrace with panoramic views over the city.

'Izzy,' a voice shouted from a table in the corner. 'We're over here.'

I suddenly felt a little shy: although I'd met Harriet and Mandy at our dinner party, I didn't know them that well and I certainly hadn't met the attractive, chestnut-haired woman who was having a fit of the giggles over something with Harriet. This must be Grace.

'Come on, you're late,' Harriet said, standing to give us both a kiss and immediately putting me at my ease. 'Now, Amanda—Mandy—you both met the other week, but this is my friend, Grace. When I told her we were coming out to celebrate your wedding she insisted on coming too. Hope you don't mind?'

'Gosh no, not at all,' I said. 'I'm really grateful you've all made the effort.'

'Effort?' Grace laughed. 'I can assure you that getting dressed up and leaving the kids with their fathers for a change is no effort. Now, we're just about to order cocktails. What do you fancy, Clementine? What a fabulous name—Clementine.'

'Her sisters are called Mandarin, Nectarine and Tangerine,' Izzy guffawed. For a moment, I froze, panic rising at the thought of Lucy somewhere dark, somewhere bad. In an alley? Down a backstreet? About to get in a car with a new-kid-on-the-block Ripper?

'Right,' Izzy said, beckoning a waiter over, 'I've seen nothing but athlete's foot, psoriasis, nits and a particularly unpleasant set of ingrowing toenails, as well as a probable dose of the clap, today and I need a *drink*.'

'Reet, ladies, ahm Gavin and I'll give your orders to the mixologist,' the rather camp waiter said, brandishing his pad and pen. He was David Walliams—albeit with a Geordie accent—to a T.

'A what? A mixologist?' Harriet giggled. 'Whatever happened to Tom Cruise?'

'Ah, think he found religion, pet, and gave up on the cocktails.'

'I think I'll have a… erm… a Brazilian…'

'Aye, man, you canna come into a posh place like this if you've not had a Brazilian already…'

'… Sunset. A Brazilian Sunset for me please,' Grace laughed.

'Gosh,' I said, 'I don't know what to have. Erm, I fancy a Cash Rebate I think…'

Mandy Henderson's blonde bob came up and she looked at me, a little smile on her lips as I named my cocktail. I felt sure she was about to say something, but she was stopped in her tracks by Izzy standing and calling over to Mel Naylor, who had just appeared at the entrance and was looking around for a familiar face.

'Sorry I'm so late,' she said, kissing those of us she'd met previously at Peter's dinner party. 'We set off from Essex early this afternoon but the traffic on the M1 was horrendous. And then it was all down to fifty miles an hour around Sheffield. If I'd had my trainers with me I'd have got out and run for it.'

'Don't *exaggerate*, Melanie. You're far too immaculate to *walk* anywhere, never mind *run*,' Izzy protested, laughing.

'Have you found a house up here?' I asked. I liked Mel, liked the way that she had been so lovely with Allegra and I liked the idea of her moving north and her being another friend. I'd not had a gang of girlfriends since I was about fourteen, when Lucy had organised and headed 'The Black Ladies'—a sort of take on 'The Pink Ladies' from *Grease*— and which was, more than likely, the start of it all.

'Yes, we're so excited. It's actually not far from Westenbury, probably about ten minutes from you, Mandy and, now, of course, you as well, Clementine. We spotted it as we drove back from Peter's place the other week, put in an offer the next day and basically had it all agreed this week. It's been a bit nail-biting because there was someone else after it as well, but as we'd sold our house and have been renting down south, we were in a good position. We'll come up fairly soon and live with Mum until we can move in.'

'Well, we have a double celebration on our hands this

evening then,' Izzy said. 'You're just in time for the first round of cocktails, Mel. Get your order in…'

'And you have a son?' I was chatting to Harriet, asking about her children.

'Bloody hell,' she said. 'Do I have a son? Well, I have *two*, but as Fin is *only* two and absolutely no problem at all—even though he *is* two and two-year-olds, as I'm sure you remember are pretty terrible—I tend to forget about him. Which is a terrible thing to say in itself.' Harriet downed her Brazilian Sunset in one and tried to catch the eye of our waiter. 'No, it's the seventeen-year-old—Kit—who is bloody hard work. He's just finished his first year of A levels and hasn't done a stroke of work as far as I can see. Nick keeps threatening to stop paying the school fees and says Kit will have to find a job and earn a living and, unfortunately, that's just what the boy wants to do. So, when Nick threatens him with this, Kit goes "yes" and high-fives anyone who is around—usually the twins or Lilian, my nanny—and so Nick has to backtrack and then he goes off back to India or China or Russia or wherever he is due next and leaves me to sort it all out.'

'The joys of teenage kids,' I sympathised. 'Actually, I could do with some advice on Peter's daughter. She's away at school most of the time but now she's home and making it pretty obvious what she thinks of Peter marrying me. I suppose it has all happened a bit quick, and I have been really lucky with Max who is lovely.'

'Yes, he *is* a lovely boy isn't he? Both Nick and I said as much after we'd been for dinner. The problem with Kit at the moment is he's always over here in Leeds. I think there's some girl he's knocking around with and, whereas he always used to tell me everything, now he's not really interested in talking to me at all.' Harriet sighed and then laughed. 'And then, when I'm in the middle of telling him off, he'll say something really funny and I just end up laughing. The other day he was eating scrambled eggs straight from the pan: "That is *appalling* behaviour, Kit," I said to him and he just said, "Mother, putting an axe into somebody's head is *appalling* behaviour; eating scrambled egg out of the pan most certainly is not," and I just laughed out loud and the moment for trying to educate him into being a civilised human being was gone.'

'Are ye ready to eat, ladies?' Gavin the waiter reappeared at our table. 'Ye can come alang now leik. Now, there's quite a lot of youngsters in toneet, but I've given ye all a table in the corner so you don't have to worry about them thinking ye're all part of the *Antiques Roadshow*. Joke, hinnies, just a joke,' he chortled, 'divvent get mad with us, leik,' and led us to the table right in the centre of the room.

'Why has every restaurant in the country jumped on the pulled pork bandwagon Grace grumbled as she studied the menu. 'I don't want to be pulling anything at my age and certainly not a lump of pig.'

'I think I'll have the Burrata with heirloom tomatoes,' Mandy said, her clipped vowels sounding particularly refined compared to our Geordie waiter.

'What the hell is Burrata?' Izzy asked. 'And *heirloom* tomatoes?'

'Ah divvent have a clue about the Burrata, hinny,' the waiter said dismissively, 'but ah think ye'll find the heirloom tomatoes are something yer grannie keeps hidden under the bed with the family silver…'

Mandy tutted. 'Burrata is an Italian mozzarella mixed with cream; the heirloom tomatoes are non-hybrid—they lack a genetic mutation that gives them their red colour.'

'Right,' Izzy said, frowning. 'Erm, do you have a steak?'

'For you, bonny lass, ah can find a whole cow if some meat is what ye're fancying toneet.'

I loved the menu and couldn't make up my mind what to have. I always felt excited when I saw food that was original and gutsy. 'I think I'll go for the crispy Westmoor Farm pig's ears with truffle mayo,' I said. I was already trying to work out how they would cook it and if I could replicate it once I was home. Home. Golly, I'd be able to experiment to my heart's content in Peter's kitchen. *My* kitchen, I reminded myself. It would be *my* kitchen as well. Mine *and* Allegra's.

'Just the poor pig's ears?' Izzy said. 'What about the rest of him?'

'Neever ye mind aboot the pig, hinny,' Gavin said seriously to Izzy. 'Ye just think aboot that cow *ahm* gan breeng for ye.'

'I know Clementine won't agree with me,' Izzy was saying confidentially to Mel and Mandy, 'but I sometimes long for prawn cocktail, steak and chips—'

'And a Black Forest Gateau to finish?' I interrupted, laughing.

'I know what you mean,' Harriet agreed. 'Restaurants do seem to jump on bandwagons don't they? Nick and I couldn't go out for a meal a couple of years ago without everything being surrounded in damned *foam*. Reminded me of cuckoo spit and really put me off.'

'I love it all,' I said enthusiastically. 'I love seeing how *daring* menus can get. But, having said that, I do enjoy cooking basic regional stuff like Yorkshire pudding, curd tarts and... erm, erm... Eccles cakes.'

'Eccles cakes? Wrong side of the Pennines, you heathen,' Izzy snorted.

'Well, you know what I mean,' I laughed. 'I'm already teaching Allegra the basics of Yorkshire cookery.'

'I'll send my kids over to you,' Harriet said. 'You can teach them as well.'

'What are you going to do now you've finished your course at university?' Mel asked. 'You *have* finished, haven't you?'

'Yes. Well, I suppose it's all changed a bit now,' I said. 'My plan was to find hotel management work—something that would fit in better with Allegra and school. That's why I decided to do the course: restaurant hours and shifts just don't fit in with having children. But now, well, I don't really know.'

I suddenly felt a bit embarrassed. All the women were looking at me, listening as I spoke. Were they all thinking I'd landed lucky? That I was only marrying Peter so I wouldn't have to work?

'I probably will end up doing some sort of hotel work,' I said stoutly. 'That's what I've trained for...'

Izzy patted my arm and then hugged me. 'It's your hen do, Clem. You're not to think about work and the future tonight.' She poured more wine as our food began to arrive. 'A toast, ladies. To Clem. All happiness for your future, darling.'

13

'**Y**ou are *not* allowed to go home at this time of night on your hen night,' Izzy said bossily as she squinted at her watch. 'I haven't got my glasses—what time *is* it?'

'It's only ten-thirty,' Grace said. 'The night's not started yet, Clementine. Come on, Harriet and I haven't had a good night out for ages. We can't go home yet—that really would be showing our ages if we're home before midnight on a hen do, for heaven's sake.'

'Are you worried about leaving Allegra?' Mel asked 'I imagine you don't leave her very often, do you?'

I smiled gratefully across at Mel. Even though she didn't have children of her own she seemed to realise, without my saying so, that I was beginning to feel a bit twitchy about leaving Allegra. 'Actually, she's absolutely fine with Peter—and she loves Max and George, the dog…' I hesitated. 'It's just that Peter's wife, Vanessa, and her husband have gone off to Australia for six weeks, leaving Max and his daughter, Sophie, with us for the duration. Max is absolutely no problem at all—he seems to have accepted that Peter and I are getting married and that Allegra and I are basically taking over his family home. Children are amazingly resilient, aren't they? Well, Max is. Sophie seems to be another story.'

'How old is she?'

'Just sixteen.'

'Ouch.' Mel pulled a face of sympathy. 'One of my nieces is fourteen and she's quite horrible—gone from a lovely little girl to a moody Rottweiler overnight. It can't be easy for— Sophie, is it?—for Sophie with all those new hormones, and you swanning in with your little girl and taking over her home.'

I nodded. 'I know all that. And she's away at boarding school in term-time so when she does come home she wants everything to be as it was, I suppose. I'm not sure how she gets on with her mother either at the moment. Vanessa seemed more than happy to leave her with us and go off to Australia with her new husband for a couple of weeks the minute Sophie arrived home for the summer.'

'Hmm, does seem a bit mean, that. You'd have thought she'd have waited for the autumn when the kids were back at school.'

'I get the impression that it's *because* they're not at school she's gone now. I don't think she can cope with Sophie now she's growing up.'

'Right,' Grace said, standing up and grabbing her bag, 'this is a hen do not a "talking about kids" do. Let's pay the bill and then go find a club and *dance*.'

And we did.

Mandy Henderson led the way until she found what

she'd been looking for down a rather grubby street just off Greek Street, and we all followed as she went down a long flight off steps into what seemed like the bowels of the earth. It probably was.

'Are you sure this is it, Mandy?' Izzy was asking doubtfully.

'Yes, yes, absolutely. My son told me about this place. Said it's quite upmarket and not at all full of young kids.'

We gazed round at the heaving crowd, sweating in the warm July night, and Harriet and I exchanged glances. '*Upmarket*?' she whispered from behind me on the stairs. 'Bloody hell, I'd hate to see his idea of *downbeat*…'

'Quick,' Mel said, pushing her way through a group of men dancing energetically to a seemingly erratic beat, 'there's a table coming free over there. Grab it quick before someone else does.'

No one else in the dancing, sweating throng seemed at all interested in sitting down and Mel bagged the table, purloining extra chairs from other tables so that we could all sit.

'Phew, that's better,' Harriet said as she sat down gratefully and kicked off her heels. 'These shoes are killing me; any dancing I do will have to be barefoot…'

Grace suddenly started laughing. 'I don't think bare *feet* will be a problem, Hat. Have you seen all the bare *chests*?'

The rest of us looked round to where Grace was indicating another group of dancing, gyrating men. They were naked from the waist up, their smooth monochrome chests, slicked with a film of sweat in the sweltering heat of the enclosed space, a direct contrast to the busy, pink flamingo wallpaper on the wall behind them.

'There is an unusually large amount of *men* here isn't there?' Mandy said in surprise as she gazed round. 'And all dancing with each other…' Her hand suddenly flew to her mouth. 'Oh my word, it's a gay bar isn't it? I've brought you to a gay bar.' She turned back to the table where the rest of us were hysterical with laughter.

'This is *so* well thought out, Mandy,' Izzy said with a straight face. 'What a brilliant surprise to bring us down here—and not let on all the way through dinner that this is what you were planning. Is this your sort of thing, then? Are you and David members?'

'Good gracious, no,' Mandy said, shaking her head vigorously. 'I really…'

'Mandy, she's teasing you,' I said, laughing. 'Do you think this is what your son had in mind for my hen do?'

'Good gracious, no,' Mandy said again.

'I don't care that we seem to have ended up in the *wrong* place,' Izzy whooped, getting out of her seat. 'This seems to be just the *right* sort of place for a hen do to me.' Grabbing both my and Mel's hands, she pulled us onto the tiny, pulsating dancefloor and began to move in what could only be described as an overtly sexual way. 'Trust me, I'm a doctor,' she said, smiling politely, and surprised, the men moved aside for her but then, grinning, shimmied back towards her, including her in their bump and grind.

'Just don't start doing the YMCA,' Izzy mouthed theatrically before going back to back in a sort of upbeat do-si-do with the smallest of the five men.

I was pleased to see we weren't the only women in the club, but we were certainly outnumbered by the men, some outrageously camp, others not so at all.

'Well, look heeah,' an unmistakable voice shouted, 'it's the *Antiques Roadshow* again. Yer gan reet upmarket, heeah, pet.' David Walliams, aka Geordie Gavin, did a sort of running leap—as much as anyone could run or leap in this seething mass of humanity—landing perfectly on Izzy's big toe before swinging her round to the music and then ignoring her as he danced with the other men.

'I feel a bit sick now,' Izzy said, trying to keep upright, but bumping into me as she recovered from spinning round, 'and those bloody swans are doing me in.'

'What swans?' I asked, laughing.

'Those pink ones on the wall,' she said, looking a bit green. 'Think I'll just sit down for a bit.'

I was really beginning to enjoy myself; it had been ages since I'd been out like this; letting my hair down, acting like a thirty-year-old without a care in the world, and Harriet, Grace, and I danced on, at times as part of the group of men, sometimes on our own. I felt free, frivolous, enjoying the evening and the music for what it was; forgetting for a while any responsibilities and thoughts of my new future that would come back to sober me up once out of this tiny, temporary microcosm that was, just for the moment, enclosing me in its very alien but womb-like world.

I glanced over to our table where Mel and Izzy were catching up, but where Mandy was sitting rather aloof and looking distinctly uncomfortable. I found my shoes at the edge of the dancefloor and made my way over to sit with her.

'It mightn't have been your intention to end up in a gay bar, Mandy,' I said, shouting over a thumping remix of 'It's Raining Men', 'but it's been brilliant. Honestly, I couldn't have planned a better night out.'

'Really? Are you sure? I feel totally mortified that I've brought you all down here. I almost had a stroke when I saw all these semi-naked men…'

'Ye fancied a stroke did ye, pet? But then ye thought, "Hands Off. No Touching." Very sensible.' Geordie Gavin on his way back from the bar, bottle in hand, came to a halt behind Mandy, chortling at his own wit. 'Now then, pet, are ye not dancing?' Gavin nodded towards the men. 'Ye see, straight men cannee dance for sheet. Gay men actuallee dance *without* having to be hit first with a cattle prod like straight men. And—' he continued sagely, pausing only to take a swig from his bottle '—gay men dance with their hands higher than their nipples.'

'Right, er… thank you.' Mandy didn't seem to know what else to say and Gavin cavorted off into the centre of the dancefloor once more. She turned to me and I thought, not for the first time, what an exceptionally beautiful woman she was. Glossy, chic, well turned out, were all phrases that could have, and probably had been at some stage, applied to Mandy Henderson. No wonder she was married to such a powerful and handsome man as David Henderson.

She turned from where she was watching the far wall, now streaming a video of Kylie Minogue, and said, 'I need to tell you again, Clementine, just how impressed David and I were the other week with your superb cooking. Would you ever consider doing dinner parties for others? David has so many contacts if you did feel you might like to go down that route.'

'That's really kind, Mandy. I really appreciate it. At the moment I think I'll have enough on being married and being a stepmother. But I don't want to be dependent on Peter too much, so—'

'Blimey, Clementine, I thought you'd got your kit off in there.' Harriet laughed and indicated the room beyond with a nod of her blonde head. 'I've just been to the loo and went for a nosey. You'll never guess what there is in that bit of the club. Seems a bit strange next to a gay club… There's a lap dancing, pole dancing sort of club. God, it's a right den of iniquity. There are half-naked women wrapped round poles and thrusting their bits and pieces into men's faces almost. I'm actually quite shocked. But the thing is, there was one of the pole dancers who I thought was *you*!' Harriet giggled and reached for her abandoned glass of rose. 'Honestly, I thought you must have had too much to drink and wandered in there and got your clothes off. I tell you, Clementine, you've got an absolute double. Come with me, come on, come and have a look…'

Heart hammering in my chest, blood pounding in my ears, I stood up, knocking over the chair, running barefoot towards the red velvet tasselled curtain that separated Rawhide, the gay bar where we'd spent the last hour or so, from Fallen Angels, its name emblazoned in red lights on the ceiling greeting me as I ran in.

A potently strong smell of cheap perfume and beer hit me head-on as my vision took in flashing neon signs:

LIVE!

NUDE!

GIRLS! GIRLS!! GIRLS!!!

It took a while for my eyes to accustom themselves to

the gloom, but I was immediately struck by any lack of joy, glamour or even sexual charge emanating from its airless depths. There were very few people in the room, and the punters that were there didn't appear to be particularly enjoying themselves. There was no clapping, or *woo-hooing* that, to the uninitiated, might have been a gauge of involved enjoyment if not an expected norm. Instead, I had the strange impression that, for the on-looking men it was more a rite of passage—something that had to be got through to ensure a good time, but with as much enjoyment as having your car engine oil changed or waiting to pay at the checkout in B&Q.

It took only a few seconds to find her. She was swaying lethargically, almost drunkenly, her long dark hair, sprayed with pink, swinging across her face as she hugged the pole. Always slightly built, she was now much thinner than when I'd last seen her two years ago but she was still beautiful. Apart from a cheap-looking pair of white, fringed ankle boots and an accompanying white, fringed thong she was vulnerably and, quite shockingly, naked.

Every so often she would perform an obligatory swing around the well-used, rickety pole, but apart from this there appeared to be a lot less pole activity and a lot more lying down, together with an accompanying, almost mindless, wiggling of legs in the air. As I watched, probably only for a couple of seconds, the totally ridiculous thought suddenly occurred to me that that was par for the course; she'd always hated gymnastics at school.

'Lucy,' I whispered, and then, as she continued in what appeared to be a fairly catatonic state, shouted, 'Lucy!'

Fleetingly aware, but not caring, that Izzy, Harriet and

Grace were standing open-mouthed but silent at my side, I rushed over to her, grabbing a dirty-looking robe that had been abandoned on the floor by the pole. 'Lucy.' I realised I was crying as I tried to cover up her pitiful nakedness with the grubby material.

Startled, she turned her big brown eyes and looked at me, her gaze becoming almost one of terror, and then, grabbing the robe from my hands, dashed towards the single door at the back of the room and disappeared down the flight of steps and out into the empty back streets of Leeds.

14

SARAH

'I do hope you're not letting Poppy run wild,' Lady Anne Sykes said in her usual clipped tones, peering at her younger daughter over her glasses as she did so. Sarah, instantly transported back to this very sitting room and to any number of scenarios where, as a dreamy, almost anxious child and then as an inattentive teenager, she was regularly on the receiving end of her mother's acerbic tongue, blushed.

'Oh no, Mummy. Really, no.'

'So why isn't she here with you then? It seems an absolute age since we saw her. And what about school in September? I do hope that you and Roger have not given in to this dreadful idea of her going to sixth-form college rather than staying on where she is? Plenty of time to be at *college*—' Anne almost spat the word '—when, and if, she goes to university.'

Sarah flushed further, recalling Poppy's last words as she'd dropped her daughter off at Harrogate station.

'Mum,' she'd said through the car's open window as she

bashed Kermit's door closed, 'I'm telling you, now, I *am* off to sixth-form college after the summer. I've got a place, and I told school I wasn't going back. I know school's been on at Dad wanting to know what's happening, but there's no way I'm going back. You know as well as I do that he's secretly relieved he won't have to fork out the fees. And don't go telling Granny or she'll bully Dad into paying up.'

That had actually made Sarah smile; she was never quite sure who was the biggest bully—her husband or her mother.

'OK, OK,' Sarah had said, her hands off the steering wheel in a gesture of acquiescence, 'I'm not the one that needs persuading. I'm more than happy for you to go to sixth-form college rather than stay on at school. Now, remind me again, because your Granny will want to know, who you're meeting in Leeds and why it's so important that you can't come to see your grandmother with me for an hour and catch a later train?'

'Mum, I'll miss the train. I've told you…'

Had she told her? Sarah tried to recall, but Poppy had been plugged into her iPod from the minute she'd got up and she, Sarah, had been so immersed in listening to *Woman's Hour* where James Martin was discussing his latest recipe book, she really couldn't be sure that Poppy *had* actually told her what she was up to. Sarah had sighed. She was such a poor mother, more interested in recipes, herbs and spices than with whom her daughter was meeting or where she was actually going.

'All right, darling,' Sarah had called out to Poppy's frighteningly tight-jeaned bottom. 'Ring me when you want picking up.'

But Poppy had already gone, disappearing through

the station entrance where, no doubt, she was already re-plugged into some alien music and wishing she could light up a fag. Sarah had sighed, reversed Kermit and, narrowly missing some old dear who, shouting 'watch where you're going, you fucking moron,' had turned out to be *not* so dear after all, had driven off to her parents' house in what had lately been dubbed the 'Golden Triangle': that area of North Yorkshire encompassing Harrogate, Wetherby and North Leeds.

'So, where is she?' The Lady Anne, as Jamie and Polly had christened her a few years ago, was insistent as she continued to peer at Sarah adding, for good measure, 'You're looking very flushed, Sarah.'

'I think it must be the menopause, Mummy. I suppose, at fifty, it's to be expected.' Trying to veer her mother away from the fact that Poppy was undoubtedly at that minute in some bar with some boy, surreptitiously smoking and onto her second alcopop or worse, Sarah asked, 'Did *you* suffer, Mummy? They do say daughters take after their mothers when it comes down to it.'

The Lady Anne snorted. 'No such thing as the menopause. Well, not in my day anyway. It's a modern invention brought in by that *Marie Claude* magazine to have something to write about as well as being in cahoots with the pharmaceutical companies to get you on to their drugs.'

'I think you mean *Marie Claire*, Mummy,' Sarah said and then, emboldened by the fact that she'd already questioned her mother's naming of the magazine, added, 'and actually there was a very good article about the menopause in last month's *The Lady*.'

'Well, that doesn't surprise me for one minute, knowing

who's in charge of it these days. The woman has totally ruined it. I cancelled my subscription years ago; can't get any decent help in there these days. Anthea Drysdale wanted a new housekeeper and all she could find was some young Russian floozy who didn't have a clue how to set a table or, apparently, even the correct way to hold her knife at dinner.'

'Why was the housekeeper sitting down to *dinner* with Anthea Drysdale?' Sarah asked, discreetly moving her sleeve in order to work out how much longer before she could get up and leave.

'Oh, it's all the way now. It's all kitchen sups and everyone—children, au pairs, housekeepers, probably the gardener even, if one is still fortunate enough to have one—eating together with the family.' Anne sniffed disparagingly and poured more tea from the Minton teapot. God, Sarah thought, what she'd give for a strong Costa coffee rather than the brackish English Breakfast tea her mother favoured.

The sitting room was stifling and Sarah, longing to draw back the heavy Sanderson curtains her mother insisted on half closing against the sun's fading of her brightly patterned carpet, felt beads of sweat begin on her upper lip.

'How are Selena and Edward?' Sarah asked, trying to change the subject. She knew from old that once her mother was on a rant about something, she'd be unable to steer her away from it unless she could head her off at the pass, as it were, and get her on to her favourite subject: Sarah's elder siblings and their families.

'Oh, of *course*, you won't know. Hugo has been chosen as PPC...' Anne tutted as Sarah looked blank. 'Prospective Parliamentary Candidate for Esher. We're all thrilled as you can imagine.' Anne's over-enthusiastic application of blue eye shadow had creased unbecomingly in the wrinkles of her eyelids, Sarah noticed, and her eyebrows were strangely higher and darker than one would have expected from an eighty-year-old woman. She looked... grotesque, Sarah thought, a clone of Barbara Cartland in her last years, and hurriedly looked away.

'Isn't he a bit young wanting to be an MP?' Sarah frowned, trying to recall the last time she'd seen her nephew—her brother Edward's son. Surely he was only about twenty-two?

'He's twenty-six,' her mother said, almost crossly. '*My* father was Churchill's right-hand man by the time he was thirty-five and *Lord* Charles Gardener by the time he was forty. I did hope Edward would follow in both sets of grandfathers' and Daddy's footsteps, but it wasn't to be.'

Too busy asset-stripping the family mill in Bradford in order to feather his own nest during the Eighties, Sarah thought, uncharacteristically sour. Not that she'd ever been in line for any of her father's inherited, if now hugely diminished, wealth. She'd well and truly blotted her copybook when she did what she did when she was just nineteen.

'We should be happy that it appears to be Hugo who is intent on carrying on the family tradition,' Anne was saying, eyes narrowed slightly as she glanced at her younger daughter. 'And actually, Sarah, we don't want to go scuppering Hugo's chances...' She lowered her voice. 'It wouldn't do Hugo's case any good if the *Express* or the *Mail* got to know about... about, well... you know...'

'I know, Mummy. I know exactly what you're getting at.' No good telling her mother then, that her yearning to find her babies was becoming almost overwhelming. That if she didn't talk to someone soon she felt she might literally burst: all the pent up feelings, shame, regrets, and thoughts that her mother and Roger simply refused to listen to, exploding out of her one morning – *boom*!—as she stood in the checkout in Aldi, or sat in church listening to yet another of her husband's quite dreadful sermons.

'I don't think it would be a bad idea for you to make a bit more use of your *title* either, Sarah. At the end of the day, with your father being in the House of Lords—as was mine—as their daughters we've always been entitled to the title "The Honourable." I've always been proud to be The Hon. and, since your father's knighthood, even prouder to be The Hon. Lady Anne. Your sister Selena makes sure she's always addressed as The Hon. Selena, particularly now that she's president of The Children's Society charity. It does add a certain something, you know. I do feel, given your... your past history, it might not be a bad idea, particularly with Hugo's present candidacy, to use it rather more than you do? Hmm? Sarah?'

Sarah jumped. 'Sorry, Mummy, I was miles away.' Forty miles away, to be exact, pleading for her daughters not to be taken away.

'You always were, Sarah,' her mother said crossly. 'That was always your problem.'

Heading south back down the A61 and home, Sarah suddenly couldn't bear the thought of doing the supermarket shop, which had been her vague intention, nor did she want to actually go home. Roger, with one of his migraines—Sarah was still not convinced they *were* actually migraines, but rather an excuse to take himself off into his study and out of the way of his family and any wandering parishioners in search of God's blessing—was to be avoided at all costs, but particularly on this humid July afternoon.

Sarah felt restless, unwanted, aimless. That was it, she thought to herself, there was no *aim* to her life. She'd adored bringing up her children but, of the three, only Jamie had ever seemed to be on her wavelength. The girls, Jennifer and Poppy, had shown no interest whatsoever in art, cooking or the garden, the three things that got her through her days now that she was no longer needed by the children. Sarah knew she had very little in common with her elder daughter, Jennifer; she knew that, as with Roger, Jennifer was soon exasperated by her dreamy way of doing things, of her lack of desire to wear smart clothes and high heels. Jennifer, Sarah thought wryly as she slowed down for traffic lights, would have loved the 'Hon.' title. She would have used it on her letter headings, and shown no scruples in using it in her ambition to run any one of the top private schools in the country.

Sarah slowed for a tiny hedgehog in the road. Totally squashed and dead, of course, but she couldn't bear the thought of squashing it further. Poor little thing. Was its mother pining for it somewhere, weeping hedgehog tears in the dusty, pollution-stunted hedge of the dual carriageway, looking for her baby? She'd Google it when she got home—find out just how maternal hedgehogs were.

Approaching her turn-off for home, Sarah indicated right and moved on to the roundabout but instead of taking the second exit decided suddenly she couldn't bear the thought of going home to Roger and his bloody head, and carried on going round and then, back where she'd started from on the A61, headed for Leeds. She hadn't been into Leeds for months she now realised, but she was going to go and sit in a bar. Yes, that's what she'd do—go find a bar and sit outside on the pavement and pretend she was young and in Paris and studying art there, as had been her sole intention once she'd finished her course in Leeds all those years previously.

Pulling into Cookridge Street, Sarah saw the amount of traffic and, realising the futility of trying to land a parking space, almost abandoned the ridiculous idea of sitting in a bar in the middle of Leeds on a Monday afternoon. But both the gods of parking and bollards were obviously on her side and she saw her chance, slipping almost seamlessly round the yellow and white plastic and neatly into a parking spot between a Porsche Boxster and a rather jaunty orange Mini.

Pleased with herself, she ran her fingers through her long, still-dark hair, decided a lick of lipstick wouldn't go amiss and, within minutes was sitting on the pavement outside a bar called Bourbon sipping a wine spritzer.

Don't pretend, Sarah scolded her reflection in the shiny metal paper napkin holder, *that it wasn't your intention to come back to the spot where it all started*. She sat back, trying to relax, shoving firmly out of her mind the sudden recollection that she'd expressly promised Mrs Lindop, one of the church wardens, she'd make herself available for a spot of church pew dusting and polishing that afternoon. She tried to assume an 'I regularly sit outside bars in Leeds on a Monday afternoon' pose, and glanced around at the surrounding pubs, offices and shops that made up this area around the college. The early Eighties pubs that she had frequented, before having to return each evening to her family home in suburban Harrogate, might have become gentrified, and quite shockingly unrecognisable to Sarah, thirty years or more on, but she knew this was the very bar. It was previously The Red Lion, where Johnny Lipton had first exploded into her existence, her life, her dreams.

Two months after returning home from almost six years of school in Leicestershire and, despite Anne Sykes's hollow insistence that her younger daughter be 'finished' at Villa Pierrefeu in Switzerland, the Hon. Sarah had uncharacteristically braved her mother's wrath, enrolling at Leeds College of Art on a one-year foundation course that she intended would then pave the way for London, or even the dizzy heights of Paris. It wasn't just the fact that she was eighteen, or her mother's realisation that Sarah was technically an adult and, as such, out of her parents' jurisdiction, that were on her side. For the previous ten years or more, her father, ostrich-like, had buried his head—as well as pickling his liver in an excess of consoling whisky—over the demise of his Bradford-based woollen mill and, as a result, money was tight.

In the Sykes family since the days of Lister's mill in Manningham, as well as the philanthropic Salt's mill in what became known as Saltaire, it was Sarah's grandfather, Albert Sykes who had first seen the commercial possibilities of the Tibetan goat hair used in the making of Kashmir shawls. By the early 1930s, Sykes Mill had a commanding lead over many of its Yorkshire competitors and, with the need for cloth to put in uniform the huge number of soldiers during the Second World War, the wily old Albert had pulled in favours, as well as metaphorical strings with the government, amassing not only a fortune for the Sykes dynasty but also becoming Tory MP for the area.

The Hon. Anne Gardener, meeting the young Gerald Sykes at one of her 'coming out' parties in Knightsbridge, had informed her parents there was no way she could entertain even an evening's invitation to dinner with 'that red-faced yokel from 'oop north.' She had no intention of marrying anyone in 'northern trade' and such an evening would be a waste of time when she could be out with more suitable men of her own ilk from London and the Home Counties in the pursuit of a future husband. Nevertheless, as was often the way with families who could trace their heritage back to William the Conqueror as well as their diminishing fortune to the bankruptcy courts, Lord and Lady Charles Gardener encouraged the wealthy Gerald's dogged pursuance of their beautiful daughter, and Anne finally succumbed to his proposal with the proviso that the young couple should live in fashionable Harrogate rather than among the dark satanic mills of industrial Bradford.

In the early Eighties, Bradford began to be known for its curries rather than its woollen fabric and Sykes Mill had gone the way of the majority of those mills still clinging to the illusion of the grandeur of their former glory, and been divided into myriad industrial units housing everything from spray-paint outlets to children's play gyms. Sarah's brother, Edward, having taken over as MD from an increasingly morose—and inebriated Gerald—showed not a scrap of familial loyalty and, by the mid-Eighties had stripped Sykes

Mill of its assets, feathering his own nest which, it seemed, was not to be built in the north but in the comfort and wealth of Surrey, with his London-born wife, Melissa.

Sending Sarah to follow the traditional route taken at eighteen by the then Hon. Anne Gardener in the 1950s was now no longer a viable option. While regretting daily that neither of her daughters would be a part of that, now dying, tradition of introducing young ladies of a certain class to English Society via The Season, Anne Sykes had also thanked God that there was no longer the expectation, as well as the prohibitive cost involved, in doing just that. As such, Sarah was allowed to enrol on her art course on the one proviso that she live at home and not get involved with any *arty types* who presumably were only there to take drugs, become a part of student sit-ins, love-ins, try to Ban the Bomb (Anne did have a tendency to harp back to the Fifties and Sixties) or because of their inability to land a place to study PPE at Oxford.

An early Saturday evening more than thirty years ago: Sarah, nineteen and deliriously happy, if not a little drunk on sweet cider and life itself. She and April, her friend from college, sitting on the pavement outside The Red Lion while Duran Duran's 'Wild Boys' belted out from the gloomy depths of the ridiculously large speakers wired up to the huge TV, brought in by the landlord specifically for some money-raising charity event.

'Could you shift a bit over that way?' Alice shouted to the back of a dark head in their line of vision, poking him rather rudely as she spoke. 'We can't see the TV.'

He turned, smiling, obligingly moving slightly to the left as he did so. And Sarah knew, knew that she would remember forever her first glimpse of that wickedly beautiful face.

He had fashionably long black hair curling almost to his collar, and decadent brown eyes. He was divine, and Sarah felt almost faint with longing, knowing that in a few more minutes tiny, blonde, gorgeous April would have made yet another conquest to add to her rapidly increasing portfolio of men.

The boy took Sarah's arm and, unable to speak over the heavy beat, simply, but expertly, moved her in front of him, pinning her against his chest with one brown arm, his chin resting on her head. She wanted the moment to go on forever, wanted to stay pulled against his white T-shirt, melting seamlessly into the muscled warmth of his chest so that she wasn't quite sure where she ended and he began.

As Frankie Goes to Hollywood exhorted the UK's young to 'Relax,' the mainly student pub crowd hollered, as much in approval at the sentiment expressed as the sheer joy of being young and intoxicated on alcohol, loud music and, from the pungent smell emanating from the pub's dark corners, pot.

'That's right,' the boy yelled, both arms now firmly clamped around Sarah's upper chest, 'Relax, don't do it,' and then, pulling her round, so that she was facing him, kissed her very thoroughly. He tasted of French cigarettes and danger and Sarah, suddenly recalling her A-level English text of *Sons and Lovers* now knew irrevocably what D. H. Lawrence meant about *swooning*. She was *swooning*, kissing the boy back, her eyes closing as she *swooned*. She was Miriam, cleaving to Paul Morrell—*swooning* in his very presence. When she opened her eyes, he was laughing down at her, the corners of his brown eyes crinkling with amusement, enjoying the effect he was having upon her.

Sarah would never again hear 'Relax' without remembering that first kiss: that first step taken down the path that would change her young life forever.

15

I was eating an over-ripe peach fresh from the market in Jerusalem, the fruit so heavy with juice I couldn't contain its sticky sweetness and it dripped from my mouth, oozing down my chin and on to his neck, tanned from the day on the beach. He moved a hand sleepily to the sudden wetness and I reached down, lifting it to my mouth, tasting the sweetness of the peach rather shockingly—wonderfully—mixed with the taste of myself on his fingers. Awake now, he smiled that slow, leisurely smile—white even teeth, skin the colour of melted caramel—and shifted his legs from the tangle of cotton sheet, moving his mouth to circle a nipple with his tongue …

'Are you awake, darling?' Peter asked cheerfully, his blond curls bobbing dizzyingly from the bottom of the hotel bed as he neared the end of some strange convoluted stretching exercise. 'Just a couple more of these—need to be as fit as I possibly can for the Newcastle muster next Sunday.' He snatched an imaginary pikestaff, bracing himself before lunging, presumably, at one of King Charles's phantom Cavaliers.

Brace. Lunge. Bob. Lunge again. Now you see him, now you don't. Brace. Lunge. Bob…

'Ten more, Clementine, just ten more and then I'll make us a cup of tea. I managed to sort that Teasmade eventually; wasn't going to let it disappoint my beautiful bride on the first day of her honeymoon.' Peter was being particularly jolly, yet seemingly unable to meet my eyes across the beige polyester throw of the Holiday Best Inn bed.

I flushed, remembering not only the dream that had woken me, but Peter's embarrassment at my attempts, the previous night, to subtly initiate rather more different moves than the ones that had become the norm—his norm—since the first time we'd slept together on the night of his proposal.

After the excitement of The Big Proposal, after the huge diamond ring had been placed on my finger, Allegra had finally drooped like an overblown peony and I'd carried her up to the girly pink boudoir where, after hugging me fiercely, she'd instantly fallen asleep, totally at home in her new bedroom.

When I'd re-joined the guests there'd been a total shift in atmosphere, an almost end-of-term jollity as more champagne was opened, poured and consumed and, as my own glass was refilled, stories of their own proposals and other, just as exciting proposals as the one tonight, were being swapped and mulled over across the detritus of the pudding dishes.

I knew I was in some sort of shock. I felt as though I

were watching a play unravel and where, instead of being the main character in Peter's proposal, I was actually in the audience, taking in every nuance, every aspect as the drama unfolded in front of my eyes, the dark-haired girl in the stunning black dress playing the lead as the other guests acted out their parts.

Oliver Cromwell and his lady wife had left shortly after the grand proposal, driven back to Harrogate by Hilary who had drunk nothing but ginger beer all evening. 'Good show, my dear,' he'd enthused, lifting my hand to his rather wet mouth. 'Jolly good show, all round. Just what young Peter needs—some stability in his home life—if he is to make Musketeer sooner rather than later. I wouldn't be surprised, my dear, if this doesn't go down very well, very well indeed, especially if we are to see rather more of *you* down on the field on Sundays? Hmm? A chap needs *support*, you see, needs to know there's someone keeping the home fires burning when he's about to do battle.'

Home fires burning? Wasn't that to do with the Second World War, rather than the Civil one? 'Right,' I'd said, extracting my hand from his moist paw and, because I couldn't think of anything else to say, repeated, 'Right, right, yes, Oliver, I'm sure you're right.'

As the guests had begun to leave, gathering up bags, phones, jackets, searching for kicked-off heels under the dining table, swapping dates and arranging times for events yet to come, I was hugged and congratulated, gathered up as a new member of this little clan. Izzy, however, usually the more vocal and outrageous of any group, had appeared uncharacteristically subdued. Despite, or perhaps because of, the rather large amounts of alcohol she'd downed over the course of the evening, she'd said nothing until it came to actually kissing me goodnight.

'I'll speak to you tomorrow,' she'd whispered as the metronome-ticking of the taxi ordered for her and Declan, Mel and Julian was heard in the drive. 'You don't have to do this, Clem,' she'd added almost fiercely, giving her a hug. 'Do you hear me? You do not.'

And David Henderson who had charmed everyone—male and female—with his apparent gift for making them feel interesting if not downright special, had not said a word about the proposal until he and his wife, Mandy, were on the point of leaving.

'Come on, David,' Nick Westmoreland had shouted, about to jump into another waiting cab. 'Get in. We'll give you a lift home—save you walking across the fields.'

'I'm coming,' David shouted back but instead of leaving he'd turned to me and, with his hand resting lightly on my arm, said, 'Be careful, Clementine.'

'Careful?' I'd asked in surprise. Thinking, not for the first time—and surely what a newly engaged woman should not—what a handsome man David Henderson was, my heart did a little flip as he held my eyes with his own shrewd, knowing ones. Dropping a chaste kiss on my cheek, he'd thanked me formally for the evening and gone down the garden to join his wife and the Westmorelands, leaving me wondering if I'd actually misheard his last comment.

Peter had waved off these, the last of the guests, and returned to the house where I'd begun the marathon task of clearing up. Anything, anything to try to bring back a semblance of normality to my senses. Because surely,

I'd thought, panic mounting, telling a man I didn't love that I'd marry him, in front of all those people, was not normal.

'Darling…? Clementine…?' Peter had said, his face pink, his blond curls bobbing in perfect rhythm with his prominent Adam's apple, 'Do you think… I mean… how do you feel…? It's just that I want you so much…'

If only he'd taken me out into the garden, I thought, pressed me up against the bark of the huge cedar tree and, with the heady scents of the May evening in my senses, kissed me thoroughly. Instead, Peter had double locked the front door and checked that the chain was on; pulled plugs from TV and lamps—'don't want a fire,' he'd said jovially— plumped a few cushions and straightened a picture in the hallway that was slightly askew before leading the way to his bedroom.

'Erm, which side of the bed do you prefer?' Peter had asked, obviously nervous. I'd smiled, trying to put him at his ease, not quite able to work out what he had to be worried about. After all, it was me who hadn't had sex since before Allegra was born, whereas he and Vanessa had only been separated a couple of years. I was, I presumed, lagging behind in the '*I've not had sex recently and might have forgotten where things actually go*' contest. He'd looked so stricken I was actually beginning to wonder if he was having second thoughts, both about inviting me to his bedroom as well as inviting me to be his wife.

Determined to make this all work, I'd taken a deep breath, walked across to my new fiancé and started to kiss him, not with any great passion—I was yet to feel any passion at all for this gauche man—but slowly, encouragingly, in the hope that a small flame of something, anything, might be kindled somewhere on my person.

'Would you like to use the bathroom first?' Peter had suddenly whispered.

'Sorry?' If there had been little, so far, to raise my feet off the ground, to have me on my way down that corridor of desire where I so longed to be heading, this one sentence, like pouring water on a barely fizzing firework, brought me firmly back to ground zero.

'Right. Yes. OK.' And I'd gone into his beautifully spacious en-suite bathroom, spending a good five minutes marvelling at the expensive tiling, the pile of fluffy towels, the array of designer toiletries on display rather than at Peter's naked body.

Once I'd stripped to my underwear I didn't quite know what else to do apart from squirt a drop of Peter's 'Cool Water' between my breasts and attempt a rictus of a smile at myself in his mirror. *Come on, Clem*, I'd said to myself, *you can do this*. I came back out to find Peter already in the bed, the sheets up to his neck. He'd looked rather like a curly-haired Christopher Robin and I had a terrible urge to laugh. *Please don't let him have pyjamas on*, I'd thought. *Or his pants. Or, God forbid, both*.

I'd pulled back the sheets and slid in beside him whereupon he'd quickly turned out the light and kissed me with a mouth smelling and tasting of a strange combination of alcohol and peppermint. Did he think I was the police, I'd thought almost hysterically, and might arrest him for being drunk in charge of a half-naked woman? Almost immediately, Peter had begun the sexual moves that now, habitually, *always* started with the twirling of my right nipple, then the left, before lurching, almost apologetically on and into me, thudding away, as if on some mission that had to be accomplished at any cost; the prolonged pumping which left him pink-faced and sweating, and me wanting to cry.

So now, on this, the second day after our wedding at Midhope Register Office, I was feeling desperately homesick for Allegra left, unwillingly I knew by both parties, at my parents for the few days of our honeymoon, and as well, for some reason I couldn't quite decide, feeling slightly physically sick.

Whether it was the bobbing up and down of Peter's blond curls reminding me of so many curls of butter on a swirling patterned sea of carpet; embarrassment at my attempts, last night—together with Peter's rebuff—to expand his sexual repertoire or the amount of wine I'd knocked back in order to actually make those attempts on his fairly fragile ego, I wasn't quite sure, but Peter's enforced jollity was making me feel worse. I didn't get it: Peter had been married to the strong, feisty Vanessa. Surely to God *she* hadn't been happy to put up with what amounted to crap, *really* crap, sex? Or had I just been incredibly lucky with my few previous lovers who not only knew what they were doing, but revelled in making sure I was enjoying it as much as, if not more than, they did? Surely there was no excuse for bad sex? There were enough manuals and films to put one on the right track if one was unsure how to go about it. But then, there were a hell of a lot of people who made crap food and that, surely was just as inexcusable as offering bad sex?

As Peter bobbed up once more, lunging towards the beige hotel curtains, I knew I was going to have to get into the shower before I threw up. Although the sex was dreadful and I was missing Allegra dreadfully and, glancing out of the bathroom window I could see grey Scottish mist with its promise of rain to come, I hugged myself as I wrapped the somewhat threadbare standard-issue towelling robe around myself and made for the tiny bathroom. I knew I mustn't allow myself to hope for one minute that the feeling of nausea could be something quite different; that there was anything but the tiniest of faint chance I was already pregnant with the baby I so longed for.

It would be so different this time. There would be no plucking up the courage to tell a horrified lover behind the huge industrial freezer in a frenetically busy restaurant kitchen; no look of disbelief, of contempt even, as I broke the news; no being told in that suddenly cold voice that he wanted no part in this mess. What about our plans to return to his native Israel? To work together in his uncle's restaurant in Haifa so that we could both become proficient in the Mediterranean and Middle Eastern cuisine to which he'd introduced me, and which I now adored? There was no way he was going to stay in fucking rainy *Leeds* with a *baby*, he'd spat, cold with anger. *Think, Clem, think*, he'd pleaded. Together we were going to become as good as, better than, his compatriot, Ottolenghi, who was doing so well with his gourmet delis in Islington and Kensington. Did I really want to end up in some council house in Leeds—because that's all that we would be able to afford with a baby—when we could be travelling, cooking together, making love in the heat of an Israeli night?

Frustration at me for not sharing his dream, as well as his fear at the possibility of losing me, made him angrier than I'd ever seen him. I'd looked at him, shocked. I'd known he wouldn't be *pleased*, known full well that he wouldn't wrap his arms round me and tell me he wanted a baby more than anything else in the world especially as it was my baby, *our* baby and conceived in Israel, but I hadn't expected this cold fury. I'd had a sudden vision of this baby with, *Made In Israel* stamped all the way through it like a stick of Blackpool rock and, despite myself, I'd smiled.

'Clem, this is not funny,' he'd said, his beautiful brown eyes devoid of any warmth, vacant almost, 'Get rid of it.' And with that, he'd stalked out onto the wet, greasy streets of Leeds despite Gianni, the head chef, bellowing at him that there was fucking food to cook and where the fuck did he think he was fucking going?

'Now, when in Scotland, do as the Scots do, I think, darling, don't you?'

'Sorry, Peter, did you say something?' Brought back to the present and the somewhat mean hotel in Scotland rather than the heat of Israel with its all-pervasive heady smells of cumin, sumac and lemon or the overheated, frenzied turmoil of La Toque Blanche in Leeds, I looked at my husband as he stood, rosy-cheeked and sweating against the window.

'Just saying, darling, when in Rome and all that…'

'Rome?'

'Well, *Scotland*, obviously. Porridge for breakfast, with salt rather than cream and syrup…?'

I fled to the bathroom.

In the end porridge, in any of its forms, had not been an option. The standard buffet of a three-star chain hotel—individual packets of processed cereal, bacon with an abundance of fat and white flecks of bone, eggs greasily fried or scrambled into dry, rubbery clumps and tepid, filthy coffee—greeted us in the dining room already packed with bad-tempered babies and truculent teenagers who, denied the option of a 'free house' at home with their mates, had been dragged out for a two day Superbreak made cheap by Groupon.

'I'm really sorry about the hotel, Clem,' Peter apologised as I ate limp toast and drank the Earl Grey tea the harassed waitress had eventually found for me. 'All the five-star places were fully booked up months ago.' He attacked with gusto the undercooked fried eggs, a string of raw albumen hanging from his fork as he did so. I looked away. 'We'll have a proper honeymoon next year: Barbados, perhaps? Would you like that? We can take Allegra with us and my two if Vanessa will allow them.'

I smiled, willing myself to feel some enthusiasm. I shook my head, as if by doing so I could clear thoughts of the past that were tumbling, like clothes in a drier, with thoughts about the present. About Lucy and her shocked, white face when she realised it was me standing there watching her, together with the equally shocked faces of Izzy, Harriet and Grace at the pole dancing club; about my marriage to this man who sat opposite me now, spreading cheap, vividly red jam onto his toast while beaming hopefully at me.

Berating myself for not living for the now, I took Peter's hand and smiled. *Make more of a damned effort,*

I told myself. I had to cheer up and try harder, show more enthusiasm, if this was going to work. I had to keep to my side of the bargain. This good, earnest man who loved me—loved me and Allegra—would never have left me, pregnant, like Ariav had. Allegra and I had a lovely future because of Peter, and I should jolly well start behaving myself if this marriage was going to work. Ignoring the leaden sky that I could just see from the restaurant window and the rather irritating noise Peter made as he sucked up his coffee, I smiled and said, 'Tell me about your mother, Peter. I'm really looking forward to meeting her.'

'Mother, I'd like you to meet Clementine Douglas—oops, silly me, Broadbent,' Peter chortled, introducing me to the diminutive figure who presided, Miss Havisham-style, in the middle of the otherwise deserted sitting room. Peter had driven the fifty miles or so in the pouring rain towards the rest home where his mother had lived for the last ten years and now stood, hovering anxiously at his mother's side, as her claw-like hand pulled repetitively at some imagined thread on her woollen skirt.

Morag Broadbent, nee Mackinlay, was tiny, a reduced, bird-like figure, and I couldn't believe that so diminutive a woman could ever have produced the man that Peter had become.

'She's a neat little thing,' Morag said, in her soft Scots burr, addressing Peter as if I wasn't present. 'I do hope she's going to be better for ye than the other one.'

'Mother, really—'

'I'm just saying, Peter. Ye were sold a pup with the first one. Y'always did go for a pretty face, and this one certainly has one of those.' Peter's mother had finally turned to take a good look at me, her bright little eyes—incongruous in the wizened, pale face—boring into me as if she could see into the very core of me.

Spooky, I thought, reddening. *It's as if she knows exactly who I am and why I've married Peter.*

'Married him for his money, did ye?' Morag suddenly asked, still staring at me.

'Mother, enough,' Peter said, scarlet. 'If you can't be civil, we shan't come and see you again.'

'Well, he's got nae one else once I've gone,' she went on, pointing her stick at her son. 'Nae brothers or sisters, nay aunts or uncles still alive and nay real cousins to speak of.'

She was beginning to sound like that Scottish bloke in *Dad's Army*. I recalled early Sunday evenings as a little girl when Lucy and I had sat with Granny Douglas watching repeats of her favourite series. Private Frazer, that was it, with his 'Wur doomed, wur awl doomed…' Blimey, I thought, wanting to giggle as I remembered Neil Manning aka Oliver Cromwell aka Captain Mainwaring. How many more characters from *Dad's Army* was Peter going to produce?

'So he'd have been in a guid position to inherit the whole of the Mackinlay fortune—we were part of the Buchanan clan,' she added proudly. 'But, I tell ye now, the money—my money that I brought to the marriage—awl gone. His father spent it awl on women and horses.' Morag fixed me with her gimlet eye once more. 'And blood's thicker than water, d'ye hear?'

'Erm, I don't think Peter bets on horses,' I said, smiling nervously. 'I don't think ye need—you need—have any worries on that score.'

'As I say, you cannae teach an old dog new tricks.' Morag rolled the 'r' on 'tricks' for what seemed forever before suddenly stopping dead. She'd fallen asleep, her head drooping, her fingers continuing to claw at her skirt.

16

I glanced around at Peter's—my—beautiful kitchen where I was in the middle of preparing supper for the five of us and then at the clock on the wall. Just a few days into my new married life, I was determined to make a go of it all, determined that Sophie, as well as Max, should start to like me and Allegra and want us in her family home.

We'd arrived back from our three-day honeymoon in Scotland the previous evening, picked up Allegra from my parents and then driven home where, to Allegra's delight and my huge embarrassment, Peter had carried both of us over the threshold. Sophie, who had been dropped off by her mother a few hours earlier, had tutted in disbelief, slouching off to her bedroom after making the obligatory sick noises and muttering, 'gross,' under her breath.

It was now six in the evening and I'd seen very little of Sophie all day. She'd refused all offers of breakfast and lunch and turned down flat any idea of accompanying the kids, George and me for a walk down into the village to the café that did fabulous milkshakes. Instead she'd spent the morning in bed—finally appearing at two in the afternoon—given me her customary sneer and, plugging herself into her phone and iPod, passed the afternoon sunning herself in the Secret Garden.

She was now stretched out on the sofa in the 'family area' of the kitchen, devouring a huge bag of chemically-orange Doritos and cans of coke while watching *Hollyoaks* at full volume as I put the final touches to what Peter had told me was his daughter's favourite food.

'What's this?' Sophie poked suspiciously at the ravioli I'd spent a good couple of hours making: mixing and forming the dough from scratch and stuffing with a filling of prime minced beef and spinach as soon as the kids and I had returned from our walk.

'Ravioli,' I said smiling at Sophie. 'Your father said it was your favourite.'

'It doesn't look anything like the ravioli that we eat at home.' Sophie dissected one of the perfectly cooked squares, pulling it apart as if she were a forensic pathologist looking for clues to how it had met its demise.

'That's because Mum gives us ravioli from a tin—on toast,' Max said, through a mouthful. 'This is tons better.'

I shot him a look of gratitude while simultaneously wiping sauce from around Allegra's mouth. 'Just try some, Sophie. It really isn't all that different from the Heinz stuff. And I'll make you some toast to go with it if you'd like.'

'It's nothing like the tinned stuff. This is wonderful.' Peter smiled, patting my hand in appreciation but, I noticed, he'd pulled specks of spinach from their little parcel of pasta and was leaving them, stark, against the white of the plate. It reminded me of an interview with Mick Jagger I'd once read in Cosmo, or some such magazine, where he said he'd had an emerald put into his front tooth but very soon swapped it for a diamond when people thought he had spinach stuck in his teeth. Peter's plate was beginning to resemble Mick Jagger's mouth, I thought hysterically. Why didn't he just devour the whole beautiful, delicious square of pasta and let the tang of the spinach mix with the delicately flavoured beef and basil-infused tomato sauce?

'Well, I'm not eating it,' Sophie said petulantly. 'I've become vegetarian anyway.' She pushed her plate to one side and helped herself to a mouthful of Peter's wine.

'Stop it,' Peter snapped. 'Stop showing off. And you're certainly not old enough at sixteen to be drinking wine. If you can't behave, leave the table.'

'Mum lets me drink wine with my meal. She says if I'm introduced to it while she's watching and in control, I'll be far less likely to binge drink when she's not there.'

Bloody stupid middle-class theories, I thought crossly, as well as in total contradiction to my thoughts expressed on this matter at Peter's dinner party. Much more likely to have kids drinking heavily with their mates, if they're given free rein and get the taste for it at home.

'Sophie,' Peter said crossly, obviously unsure whether Vanessa did allow their daughter to drink at meals or whether Sophie was making it up, 'you're acting like a child. Look at Allegra—she's thoroughly enjoying this lovely food.'

'Well she would, wouldn't she? She's used to this sort of stuff.'

I glanced at Allegra, who was gazing wide-eyed at her new stepsister. The last thing I wanted was confrontation at our first real family meal together and I certainly didn't want Allegra, who was clinging on to Hector elephant, upset. Max came to the rescue by telling us all about how many goals he'd scored at his football tournament that morning and how he'd been given Player of the Day award.

I fetched the lemon meringue pie I'd made for pudding—surely all kids loved lemon meringue—and started to cut it into slices. 'Sophie? Will you have some? Your dad said it was your and Max's favourite.'

'I think he must be going back several years,' Sophie almost sneered. 'Anyway, Mum says puddings like this are full of sugar—even Jamie Oliver now says they're no good for you. There was an article in the *Sunday Times* yesterday about him not eating sugary stuff anymore. You shouldn't be encouraging little kids like her—' Sophie indicated Allegra with her unused napkin '—to eat them either. All her teeth will go rotten and drop out...'

'Enough, Sophie,' Peter said, as he saw Allegra's face crumple and tears well up in her huge brown eyes before plopping, hugely, onto her meringue. 'Go to your room, go on.'

'It's fine, Peter.' I smiled at Allegra, encouraging her to get on with her pudding. 'We all have principles when we're sixteen. I certainly did. Didn't you?'

'Erm, I think I was too busy studying for GCSEs and looking at the stock market to have principles,' Peter said vaguely, still glaring at Sophie.

'The stock market at sixteen?' I said, surprised. 'You were playing the market even then?'

'That's how Dad made all his money,' Max said proudly, tucking into his meringue in the manner of all eight-year-old boys when faced with a delicious pudding. 'Once I get to be a teenager, Dad's going to help me get started—'

'Boring, boring,' Sophie interrupted.

'Not so boring when it pays for your school fees and your iPhone etc, etc,' Peter said, mildly.

'Yeah, well, I can't wait to get back to school,' Sophie said, nibbling a fragment of sweet, buttery pastry that had fallen from Max's plate and onto the table. 'I can't think of anything worse than having to go to *state* school and live at home *all* the time.'

Hours later, after Peter had gone to his study with coffee, apologising that some problem had arisen with work that had to be sorted, I bathed Allegra and tucked her up in the pink boudoir and read *We're Going On a Bear Hunt* for the zillionth time. Cross with myself that I'd been unable to make any headway with Sophie, I took George out into the garden and walked the grounds, enjoying the cool night air on my arms and legs. Oh God, what had I done in marrying Peter? In trying to find security for Allegra and myself had I, in effect, made things worse? Would I have been better just moving out of Emerald Street as I'd always planned to do and being in the process of, hopefully, starting a new job now that my degree was finished? But what if I'd not been able to find a job that fitted in with Allegra's school day? And, what about the holidays? Where did kids go during the long school holidays while their mums worked? Other single mothers worked, I told myself crossly—I would have sorted something. My thoughts, like a tennis ball on centre court at Wimbledon, flew from the positives to the negatives of being married to Peter Broadbent.

'Sort it, Clem,' I told myself, speaking out loud so that George looked up at me expectantly. 'Man up and sort it. You've made your choice; bloody well live it.'

I gazed up at the clear inky-black sky, breathtakingly full of countless stars now that it didn't have to compete with the sodium streetlights down in town. I breathed in the scents of late summer: the heady tobacco reek of the white Nicotiana Sylvestris; the fruitily delicious honeysuckle; the resin-y smells of lavender, basil and rosemary that I had planted myself only recently.

Somewhere out there, under those same stars, Lucy was living an entirely different life.

I shouted for George who had run off, following a badger trail in David Henderson's fields, and together we walked back to the house. The walk, along with the almost exotically scented night air had lifted my spirit, and the panic I'd felt at making the wrong decision in marrying Peter had subsided once more. I determined to have a Jo Malone scented bath before having another go at gently seducing my new husband and encouraging him to let me take an actual part in our sex life.

Through the kitchen's French windows I caught sight of Sophie. She was stuffing her face with leftover ravioli before starting on a huge piece of lemon meringue, eyes closed and a look of pure ecstasy on her face as the delicious food was consumed. Grinning to myself, I went to find Peter.

17

On the first Wednesday morning in September, I received two phone calls that had me jumping around the kitchen with delight. The first was from the headteacher of the local village school who had, somewhat witheringly I thought, peered over her glasses and informed me, only a couple of weeks previously, that to be given a place at her school a child had to have had its name down for years. As I had only recently moved into the area, and Allegra had no sibling in situ in her school but *did* have a perfectly good school place down near Emerald Street—here the head had almost shaken her head at the thought of any child being educated in that part of town—she couldn't see any chance of her becoming a pupil at her school in the foreseeable future.

Just as I was making a list as to which bits of Allegra's uniform needed renewing for the new term at her old school that, I'd suddenly realised with a guilty start, was only a few days away, Mrs Theobold, the village school head, rung to say a place for Allegra had unexpectedly been made.

'A family that was moving across from Cheshire has given back word only in the past five minutes,' Mrs Theobold said in that same sniffy, nasal tone she'd previously used to turn down Allegra from the school. 'I need to know if you want to accept the place for Allegra, Mrs Broadbent, as I have a list here of children who are *clamouring* at the door for a place at Westenbury Church of England.'

'Oh, right, er, well, yes please then, Mrs Theobold,' I stuttered, feeling that same mixture of awe and intimidation I thought I'd left behind once I hit adolescence and realised teachers, along with traffic wardens and the police were just ordinary people in a mantle they assumed for the duration of their working day. Having said that, I couldn't imagine this woman on the other end of the phone in any other role but that of bossy headmistress. For a split-second I hesitated. Did I really want Allegra going to this white middle-class oasis when she'd been totally happy spending her days with the multicultural, somewhat dysfunctional clientele of Beaumont Street Community School at the bottom end of town? But what bliss to be able to walk Allegra down into the village every day rather than fighting the traffic each morning to get her across town to her old school.

'Thank you so much, Mrs Theobold,' I said in my most grownup, married-lady voice. 'Of course I accept.'

'Well, you need to call in today to pick up the uniform list and all the other information we have for new parents. I'll leave it all at the office for you—someone will be here until midday. The new term does start on Monday, you know.'

I'd only just put the phone down and was calling Allegra in from the garden to tell her the news when the phone rang once more.

'Clementine? Ah, good, caught you in. David Henderson here. I was wondering if you'd thought any more about doing a spot of cooking for me?'

I had a sudden vision of the 'Richard Branson of the north' sitting alone at a table, napkin around his neck, knife and fork at the ready in the manner of some hungry cartoon character, and stifled a giggle. I needed to be grownup about this—I'd just chatted with the headteacher from hell and now here I was talking with the number one businessman in the north of England.

Before I could say anything, David went on hurriedly, 'Well, not me by myself, of course. An odd lunch or two for business clients over from Italy or Russia?'

'Well, that sounds really like something I'd love to do…' I tailed off, not quite sure what else to say.

'Look, why don't you pop over to the barn with me and I'll show you around and together we can decide what might be best.'

'The barn?' I asked, puzzled. I could see the Hendersons' beautiful old manor house across the fields. It certainly didn't look anything like a barn.

'The company has a house—an old barn that was renovated just a couple of years ago. My son lives a bachelor life in it most of the time but he knows if I need to butter up clients, he has to move back in with us for the duration so that the clients have a home from home while they are in the area. They seem to prefer it to the third-rate hotel that masquerades as Midhope's most salubrious place to stay. I thought it wouldn't be a bad idea if you could seduce them into spending obscene amounts of money with us by cooking wonderful lunches for them?'

I felt a frisson of excitement and prayed it was the thought of creating a marinated brochette of swordfish perhaps, together with a strawberry crème brulée and rosewater shortbread, and not the thought of the great man himself. I shook my head to get rid of the vision of David Henderson pulling a black cashmere sweater, the colour of his hair, over broad, tanned shoulders and said, 'That sounds really great, David. I'd love to.'

'Brilliant. I'm actually off to Milan this afternoon, so I'm glad I caught you before I leave. How about I pick you up next Tuesday morning and drive you over and you can see the kitchen and dining area and see if you think it's feasible?'

'That'll work well,' I said. 'I'm really excited because I've just got Allegra into the village school after being told there wasn't a place for her. She starts next Monday so Tuesday would be good.'

David laughed. 'Oh, is she starting with The Fear-Bold?'

I giggled. 'The Fear-Bold? Brilliant name. You know her?'

'Oh God, yes. She's run that school with a rod of iron for years. Seb, my son, went there as a little boy until he went to King Edward's at eleven. She's a tyrant but, I tell you, it's a fantastic little school. I'm actually a school governor there.'

'Really? I wouldn't have thought you'd have time with everything else you do.'

'Well, I don't do much else for the village—it's my one bit of voluntary work and I'm part of the furniture now. Probably once The Fear-Bold leaves, I'll go too.'

★

I'm happy, I thought later that afternoon as I cut bunches of basil and rosemary from the pots of herbs I'd planted outside the kitchen door just after Allegra and I had officially moved in with Peter. I'd taken Allegra into Midhope and kitted her out with the navy skirts and sweatshirts as directed on the new school list. I still wasn't used to having a bankcard that I knew wouldn't be handed back by embarrassed shop assistants, and had kept the expenditure on Allegra's uniform down to a minimum. The little white shirts and black school shoes she'd had at Beaumont Street Community still had plenty of wear in them, but I'd treated Allegra to a pair of navy long socks with a navy frill around the top that she'd coveted from the moment we stepped into the queue, waiting our turn with other last-minute, harassed mothers to purchase garments a size too big in order that 'they'll grow into them soon enough and last that bit longer.'

'I'm happy,' I repeated, aloud this time, refusing to think, at least for that moment about Lucy. Once I'd got Allegra started at her new school, and Sophie and Max had also started back at their respective schools, then I would really begin in earnest to think about what I was going to do about her. I felt the despair over Lucy begin its pernicious attack on my senses once more and tried desperately hard to savour the moment of the early September afternoon warmth in this beautiful haven of peace. I breathed in the scent of newly mown grass as Eric Williams, Peter's gardener, moved methodically across the vast area of lawns.

Peter had been up early, had left the house before I was even awake and now, with Max and Sophie both back at their mother's for several days and Allegra sitting at the kitchen table cutting out her new 'paper dressing-dolly', I revelled in having the house and garden to myself. I lay on the soft grass, book and mug of tea to hand and, closing my eyes knew, for a couple of moments at least, if not happiness then certainly contentment.

I realised I hadn't actually seen much of Peter over the past few days. He'd appeared preoccupied, anxious almost— 'nothing for *you* to worry about, darling,' he'd smiled—and was forever on the phone or disappearing into his study for hours on end, emerging only to eat distractedly before apologetically absenting himself once more. I knew, because he'd told me, he was having problems with Vanessa who, he said, was being totally unreasonable over maintenance and the children's school fees. He said at some stage soon he was going to have to have a showdown with her in order to sort it all out. But that was Peter's problem, I told myself, reaching for my tea and the chocolate and pistachio muffin I'd baked from a new recipe that morning. This afternoon, in *my* garden, sitting on *my* grass, eating *my* recipe muffin I was happy.

The following Tuesday, as I was waiting for David Henderson to pick me up to show me his barn and discuss my working for him, Harriet rang to suggest that as I'd be only two minutes away I join her and Grace for lunch at her place. When I told her I'd actually arranged to meet up with Izzy she said no problem, she'd ring Izzy too, and as it was such a beautiful day we should be able to all eat in the garden.

I so loved having a bunch of girlfriends after years of

really not having anyone and, what with seeing Allegra trot confidently into her new classroom, the invitation to lunch with these women with whom I felt a real affinity and friendship, and the imminent meeting with David, I started to think my life might really be beginning to improve at last. I moved a hopeful, tentative hand over my stomach; there was still no sign of my period and, while my constant worry and fears with regards to Lucy meant I could never totally relax and be truly happy, just for this moment, on this beautiful autumn morning, I was at one with myself.

'You're looking well,' David smiled as he leaned over me, expertly fastening the seatbelt I'd been unable to find on the wrong side of my seat.

He looked and smelt divine. I glanced across at him, taking advantage of his turned head as he reversed down Peter's drive to the country lane that bordered both our properties. He had a full head of very dark hair, greying now at the temple, olive skin and eyes I assumed also to be dark behind the expensive looking Ray-Bans that were shielding his eyes against the late summer sun.

Although not usually overly vain about my appearance, I knew I was looking good. I'd made a big effort washing my long dark hair, drying it upside down so that it hung in a layered curtain below my shoulders. I'd paid particular attention to my makeup, outlining my brown eyes in soft brown kohl and my mouth in red, rubbing it off crossly—I was going for a job interview for heaven's sake—before defiantly re-applying it once I heard David's knock on the kitchen door.

'I'll give you a bit of history on the barn,' David was saying as I found myself unable to shift my gaze from his competent-looking hands deftly steering the upmarket four-wheel-drive round substantial hedgerows grown dense following the recent warm weather. Feeling guilty, I tried hard not to compare David's large, olive-skinned hands with Peter's small, white, almost pudgy pair, but was finding it difficult not to.

'History?' I asked, pulling a face. 'Can't say I was overly good at history at school. I seem to remember I was sent out of a lesson on The War of Jenkins' Ear for writing "I Love Robbie Williams" in the margin of my history book.'

David laughed. 'It was Kim Wilde for me. God, she was gorgeous—I had a huge poster of her on my wall in the dorm at school. But I'm talking history as in how I've ended up with the barn. As I'm sure you know, now that you've met her, Grace and Sebastian, my son, bought the house together when it was a total and utter wreck. Once Grace had Jonty, my grandson—I still can't believe I'm a grandfather for heaven's sake—she really wasn't well and they all ended up staying with Mandy and me while it was gutted and done up. And then, Grace and Seb split. By then, because *I'd* actually ended up taking on the renovations, I couldn't bear to let it go and decided it would be a good place to put up clients from abroad rather than in The King's Head down in town. As I said to you on the phone, Seb stays there a lot of the time but is more than happy to move out if we're putting people up. Your way with food, Clementine, is so exceptional, I thought it would be an added bonus to get you to cook on an ad hoc basis, if it's something you might like to do.'

'My plan—before Peter came along and swept me off my feet—was to look for hotel management work once I'd finished my degree. I have to say, it never occurred to me to do outside catering—I assumed if I was going to go back to cooking it would have to be in a restaurant with restaurant hours and I just couldn't do that with Allegra being so little. Now that I don't have to work full time to keep us both, this sounds perfect.'

'And how is married life? As I said, you're looking very well on it...'

'I'm so lucky. Peter has been very kind.'

When I didn't say anything else, David, who had stopped at traffic lights, looked across at me. He didn't say anything else either, but gave me a sympathetic smile, patted my arm and then drove the rest of the journey telling me about his various businesses but particularly L'uomo, the company he and Nick Westmoreland had started only a couple of years previously but which had exceeded all expectations, expanding into Russia, China and soon, Brazil.

'Yoo-hoo. We thought we'd come down and meet you and walk you back up to our place for lunch.' Harriet Westmoreland, holding the hands of two ravishing blond-haired toddlers appeared at the French window of the barn. 'Although with these two, who insist on walking everywhere instead of riding in their buggy, it might be suppertime before we get back. What do you think of this place? What a brilliant idea to cook fabulous lunches for rich businessmen.'

'I'm so excited. If it's what these people want then, yes,

I'd love to do it. David says I can have free rein with the menus so I'll be in my element planning it all. It will fit in so well with Allegra too—she's just started at the little village school in Westenbury.'

'Has she? Ooh, well done. It's a great little school by all accounts… Fin, come away from the wall. Oh, and Jesus, the cowpat too.' Harriet dashed across the lawn to the adjoining meadow and grabbed her little boy who was poking an experimental sandal-shod toe into its crusty perimeter. 'Hi, David,' she called as David Henderson stopped to lock up before stepping into the garden. 'Have you finished here? Can I take Clem away now?'

'Absolutely.' David walked over to us, kissed Harriet briefly and patted her daughter's blonde curls before turning to me. 'I'll be in touch, Clementine.' He smiled. 'I think I've just acquired another business partner.' His eyes held mine for longer than was necessary and I felt myself blush. He waved a brief goodbye and made for his car parked up against the wall of the narrow lane.

I felt ridiculously happy.

'Right, are you ready?' I was brought back to earth as Harriet pulled Fin away from an ancient stone water trough almost completely hidden in the seeded long grass. 'God, these two are exhausting… yes, darling, it's a slug but put it back where you found it…'

'Are you going to tell us, Clem?' Izzy asked gently. 'Tell us about the girl in the nightclub on your hen do?' I felt my heart begin to beat faster as Grace, Harriet and Izzy turned as one towards me.'

'That's not fair, Izzy,' Grace protested. 'Clem hardly knows Harriet and me.'

'No, it's OK. It's really OK, Grace. It's about time I talked about Lucy…'

18

I took a deep breath, a too big gulp of wine and said, 'It would actually be really good to tell someone about all this. It's been years since I've had a gang of girlfriends. Oh God, that's presumptuous of me, isn't it, assuming you are all my mates suddenly, after only knowing you all—apart from Izzy of course—for a couple of months or so?'

'No, no,' Harriet said, beaming. 'You really are our new best friend, and I'm not saying that in that awful affected way people go on about their new "bezzie'—bloody stupid handle when used by anyone over sixteen, I reckon. Honestly, Clem, Grace and I were saying only the other day how much we really liked you and how we wanted to see more of you. Women really *need* other women; well, I certainly do anyway. I'm a big believer in that.'

Grace, who could obviously see I was quite affected by Harriet's little speech, patted my arm and filled my glass. 'Hat and I have been friends since we were eleven. We've nothing left to talk about—in fact I don't think I even like her very much really.' She ducked as Harriet threw a child's soft toy frog at her. 'I certainly welcome *any* new coven of women friends.'

'We could form a book club and… and go to more gay bars in Leeds,' Harriet laughed. 'I really enjoyed that night.'

'Don't forget Mel,' Izzy said. 'She's new to the area—well, not new, she was born here, of course—and she will need new friends.'

'Right, that's sorted then. I think we should drink to that.' Grace smiled, lifting her glass.

I swallowed hard. Gosh, I really did feel quite tearful.

'OK. The girl you saw at the lap-dancing club was—is—my sister, Lucy.'

'Blimey.' Izzy took in a sharp breath before exhaling deeply. 'You've kept that to yourself, Clem. I've known you four years and you've not once mentioned a sister, let alone her name.'

'Well, you can certainly see the family resemblance,' Harriet said, obviously remembering how she'd come across the almost-naked girl when she'd wandered into the club and seen her swaying around her pole.

I smiled and bit my lip. 'Lucy's actually my twin. My identical twin.'

'Oh, you *poor* thing,' Harriet exclaimed. 'No wonder you looked as if you'd seen a ghost when I said you had a double dancing round a pole. Did you know that she was in Leeds? That she'd taken up…' Harriet paused, desperately trying to think of the right words '… dancing as a career?'

'No, Harriet, I didn't. The last time I saw her—two years ago—she was working the streets down near the centre of Midhope.'

'The streets...?'

'She's a prostitute, Harriet. A sex worker. A whore. Call it what you will.'

'Harriet, do you want this food out here?' A tall, motherly-looking woman appeared at the door with Fin, Harriet's little boy, giggling and clinging on to her back. 'It's ready.'

'Thanks, Lilian. Sorry, Clem, Izzy, this is St Lil of Desperate Mothers. Please don't try and pinch her, anyone, because I will have to shoot you if you do.' There was real affection in Harriet's voice and the woman smiled.

'Aw, get on with you,' the woman said in a rich Southern Irish brogue. 'I'm going nowhere except upstairs to put this one down for a nap. Thea is already asleep upstairs and Jonty—' the woman smiled at Grace before nodding back towards a pushchair in the kitchen '—is still spark out as well. Enjoy the peace while you can, ladies.'

'I'll come and get it, Lilian.' Harriet pushed her chair back. 'Sorry to interrupt, Clem,' she apologised. 'Don't say any more until I get back.'

'I'll help you.' I jumped up from my seat and followed Harriet into a homely, comfortable kitchen. It wasn't a patch on Peter's for either grandeur or size but I immediately fell in love with the cream and oak units adorned with children's lovingly executed and displayed drawings and scribbles; with the mass of wild flowers haphazardly arranged in blue pottery jugs; the general untidy paraphernalia of a family with five children.

'Now, this Caesar salad is not going to be anything like *you* can produce—' Harriet held up a hand as I started to protest '—but the date and walnut bread, which

I am passing off as my own—note the lengthening of my nose—will be brilliant because it's from that fabulous little artisan bakery that David Henderson is always recommending.'

'It looks wonderful. Shall I add this parmesan, Harriet?'

'Oh yes, do. I'd have forgotten all about that.' We gathered up plates and dishes and headed back outside. 'I'm really pleased David is recommending *you* too, Clem,' Harriet added. 'If you've got him on your side, you can't go wrong.'

Once we had passed round the salad and bread and filled glasses of wine and water, Izzy said, 'So, Clem, how come you've turned out so well but your poor twin has ended up on the streets?'

'That's bit harsh, Izzy,' Grace said. 'Maybe Lucy has chosen it as a career path?'

'Oh, don't be daft, Grace,' Harriet admonished her friend. 'No one ends up as a sex worker through choice. No one goes to the careers officer and says, "I'd like to be a sex worker please. What training would you suggest?" God, do you remember those awful sessions when you were fourteen and just wanted to be an air stewardess or the next Madonna or… or Christie Brinkley and the guy peered over his glasses at you and said the same thing he said to all of the class: "Teaching? Banking? Secretarial?" And you agreed to all his suggestions because you didn't dare tell him you were going to marry George Michael and become a film star acting alongside Richard Gere…'

I put down my fork and took a long drink from my glass of water. 'Lucy and I were adopted from birth.'

'My God, Clem, you never even told me *that*.' Izzy stared at me in surprise.

'We had a normal, happy—I suppose—childhood. Lucy was always the naughty one, particularly at school. She was constantly in trouble, even from when we started in infant school. She wouldn't sit down at circle time, was always thumping the other kids, pulling the ribbons from the other little girls' hair and making them cry. She was very bright, could read even before we went to school, but had absolutely no interest in schoolwork whereas I loved it all. Loved the books, the colouring, the singing...'

'How strange that you should look so much alike and yet have such different personalities,' Izzy said through a mouthful of salad. 'I thought identical twins always thought alike and did things together?'

'A bit like the Kray Twins, you mean?' I said seriously and then smiled at the faces of the other women who, I could see, were slightly uncomfortable at my words.

'Sorry, that was a bit crass of me. Don't get me wrong— as young sisters we were close. I adored her. I've often wondered if it was because my mum—obviously—told us we were adopted; that even though she said she and my father had chosen us because we were special—you know how the adoption people at social services would have told them to tell us—that Lucy just couldn't hack it.'

'Well, you must have discussed it with her over the years,' Harriet said. 'What did she say?'

'She never really wanted to talk about it. All she would say, particularly as we got older and hit our teens, was that some bitch of a woman had had us and thrown us away.

That's how she always saw it. I mean, I always wanted to find out who our mother was but Lucy was adamant, would actually fly into a rage if I suggested, once we were eighteen, that we look for her.'

'And you still haven't? Looked for her, I mean?' Harriet asked. 'Maybe she's desperate to find you too?

I smiled, but I could feel my lip begin to wobble. Shit, I didn't want to cry. 'I doubt it very much, Harriet.' I hesitated, unsure whether to carry on. 'Look, there are very few people who know this and I'm not sure why I'm telling you all now. It must be the wine I've drunk, and I'll probably regret it because you might not want to know me after this...'

'After what?' All three women stared at me.

'My mother—my adopted mother that is—would never tell us anything about our *real* mother. Lucy never really wanted to know anyway but, even though I always did, my mother said she knew nothing, had no idea who our real mother had been. And then, when Lucy and I were about fifteen, Lucy came up with the idea of forming a sort of gang. All the naughties—and even though we went to this little private school, there was a real set of *incredibly* naughty girls—were in it and Lucy was in charge. She was incredibly rude to the teachers, did no homework, skived off school and went into town after school with her gang, hanging round the bars, drinking and smoking and, eventually, dabbling in drugs. The Black Ladies, as they dubbed themselves, were warned if they carried on they'd all be expelled. Lucy didn't care; she hated school anyway.'

'What about you then, Clem, in all this?' Grace asked, gently. 'Were you in the Black Ladies as well?'

'Yes of course. It was great fun to begin with, but then it all seemed like a lot of hard work skiving off and deliberately not doing homework when actually, because I was interested, especially in the arts and English, I wanted to go to lessons and do well. Lucy used to get angry with me, tell me I wasn't being loyal to her and the gang, but I really wanted to do well at school because I enjoyed it and particularly because I wanted to go to the really good sixth-form college here in Midhope. Lucy thought I was mad and played up even more. Then she started staying out really late, hanging out with a new set of kids she'd met from the comprehensive in our village and doing drugs. Only cannabis, I think, to begin with, and maybe Ecstasy occasionally. It got to the stage where my parents started ringing the police when she didn't come home until two in the morning. She was only fifteen.'

Everyone had finished eating but seemed too engrossed in listening to what I was saying to think about clearing plates or making coffee.

'It must have been awful for you,' Izzy said, squeezing my hand. 'Oh, God, of course...' her hand flew to her mouth. '*That's* why you insisted on living down on Emerald Street. To be near Lucy?'

'Well, yes, but that was only in the last year or so. Anyway, one night, the police had picked Lucy up once again and brought her home, of her head, about three in the morning. We were both sixteen by then and had just left school. I'd started sixth-form college but Lucy was basically doing nothing apart from staying in bed all day and staying out most of the night. Well, my mother absolutely lost it. She just lost her temper and let rip and said it was history repeating itself, Lucy was no better than the trollop who'd given birth to us. That…' Here I stopped and couldn't say anything for a while. 'That our mother was a drug addict who'd been sent to prison for assaulting the police and smuggling heroin into the country… and that… and that… Lucy and I were born in prison.'

'In prison? You were actually born in prison? Oh my God, Clem, how awful for you to be told that.' Harriet was genuinely distressed. 'Had your mother known that all along, do you think?'

I smiled at Harriet's concern. 'Oh yes, absolutely. Social services don't keep anything from prospective adopters these days. Knowing my mother, it never ceases to amaze me that she took the children of a violent drug addict on in the first place. But apparently, she and my father had been married for fifteen years and she was pushing forty and just couldn't get pregnant herself. I suppose when she was offered us by social services she realised that it was her last chance to actually have children. She's not overly maternal so it's always made me wonder why she wanted to take us on. Anyway, she did but, as she tells me now, taking Lucy was the biggest mistake of her life. I often think she wishes she could have taken just me. She's refused to have anything to do with Lucy for years.'

'I wonder where your real mum is now?' Grace asked. 'Have you never tried to find out?'

'No. No, no.' I shook my head vehemently. 'Once I'd been told what sort of woman she was, I think I was frightened to find out more. Worried that she'd gone from bad to worse; that she might *still* be in prison somewhere. That maybe she had mental health problems. I was frightened I'd find her, meet her and see what I might become in the years ahead.'

'I see absolutely no reason why you should turn how to be a violent drug dealer.' Harriet smiled. 'You seem to have done pretty well so far. I mean, Allegra is absolutely gorgeous and you are a brilliant cook and—I'm sure this is the wine talking again—although I wasn't sure at the time about your marrying Peter, I'm sure it's going to work out well. You seem happy?'

'I'm getting there,' I smiled. 'If I could just find Lucy and sort a few things out…'

'But you've managed to have some contact with her over the years?' Grace asked gently.

'Oh, yes, yes, of course. I saw her on and off throughout our early twenties: she'd get clean, off the drugs, off the street, come back home to Mum and Dad's for a while, but then something would happen and she'd start using again. She'd meet some man, move to another town…'

'But why doesn't she want to see you?' Izzy asked. 'You're her sister, her *twin* for heaven's sake. But, Jesus, she ran like a frightened rabbit when she saw you the other night.'

I didn't say anything for a couple of seconds, knew I didn't want to explain further. 'It's complicated,' I said finally. 'Just a bit complicated. Look, would you all mind awfully keeping all that I've told you today to yourselves? I mean, David Henderson has just offered me this little job— maybe he wouldn't if he knew my background…'

'Oh gosh, absolutely…'

'Yes, yes, no problem…'

'It's got absolutely nothing to do with anyone else…'

The four of us sat in silence, not one of us wanting to break the mood of complicity that suddenly seemed to bind us together, until Harriet asked, 'Does Peter know about Lucy, Clem?'

'Oh yes, he knows everything. I told him on the night of the Big Proposal. I needed him to know so that he could change his mind about marrying me if he couldn't cope with the idea of me being born in prison and my sister being a sex worker. It was quite a lot for him to take in. But he did. He's not really mentioned it since which I know must seem very, very strange. I get the impression that he feels if it's not talked about then perhaps it will all go away. He's certainly never offered to walk the streets of Midhope with me looking for her. And now, she appears to have moved on. I don't know where she is and I don't think I'll get any help from him when I start looking for Lucy again.' I could feel my traitorous lip beginning to wobble again and I quickly drank some water. 'And that's fine, it really is. Peter's taken on Allegra and me; I really don't expect him to take on all the baggage that goes with us.'

'Isn't that what marriage is all about though?' Grace asked. 'Taking on all the baggage, I mean?'

She was interrupted by a sudden whimper that very quickly became a strident yell. 'Jonty,' Grace said, immediately getting up from the table and making her way to the kitchen. 'Another male needing attention.'

I glanced at my watch. 'Gosh, I need to go—I've got to pick Allegra up from school and Vanessa is dropping Peter's two off in an hour. Are you OK dropping me off, Izzy? You're all right to drive?'

'Yes, of course. I've not had anything to drink. Hell, we *are* late…'*

I love it that I've suddenly got these bright, generous women as new friends, I thought as I poached salmon, wilted spinach and grated cheese for fish pie. *I love it that Allegra seems already to have settled so well at her new school and I love it that I appear to have got a new job with David Henderson.*

I'd been ten minutes late picking Allegra up from the village school, running in from the adjacent lane where Izzy had dropped me off, horribly conscious that on the second day at Allegra's new school I was running late, exhaling, I was sure, alcohol as I ran. I *had* drunk too much wine, and as I panted across the tiny playing field and into a playground full of waiting, chattering mothers, I suddenly panicked that I'd revealed too much. Oh God, I really had opened up to these women who, let's face it, apart from Izzy, I didn't really know.

What if they were, even at this very moment, telling husbands, nannies, mothers, neighbours-over-the wall: 'Listen to *this*: we had lunch today with this woman whose sister—*twin*—is a, would you believe it, a common *prostitute*… and *she*, this woman, she's not that much better. She's married this man who is a bit strange, does those re-enactment things, you know racing up and down fields with pikes, thinking they're Charles the First—or is it the Second? Anyway, he's very, *very* wealthy… huge house… well, she's obviously only married him for his money… and if that's not prostitution as well, I don't know what is… and *listen*, this is the best bit. Where do you think she was *born...?* No, not London or Birmingham. No, not Russia or Timbuctoo...' A triumphant shaking of head. '*Prison*! ... Her mother was a drug runner, a violent heroin and crack cocaine smuggler who apparently kept most of Yorkshire supplied with its drugs... Probably still does..."

I shook my head as I ran, desperately trying to rid my brain of thoughts and pictures of women sharing delicious morsels of gossip—*my* gossip—and, searching for Allegra in the throng of heaving children, ran straight into The Fear-Bold.

'Ah, Mrs Broadbent,' Mrs Theobold said, glancing at the watch on her plump, freckled wrist. 'I'm glad I've caught you.'

I smiled, but kept my mouth clamped shut, conscious of the alcohol fumes wafting towards this fearsome woman if I didn't. The last thing I needed was more gossip starting about how that violent, drug smuggler's daughter had picked her own daughter up, 'obviously quite *drunk*, darling, on only the poor little mite's second day at Westenbury C of E."

'Just a quick word, Mrs Broadbent, if I may? About Allegra?'

My heart sank. 'Is there a problem?'

'No, no. On the contrary. I just wanted to pass on to you Miss Fisher's comments about Allegra, about what an extremely bright, personable little girl she seems to be and how well she's settled in with us. Miss Fisher would have come out herself but she's had to go off to a twilight training session on Safeguarding.'

Relief spread through my whole body like a sudden ray

of sunshine on a dull day, and I was just about to utter my thanks to the headmistress—I could actually have hugged her—when I remembered the alcohol fumes and, instead, beamed beatifically in what I hoped gave the impression of pleasure rather than insanity.

'I'm so pleased, Mrs... erm, Mrs Theobold,' I said out of the side of my mouth. 'Thank you so much for that. I won't come too near. I'm prone to... to er... tonsillitis and I can feel a bout coming on. I would so hate to pass it on to you so early in the term.'

Mrs Theobold hastily stepped back as Allegra came running, leaping into my waiting arms before wrapping her legs expertly around my middle.

'Careful now, Allegra, Mummy's not too well,' she said to Allegra before adding, 'Honey and lemon, Mrs Broadbent. Works a treat, I always find.'

But even more so with a good tot of whisky, Mrs Theobold, the tipsy little devil inside me was daring me to reply but, quitting while I was ahead, I beamed again and, swinging Allegra's sticky little hand in my own, we made our way across the village and home.

Any disquiet I might have been feeling about sharing my shady past with the women at lunch was wonderfully squashed by two text messages that came through within minutes of each other as I unlocked the kitchen door.

Lovely to have you for lunch, Clem. Sorry if we poured too much rose down you. If you're regretting sharing what you told us today, please don't. Anything you told Grace and me goes no further. For a start, it has

absolutely nothing to do with anyone else and, secondly, we all have something in our lives we might wish to keep to ourselves. I certainly have.
Hat

And:

It's so good to meet people that one immediately feels an affinity with, Clem. Really enjoyed your company and talking to you again. Anything we discussed remains, of course, absolutely confidential. Hope to see you soon.
Grace

Even the knowledge that Sophie had come in and gone straight upstairs without acknowledging me, together with the loud thump of unrecognisable hip-hop music emanating, it appeared, through every wall in the house, couldn't dampen my happiness as I assembled the fish pie, topped, tailed and sliced green beans and washed lettuce for salad.

'Clem? Darling?' Peter had to raise his voice above the insistent and seemingly increasing noise from Sophie's room as he came into the kitchen, taking off his black pinstriped suit jacket and loosening his scarlet tie. 'Goodness, what *is* she listening to up there?'

I laughed. 'Oh, the equivalent of what *we* listened to as fifteen-year-olds. You remember? The Vengaboys' "Boom, Boom, Boom, Boom!!" And Ricky Martin? God, I loved Ricky Martin's "Livin' La Vida Loca".' I started singing, shaking the wet lettuce like a single maraca, droplets flying over my head and onto Peter.

Peter frowned, shaking his shirtsleeve of water before searching in a cupboard for a glass. 'I *never* listened to dreadful stuff like this. Have you heard the words? I can't even repeat them…'

I laughed again. 'Bad day?' I found the bottle of Royal Lochnagar he'd been searching for and passed it over. 'You seem a bit tense.'

'Not the best day in my life, no, Clem.' He tried to smile. 'But nothing to worry *your* lovely head about, darling.'

'Don't be daft, Peter. Tell me.'

'Problems at work. I mean, that's bad enough, but it's Vanessa now as well. I'm going to have to go and see her after we've eaten. She's being totally unreasonable about money—just wants more and more all the time, ringing me constantly at work. She even came to the office today demanding I leave what I was doing and speak to her. Well, I'm not going to her and Justin's house, I can't abide the man. Don't want *him* putting his damned two penn'oth in as well.'

'What does he do, Justin? For work, I mean?' I was curious. 'He seems to have plenty of money himself, swanning around in that huge Merc.'

Peter frowned again and downed the glass of whisky in one. 'God knows. He's a total shyster, total waste of space. He certainly didn't have a Merc until he married Vanessa…' He poured two more fingers. 'It'll be him that's put her up to this, demanding more and more all the time.'

'Don't have any more to drink if you're going out,' I said, taking the bottle from him. 'Where are you meeting her?'

'I said I'd pick her up outside the house—I am *not* going in. It's bad enough seeing Justin's smirking face on the field at weekends. You know, Clem, I'm seriously thinking about moving companies—the Marquess of Newcastle's Regiment of Foote in Northumberland are still willing to have me. I think you'd like it there, too.'

I don't think I would, I thought, but instead said, 'Oh don't do anything hasty, Peter, You'd miss Neville and Beefy Brenda if you left your lot and started again further north.'

'Beefy Brenda…?' Peter looked perplexed for a moment, but his mind was, for once, apparently on more pressing problems than my lack of respect for the pack's current 'Good Wife'. He looked at his watch. 'I said I'd pick Vanessa up in an hour. Is that all right with you, Clem? Have you had a good day, darling? Has Allegra enjoyed school again?'

While I laid the table, enjoying the sensation of being happy, content, almost at one with my new family and situation, I chatted to Peter telling him about lunch; what The Fear-Bold had said about Allegra; how David Henderson had offered me a little job only to realise, as he tapped away on his laptop at the kitchen table, he really hadn't listened to a word I was saying.

'Peter, are you all right?' If he hadn't even taken in that David Henderson had asked me to work for him, he really wasn't himself. 'Peter…?'

'Hmm?' He continued to scan his screen, not even looking up when Sophie slouched into the kitchen finishing what was left of a McDonald's.

'Sophie!' I couldn't stop the disgruntled tone even though I'd sworn to myself I wouldn't rise to Sophie's behaviour.

'That's *me*.' She smiled at me with raised eyebrows, daring me to question what she was eating.

'We're just about to eat. Why on earth are you eating a burger now?'

'Well, it's a good job I got Mum to drop me off at the drive-in down on Elm Lane. If I'd known you were cooking *fish*—' Sophie shuddered as if she'd been told she was about to be served a cup of cold sick '—I'd have got Mum to buy me *two*.' She shuddered again. 'You know what they say about fish. Like guests—' she held my gaze, looking me up and down as she methodically chewed on her burger before swallowing '—they both begin to stink after three days.'

'Whatever, Sophie.' I managed to speak calmly. 'But I thought you were vegetarian, and junk food, you know, is particularly bad for *spots*.' Shit, why had I said that? Why had I come down to a just sixteen-year-old's level? 'I'm sure your dad and Max would like you to sit and eat with us.' I smiled. 'Particularly as they won't see you for a few weeks once you're back at school.'

Ignoring me, Sophie went over to Peter and put her arms round his shoulders. 'Daddy, I think I'll come with you when you go to meet Mummy. It would be really nice for the three of us to be together again. We could go to that champagne bar Mummy goes to with Justin.'

'Hmm?' Peter looked up, distracted, one eye still on his screen. 'Sorry, darling, your mother and I have a few things to sort out. You can't come with us tonight. You stay here with Clem? Hmm? Maybe there's some girly things you... you *girls* can do together? Do each other's nails or... or... hair or something?'

If I hadn't been feeling so cross with Sophie, I'd have laughed out loud at that. I stored the little snippet to tell Izzy next time I saw her, and started to load the dishwasher.

'Food is just about ready, Sophie. Would you go and tell Max and Allegra? They're in the snug watching TV.'

Tutting, Sophie dropped the yellow Styrofoam takeaway box with its greasy remains onto the kitchen table and stalked from the room, yelling to Max that his *fish* was ready. Of Allegra, she made no mention.

Later, much later, when the younger children were in bed, when I'd dissected the events of that day's lunch on the phone with Izzy and when I'd asked Sophie if she'd like a cup of tea with me and been royally turned down, I went out into the garden, George at my heels, breathing in the intoxicating smells of the early autumn night. Walking down towards the Secret Garden, as Allegra had christened it, I glanced across the fields to where I could see the lights in David and Mandy Henderson's house. The downstairs rooms appeared dark but one of the upstairs rooms gave out a gentle glow of light.

I had a sudden vision of David Henderson in that upstairs bedroom, slowly undoing the buttons on the front of a woman's white shirt while kissing her neck with an oh-so-soft mouth, his dark hair brushing against her skin…

Stop it, Clem, you silly bitch, I warned, knowing the woman to be myself. *Bloody well stop it.* I pulled a couple of pernicious weeds from my rosemary patch before realising all the herbs needed a good watering. I was just deciding whether to make do with the watering can or if I could be bothered, as I really ought, to unravel the garden hose, when I heard the sound of a car coming to a halt on the gravel at the front of the house.

I walked, with George in my wake, down the path that led from the back to the front of the house to meet Peter. I'd bring him out here to the herbs, fill his senses with the heavenly smells of the garden, get him to discard his shoes and socks even and walk with me, barefoot on the dew-laden grass.

'Mrs Broadbent?' The woman, and obviously senior of the two police officers, came towards me. 'Could we have a word?'

19

SARAH

Sarah had spent the next few weeks of that hot summer of 1984 looking for him. She dragged April back to the Red Lion most lunchtimes and as soon as lectures were over. She stayed behind in the cavernous art rooms until long after most of the other students had left for home or their digs in the hope that he was a final-year student and would be, like so many others, behind with a final project, panicked into working late on an unfinished sculpture or canvas.

Sarah's own art work became more and more erratic as she veered away from the safe set pieces she'd been working on, compelled, instead, to fill huge—and expensive—canvases with the crimson, cadmium yellow and vermillion oils that flowed effortlessly: an extension, it seemed, of the fire inside her, ignited when those strong brown arms had held her in a tight embrace, and fuelled daily by a longing to see him again.

For the first time in her nineteen years Sarah felt alive as opposed to just existing. She tried to think of other times down the years when she'd felt anything like the excitement and longing she was experiencing during these last few weeks leading up to the long summer break but, apart from the birthday when she'd been given Raffles, her much longed for spaniel puppy, and the anticipation of holidays and exeats from school, nothing compared to this.

She took to rereading D. H. Lawrence together with the poetry of Christopher Marlowe and Andrew Marvell, and lost the half stone of puppy fat—a tenacious reminder of the white sliced bread and cake she'd eaten in abundance at boarding school out of boredom and longing to be free from its confines.

So when, almost ten days later, she spotted him on Albion Street in the city centre, she found herself frozen to the spot, her brain apparently unable to send a message to her legs to move away from the double glass doors of Boots she'd been on the point of going through in order to buy Tampax.

He was with a group of men and women handing out leaflets to the afternoon shoppers but as Sarah stood, rooted as any tenacious weed, he reached into the back pocket of his denim cut-offs for cigarettes and, in the act of lighting up, looked up and saw her. It was plain he knew Sarah's face, had come across her and recently, but also obvious he couldn't quite place her. He said something to the others, handed one of them his pile of leaflets and walked over to where Sarah stood in the doorway, obstructing customers intent on their purchase of toothpaste, cosmetics or their picking up of a prescription for hay fever or haemorrhoids.

'I know you, don't I?' He smiled, puzzled.

'Erm... yes, you had your... I mean... it was in The Red Lion... erm... the night of that charity do...'

He laughed, showing perfectly straight white teeth. '"Relax"? Right?'

'You kissed me,' Sarah said, and then blushed furiously at her inane comment.

'I'm not surprised,' he laughed again. 'You're gorgeous.' He continued to smile down at her from his six-foot height until she thought she might just fall to the street, lying in a heap until she was swept up at the end of the day together with the abandoned tab ends, sweet wrappers and spilled ice cream cones.

'What are you doing now?' he asked. 'Do you have to be somewhere?'

She didn't like to say she'd just been going to buy tampons, and shook her head. 'I've just about finished here,' he said. 'Do you fancy a drink?'

'That would be lovely,' she said, longingly. 'Really lovely.'

'So how come, if you're a Yorkshire girl, you've got such a posh voice?' Johnny asked as he handed Sarah a half pint of cider and took a long, thirsty pull on his pint. His own accent was southern, London probably, Sarah guessed as they made their way to the tables outside Whitelock's Ale House in Turk's Head Yard and found a couple of spare seats.

'Boarding school,' Sarah said, slightly embarrassed, and then, to change the subject, asked, 'What were the leaflets you were handing out?'

'Oh, just trying to get support for the miners,' he said. 'The strike doesn't really seem to have affected the people of Leeds. We thought we'd try to get the people round here to see what's happening just a few miles away in Barnsley and Doncaster.'

Sarah reddened as she recalled her father, only that morning, harrumphing behind his *Telegraph*, denigrating Arthur Scargill and the 'bloody, idle miners.'

''Bout time Margaret got the damned army in and sorted them out,' he'd muttered through a mouthful of toast and ginger marmalade to anyone who was listening. As her mother had already left the dining room—there was only so much of Gerald Sykes's insistently noisy mastication she could take at any one time—and Sarah wasn't hearing anything except the continual replaying in her head of the few minutes she'd spent in the arms of the beautiful boy in The Red Lion, it was left to a now ageing Raffles to bear the brunt of Gerald's scathing diatribe.

'So, you're an art student?' Johnny Lipton was asking. 'I got kicked out for not doing any work a couple of years ago but decided to stay round here in Leeds rather than go back to London.'

'But how do you live?' Sarah asked. 'What do you do?'

'Oh, bit of this, bit of that. There's always someone wanting something doing or wanting some gear scoring.'

Gear? Did he mean clothes? Sarah glanced at his faded knee-length cut-offs and oversized white T-shirt; there was nothing there to give her any clue that Johnny Lipton might be any sort of fashion trendsetter.

'You really are incredibly sexy,' Johnny said, taking a length of Sarah's dark curly hair and winding it round his finger, the effect of which brought colour to her cheeks as well as her face nearer to his. 'How on earth did I let you out of my sight the other Saturday?'

'You sort of just disappeared,' Sarah said shyly, her heart hammering as he began to stroke her face. 'One minute you were there and the next you were gone.'

'Well, I can't believe that. I must have had something on or I would have whisked you off to bed.' He smiled lazily, enjoying her discomfiture at the suggestiveness of his words as well as the effect he knew he was having on her. He reached for his cigarettes and offered her one.

'Oh, I don't smoke,' Sarah said hastily.

'Cigarettes?'

'Anything...'

'You're not going to tell me you're a virgin as well, are you?'

Sarah hung her head in shame. 'There's not been a great deal of opportunity to... you know... to lose my... you know my ...'

'Virginity?' he asked.

'Yes, that.' Sarah was scarlet-faced, unable to meet his mocking eyes. Oh God, he'd never fancy her now knowing she was so inexperienced. He must have hundreds of beautiful, *experienced* women knocking on his door. She took a too large gulp of her cider and, in doing so, spilled some down her face and onto her hands.

Johnny took her hand, licking the spilt alcohol from between her fingers and Sarah felt a warm excitement spreading in the region of her knickers.

'I'd better go,' she muttered. 'My mother is expecting me for supper.'

'You live at home? And you're an art student?' Johnny was genuinely puzzled.

'All part of the bargain,' Sarah said miserably. She knew

she'd lost Johnny Lipton now; what could this god, this *Adonis* want with a nineteen-year-old virgin who had to go home to Harrogate to eat her mother's excuse for shepherd's pie?

'Bargain?'

'My parents agreed to my doing art college rather than being finished in Switzerland as long as *I* agreed to live at home.' Miserably Sarah bent to collect her bag and art portfolio and made to leave. She'd ruined everything by not being the sophisticated, experienced woman he was so obviously used to. 'Thanks for the drink.'

'But, Sarah, I *have* to see you again. You can't desert me for a second time.' He was laughing at her, teasing her. 'Come out with me tomorrow night?'

He was asking her out: a date. Sarah felt happiness flood through her. She was going to see him again. She left him ordering another pint before moving over to join a group of people who had hailed him as they walked in, and floated to the station to catch the Harrogate train, a ridiculous grin on her pretty face.

Johnny Lipton monopolised Sarah for the next couple of weeks, waiting for her outside the art college at lunchtime, refusing to let her go back to lectures and the unfinished projects that were necessary to complete her foundation year. Any guilt Sarah felt at abandoning both her studies and her friendship with April—who, furious at Sarah's getting off with the enigmatic Johnny Lipton when it was quite obvious it should have been herself and not the gauche, inexperienced Sarah, had turned quite unpleasant—evaporated like early morning mist the minute she saw him lounging against the wall waiting to whisk her away.

They spent the long afternoons of that wonderfully hot June in, or sitting outside, The Red Lion or Whitelocks or any number of bars where Johnny was always hailed with great enthusiasm by both the landlord as well as the, mainly student, clientele. Johnny would never have been left shivering on the hockey field or netball court desperately waiting his turn to be chosen, Sarah mused one afternoon as Johnny was accosted by a group wanting to buy him a drink the moment they walked into a bar.

'Well, who left *you*?' Johnny asked once he'd become free and joined her outside at their table and she'd laughingly told him her thoughts. 'I'd have chosen you every time, straight away, number one on my list.' And he'd kissed her so tenderly, Sarah had flung her arms round him, hugging him fiercely.

Sarah's happiness was marred, however, when, after drinking rather too much sweet cider, she'd made her way to the Ladies', tipsily cannoning off a couple of tables as she went. Waiting for a toilet to come free, she gazed at herself in the chipped, dirty mirror, hardly recognising her face, tanned from a week of sitting in too many pub yards and gardens, or her brown eyes, pupils huge with love for Johnny Lipton.

'I see Johnny's got a new girlfriend.'

Sarah stiffened as the words drifted over one of the engaged cubicles.

'Yeah, I saw,' came the response from the adjacent toilet. 'Not his usual type, is she? Very pretty though, don't you think, with all that cloudy dark hair? Johnny must be going for the virginal Madonna look this week.'

'Well, it was Theresa Adamson last week,' the disembodied Irish-accented voice returned, 'and she's certainly no virgin. She reckoned he was the best ride ever.'

'Well, whoever the virgin *is*, she won't *be* much longer.' Both of them cackled and, heedless of her need to pee, Sarah fled.

'Are you OK?' Johnny, taking advantage of her absence, was once more chatting to two men inside the pub. He quickly put what looked like a wad of notes into his back pocket, grabbing Sarah's arm as she dashed past him. 'What's up?'

'Nothing, nothing.' Sarah tried to smile but instead, to her horror, found she was crying. 'It's just something someone was saying in the toilet.'

Johnny glanced up as two girls walked from the Ladies'. 'About me?'

Sarah nodded miserably. 'And me.'

'Come on, let's get out of here.'

As they walked down The Headrow, busy now with afternoon shoppers, Johnny took her hand. 'Look, people round here know me. They talk.' He stopped and turned her face to his. She was quite adorable, he thought. He really had to have her.

'I can't tell you what you're doing to me, Sarah. Look.' Subtly, he moved her hand to his crotch and, mortified, she jumped back in embarrassment.

'This is the effect you have on me.' He grinned. 'Come back with me, now. Come on'

'Back with you? Where?' Sarah was playing for time. She longed to be with him, to go anywhere with him but it was a bit like being with a sleepy black panther. She didn't know what he was going to do next and, more worryingly, apart from the basics she'd gleaned from the more adventurous girls at school, she'd no real idea what she was supposed to do in return.

All the while, they'd been walking away from the main streets and through a maze of litter-strewn side streets, grubby in the heat of the day. Johnny stopped suddenly outside a betting shop.

'Come on,' he said again, smiling down at her.

'You want to make a bet?' Sarah asked surprised.

'Not particularly. I'd far rather make you.'

He took out a key from the front pocket of his jeans and used it to open a sludge-coloured door to one side of the shop's entrance. 'I live here.'

'Here?' Sarah glanced up at the dirty, net-curtained windows above the betting shop. It didn't look much like a home.

'Now don't go all uppity on me. See how the other half live—I'll make you tea if you like.'

Terrified of being thought a snob, Sarah went into overdrive, commenting enthusiastically on the battered velvet sofa, the large dusty rugs and pine table that were crammed into the tiny living room.

Johnny handed Sarah a huge chipped mug of strong tea. 'Come and sit down, Sarah,' he said, patting a cushion next to him on the sofa. 'You're making me feel carsick, circling round the room like that.'

He didn't lunge for her but simply stroked her face with practised yet nonchalant fingers until she was almost trembling with longing for him, terrified he was going to take it further and whisk her off to the bedroom, but equally terrified he was not.

'Don't be frightened, lovely Sarah,' he eventually said. 'I promise you'll wonder why you left it so long.'

After that afternoon in the flat above the betting shop, she couldn't get enough of both Johnny and the things he did to her body. He persuaded her that having sex at the same time as smoking a joint made the whole thing even better and after a week's initiation into both the pleasures of the flesh and the use of cannabis, she felt as though she were an old hand at both.

Sarah knew she should be working on her final pieces of art if she were to take up the provisional offer of the degree course at The National School of Fine Arts on the Rue Bonaparte in Paris in the autumn, but every day, by early afternoon, the longing to be with Johnny broke her resolve and, ignoring both April's disapproving looks and her tutting, would dash to the loos, fill her generous mouth with lip gloss, outline her huge brown eyes with kohl and be off in the direction of The Headrow and the flat above the betting shop.

One weekend towards the middle of June, Sarah stayed over at the flat, telling her parents she'd been invited to April's parents' silver wedding celebrations at their house in Midhope and wouldn't be home until the Monday teatime after college. Anne and Gerald accepted this lie without question and even gave her a bottle of Gerald's best Veuve Clicquot that Anne ordered Gerald to—somewhat grudgingly—bring up from his wine cellar for April's parents by way of thanks for having their daughter stay with them.

By Friday evening the champagne had been drunk and Johnny was restless. Sarah didn't see much of him during the Saturday—he had business to see to, he said and would be some time—and, missing him, spent what was left of her allowance shopping in Leeds Market for and then cooking a fabulous three-course meal for him on his return. By the time he finally rolled up at midnight, Sarah was convinced he was lying dead in a gutter somewhere and was on the point of setting off for A and E at Leeds General to see if he was there.

'Sorry, sweetheart, I ended up with a couple of mates I'd not seen for months and one thing led to another.'

Sarah was so glad he was back, in one piece and not lying somewhere with a knife in his back, she didn't even notice the faint scent of an unknown, but very feminine perfume that came in on the warm night air with him.

On the Monday morning Sarah knew she just *had* to go in to college and work nonstop until the evening if she were to complete her final pieces, although the very thought of leaving Johnny in the September, even for the wonders of three years in Paris, was anathema to her now. Reaching out across the bed for him, the sun's rays already illuminating the shabbiness of the womb-like room above the bookies, Sarah was surprised to find him gone. She'd never known him rise before midday—he did most of his business at night, he'd assured her and, as such she must think of him as a shift worker—and here he was, fully dressed, munching on a bowl of dry cereal.

'What are you up to?' she asked sleepily, torn between

the desire to pull him back into the bed with her and the knowledge that she had to be back in college later on. She looked at her watch. 'Johnny,' she laughed, 'it's only six o'clock. Come back to bed.'

'We, my darling Sarah, are having a day out. Come on, get your clothes on. We need to move.'

'I can't, Johnny, I *have* to finish my course work. I'm way, way behind.'

'Sarah,' he said, patiently, 'what is more important? A few pieces of artwork that you can catch up with tomorrow, or a day showing that bitch, Thatcher, we won't be moved?'

'We?' Sarah was puzzled. 'I don't know what you're talking about.'

'Sarah,' he said, a note of impatience creeping into his voice, 'just get your face washed and your jeans on and I'll buy you a coffee on the train.'

Sarah hated it when she heard that petulance in his voice. She was always frightened he'd go off and leave her, find someone more adventurous, more experienced to take her place.

Oh, what harm could one more day playing hooky make in the larger scheme of things? The sun was shining, she was young, she'd have a whole day to herself with Johnny. Sod it. She jumped out of the grubby sheets and made for the bathroom.

'So where are we going?' she shouted through a mouthful of toothpaste. 'Scarborough? Whitby? Filey?'

'Rotherham. Come on, the train goes in twenty minutes.'

Two men in an ancient Toyota Corolla met them at

Rotherham Central. 'Why've you brought *her*?' the taller of the two asked impatiently, nodding towards Sarah as she climbed into the back of the car. 'There'll be very few women coming.'

'Sarah's OK,' Jonny said. 'I thought we'd look a bit less conspicuous if we had a gorgeous girl with us.'

'Don't get your logic there,' the man snapped. 'It's not a place for women.'

'Never mind,' the smaller man said, turning from the driver's seat to give her a brief smile. 'Just keep your head down when we get there, love.'

It was a five-mile drive to the British Steel coking plant at Orgreave, South Yorkshire, and by the time they joined the ten thousand or so pickets from around the UK, Sarah had been well and truly brought up to date on what the men thought about the miners' strike in general and Margaret Thatcher in particular.

The police were waiting for them but, unlike most of the strikes at this time where pickets were kept well away from their intended positions, they were escorted along with the thousands of others to a field to the north of the plant. Sarah clung tightly to Johnny's hand and, although she was terrified at being here among miners and pickets she'd only seen previously on the evening news programmes, she felt a mounting rush of excitement that she was helping the workers against Johnny's hated Margaret Thatcher. The field was flanked, it appeared, by as many police as strikers. Sarah couldn't believe the number of dark blue and black uniforms in so small an area, couldn't believe so many police could actually exist.

'Why here, Johnny? Why aren't we outside the mines?'

Sarah panted breathlessly as she stumbled after him, trying desperately to keep up as he strode ahead to get a good position.

Johnny didn't seem overly sure himself, but the driver of the Toyota slowed down his pace to hers and they walked on together. 'The British Steel plants have been receiving "dispensations" or picket-permitted coal so that their furnaces don't end up damaged,' he explained. 'But it seems they've been shifting far more coal than was agreed with the NUM—the miners' union. That's not on, love. If the steelworkers' union won't cooperate with us then we'll just have to take it on ourselves to stop the fucking delivery of coal from the coking plant. When the lorries arrive to fetch the coal from the plant up there,' he nodded in the direction of the road past the fields, 'to take to the steelworks, we're not going to let them through.'

'But how will you stop them?' Sarah asked. 'Won't it be dangerous?'

'How've *you* got involved with this lot, love? You've absolutely no idea, have you? What are your mum and dad doing letting you come out like this? Why don't you just go back now? Go on, love, it's a five-mile walk back to the station, but you're better out of it. I've never seen so many police all at once. It's going to get really nasty, I can tell.'

'She's all right, Davey,' Johnny called over his shoulder. 'She needs to see how the workers live, what shit they have to put up with.'

'And you're a bloody worker yourself, are you…?' Davey muttered, at the same time as the strident call, 'Lorries' went up from all over the field. This was the cue for the pickets to charge towards the police in an attempt to break the lines. Sarah found herself in the middle of a terrifying crowd hurtling down towards the road where it was met by an even more terrifying group of mounted police.

'Oh, those poor, poor horses,' Sarah cried as stones were lobbed over her head.

'Never mind the fucking horses, you stupid bitch,' a man yelled furiously in her ear. 'The fucking lorries are getting through.'

After ten minutes the crowd surged again and was met by a second mounted response. Sarah had lost both Johnny and the two men from the car by this time and found herself on a tide of pickets, being pushed forward to meet the police before being carried back up the field. She felt something hit the back of her head and had a few seconds to realise she was bleeding before being swept down towards the line of police once more. *We should have gone to Filey*, she kept thinking, dazed and battered. The waves there would have been just as good.

Sarah managed to look at her watch; it was only nine-twenty-five but she felt she'd been in that field and that crowd for a lifetime. There was a shift in the mood of the men around her and she saw that the fully laden lorries of coal were beginning to leave the coking plant. Once more the miners surged and once more Sarah found herself taken along with them. And then, mercifully, there was a lull in the proceedings.

'Go, Arthur,' someone shouted and she realised it was Johnny standing just behind her, thoroughly enjoying the whole thing.

As the NUM leader, Arthur Scargill, walked defiantly in front of the police lines for just a few moments, Johnny grabbed Sarah's hand and pulled her, running down towards the crowd who were making their way towards Orgreave village itself.

'Where are we going?' she yelled. Her head was throbbing badly and she had cuts to both arms and legs but she felt safe now that Johnny was holding her hand.

'Someone's just said there's drink and food in the village,' he yelled back. 'Come on, I'm starving.'

The stone throwing had abated for a while, but as they ran towards the waiting police a brick was lobbed over her head, catching the nose of one of the huge mounted horses. Its training prevented it from rearing, but Sarah, unable to see any animal in pain, instinctively let go of Johnny's hand and dashed towards it. As she reached a hand to the frightened beast, something hit her around the back of her legs and she fell, stumbling into the cordon of mounted police.

20

'Lucy? Is it Lucy?' My hand, still clutching the weeds I'd plucked from my rosemary patch moments before, was instantly sweaty and my stomach churned as adrenalin coursed through every inch of me at the sight of the two police officers walking towards me.

'Can we go inside, Mrs Broadbent? Are you by yourself?'

'The children are here with me. My husband is out with his wife…' My mouth couldn't seem to form the words properly. 'His first wife, I mean…'

The officers followed me as I turned and went to open the huge oak front door that was, as always, locked. 'I'm sorry. I was out in the back garden. I don't have a key… We need to go back this way.'

I led the way back down the pebbled path, George sniffing interestedly at the officers' legs as they walked round to the back of the house, through the open French window and into the kitchen. A faint reminder of the fish I'd cooked earlier still lingered and I would, from then on, always associate that particular smell with the same sensation of doom I was feeling now as the police followed me, unsmiling, into the house.

'We're sorry, Mrs Broadbent, to bring bad news, but I'm sorry to have to tell you...' the young policeman hesitated, obviously torn between the enormity of being allowed by his senior officer to break such terrible news to me and anxiety at carrying out such a task. 'I'm afraid your husband, Peter Broadbent, is... is significantly unresponsive.'

My head, bowed as I waited for the inevitable about Lucy, shot up and I stared at the young rookie. He looked about sixteen, his acned face, already crimson porridge, flushing uncomfortably as he spoke the words.

'Peter? He's what? *Significantly unresponsive...*? Oh God, has he been done for drink-driving? Has he passed out somewhere? He was upset when he drove off. I told him he'd had too much whisky before he left...'

Tutting at the now totally embarrassed young police officer, the female constable took my arm and steered me towards the chair she pulled out from the kitchen table.

'I'm sorry, love, I'm afraid your husband was involved in a car accident earlier this evening. He died instantly.'

My hand, still clutching the now wilting weed, flew to my mouth. One's hand really did fly to one's mouth, I thought stupidly, recalling myriad characters' invariable reaction to loss and tragedy in the novels I'd devoured over the years.

'Oh God, no. Max and Sophie...they adore their father. Allegra too... she's only known him a little while, you see, but she loves him too. He's the only father she's ever known.'

'Is there someone we can get in touch with for you? You shouldn't be by yourself,' the woman officer said. 'I'm not sure yet, but we may need a formal identification at some stage. Mr Justin…' She took out her notebook and riffled the pages until she found what she was looking for. '… Sanderson is already on his way to identify his wife. He may be able to identify your husband as well.'

'His wife? Vanessa?' My hand went involuntarily to my mouth once more.

'Mrs Vanessa Sanderson died too. I believe she was your husband's first wife?'

'Yes, yes. Oh, Jesus, how am I going to tell Max? And Sophie?'

'Mr Sanderson said the children are with you at the moment?'

'Yes, yes, they're asleep upstairs. Well, at least Max is. I doubt that Sophie is in bed yet…'

'Are there grandparents? Can they come and be with them?'

I shook my head, as much to confirm that no grandparents existed apart from the old woman up in Scotland (dear God, did *I* have to inform her? Would I have to ring her, speak to her on the phone: did I even have a number or would I need to drive up to Aberdeen and tell her face to face that her son was no longer), as to try and assemble some sense of what had happened and the implications for myself and those poor, poor children now that Peter had died.

I suddenly remembered Vanessa's mother was alive too, but somewhere in a home with Alzheimer's.

'What about *your* parents? A friend? You need someone here, love.'

'What's going on? What's happened?' Sophie suddenly appeared, almost silently, in the kitchen. 'Where's Dad?'

'Sophie, come and sit down. I'm so sorry, darling, I have some really dreadfully bad news to tell you…'

'I'll come with you,' Izzy said. The Indian summer that had gloriously taken care of most of that September had, overnight it appeared, gone back to the subcontinent leaving a cold and miserably wet October in its wake.

'Would you, Izzy? That is so kind. I have to be there at one this afternoon. There's so much paperwork to sort out, so many bills that need paying that I can't just bury my head anymore. I need to see Peter's solicitors for help with it all. I need to sort out bank details, mortgage deeds on the house, a ton of stuff that Peter sorted automatically that I'm afraid I just let him get on with.'

'Well, why wouldn't you?' Izzy asked, moving to finish making the coffee that I'd started on ten minutes earlier but which, it seemed, I'd now forgotten all about. 'You'd only been married, what, six weeks? Why would he have told you everything about his financial situation when it was pretty obvious to anyone who had a pair of eyes—' Izzy flung her arms in the direction of the kitchen and beyond '—that *you* didn't need to worry your head about it whatsoever. I mean, let's face it, Clem, and I don't wish to sound crass, you're not going to have any financial worries for the rest of your life, are you?'

'But I'm a grown adult, an intelligent woman. I *should* have been aware of things: money, mortgage etc. I mean, as far as I know, there *is* no mortgage on the house—I do seem to remember Peter being very proud of the fact that it was paid off years ago. But I don't even know if he had life insurance or… or what was being paid to Vanessa each month. And now *she's* dead as well. I mean, the children…? Am I in charge of them now? Do they belong to me?'

'That's why I'm coming with you this afternoon. You have to find out what was written in the will—what Peter and Vanessa had put in place. I mean people usually name someone to be guardian of their children in the event of their death, don't they? There's probably an aunt or uncle or… or university friend or someone who agreed to take them in the event of their being left alone. Vanessa must have girlfriends you don't know about.'

'But there was no one at the funeral who made themselves known, was there?' I said. 'No one came up to us, to Sophie or Max, I mean, and said, "Your mum and dad appointed us guardians in the event of their death. Come home and live with *us* now".'

'Isn't it usually godparents?' Izzy asked, frowning. 'You know, when you're christened, don't godparents agree to take you on if necessary…?'

I looked doubtful. 'I've no idea. Don't godparents just agree to send you to church every Sunday and buy you an especially big Christmas and birthday present…?'

Izzy frowned again. 'Haven't got a clue. We never even christened our three, and my own godmother apparently sloped off to live in Slough with some ex-nun she actually *met* at my christening. It's a legendary tale that is brought out and aired at dinner parties every now and again. Anyway, you're still not yourself at all, Clem, and you won't be able to take it all in. Oh, there's a man just walked past the window. Are you expecting someone?'

I looked up, startled by the brief knock on the door.

David Henderson walked into the kitchen, taking off his raincoat and shaking it through the still-open door before closing it against the rain.

'God, it's foul out there. Needed some fresh air, so thought I'd walk over and see how you're doing, Clem. Are you OK?'

I'd not seen him since the funeral two weeks earlier when everything had seemed a blur; when the whole day had gone so unexpectedly quickly. And yet, in retrospect, there were enough persistent single clips that kept replaying themselves in my head during the long days and the sleepless nights since, to make an endlessly long film of the whole bloody awful occasion.

At the crematorium Max had held my hand throughout, desperately trying but unable to stop the tears from rolling down his pale, freckled face. 'It's really OK to cry,' I'd whispered. 'It really is.' To Max's left, sitting rigidly on the painfully hard chair (provided surely, I surmised, to get one grieving set of mourners out the front door as quickly as possible before the next set were allowed in at the back) Sophie had said little, refusing to meet my eyes, unable or unwilling to give comfort to her younger brother. I'd debated long and hard as to the wisdom of allowing a five-year-old to go to a funeral, but Izzy had assured me that while we might live in a culture of wanting to protect children from everything, from losing at games, from being bullied at school, from boredom even, she found no reason—and this, she assured me, came from both a maternal as well as a medical stance—to protect them from the very fundamentals of life and death. Allegra, then, had been allowed to attend her stepfather's funeral and had held onto my other hand throughout, quietly taking in all that was happening around her. I had assumed I would cry myself but, apart from the shock of the coffins themselves that made me catch my breath as they were carried to the front, I had remained—according to Izzy—passively poker-faced throughout.

'Is she OK?' David now asked Izzy when I couldn't reply, when it seemed I didn't appear able actually to speak.

'I'm all right, David. Really.' I took a deep breath. 'I'm sure you must have realised that I didn't love Peter, that I married him because... because he asked me. But I'm so sad for him. He was a good man, a very kind man and he shouldn't have died like that.' I really didn't know what else to say and I clammed up once again.

'We've an appointment at the solicitor's in an hour,' Izzy said, handing David a mug of coffee and looking at her watch. 'I think Clem will feel better when she's been able to sort out a few things.'

'And the children?' David moved over to the table and sat down with me. 'It must be so hard for them.'

'Sophie insisted on going back to school as soon as she was able. My mother came over to be on hand to pick Max and Allegra up from their respective schools when I drove Sophie back up to North Yorkshire last week.'

It had been a nightmare journey. I'd found I was able only to elicit grunts and shrugs from Sophie all the hour and a quarter it had taken us to get there. The new term had started the previous week and, as we drove up the long drive that led to the school, girls were already entrenched on the playing fields, wielding lacrosse sticks—a parody of *Malory Towers*.

'You really don't have to come in with me, Clementine,' Sophie had finally said, her heavily mascaraed blue eyes large in her pretty, pale face.

'Don't be silly, Sophie. Of course I'm coming in. I need to speak to your headteacher—we arranged it on the phone a couple of days ago.'

'I really don't think it appropriate that someone born in prison, someone whose twin is a *prostitute*, should be accompanying me into *school*.' Two pinpricks of red appeared in Sophie's cheeks as she turned to glare at me. 'You might have conned Daddy into marrying you,' she hissed, 'but don't think you're going to end up with all his money, with his house. It belongs to Max and me now, not you and your snotty little kid.'

I actually felt as though I'd been physically hit—winded and mentally staggering from the blow of Sophie's attack. Before I could gather my senses to say anything, Sophie launched once more.

'Mum told me. She said I had to be *nice* to you as you'd had such a terrible *real* mother and that you were living in the red-light district of town because you were probably a prostitute like your sister. Well, I don't want my friends at school to know that, thank you very much. So, if you don't mind, just drop me off here. I'm more than capable of carrying my cases up to the main entrance.'

Sophie had jumped out of the car, dragged her luggage from the boot of the Mini and walked slowly up the drive without a backward glance. Through a veil of tears I'd turned the car, crashing the gears and mounting the kerb before driving back home to Midhope. By the time I arrived at the house, the pounding headache I'd acquired on route had been joined by a familiar low-down gnawing pain in my abdomen and I knew instinctively any hope I'd been harbouring, despite Peter's death, that I might be pregnant, were in the throes of being dashed.

'It's all such a mess at the moment, David,' I now said, trying, but unable, to smile. 'I'm hoping that by the end of this afternoon it'll all be a lot clearer and we can move on a little. The main thing is to know who has guardianship of Peter's children and all the legal ramifications that go with that. Poor Max just keeps asking what's going to happen to him. I can't make any decisions or try to reassure him until I've seen Peter's solicitor. I'd like to have gone sooner, but every time I've rung he's put me off, telling me there is more and more paperwork to sort.' I looked at David who was gazing at me so intently I could feel myself start to blush. What was it about this man that he had such an effect on me?

'Look, Clem, I know Izzy is going with you, but if you think another pair of eyes and ears might help you to grasp what is happening, I'm more than happy to come with you as well.'

'That's so kind, David, but I'm sure it will all be OK. If there *are* some areas I don't understand then, yes, please, I'd love you to tell me what you think.' I took a deep breath. 'I need to get on with things, so if you have any cooking for me to do over at the barn…?'

David smiled. 'I was hoping you'd say that—it was one of the reasons I came over, but I didn't like to ask you. Didn't know if you'd be up to it…?'

'Life goes on. I mean… it has to, doesn't it?'

★

'Jesus, Clem, we need a drink.'

'There's a Costa over there,' I said, walking automaton-like down the stairs from the rather plush offices of L. W. Montford (Solicitors) before turning into Midhope's main high street and the rain. 'Should have brought our brollies,' I added numbly, 'or at least one of those plastic rain-mate things like your granny used to fish out of her bag as soon as it started raining. Did *your* granny have one?'

'Gin, we need gin,' Izzy said, taking my arm in a tight grip and steering me across the road and into the nearest bar. 'You've had a shock, Clem. You can't go home like this just yet.'

'So basically,' I said, grimacing as the gin hit the back of my throat, 'Peter didn't have a penny? Is that what the man's just told us?'

'Well, not just that he didn't have a penny to his name, unfortunately he also *owed* thousands and thousands and *thousands* of pounds.' Izzy took a good mouthful of her own drink, blew out a long breath and looked at me.

'Would you *ever* have guessed that he was a prolific gambler, Izzy?' I asked, and I know I sounded icily calm. How was I calm after what the solicitor had just imparted? 'I mean, when did he do his gambling? *Where* did he do it? He never once said he was off to… off to the bingo or the… the dogs?'

'Rather more serious than two fat ladies and clickety click, Clem, I reckon,' Izzy said grimly. 'Where the hell does all this leave you, sweetie? That's the question?'

I smiled, still weirdly calm. 'Back where I started, I suppose. The man said the house will have to be sold to pay off what Peter owes. But can you believe he was taking money out of his company to gamble? Having said that, surely if it's your own company you can do what you want with the money in it…?'

'Bloody hell, Clem, no, of course you can't do that. People give financial companies like Peter's money to invest, to work for them, not to gamble it away. Every little old lady who has trusted Peter with her pension pot is entitled to just that: trust. You can't fiddle the books and play about with money that you are looking after, like Peter's done. It's against the law. Those solicitors were right—there will be a *huge* investigation started into financial malpractice. You'll have the law, the taxman, creditors, every man in the street on your back wanting their slice of the cake. It's not just as simple as selling the house and paying people back, Clem. He's been fiddling the books for years, it seems. Those solicitors seemed to think even if he hadn't died it was all about to blow up in his face…'

'The house is only bricks and mortar.'

'Oh, don't be daft, Clem,' Izzy said crossly. 'It's your home. It's Sophie, Max and Allegra's home too.

'Not anymore, it's not. Oh, Izzy, what a mess.'

'Yes but, Clem, the big decision you have to make is the children. Nothing had been put in place about what should happen to them if Peter and Vanessa died. And they have; they've bloody well gone and died and been so fucking irresponsible as to not say what should happen to their own kids in the event of their death.'

'Well, that's not a problem,' I said, vaguely. 'I'll have them. I'll look after them, of course...'

'And where are you going to *live*? And what on? It was bad enough you trying to house, feed and clothe one little girl all by yourself when you had no job. Now you're going to have a stroppy teenager who hates you and will expect a fortune spending on her, plus one small boy who will grow up into another stroppy teenager eating you out of house and home... Think about it, Clem. For God's sake, think about it.'

'But Sophie and Max are *my* stepchildren,' I said. 'Don't I have a legal obligation if not a *moral* one to look after them?'

'Oh shit, Clem, I really don't know. And if you do have a legal obligation surely that's only six weeks down the line and might not count? I can't remember what that second solicitor said, can you?'

'He said something about I had enough on my plate to think about with regards to the shock everyone's had about Peter and what he's been up to and that that will need some sorting before a decision is made about the children. Didn't he say he's coming out to the house tomorrow?'

'Yes, he gave me a card because you just sat there in a trance.' Izzy delved into her bag and brought out an appointment card. 'Oh God, I haven't got my glasses.' She squinted at the card. 'Eleven in the morning; I can't be with you, Clem, it's one of my full days at the surgery. Maybe your dad could come over?'

'Yes, maybe. Right, I need to get back to pick up Max and Allegra.' I paused, frowning. 'Izzy, Max isn't going to be able to go away to school now in the next few years, is he?'

'Nope. And I think you'll find you have Sophie back with you by Christmas—if not before. Depends if her school fees have been paid.'

'They haven't. When I spoke to Sophie's headmistress last week and told her about Peter and Vanessa she said it probably wasn't wholly appropriate to be mentioning it at such a terribly sad time, but Sophie's fees hadn't been paid for last term or for the coming one. I never thought anything about it at the time—assumed last term's was just an oversight on Peter's part and this term's hadn't been paid because Peter was dead.'

Dead. Such a final word. I'd had a husband for all of six weeks, and now he was dead. I shook my head, trying to erase the word from my brain.

'Well, try not to worry about that at the moment: it's possible the school will have contingency plans for times like this. I don't think they'll just throw a bereaved child out in the middle of a term. Wait until they get in touch with you again.'

'It's all a bit of a mess, isn't it?' I said again, blankly.

'You could say that,' Izzy sighed, resolutely gathering bags and coats. 'In fact, Clem, I'd say you've hit the nail right on the proverbial bloody head.'

21

SARAH

Possibly because she was so young, and one of only a few females at Orgreave that hot June day back in 1984, or possibly because she'd actually been assaulted by one of the many thousands of police officers on duty, the police didn't go ahead and charge Sarah with anything, but once they'd arrested her, hauled her into a van and taken her to one of the local police stations—dazed, she never really knew quite where—she was patched up and given a police caution.

Concussed as a result either of the earlier stone throw to her head or, more likely from her fall to the road, Sarah was unable to prevent the woman officer at the police station searching in her—now rather battered—bag for her name and address and, by late afternoon, Gerald Sykes accompanied by Desmond Whittaker, the family lawyer, had arrived to sort out the mess his younger daughter had apparently got herself into.

'Unbelievable, Sarah, truly unbelievable,' Gerald Sykes ranted once he'd convinced the custody sergeant that Sarah was of impeccable character; that his daughter was actually the *Honourable* Sarah Sykes and that she'd obviously been influenced by lefties at that damned art college to make her behave in such a way.

The custody sergeant, on his feet for the last fourteen hours and with not even a sniff of a coffee and a Wagon Wheel, let alone an end to this bloody awful day, was more than happy to be relieved of at least one of those arrested. He still had his share of the ninety-five pickets arrested and brought to his station to see to, and he packed Sarah off with Gerald and his solicitor, but not before giving her a formal caution that in effect, he advised her father, now gave her a police record.

'Unbelievable, Sarah,' Gerald repeated furiously as they drove north back to Harrogate. 'Who were you with? Who persuaded you to go there? How dare you besmirch our family's good name? Your mother is beside herself. And your sister is furious—afraid that if the Hamley-Smiths get to know about this they'll want Jeremy to cancel the wedding.'

'Oh, come off it, Gerald.' Desmond Whittaker turned to smile at Sarah who sat sobbing, head throbbing in the back seat of the Mercedes. 'It's the sort of thing all students do. I seem to remember myself being on the edge of the Grosvenor Square riots when I was up at UCL in '68. We've all been there and done something daft when we were teenagers. No harm done, hey, Sarah?'

'No harm done?' Gerald glared across at Desmond, narrowly missing a lone cyclist who had the temerity to hog Gerald's side of the road. 'My daughter has been mixing with damned Commies, lefties and… and… Bolsheviks and now has a police record, and you say there's no harm done? Good God, man, if Margaret gets to hear about this she'll have me in her office and over the coals.'

Desmond hid a smile. 'Bad choice of words there, Gerald.'

'Well, I tell you now, Missy,' Gerald barked over his shoulder, ignoring Desmond's attempt at levity, 'there'll be no Paris for you in September. Damned if I'm forking out for you to mix with Frog revolutionaries and lefties in *France*.'

Anne Sykes said Sarah had burned her boats, taken one step too far, and the unfinished pieces of artwork would have to stay just that—unfinished. There was no way she could trust her younger daughter's going to Paris if, for heaven's sake, she couldn't even behave herself going to Rotherham, so there was no need for Sarah to be going into Leeds to finish her course work.

After two days of being given the cold shoulder at home, Sarah showered, dressed in a way she knew her mother would approve rather than 'the endless denim you always have on your backside' and went downstairs.

'Mummy, I know you're cross with me for what I did, and I agree, it was silly to go, but I just tagged along with the photography group from college who were hoping to get some incredible pictures that they could perhaps even sell to the newspapers…'

Anne Sykes snorted disparagingly over her coffee and Bath Oliver but left off reading her article in *The Lady*.

'None of us had any idea that it would turn out to be such a *frightful* day,' Sarah went on. 'Do you really think we'd have gone along if we'd known those *dreadful* miners were going to do such horrid things to those *poor* policemen and those lovely horses? I'd had enough of being there, wished I hadn't gone and was just on my way home. I was leaving to walk to the station when I just *had* to go and help one of the horses…' Sarah looked at her mother in desperation. '*You* couldn't bear to see a horse hurt, Mummy, could you…?'

Anne still didn't say anything, but Sarah knew she was relenting and pushed her advantage. 'Mummy, I'm nineteen. I'm a grownup. You really can't keep me locked up here for ever.'

'Don't be ridiculous, Sarah, no one is keeping you locked up, for heaven's sake. When does term at that place in Leeds actually finish?'

'Mummy, I need to go in every day for the next week. If I don't, I won't pass my foundation course. I know you're not going to let me go off to Paris now after what I've done to you and Daddy, but please don't stop me now when I've worked so hard.'

'Sarah, as you say, you are an adult—although for the life in me I don't know why you don't act like one. There are some lovely young men in the county just waiting to be snapped up. So, I suggest you get off to that art place, finish your course and then we'll sit down with Daddy and decide what you should do next… perhaps a secretarial course at the North of England like Selena did once she came back from Switzerland?'

Sarah breathed a secret sigh of relief and smiled at her

mother. 'That might be a good idea, Mummy. Selena hasn't looked back since doing that, has she? Now, I'm going to catch the ten o'clock train and I'll be back for supper. If I can work hard every day this week, the lecturers should let me through, I think.'

Sarah kissed her mother's Max-Factored cheek, inhaling the Estee Lauder 'Youth Dew' Anne Sykes had insisted on wearing ever since it made its debut in the 1950s and which always made Sarah feel slightly nauseous. 'Thanks, Mummy and I *am* sorry I've caused you and Daddy so much upset.'

Sarah escaped, running for the bus that would take her to the station, abandoning her skirt and blouse for the Levi's, T-shirt and Doc Martens that she managed to change into in the Leeds train's malodorous toilet cubicle and, once in the city, ran the three-quarters of a mile to Johnny's flat.

He was asleep and it took a good three minutes' hammering for Sarah to waken him and bring him, naked except for a pair of 'Ban the Bomb' underpants, to the door. He squinted against the bright sunshine, rubbing his eyes and yawning loudly, peering at whoever it was mad enough to be up at so early an hour.

'Fuck, Sarah. Where's the fire?'

'Oh, Johnny, you're OK?'

'OK? Yes, I'm fine, apart from some idiot waking me up in the middle of the night.' He took in her pretty face, red from running in the warm sunshine; the large breasts and long legs encased in denim; her huge brown eyes, her full mouth just waiting to be kissed. 'Christ, you're gorgeous,' he said, burying his face in her long dark hair and pulling her into the flat. 'Where've you been the last two days?'

'I searched all over for you, Sarah,' Johnny said as she lay, sated with sex and love for this beautiful man who was now in the middle of meticulously rolling a joint for them both.

'I'm really sorry I lost you but, that poor horse... Didn't you see it? It was hit on the nose with a brick and it was so brave, it just stood there. I had to go and help it, and then someone, or something, hit me in the back of the legs.' Sarah turned to show him the huge bruises, yellowing now and in hues of purple and ochre. 'I just sort of fell forwards and lost consciousness for a while.'

'Bloody hell,' Johnny said, squinting through the pungent smoke of the joint, 'I hate horses—they're huge big things. One stood on my toe once and it's never recovered.' He lifted a grubby-looking foot from the sheet, examining it for proof of the horse's clumsiness. '*And* I'm totally allergic to them; I sneeze if I even see one—that's why I kept well away when you ran off towards them.'

'Didn't you come back to find me?' Sarah asked sharply. 'Didn't you see what happened?'

'No, no, I didn't,' Johnny said too quickly, pinning her arms back against the pillow so he had unhindered access to both delicious, full breasts and could continue from there to kiss up the inside of her arms. 'I kept running all the way down to the village and assumed you were behind me. When I realised you weren't there, I ran back but couldn't get past the cordon of police that had turned really nasty by then.'

'But didn't you look for me? Didn't you wonder what had

happened to me? Didn't you... *care?*' Sarah's lip trembled and she tried not to cry.

'Sarah, lovely Sarah, I've been searching everywhere for you for the last couple of days. You've never allowed me to have your phone number so I couldn't ring your house. I sometimes wonder if you aren't a bit ashamed of me. I mean you've never asked me back to meet your parents.'

Sarah flung her arms round him. 'No, no, it's not that. No, you mustn't think that. It's just that Mummy and Daddy are a bit old-fashioned... They're a bit protective of me.'

'That's all right then,' Johnny said comfortably, kissing her nipple so lightly Sarah thought she'd go mad with longing for him. He didn't say anything for a while but then suddenly smiled. 'Tell you what, Sarah, I'd love to take you away for a couple of days. Have you ever been to Amsterdam?'

'So what did you tell Mummy and Daddy?' Johnny asked as Sarah strapped herself into the cheap afternoon flight from Manchester airport to Amsterdam. He seemed distracted, nervous even, and Sarah assumed it was because she'd been really late getting to the airport, arriving just as the gate had been about to close.

'Suzy Sinclair,' Sarah muttered, so rigid with nerves her teeth were actually chattering. She took a deep breath and tried to speak slowly. 'I was at school with Suzy—she was one of the naughty ones, but for some reason she always seemed to like me.' Sarah shook her head as if still unable to believe that any girl as enigmatic as Suzy Sinclair could have elected to have her as one of her buddies. 'I think she

liked the idea of hanging around with "an honourable'"
more than anything else.'

'An honourable? An honourable what?' Johnny stared at
her, puzzled.

Sarah blushed. 'Oh, because Daddy is a life peer, it means
I'm allowed the title. I never use it, but Suzy seemed to think
it was something special.'

Johnny looked at her and whistled. 'So my girlfriend is
The Honourable Sarah?' He grinned. 'Well, what do you
know?'

'As I said, I don't use it, it doesn't mean anything,' Sarah
said hurriedly, embarrassed. 'Anyway, Suzy had invited me
ages ago to some party of hers down at her parents' house
in Lincolnshire and I said I wasn't going, but then I told
Mummy I'd changed my mind. Mummy was delighted that
I was back seeing friends from school rather than the *scruffy
lefties* she assumes I'm mixing with in Leeds…'

Johnny laughed out loud at that. 'Scruffy lefty? Well, I
think I've been called everything now.'

'Anyway, I couldn't think of any other way of coming
away with you, so told Suzy everything and asked her to
cover for me. She loves any sort of intrigue and even spoke
to Mummy the other night when she rang and Mummy
answered. Mummy said she was so pleased I was going
down for a few days because she felt I'd been mixing with
some very strange characters and it would do me good to
mix with *my own sort* once more. I do feel horribly guilty—
Mummy gave me some money to buy Suzy a present and
dropped me at Leeds station so I could catch the London
train to Peterborough. Suzy's mother is supposed to be
picking me up from there. Well, I mean, obviously she isn't

because she doesn't know anything about it. Oh Johnny, I feel so nervous. Mummy insisted on waiting with me at Leeds until the London train came and then I had to dash to the other platform to get the Manchester train and then I just missed one and...'

Johnny patted her hand, but still seemed distracted. It must be her own nerves that were catching, she thought, and again tried to relax by taking deep breaths.

'Christ, I need a drink,' Johnny said, once they were airborne. 'Where's the drinks trolley?'

'Where are we staying?' Sarah asked. 'Is it somewhere you've stayed before?'

'Well, I think I need to introduce you to the pleasures of the coffee bars in the red-light districts before we think of finding somewhere to kip for the night.'

'Coffee? I thought you'd have preferred the bars.'

'The Amsterdam bars are not a patch on their coffee bars,' Johnny grinned. 'Just you wait and see.'

They spent the rest of that day and the next in the coffee bars, getting so high Sarah couldn't imagine any other world except this one cocooned in the smoky, overcrowded, almost subterranean world of music and pot, immersed in Limahl, Howard Jones and the Thompson Twins, while giggling uproariously at anything remotely funny that Johnny said.

'I'm supposed to be going to the Burghley Horse Trials with Mummy sometime in September,' Sarah was telling Johnny, suddenly feeling emotional about the lovely chestnut horse that had been hit on the nose. 'I wish you could come but you'd hate it, wouldn't you?'

'Not if the horses were all found guilty,' Johnny said with a straight face. 'That would be fun.'

Sarah was giggling so much, hiccupping at the thought of horses parading in front of judge and jury, she didn't acknowledge, for a couple of seconds, the tall, Middle-Eastern looking man who had joined them, sliding into the spare seat and shaking Johnny's hand.

'Sarah, this is Felix, an old friend of mine.'

'Oh, fancy bumping into someone you know,' Sarah exclaimed, still tittering. 'Excuse me, Felix, must find a loo,' and she was off, floating through the crowd, laughing to herself.

When she got back, Felix had disappeared. 'Oh, has your friend gone?' Sarah asked, surprised.

'He's not really a friend. Just someone I knew years ago.'

'I wish we could stay here forever,' Sarah sighed. 'Do we *have* to get the plane back tonight?' She looked at her watch. She'd been determined to visit the Van Gogh museum on Paulus Potterstraat 7, a good twenty minutes' walk away from the rather seedy hotel in which they'd stayed the night, excited about seeing some of the artist's earlier, lesser-known work. But, as she'd tentatively made to rise from the bed, head woolly from an overindulgence of weed and Jenever, the city's infamous liqueur, Johnny's hand had snaked out to catch her wrist and tumble her back into bed. Now there was no time to make the visit.

'Oh, Johnny,' Sarah suddenly exclaimed, 'my overnight case—it's gone.' She scrabbled around the table and chairs, searching through myriad feet and other people's bags and jackets. 'Where is it?'

'What have you done with it? Did you take it to the loo?'

'No, I wouldn't take my case for a wee. Or did I? Golly, I'm so floaty, maybe I did.' Sarah giggled and once more made her way through the crowd to the bathroom three floors up.

'No, it's not there,' she sighed, ten minutes later. 'Oh bugger, have I lost it or has someone stolen it?'

'You didn't have much in it, did you?'

'No, not really: a couple of pairs of knickers, my Thomas Hardy and my toilet bag. Oh and my best jeans—damn, I love those jeans. Do you think we should go and tell the police?'

'Not in the state *you're* in,' Johnny said. 'It might be legal to smoke in these coffee bars, but you're pretty much off your head, you know. Wait there and I'll go and have a good look round.'

More than fifteen minutes had gone, and Sarah was beginning to think he must have passed out somewhere, when Johnny returned, triumphant.

'This is it, isn't it? I checked inside and your book is still there. I don't think anything's gone. I reckon all these people have just kicked it around, like a football. We're going to have to get a move on to the airport if we don't want to miss the plane. Come on. Don't bother checking it, everything's OK. I looked.'

Sarah slept most of the way back to Manchester, exhausted by the excitement and guilt of telling lies in order to spend a night away with Johnny. The last thirty-six hours or so had only reiterated how much she wanted to be with him, and she couldn't bear the thought of leaving him back in Leeds in order to return to Harrogate. Her parents were out for dinner at some charity do in Wetherby that evening and her mother, really pleased at Sarah's decision to go to the party in Lincolnshire, had given her money—unfortunately blown on Jenever—in order to get a taxi back to Harrogate once the return London train arrived back in Leeds.

'I wish I could come back to the flat with you tonight,' Sarah said, clutching at his hand as they queued at passport control. She was feeling hungover and depressed at the thought of leaving Johnny, as well as anxious at the thought of having to be jolly in front of her mother who would order a full inquest, wanting to know everything about the party: what the other girls were wearing, who had actually been there, which young men had talked to her.

'I'm just going to nip to the toilet, Sarah,' Johnny was saying as he scanned the queue up ahead. 'Don't worry about waiting for me. I could do with a coffee though. Once you go through customs there's a café on the other side. Order me a black one, would you, and I'll catch up with you?'

As the queue inched forward, Sarah opened her handbag to check how much money she had left in her purse. Her allowance, together with the money her mother had given her, seemed to have been spent, but she was relieved to see she had a couple of pounds left that would buy them a coffee apiece. Once through passport control, she turned left, aiming for the green Nothing to Declare symbol, at which juncture a hand was placed on her arm.

'That was quick,' she began to say, at the same time as the owner of the hand, a tall, blue-shirt-clad man said, 'Would you come with me, Madam? We'd just like a quick look in your bag.'

Sentencing Sarah Sykes to two years and six months for Fraudulent Evasion of a Prohibition by bringing almost three kilos of heroin into the country, His Honour Judge Bernard Linford, said at Leeds Crown Court that this was obviously the case of a young woman determined to rebel against her excellent upbringing, her caring parents, her privileged and elevated place in Society. Only the week before blatantly smuggling drugs with a street value of a hundred thousand pounds into the country, he told the packed court, she'd been arrested at 'The Battle of Orgreave', thinking it great fun to throw bricks at innocent police and their horses in the course of their duty. He had no alternative, he said, but to impose the maximum sentence open to him.

As she was taken, frightened and weeping, back down to the cells to wait for the transport to take her to HMP Styal, the cub reporter on *The Yorkshire Post* triumphantly came up with the headline that had been evading him throughout the days of the trial.

NOT SO HONOURABLE NOW!

the newspaper proclaimed next morning to the good people of Yorkshire over their bowls of muesli and plates of scrambled eggs. It was debatable whether the readers of this venerable rag would have been more sympathetic or, conversely, more outraged, had they known that not only was the local MP's daughter a leftie police basher and drug smuggler but would also, in the months to come, become even more of a burden on the state when she became a single mother of twins.

22

'OK, George, you win.' I knew I should really be replying to the many letters of condolence; throwing out the over-the-top bouquets of flowers that were drooping and, in some cases, beginning to smell, their greenery rotting to a putrid slime in the weeks-old water; putting a load of washing on and tackling the basket of ironing that was threatening to topple.

And that, I knew, was absolutely nothing compared to all Peter's stuff I had to do something about: his wardrobe upon wardrobe of designer suits, his cashmere jumpers, his hand-made Italian leather brogues. Mrs Atkinson, Peter's cleaning lady, was due in later but I was going to have to tell her I could no longer keep her on, that the house was being put up for sale and that I had no money to pay her for future work.

'Bother,' I mimicked in what I hoped was an accurate impersonation of Mole in *Wind in The Willows*. 'Oh blow.

Hang spring cleaning…' I grabbed George's lead. 'Come on, George, let's run away together.'

The early morning mist of the October morning was beginning to dissipate, a watery sun taking its place as I strode out across the fields, trampling wet grass, breathing in the smells of autumn. The leaves on the giant oaks in the wood to my right, although a long way from dropping, were turning crimson, yellow and brown—harbingers of the winter ahead. I ignored the overripe, deeply purple blackberries begging to be picked in the hedgerows—it was pointless cluttering the house with jars of homemade bramble jelly when in a few weeks I'd have to be throwing stuff out, but then I relented, searching in my pocket for the poo-bag I always carried when walking George. Filling the pantry with serried rows of jars of jam might not be a good idea at the moment, but we could at least have an apple and blackberry pie for supper that evening.

'Do *not* crap anywhere now, George,' I warned, filling the small black plastic bag with the luscious fruit. 'Or at least, if you do, go under a hedge where no one can see you.' I filled the bag, my fingers, lips and teeth soon a lividly imperial purple as I picked and tasted the pulpy berries.

Wiping my hands on my jeans, I whistled for George who, I soon realised, was delightedly absorbed, rolling in fox crap. 'Oh God, George, not again. Get out of there, you disgusting beast. Oh God, you stink.'

Keeping a good distance from the now fetidly reeking dog, I set off at a cracking pace, hoping that the speed might help to block out all the thoughts and images that were crowding, Piccadilly-Circus like, into my head. Max's face, drained of all colour when I'd told him as gently as possible that we would probably have to put the house up for sale; the phone call that I still had to make to Sophie's headteacher in order to tell her the financial position the family was now in; Allegra's repeated questions as to why Peter had died and where he was now; and Lucy. My plan to concentrate my efforts on looking for Lucy in Leeds had been scuppered for the time being with so much else suddenly and unexpectedly to sort out.

Leaving the fields and approaching a lane I'd not come across before on my previous walks with George, I turned to put him on the lead.

'Oh bloody hell, where is he?' I called, several times, but no black curly-haired rocket came hurtling towards me as was the norm when he'd wandered off by himself. I called again, retracing my steps to the last dry-stone wall I'd crossed, climbing back over the broken, wooden stile in the hope that it was a simple leg-up he needed in order to join me. He wasn't there.

'Shit.' I looked at my watch. I needed to be turning round and going back home if I was to prepare food for the children, see Mrs Atkinson and keep the appointment with Max's headteacher who, concerned about how Max was coping after his parents' death, had asked to see me.

'Of course he's not *coping*,' I shouted angrily to the skies, almost losing my balance on top of the wall as I scanned the fields for sight of George. 'He's a little boy who has just gone through the trauma of losing not one, but both his parents. Of course he's not sodding *coping*.'

I jumped down carelessly from the wall, wrenching my ankle a little as I landed and, limping slightly, headed once more to the lane up ahead. Maybe the damned dog had beaten me to it and was now on the actual road. Swearing under my breath, I ran as best I could, knowing that having to tell Max and Allegra that a speeding tractor had squashed George, that he too was in heaven, would be just one step too far.

'Oy, is this your bloody dog?' A tall, dark-haired man was standing over George, holding onto his collar while George, delighted at seeing me, pulled madly in my direction.

'George, there you are. Oh, thank you so much for finding him.'

'I didn't bloody find him,' the man said furiously. 'He found me—*and* my mother's chickens.'

'Oh gosh, are they all right?'

'Well, if by all right you mean the whole flock scared shitless and one dead then, yes, they're *all right*.'

'I am *so* sorry.'

'Jesus, this dog of yours stinks.' The man let go of George, holding up his hands in disgust whereupon George bounded over to my side and lay, panting, at my feet.

'I am really, really sorry,' I said again, unsure of what else to say. 'I mean, he's just a puppy... he's never done anything like this before.'

'Why isn't he on a lead if he's a puppy?'

'I am so sorry, he just ran off.'

'Why aren't you training him properly? You're obviously not fit to have a dog...'

I'd suddenly had enough. 'Look, it's one sodding dead hen, for heaven's sake. What does a chicken cost in Aldi? A fiver? Right, give me your name and address and I'll send you a fiver or, if you prefer, I'll buy you another hen, live and squawking, plucked and oven-ready or... or made into a... a coq au vin...'

'You could not even *begin* to replace this one. It's my mother's favourite, her pride and joy.'

'Well then, as far as I can see, you both need to get out more.'

The man glared. 'The chicken that *your* dog has just mutilated is an Ayan Cemani—'

'Well, if your mother is daft enough to keep chickens with such bloody stupid names—'

'—and is the Lamborghini of poultry—'

'Well, tell her to get the Corsa version next time—'

'—and is—*was*—worth over two thousand pounds.'

'Oh, don't be so ridiculous.' I laughed out loud at the man's hyperbole. 'No chicken is worth that much.'

'I suggest,' the man said through gritted teeth, replacing his tweed flat cap on his dark hair, 'that when you get home, you Google "Ayan Cemani" and then, when you've done that, you tear up the cheque you've made out to me for a fiver and write another one, but this time for two thousand pounds. Oh, and may I also suggest you look in the mirror? You appear to be turning purple, no doubt from my blackberries you've obviously helped yourself to.'

Jesus. I clipped the lead onto George's collar, playing for time. 'And you are?'

'Rafe Ahern. I live here, and you and that damned *poodle* are on my land.'

'Firstly, Mr Ahern, George is a Labradoodle, i.e. only *half* a poodle and you insult him by calling him the former. Secondly, how is this *your* lanyd? Have you swallowed it? Is it inside you? And thirdly… thirdly—' great sobs suddenly burst, unbidden, from my throat '—my husband has just been killed and I've no home and no *money*.' I pulled the bulging black poo bag from my pocket, swung it by its handles and threw it at the astonished man. 'And here's your fucking blackberries back. I don't want them now.'

'Gosh, did you really throw the bag of blackberries at him?' Harriet giggled as she helped me take dishes from the dishwasher. 'And after you'd just murdered his chicken, too? Brilliant.'

'It's not funny, Harriet,' I admonished, giggling too. 'When I got home, I looked up his damned Ayan Cemani and he's absolutely right about how much they cost. They're all black: black feathers, black tongue, black beak, black plume. The only things that aren't black are the eggs they lay. And two thousand pounds *is* the going rate.'

'Well, he's rich enough to cover it. Or he'll be insured.'

'Do you know him?'

'Not really. We met him once at David and Amanda's, but he left early; he had to leave for the Middle East apparently.'

'The Middle East…?'

Grace and Mel Naylor came into the kitchen, bearing huge cardboard boxes and a bottle of wine. 'Don't worry, Clem,' Grace smiled, 'I promise we won't all get merry like we did at Hat's place the other week. We're here to work, to help you.'

'But work always goes down better with a glass to help it,' Mel finished. 'Where do you want us to start, Clem?'

'We were just talking about Rafe Ahern, Grace,' Hat said.

'I was telling Clem, the only time I met him, at David and Mandy's, he had to rush off.'

'Oh, he's always rushing off. He's the BBC's Middle Eastern Foreign Correspondent or something like that. He's always on TV. You'd recognise him if you saw him.'

'I did see him. Last week. I encroached on his land, nicked his blackberries and murdered his mother's chicken.'

'Gosh, good going,' Grace laughed. 'My mother is friendly with his mother. Annabelle Ahern is wonderful: she was a Sixties model alongside Jean Shrimpton. If you believe all her stories, she used to go out with Mick Jagger and slept with all of the Beatles at one point or another.'

'She sounds a lot more fun than her son,' I smiled. 'Right, what do you all want to do? Eat or pack up Peter's stuff first?'

'Let's work first,' Mel said. 'Then we can relax. Show us the way, Clem, and Grace and I can make a start.'

'Wow, what fabulous clothes Peter had,' Harriet whistled. 'Some of this stuff must have cost a fortune.'

'I know, but it's no good to me,' I said. 'Look, if there's anything you'd like, just take it.'

'Get it up on eBay,' Harriet said firmly. 'The RSPCA or Help The Aged would lap it up, I know, but at the end of the day charity begins at home and you need to think of yourself and the kids at the moment, Clem.'

'I don't have the time to start selling on eBay,' I frowned. 'And actually, I'm not sure if I *should* be getting rid of it. I think Peter's creditors might have a legal right to it.'

'Oh, that's a point, you might be right. How about if we

box up and label everything of Peter's that you don't want and store it in the garage next to his cars. And then if bailiffs and creditors do come round you can show them where it is and you will be legally above board. If they don't, then you can eBay it and pocket the cash.'

'It all sounds a bit mercenary,' I said, taking the fifty or more silk ties from their hangers and laying them gently in an open box. My eyes suddenly filled with tears. 'Oh, poor Peter. Poor, poor, misguided man.'

'Mel, get the girl a drink. For medicinal purposes of course.' Grace patted my arm. 'It's a rotten thing to have happened, Clem. Just take your time. There's no rush. I can't believe there's no one else to help you. Did neither Peter nor his wife have any family at all?'

I shook my head as I folded a beautiful Hilditch & Key navy and white striped shirt. 'Both Peter and Vanessa were only children. There are no siblings, no grandparents left—apart from Peter's mother up in Aberdeen and Vanessa's mother in a home near Upper Clawson with Alzheimer's—and, according to Morag Broadbent who talked about her family when we were up there, no cousins to speak of.'

I suddenly sat back on my heels. 'Gosh, talking about Morag Broadbent—Peter's mother—it's just come back to me something she said when we were up there. She said Peter's father had spent all her family money—the Buchanan Clan's—on women and horses. Gambling must have been a family trait.'

'Well, just keep an eye on Sophie if she wants to play Snap.' Grace smiled. 'How is she anyway? Have you heard from her?'

I sighed, feeling a tight knot of anxiety. 'She's due home

for good at half-term in two weeks' time. The school has said she can stay until then but if no fees are forthcoming she'll have to leave. I'm dreading it. She hates me and… and she knows about my past history. About where I was born and about Lucy…'

'No! How does she know that?' Harriet, Grace and Mel all looked up from their packing.

'For some reason Peter told Vanessa and Vanessa told Sophie.'

'Well, how stupid is that?' Harriet said crossly. 'How ridiculously stupid. The woman should be shot.' Harriet's hand flew to her mouth as she realised what she'd said.

'Bit late for that, Harriet.' I smiled and Grace tutted and then, unable to help ourselves, we both began giggling.

'Oh God, I don't know why I'm laughing,' I said, wiping my eyes. 'I am dreading Sophie coming home. Am dreading telling her we'll all have to move into a much, much smaller house somewhere.'

'So, the children are staying with you, then?' Mel asked. 'That's a huge thing to take on.'

'I've no alternative; I'm Max and Sophie's stepmother. Anyway, I wouldn't dream of not looking after them or handing them over to social services, which is where they would end up if I just walked away with Allegra.'

'And where do you think you'll end up?' Harriet asked. 'I do hope you manage to stay round here somewhere.'

'It all depends on how much money, if any, is left over. This house, thank God, has no mortgage on it and must be worth a small fortune so, once all Peter's creditors have been paid, I'm hoping there will be enough for a small semi somewhere.'

'You'll need four bedrooms,' Mel said.

'We can manage with three: Allegra can always share with me. Sophie is sixteen now and hopefully will be off to university in a couple of years…'

'Well, rather you than me,' Grace said. 'From what you've said about her she sounds horrendous.' And then, obviously seeing how I was feeling, hastily added, 'It will be all right. Really. I'm sure it will all work out in the end.'

'It's just that I adore this house,' I said wistfully. 'I know I have absolutely no right whatsoever to feel put out at having to leave it. I mean, it was never mine really to begin with. But I've just grown to love it.' I stood up, looking for the shoes I'd kicked off as I packed boxes. 'I'll just have to think about it being a two-month holiday that came to a sudden end. Right, lunch. The final supper, as it were. Give me ten minutes to make a dressing for the salad and then leave all this and come down.'

'I don't think I've ever met anyone who has such a way with food as you have, Clem,' Harriet sighed, greedily mopping up the remains of the tarragon and mushroom sauce on her plate. 'At least you'll still be able to work for David, won't you?'

'Yes, he popped round before I went to the solicitor last week. I'm cooking a lunch for some Russians next week.'

'You'll knock 'em dead with your fantastic cooking,' Mel said. 'So, what do you think of David Henderson? Rather gorgeous, isn't he?'

Harriet smiled. 'Oh everyone has a little crush on David. We can't help ourselves.'

'You as well?' Mel asked.

'I don't know any woman who doesn't look at him twice. It's the power thing, I think. You know, even if he was plug ugly—which he *obviously* isn't—I still reckon women would flock to him. But he only has eyes for Amanda, so there we go.' Harriet sighed. 'We can look and fantasise…'

'Clem, what's happening about Lucy?' Grace asked, collecting dirty plates from the table. 'I don't suppose anything at the moment?'

I shrugged. 'No, I've just had too much to think about with all this mess. I can't just swan off to Leeds and, to be honest, I'm not sure I can cope with her at the moment/'

There was a silence from the others.

'I know that sounds an awful thing to say about my own twin…' My voice caught in my throat as I spoke 'But I just have to think about Allegra and Max at the moment. And Sophie as well, of course.'

'You've missed someone,' Mel said, pouring water for me. 'You. Think about yourself for once. When you're all sorted, when you've found a house and you're becoming famous for hosting rich businessmen's lunches, then start again looking for Lucy. And this time we'll all help you find her.'

'Absolutely,' Harriet said. 'Honestly, Clem, we really will.'

23

The Reverend Roger had been in a foul mood for weeks. Furious that Jamie, his son, had turned down his place at Durham so that he could remain in France eagerly assimilating more and more of the French cuisine he adored, he'd taken it out on the Rabbitt household until even Mrs Scatchard, parish stalwart and chair of the WI, who had been in love with Roger for years, had had enough.

'Don't know what's up with His Nibs lately,' she sniffed to Gloria McEwan over toasted teacake and a pot of tea in Betty's. 'If he carries on much longer like he is, I shall be resigning from the church council *and* the flower rota.'

'Oh, you don't want to do that, Susan,' Gloria said, mentally taking note of how much jam Susan was taking for the second half of her already lavishly buttered teacake. 'It'll be Droopy Drawers that's getting to him again. She was supposed to have ordered the bread wheat sheaf for the centre of the Harvest display but totally forgot to ask Brian at the bakery. We had to find a giant swede to put in the middle to offset all the tins of beans and tuna that people seem to think it OK to donate for Harvest these days.'

'Hmm. Well, I have to say, she doesn't deserve Rev. Roger. I know he can be prickly at times, and recently he's been worse than a holly bush, but she does nothing to help him, the church or the village as far as I can see. She doesn't understand his caring nature, you see, doesn't see his sensitive side like we do. If she had an ounce of get up and go about her she'd have taken on the Brownies now that Brown Owl appears to have run off with Akela. The poor little mites are crying out for someone to take them on Tuesdays, but will she lower herself? No, not Madam. Too busy floating about like some ageing hippy, growing herbs and orgasmic veggies in the rectory garden. "Mrs Scatchard," Rev. says to me, only yesterday, "sometimes I long for a bit of plain cooking, a bit of roast beef and Yorkshire pudding…".'

'Nowt wrong with a bit of Yorkshire pudding.'

'"But Sarah," he says, "is intent on cooking only vegetarian stuff or foreign stuff".'

'Foreign?' Gloria frowned.

'Osama Bin Laden stuff. You know, Middle Eastern.'

'Well, I reckon we'll all have to get used to that sort of muck soon what with this invasion going on.'

'Invasion, Mrs McEwan? What invasion's that then?' Ben Carey, the mature student chaplain on work experience in the diocese, pulled out a chair and sat down with a sigh of relief.

'Well, the Iraqis.'

'I thought we invaded *them*? Ben raised an eyebrow and reached for the menu.

'You know what I mean, Ben.'

'Actually, I'm not sure that I do, Mrs McEwan, but never mind that, I need coffee and sugar.'

'Hard morning?' Mrs Scatchard asked, with only a modicum of sympathy.

'You could say that. Rev. Roger has had me all over Harrogate putting up posters for next Sunday's Harvest Festival. He's even thinking about bringing the service into the pubs in the town centre.'

'Posters? Pubs? That's a bit modern for Roger, isn't it?' Gloria peered over her spectacles.

'Oh, Roger can be *very* up with what's *in* at the moment,' Susan said proudly. 'I'd describe him as quite a forward-thinking Luddite…'

'Right.' Ben tried to hide a smile. 'Actually, I reckon the bishop's been on at him again to rally the troops as it were.'

'Well, if *Mrs* R would just stir herself to help a bit more in the parish he might not have to resort to hanging around in pubs to spread the word.'

'She's lovely, isn't she?'

'Who?' Both women stared at Ben in surprise.

'Sarah,' Ben said, still scanning the menu. And, when no response came, looked up and smiled, stroking his beard. 'Sarah? The vicar's wife?'

'Is she? I wouldn't know,' Susan Scatchard said, almost primly. 'She rarely puts in an appearance these days in the village or in church—even on Sundays.'

'She's been wonderful to me,' Ben enthused. 'She is the most *fantastic* cook. I'm vegetarian and people are sometimes stumped about what to give me if I'm invited round for supper. More often than not, I'm offered cheese on toast, a boiled egg or a roast dinner without the roast. Not that I'm complaining,' he added hastily. 'I'm more than grateful to *anyone* inviting me to eat with them.'

Susan's and Gloria's eyes met in silent but mutual agreement: *their* respective dining rooms wouldn't be entertaining this young intern with his lefty, bearded, veggie notions, thank you very much.

'I'm actually on my way to the rectory after this,' Ben said, wolfing down his wholemeal egg mayo wrap. 'I said I'd pop in and see Sarah, take her some sumac and baharat for her salads, from the wholefood shop on Kirkham Road.'

'Very nice, I'm sure,' Gloria said, her mouth a pursed dog's bum. 'Although I have to say, I prefer a soupcon of salad cream or Branston Pickle, myself.'

The first time Roger squeezed her arm with enough force to leave vivid fingerprints on the pale skin around her wrist, Sarah assumed he'd done so without realising just how strong his grip could be. They'd been married only three months and were living in Cheltenham, a town Sarah had immediately adored even though it reminded her very much of Harrogate with its associative memories of her parents' and siblings' virtual abandonment of her while serving her prison sentence near Manchester.

It was Christmas, their first Christmas together as a married couple after moving to the south west on Roger's new appointment to the Gloucester diocese. His promotion, after four years as vicar in the small Manchester parish that had included in its mandate the chaplaincy of the nearby women's prison, was, Roger felt, long overdue and he accepted with alacrity, feeling that he could now ask Sarah to marry him on her imminent release, taking her to a town where no one would know anything of her shameful past.

Roger had fallen in love with her the minute her sad, haunted eyes had met his. With her mass of dark, cloudy hair and large, full mouth just waiting to be kissed, Sarah Sykes filled his dreams, his every waking moment and what had, at first, appeared daunting, thrice-weekly visits beyond the huge prison gates, were now looked forward to with eager anticipation. Once he'd come to terms with the gauntlet of shouting, cackling inmates and had even learned to parry their blatantly coarse comments with some ribald backchat of his own, Roger began to thoroughly enjoy his afternoons with the women, and particularly with Sarah.

In the last year of her sentence, and with a reputation among the prison staff for impeccable behaviour, Sarah had been assigned to help the visiting art teacher in the educational wing. It was here that Roger would find himself heading every week on the pretext of speaking to the women who had, so far, avoided his offer of talk and prayer. Tall, good-looking and with the athletic frame of one who had fully immersed himself in all sports both at his minor public school and university, he was doted upon by inmates and staff alike and many a prison guard made sure her Carmen rollers and Wonderbra were ready for action on the mornings of the Rev. Roger Rabbitt's visits.

That first time, it had been Roger's first Midnight Mass in his new church and, anticipating a huge crowd inspired as much by an over-imbibing of Christmas cheer as a desire to participate in the yearly ritual of welcoming the divine Child, he had been nervously rehearsing his intended message to the good people of Cheltenham for days.

'Sarah, I can't find my new surplice,' Roger had shouted up the stairs to the bathroom where Sarah was having a bath in readiness for her Christmas appearance as 'new young vicar's new young wife'. 'The new one I wore last week, but asked you to wash specially for Mass tonight?'

'I bet it's still in the washing machine,' Sarah had called back down. 'If you fish it out and put it to dry on the creel, it should be ready for me to iron later on…'

Sarah had just been pulling herself out of the bath when Roger calmly walked in with a blue sheet in his hands. She'd stared at it for a second, trying to place which bed it must have come from, and then, realising it was Roger's new surplice, got a fit of the giggles. 'Oh, God, Roger, I'm sorry,' she'd laughed. 'I must have washed it with those new navy towels Rosemary gave us for a wedding present. I know, perhaps you can wear it with a white tablecloth wrapped round your head and pretend to be the Virgin Mary. It would be very authentic; go down a storm.' Sarah had laughed again, reaching for a towel to dry herself at the same time as Rev. Roger had reached for her wrist, twisting it as he dug his powerful fingers and nails into her.

She'd dropped the towel, squealing in pain and shock as he continued to twist her arm. 'Roger, what the hell are you doing?'

'You stupid girl,' he'd hissed close up, flecks of spittle landing on her face. 'Don't you *ever* try to make me look stupid again…'

Her legs had been shaking as he suddenly let go of her arm, and she'd stumbled backwards onto the cold metal of the ancient bath. Roger had thrown the surplice at her and walked out, just as calmly as he had entered only a minute earlier.

Numbly, Sarah had pulled the plug on the cooling scummy bath water, held her aching, reddening wrist under the cold-water tap for a couple of minutes and then dressed and gone downstairs.

'Roger?'

'Don't worry, darling.' Roger had smiled across the kitchen at her. 'I can wear one of the other surplices. Kettle's on. Tea?'

'Roger, you really hurt me. Look.' Sarah had held out her wrist where tiny pinprick blood blisters had appeared.'

'Our first tiff, darling. Let's make sure we don't have any more.' Roger had pulled the sleeve of Sarah's sweater down over the offending wrist and, placing a hand at the back of her head, pulled her towards him and kissed her so gently she could almost believe the events of the last ten minutes had all been in her imagination.

Maybe she was overreacting, Sarah had thought to herself later that evening as she sat on the front pew while Roger—in his next-best surplice—wooed a full house with his good looks and humorous narrative. She'd always been too sensitive, she'd told herself. Look how she'd cried those first weeks when, as a terrified gangly eight-year-old, she'd first been sent off to boarding school; how she sobbed every time Bambi fell on the ice; the months and months of protracted weeping for the two little girls she'd given away…

The second time it happened was over six months later. Heavily pregnant with Jennifer, Sarah had left the preparations for their evening meal and gone into the garden in search of rosemary for the garlicky roast potatoes she was planning on cooking. Breathing in the heady scent of lavender, she'd plucked a couple of the lilac-coloured sprigs and, threading them through the undone buttonhole of her loose cotton frock, had lifted Gandalf, their inherited rectory cat, onto her lap and sat down with him, closing her eyes against the August late-afternoon heat.

She'd been rudely awakened by a strong grip squeezing her shoulder, shoving her upwards from the deckchair, Gandalf fleeing to the safe haven of the nearby apple tree.

'Get *up*,' Roger had hissed in her ear and, dazed, she'd lumbered awkwardly to her feet, pulling the bulk of her pregnant belly up with her. 'While you're *sunbathing* yourself, there's a pan that's boiled itself dry on the stove. And the kitchen is a tip.' Still holding her in a vice-like grip, his fingers sinking into the soft flesh of her upper arm, Roger had dragged her from the balmy warmth of the garden back into the cool depths of the rectory kitchen.

'Is this the thanks I get for taking you on?' he'd said coldly. 'For marrying a drug smuggler? A slut who gave birth to her bastard children in prison? Clean the kitchen, Sarah. It's an absolute disgrace, as are you.' This time he'd not left her to it but had stood, arms folded over his blue short-sleeved shirt, his white dog collar the only sign of his being a man of God, as she lifted the burned, acrid-smelling contents of the pan from the stove over to the sink.

She'd thought then about leaving him. Of packing a case and walking out. But where to? Where would she go? Her parents, while not quite believing a lowly C of E vicar to be good enough for the Honourable Sarah Sykes had, nevertheless, been grateful for Roger's taking on their wayward younger daughter and had given their blessing to the union, relieved that by moving down to Cheltenham with Roger she would be out of their hair, no longer their responsibility.

Gerald and Anne Sykes, together with Rosemary, and Roger's mother, Iris, had been in attendance at the very simple ceremony at Roger's own church in Manchester and had coughed up for the celebratory meal in an up and coming restaurant on the outskirts of nearby Cheshire afterwards. Immediately the meal was over, Roger had driven his new wife down to Cheltenham, leaving Rosemary to accompany their mother to the station and her train back to Birmingham.

For Sarah to arrive back on Gerald and Anne's doorstep, seven months pregnant and with a suitcase but no husband, would not, she knew, be greeted with any modicum of either sympathy or joy. Anyway, her parents, she suddenly remembered, as she stood, dry-eyed, crushing garlic at the kitchen unit, were away in South Africa, enjoying a two months' stay with the British High Commissioner—a friend of Anne's from her London days—in Cape Town.

She was, Sarah reflected dully, as much a prisoner here as she had been in Manchester. Perhaps once her baby was born she would be in more of a position to sort herself out, to put the baby in a nursery, to find a job to keep them both.

Over the ensuing years, with Jennifer, Jamie and then Poppy to look after, Sarah's resolve to leave grew weaker. She adored her children, couldn't countenance abandoning them as she had once abandoned those other two tiny little girls, but with each passing year of being married to Roger something in Sarah died.

Once the family moved back north to the village between Harrogate and Leeds, Roger railed daily against the lack of any further promotion while Sarah was reconciled, to some degree, with her parents.

Sometimes years would pass without incident from Roger and then, out of the blue, when her guard was down, something would provoke his anger and Sarah would find herself gripped and squeezed, her wrists twisted, her arms pulled behind her, her fingers bent back.

On only one occasion had Sarah ever retaliated. Poppy was just a tiny baby and Roger, unable to concentrate on writing his sermon because of her constant, colicky crying, had burst from his study and, grabbing Sarah's long hair, had twisted it round and round his hands until she thought she must surely be scalped. Sarah had suddenly lost it: all the unfairness of her imprisonment; the forced giving up of her little girls; the years of fear over Roger's outbursts suddenly coming to the fore in a red mist that obliterated everything except the uncontrollable rage to hit back. Once he'd let go of her hair she'd stood, trembling with fury and, bringing up her clenched right fist, hit him with such force he'd stumbled back in surprise.

'If you ever, *ever* touch me again,' she'd screamed, hitting him once again, this time with a left hook, 'I will go to the bishop... the *News of The World*... the... the Archbishop of fucking Canterbury, if necessary, and *you*, you pathetic bully will be sacked, *ex-communicated...*'

Roger, instead of hitting back as she'd expected, had slunk from the house like a whipped dog only to appear, an hour later, bearing flowers. Since then, there had been the occasional arm twisting, the Chinese-burn type attacks on her wrist that left bruises, but she dealt with it, closing her eyes and her inner self until the storm had passed, knowing that her children, her precious babies, had no knowledge whatsoever that their father behaved in such an appalling way. One day, she always promised herself, one day when the children had all finally left home, then she would go; take a boat, a plane to somewhere, anywhere she could live a simple life in a tiny cottage by herself, grow her own food, create new recipes, paint and draw and forget the past, find a new future, find her babies even…

Ben Carey pushed open the rusting gate that led through to the back garden of the rectory and watched Sarah as she reached a pale, slender arm to the last of the plums from one of the three gnarled fruit trees. She was singing to herself, swearing occasionally as she dropped a flyblown purple fruit, no idea she had an audience. God, she was beautiful, he thought wistfully, one of the most beautiful women he'd ever seen and yet she was totally unaware of her own allure.

'Hi, Sarah, I've got the stuff from Harrogate you wanted,' he called and she turned, smiling as she saw him standing there.

24

On a dreary Monday morning during the October half-term holiday, Ferguson, Harvey and Williams, the estate agents instructed by Peter's solicitors to sell the house, descended en masse with tape measures, cameras and clipboards to case the joint. At least that's how it appeared as I left Max and Allegra watching some dreadful, mind-rotting TV I wouldn't normally have allowed and went upstairs to try, once more, to prise Sophie from her bed.

'Sophie, darling, you really must get up now. The estate agents are here to measure up; you don't want them to see you in your pyjamas.'

Not a sound came from behind Sophie's closed bedroom door; nothing at all to indicate that a sixteen-year-old girl was in there.

'Sophie?' I knocked once more and went in, drawing a sharp intake of breath at the disarray, the total and utter dishevelment that met my eyes once they were accustomed to the almost blackout-darkness of the room. 'Sophie, you have to get up. I'm going to pull the curtains.'

'Sod off. It's the middle of the sodding night.' The hump in the middle of the huge king-sized bed turned, pulling the duvet to block out the weak October daylight that filtered through as I pulled up the blind and drew the curtains. A hurricane, a tornado, a tsunami even, must have passed through the room. The utter mess in Sophie's room could not, surely, have been created by one teenage girl. Half-full cups of coffee and dirty plates littered every surface—I spotted the remains of at least two meals Sophie had sneeringly rejected down in the kitchen—and drawers and cupboards trailing scarves, tops and jeans yawned wide, spewing their contents onto the makeup-smeared cream carpet. Dirty pants, miniscule thongs and the feats of engineering that were Sophie's bras hung from every available door handle or lay, scattered randomly, on the floor and the bed, while the huge trunk that had accompanied Sophie back from boarding school a week earlier remained unpacked. Bottles of foundation and nail varnish remover had lost their lids, and a dusting of bronzing powder had spread tenaciously over the top of the dressing table like a sprinkling of exotically coloured icing sugar. And over everything hung the cloyingly sweet smell of cheap perfume and stale cigarettes.

'Jesus,' I breathed, taking in every aspect of the room. 'Jesus Christ…'

'Sorry to disappoint you,' the disembodied voice rebuked from the depths of the bed, 'but it would appear the events of the last few weeks have proved beyond doubt that, like Santa, the Tooth Fairy and the Easter Bunny, the great man is yet another figment of adult imagination.'

While Sophie, I mused, might run true to teenage form with regards to her disgusting bedroom and appalling behaviour, her way with words could be amusingly adult. Maybe that's where I was going wrong in my handling of my stepdaughter; maybe I should try harder to treat her as an emerging adult rather than the recalcitrant child she so often appeared. With this in mind, I walked over to the spacious en-suite bathroom that was a feature of all the bedrooms in this fabulous house that very soon we would all have to leave.

'Jesus wept.' I jumped back in horror at the prevalence of dead insects conglomerating in the white basin at the far side of the bathroom.

'If he doesn't exist he can't weep.'

Tentatively, I walked over to get a better look.

Over the past week I—and Izzy when she was round—had watched in wonder as Sophie had, daily, added several more layers of mascara to her already sooty eyelashes until, by the end of the week, she was beginning to resemble a pantomime dame. Izzy and I had even taken bets as to how on earth she was going to remove it all without the eye-makeup remover I'd offered but which had been witheringly turned down. I now realised just *how* she'd removed a week's build-up of gunk: in and around Sophie's bathroom sink and mirror were myriad spiders' legs of mascara, painstakingly and patiently pulled off and abandoned without a care.

'Right. Enough, Sophie,' I snapped, pulling back the duvet. 'Up. Now. There are men coming up to the bedrooms very soon.'

'Oh, just up your street, Clem. *You'll* know what to do with them up here, won't you?'

My hands itched to crack her legs, and I found myself about to rise to the bait when Allegra appeared round the door.

'Mummy…'

'Oh, is that the little car? Hello, little *Audi*—oops sorry, wrong car name.'

'Cut it out, Sophie,' I snapped again, but this time seizing the duvet and, with one swift move, dragging it off the bed and behind me. 'What is it, Allegra? What's the matter?'

'It's Max, Mummy. He's crying.'

I ran down the steps with Allegra on my heels and found Max on the sitting-room floor, curled like a foetus around a large framed photograph of Vanessa, while two estate agents looked on, embarrassed.

'Darling, come on, up you get.' I had to get down on my knees and gently prise the frame from Max's hands before pulling him onto my knee. 'Shh, now, shh. I know, I know,' I crooned as Max continued to sob, great fat tears that splashed onto my jeans turning the light blue denim dark.

'Would you mind measuring up somewhere else for just a few minutes?' I asked the men. 'I'll take the children out for a walk with the dog.' I stroked Max's hair and kissed his cheek. 'Shall we do that, you two? Come on, let's grab our willies and jellies… oops.' I giggled 'Silly me… wellies and gilets, and walk down to the village and get a hot chocolate.'

If only, I thought, as the three of us, plus George, ran through the long wet grass of David Henderson's fields and down to the village café, *if only I could distract Sophie with the promise of hot chocolate as easily.*

★

'Well, if you think *I'm* going to live in a house like this, you are much mistaken,' Sophie snapped, gazing around the second double bedroom with raised eyebrows. 'Where's the en-suite?'

I'd brought the children—insisting that Sophie should come along as well—to look round a house that had come up for sale near Izzy, and which Izzy had rung to tell me about the day before. It was the last day of the half-term holiday and I still had to drive over to the nearby sixth-form college to show Sophie where she would be starting the following Monday morning, as well as buy her some bits and pieces that she'd need for her new school. I'd ended up having a couple of heated arguments with the headteachers and office staff of the two most highly rated—and nearest—high schools who had assured me, in no uncertain terms, that, as oversubscribed schools, they were full to capacity and their doors were closed to any new pupils regardless of the fact that their address might be within a stone's throw of the actual campus.

'But that's the problem, Izzy, I don't know where our address is going to be. We're only really looking round this one to get us all out of the house for a couple of hours and to get some idea of what we can afford for our money. The solicitors aren't even sure how much is going to be left. I mean, according to them, Sophie's school fees hadn't been paid for almost a year and Peter was way behind with gas and electricity—and that's just the tip of the iceberg. It's all such a mess.'

'Well, why don't you just batten down the hatches and stay put where you are for as long as you can?' Izzy asked, as she tried hard not to convey her dismay at the meanness of the rooms we were being shown round. 'Blimey, where do people actually *eat* in these houses? There's no room for a kitchen or dining table in any of these rooms. At least down on Emerald Street you had a couple of decent-sized rooms.'

'Are you suggesting we all go back down there?' I smiled. 'After all the times you tried to get me to move out?'

'Not at all, no, don't be daft. But you might be better looking at a Victorian terraced again rather than one of these ridiculous modern dolls' houses. Anyway, I wouldn't have thought a stonking great place like Peter's is going to sell straight away. Just stay put as long as you can.'

'I wish I could—at least I can lose Sophie in all of those rooms. Can you imagine having to share a house like this with her?'

'Maybe a bit more sympathy is needed, Clem?' Izzy asked gently before knocking on the kitchen window at Sid who was advancing on Allegra with what looked like a worm. 'She's had a terrible shock, poor kid. They both have.'

'Shh,' I warned as Max sidled up and put his hand in mine. 'Hello, darling, have you had a good look round? What do you think?'

'I think I'd like to stay at home please, Clem. Can we go back now?'

Much later that evening, I lay, eyes closed, on the sitting room sofa, an almost empty glass of white wine balanced on my stomach. There was nothing at all I wanted to watch on TV and I'd tried and failed to get into the new Patrick Gale—an author I normally adored. I was, I realised, absolutely shattered and I sent up a little prayer of thanks to whichever deity had seen fit to send over the mother of a prep school friend of Sophie's, picking Sophie up and taking her home with them for the night. Allegra had been fast asleep in her pink boudoir for a good hour and Max, after another bout of sobbing in bed, had finally cried himself to sleep while I held his hand and stroked his hair.

I was dozing, the wine starting to work its soothing magic on my body, and I felt the alcohol beginning to smooth out the over-crowded thoughts in my head like an iron on creased linen, calming my horribly jangled nerves, suppressing worries—old and new—that were making a futile attempt to disrupt the descending peace. I was floating away: I was in Israel, in Jerusalem, eating a peach, its sticky juice running down my chin...

I jumped, heart pounding, the ringing of the front doorbell making me instantly awake as George, who had been at my feet, sent up a volley of barks and rushed out of the room.

'Shut up, George, you'll wake the children,' I admonished as I swung my legs onto the floor, found my shoes and followed him down the hall. The insistent, strident ringing came again, louder this time, as I searched for the door key. Where the hell was it? We never usually used this entrance. I eventually found it in a silver ashtray on a nearby table and opened the heavy door on its safety chain, peering round it, but not yet able to work out who it was standing on the step, hand on the buzzer.

'Oh, Justin—I didn't recognise you. Could you stop ringing that bell? The children have only just got off to sleep.'

He raised a bottle of vodka, holding it aloft as if it were a prize. 'Thought I'd come and see you, Clem. See how you are. You know… keep you company and all that.'

Shit. That was all I needed. I'd met Justin only a few times, on the occasions I'd gone along to the re-enactments with Peter and, of course, at the funeral, but apart from that I didn't feel I really knew him at all.

'Look, Justin,' I said, still not fully opening the door, 'I'm really rather tired.'

'Come on, I've brought a bottle.'

'It's getting very late, Justin. Another time, yes?' I looked beyond Justin to the drive. 'Where's your car?'

'Had a drink… got a taxi… so are you going to invite me in?'

I really could do without this. 'You need to go home, Justin. I'll ring for a taxi for you.'

'Been to the solicitor today, Clem. We've things to discuss, you and me. The children for a start.'

'The children?' I looked at him in surprise. But then, I supposed, Sophie and Max were just as much his stepchildren as mine. 'Look, come in for a minute or two and you can tell me what the solicitor said. If it's anything about the children then I need to know, but I'm going to have to throw you out then. It's been a pretty tiring couple of weeks.' I pulled the chain and Justin almost fell through the door.

'Oh my darling, oh my darling, oh my darling Clementine,' he murmured, squinting slightly at the bright lights in the sitting room. 'I think, Clementine,' he belched slightly, 'excuse me, sweetheart—I think you and I need to support each other because we've both been widowed. At least you've been widowed... I've been *widowered*... is that the right word? Anyway we've both been left by ourselves, broke.'

'So what did the solicitor say to you about Sophie and Max?'

'Hmm? Oh, nothing much, really. I mean, they're not my kids, are they?' He picked up my empty wineglass and poured himself a good measure of the vodka, then turned to the book I'd been unable to get into. 'You're a reader? I'm a bit of a reader myself, you know...' He sat down heavily on the sofa and sank into the cushions. 'Yep, Clemmy, I'm reading a book called *Necrophilia*—it's dead boring.'

Right.

Without his black Cavalier curls, Justin appeared much smaller than I remembered. His reddish thinning hair was greased back, and waves of halitosis mixed with some powerful aftershave wafted towards me as he spoke. The waist of his expensive-looking jeans, held up with a Dolce and Gabbana leather belt I bet had cost more than the jeans itself, rested snugly on his gracile hips above the emergence of a pot-belly. Jesus, what on earth had Vanessa seen in him?

'So you've come over in a taxi at this time of night to basically tell me nothing I don't already know?' I looked at my watch. It was after nine and I was suddenly so fatigued, so drained, all I wanted to do was go to bed and sleep forever.

'Clementina, *Clem*,' Justin purred, 'I've come to see you. *You*. The minute I saw you with Peter I fancied you. You are one very *hot* lady. Come on, come on, have a drink with me. Relax.'

'Look, Justin, I don't want to appear rude, but I'm tired. I've had enough today. I'm going to call a taxi for you.'

'And leave you all alone in this big house? You don't want that, Clem.' His eyes suddenly narrowed. 'So I suppose you get all of *this*?' Justin raised an arm and swung it round, knocking Patrick Gale onto the carpet. 'Hey, not bad going, Clemmy. All of this—' he swung his arm again '—for what? Six weeks of shagging Peter Broadbent?' He pointed a bony finger at me and grinned. 'Not a bad rate at all for one of *your* lot.'

'One of my lot?' I felt as if a block of ice had shot down my spine and I was suddenly alert, no longer tired.

'You know what I mean. I know *all* about you and your sister, Clementine. *Clementine*?' He grinned. 'Bet that's not your real name, is it? What is it? Jessica? Deirdre? Samantha? Well, I shall call you Fifi. Like a poodle. Bet you like it doggy-style don't you, *Fifi*?'

Without warning, Justin launched himself from the sofa, grabbing my wrist before attempting to plant his wet, slobbering mouth on my own.

'Get off, you disgusting creature,' I yelled, shaking him away, angry more than frightened at his sudden lecherous lunge.

'You want it, you know you want it. Girls like you can't go more than a couple of weeks without it.' Justin suddenly grabbed at my right breast and shoved his hand painfully into my groin, backing me onto the opposite sofa. 'That's better, *Fifi*,' he panted as I lost my balance, falling against the cushions. 'That's it. Now then, what's the going rate, these days? A tenner for a hand job? How about a blow job? Twenty quid?' Flecks of spittle landed on my cheek as he pulled at the Dolce and Gabbana belt and attempted to unzip his jeans. Frightened now, I desperately tried to push him off.

'Get off, get *off*,' I said furiously, trying not to raise my voice. The last thing I wanted was Max and Allegra coming down and being scared. 'George, George,' I hissed. Where was the damned dog when I needed him?

'Never mind *George*,' Justin breathed heavily. 'I'll have you shouting, "*Justin, Justin*" in just two minutes. 'Oh yes, *Fifi*, let's do it...'

The next second, three things happened almost simultaneously: George, thinking there was a jolly party going on to which he'd not been invited, launched himself on top of Justin. Caught off guard, Justin fell off the sofa, his jeans and pants slipping down around his skinny backside, scant ginger pubic hair and flaccid penis on view to anyone unfortunate to catch sight.

And David Henderson walked into the sitting room.

All four of us—George included—froze for a second, and then David grabbed Justin's shirt, dragging him up from the floor, twisting the collar round his throat.

'What the fuck do you think you're doing?' David said, shoving him up against the wall, seemingly oblivious to Justin's boxers and trousers now around his ankles.

'And who the fuck do you think *you* are?' Justin managed to gasp out of the side of his mouth. 'Barging in here like... like Kevin Costner...'

Kevin Costner?

David paused in his manhandling of Justin and glanced across at me. I could see it suddenly dawned on him that maybe I'd been fully cooperating in Justin's attentions.

That when he'd knocked on the kitchen French window, when he'd realised it was unlocked and been able to let himself into the kitchen and heard me shouting, 'Get off,' I might have actually been shouting at the dog to get off the pair of us so we could carry on with what we were doing unhindered.

'Oh, David, thank God. I'm not sure how you got in… and it's…' I glanced at the wall clock 'Almost ten…' I couldn't say anything else. I tried to stand up, pull myself off the sofa, but I suddenly felt terribly sick and had to sit down again, putting my head between her knees. I felt wobbly, a bit like having low blood sugar when you've done too much and forgotten to eat. 'Just get him out of here, David, would you?'

'Clementine, he's assaulted you…' David grabbed hold of Justin again, shaking him like a dog. 'For fuck's sake, you little weasel, get your trousers up.'

'That's just what I was trying to do before you pushed me against the wall. If you don't mind…' With whatever dignity he could muster, Justin turned away from David and zipped himself up.

'You need to ring the police, Clem.'

'The police? The police?' Justin blustered, like a politician cornered on *Question Time*. 'What on earth for? I came round here tonight to offer a little comfort to my dear widowed friend and the next minute you're assaulting me. Who the hell are *you* anyway, letting yourself into this poor lady's house uninvited?'

'I'm David Henderson.'

'Yeah, yeah,' Justin sneered drunkenly 'And I'm… I'm Prince Rupert.'

'Ring the police, Clem,' David said calmly. 'We'll have him arrested for sexual assault and attempted rape.'

'No, no, please no,' I said, attempting to lift my head. 'I'm fine, David, really. This is Justin, Vanessa's husband.'

'Absolutely,' Justin said, confident now. 'I'm *family*.' He wagged a finger at me. 'And don't tell me you didn't want it. You were *gagging* for it. It's what you're used to. And now that all *this* has probably got to go—' he waved a hand dismissively around the room '—you'll be back on the streets with your sister. Tell you what, *Fifi*, I'll see you down on Emerald Street in a month or so. You'll be opening your legs for me then…'

David launched himself on Justin, shoving him out of the sitting room door, down the hall and out the way he'd entered only twenty minutes earlier.

'You're no family of mine,' I managed to shout after him, getting up from my seat. 'Get out of here, you snivelling little rat and don't ever, ever, ever have anything to do with me or my family again. And that means Sophie and Max. Keep your disgusting hands off them too.'

'I *am* actually going to report this to the police, Clementine,' David said, brushing himself down and running his fingers through his thick dark hair as he came back to join me in the sitting room. 'I'll call in at the station in the morning. Let me have his name and address and they'll send someone round. Frighten him, at least, if you won't take it further.' He frowned. 'What the hell was all that about Kevin Costner and Prince Rupert?'

'Dunno about Kevin, unless he thought you were my bodyguard.' I smiled weakly, stroking George's silky ears, feeling suddenly shy. 'But he actually *is* Prince Rupert…'

'Huh? Here, drink this, for the shock.' David had poured us both a brandy from Peter's drinks cabinet and I sipped mine gratefully, while he downed his in one.

'He's one of Peter's re-enactment lot. That's where Vanessa met him and ran off with him. What in God's name did she see in him?'

'Are you OK, Clementine?' David made to take my hand, but then seemed to think better of it. 'While I can't believe you left the kitchen French windows unlocked, thank goodness that you did.'

'I'd have been able to kick him off,' I said. 'He was so pissed. I just didn't want to start yelling and waking the kids. Max has had enough to deal with without seeing his stepfather with his pants down.'

David carefully placed his empty glass on the table next to him, leaned over to pick Patrick Gale from the floor and then turned to me, this time actually taking my hand.

'Clementine, this wasn't a social call, as such, tonight. I should probably have left it until the morning, but once I've made a decision about something, I need to get on with it straight away. I just had to come over and talk to you as soon as possible.'

I stared at him, heart thumping. God, he was gorgeous.

'I've a proposal for you, Clementine…'

25

'You're going to do what?' I looked at David Henderson in astonishment.

'If I can get it at the right price, I'm going to buy it.' David smiled at my obviously stunned face. While I hadn't been sure what his 'proposal' was going to consist of, the last thing I'd anticipated was that he was thinking of buying Peter's house. I actually felt a pang of disappointment; a tiny part of me had hoped he was going to tell me he'd fallen totally and utterly in love with me and he just *had* to leave Mandy and whisk me off to some far distant land with Allegra, Max and George where we would all live happily ever after. What was going to happen to poor old Sophie, I hadn't really thought through in the five-second timeslot between David telling me he needed to talk to me and then my being told he was thinking of buying Peter's house.

'But why? Your house, I'm sure, is just as wonderful as this one? Why on earth do you want to move across the fields? Oh, is it the tennis court? Are you a tennis player?'

'Clem, will you just shut up for two minutes?' David grinned again. 'And let me tell you my proposal?'

Oh God, here we go again, I suddenly thought. I could see it all now. David Henderson was another one apparently in the know about my past. Obviously thought that I was a prostitute like Lucy. Why else would I have been living on Emerald Street? Have married Peter? So what was *this* one proposing? Turning the house into a brothel or just setting me up as his mistress? Bit stupid, that, five hundred yards from his Mandy in his own backyard

I suddenly saw red. 'So who told you?' I demanded angrily. 'Peter? He seems to have let it slip to every other man around here. Or was it Harriet and Grace who thought it shockingly amusing to tell you and Mandy?' I knocked back the huge glass of brandy I'd previously been only sipping at, coughing as it went down the wrong way. God, the brandy really had missed its mark. Spluttering, my eyes streaming, I began to cough in earnest, unable to catch my breath. 'Don't suppose it will be long before Oliver Cromwell... comes a-knocking...'

'Are you all right?' David jumped up from the sofa and started to slap me on the back, but I knocked his hand away in fury and started singing that old country and western song about the path being well worn from men's footsteps leading to somebody or other's cabin.

I managed to sing the words I could remember through bouts of wheezing and spluttering and then, turning to David, I said, 'I say "no", *Mr* Henderson. "No" to your damned proposal.'

David looked at me in astonishment. 'But you don't know what it is yet, Clementine.'

'I've got a jolly good idea, *Mr* Henderson,' I interrupted him. Jesus, I was beginning to feel a bit strange again. 'I need to sit down, I feel a bit sick again...'

David grabbed me as I started to sway and pushed me back down to the sofa, shoving my head between my knees.

I felt him stroke my hair and then, as the nausea passed and I began to lift my head, he stood up and left the room, coming back a minute later with a glass of water.

'Here, drink this,' he commanded. 'Now,' he went on as I drank the water and placed the glass on the floor, 'what the hell was all that about? Why in God's name did you suddenly start singing? If you can call that wheezing and coughing actually *singing*...?'

'So who told you about Lucy? And where I was born?' I felt almost calm now and looked at David with some defiance.

'Lucy? Lucy who? And I've no idea where you were born... I assume somewhere around here? Is it important in the general scheme of things?'

'OK,' I said, wearily. 'Tell me your plan. Tell me your *proposal*.'

'I'm not sure I want to now. Probably a silly plan anyway.'

'Oh, don't sulk. Don't take your bat home.'

'I can assure you, Clementine, I never sulk.'

'OK, OK, hit me with the big proposal. So, you're going to buy this house? For what purpose? Hm? Hmmm?'

David looked at me with raised eyebrows. 'So that between us, you and I can turn it into the most amazing restaurant-cum-cookery-school-cum-extremely-expensive-retreat-cum-wedding-venue-cum... whatever else we think will make us lots of money...'

'Sorry?' My head shot up and I stared at David.

'Do you want me to repeat all that? OK. So that between us, you and I can turn it—'

'Sorry, sorry, I heard you the first time.' I continued to stare at David, at his handsome tanned face: his genuinely kind, *lovely* face. 'Oh my God. I thought, I thought…'

David was truly puzzled. 'What? What did you think?'

'I thought you…' I took a deep breath. 'I thought you were trying to set me up as some sort of madam in a brothel. Or… or…' I knew I had to tell him the truth. 'Because you'd found out that my sister is a prostitute, you thought *I* was too and were trying to set me up as your mistress, your whore even.' I felt myself go scarlet with embarrassment.

David looked at me, eyes wide in astonishment, and then threw back his head and roared with laughter. 'Clem, this is the twenty-first century. Does anyone set oneself up with a mistress these days? You've been reading too many Mills and Boon romances.' He laughed again and then took my hand. 'Clem, I didn't know your sister was a prostitute.'

'She's not just my sister. She's my identical twin.'

'OK, I didn't know your identical twin is a sex worker— it makes absolutely no difference to me what your family is. I just know that you have a gift for creating the most delicious, original food and this is one of the most beautiful houses in Midhope. Put the two together and I have every intention of turning them both into an extremely lucrative business.' He paused for a second. 'Ah, now I see what all that was about tonight with Vanessa's husband. And then I come along with *my* proposal… I can see what you must have been thinking.'

I giggled. 'Oh shit, and then I started singing "Hickory

Holler'sTramp" in your face. You must have thought I'd gone mad.'

'Well, I did wonder. Assumed you were still in shock from that nasty little weasel's performance. So, tell me about Lucy. Where is she? Why aren't you helping her to get off the streets? Presumably she *wants* to get off them?'

'It's a bit complicated, David.' I hesitated. 'I've had to put her out of my mind for a while what with marrying Peter and everything. Harriet and Grace know the whole story. Well, almost. Anyway, they're going to help me to find her and… she's a heroin addict, you see… it's a bit like trying to help an alcoholic. You have to *want* to be helped. So, now you know that Lucy is out there and that I need to spend time trying to find her, to help her if I can, do you want to abandon this plan?'

David frowned. 'No, of course not. But, Clem, this *will* be a lot of hard work. Do you want to think about it?'

'Well, obviously I need to know what you have in mind. I mean, will the kids and I still be able to live here?'

'Of course, yes. Absolutely. This is your and their home. Look, Clementine, I don't take on any project I don't think will be a success.'

'Golly, you should be on *Dragons' Den*.'

'They did ask, but I turned them down—can't stand that Peter Jones fellow. So, what I envisage is that my company will buy the house, and Peter's estate can be settled with that money—'

'You know all about that then? That Peter gambled most of it away?'

'I've known about Peter's, erm, shall we say, *little problem*, for years.'

'Years?' I was shocked. 'I thought it was all fairly recent.'

'Oh, I don't know the whole ins and outs of what Peter was up to, but I was very concerned about your getting yourself mixed up in the whole mess. I wasn't at all certain what future there was actually going to be for you and Allegra with Peter.'

'That's why you told me to be careful? The night of our dinner party after Peter proposed so publicly?'

'Yes. I think, Clementine, that had he lived, Peter would have ended up in prison. I think he knew that too.'

I felt tears well. 'He wasn't a bad man, you know, David. I think he wanted to try and get Vanessa back, but that involved making a lot more money than he was doing. Probably things just got out of hand and then…'

'And then he met you and fell in love with you. He did, you know. He really loved you. I think he probably thought you were like Vanessa and needed the designer cars and handbags to stay with him.'

'Well, they didn't keep Vanessa, did they? She left anyway.'

David smiled. 'From what I know of Vanessa she would have assumed she would end up with half, or more than half, of everything that Peter owned when she left him. Even *half* of what she thought he had would have kept her happy over the next few years. That Justin fellow obviously jumped on the gravy train, and imagined he'd have a life of luxury with an extremely rich man's ex-wife.'

I was mortified. 'Put like that, I'm no better than Justin…' I hesitated. 'I didn't love Peter, David.'

'I know,' he said gently. 'I know that. But you *do* love your little girl. I'm sure she was the big reason for your accepting his proposal?'

'I really wanted it to work, David. And it was doing, it really was. Allegra and I were actually really settling in here. We had a ready-made family and for the first time in years I was beginning to feel safe.'

'Safe?'

'Yes. I know that sounds a bit melodramatic. You see—you may as well know my whole past—Lucy and I were adopted.'

David raised his eyebrows but said nothing.

'We were born to a violent drug smuggler. We were born in the women's prison near Manchester. This woman—our *mother*—obviously didn't want us and basically gave us away. When you don't really know who you are, when you see your identical twin totally going off the rails, become a drug addict, you really begin to wonder which gene pool you've sprung from. And with Peter I actually did feel safe. Not that it lasted very long,' I added wryly, and David squeezed my hand.

'Well, I see no reason why you and Allegra shouldn't continue to feel safe again here. And Max, of course. Poor little chap. He'll be delighted to stay, won't he?'

'But David, I'm not sure I can do all this.' I suddenly felt panicky at the thought of being given so much responsibility by the notoriously ball-breaking David Henderson. 'What if it doesn't work? What if no one wants to come to a cookery school? There must be hundreds of restaurants going under on a daily basis.'

'You sound just like Harriet Westmoreland did when Nick and I started L'uomo—and I fully understand your fears. But you have to remember I have really good financial advisors and I will be just over the field. I'm getting a bit fed up swanning all over the world with Nick. It will be great to walk to work occasionally instead of flying off to Milan and China so much.'

'But I'm really not sure I'm the best person for the job. I've never done anything like this.'

'Haven't you just completed your degree in hotel management?' David asked patiently.

'Well, yes…'

'And you've learned about, what? Finance? Managing employees? Health and Safety?'

'Well, yes, I suppose so.'

'So what's the problem? I'm hoping that most of the time you will be cooking and showing people *how* to cook. A fabulously expensive place to come and learn from a superb master.' His eyes gleamed at the prospect and I began to feel his excitement. 'OK, put it this way,' he went on. 'Let's say you and I had never met. Let's say you saw an advert in *The Telegraph* or *The Times* or even the local paper advertising this job. To be part of an exciting, innovative new business backed by me, and my company, where you would do lots of cooking, some teaching, some management. Where basically you would be in charge of the whole kit and caboodle. Would you apply?'

I swallowed, terrified at the very thought. 'Well, no, I'd have had no experience and… I'd be shit scared of you.'

'Of me?'

'Well, you do have a bit of a reputation.'

'All unfounded as you now know.'

'Well, all right then, yes, obviously. It would be a *dream* job.'

'So there you go. The job's yours and you don't even

have to fill in an application form or send me your CV.' He grinned. 'I think I've found out more about you this evening then I ever needed to know.'

'Why are you doing this, David?'

'Believe me, Clem, I don't take on any new project that doesn't have an extremely good chance of succeeding. L'uomo, Nick's business, went through the roof in an extremely short time. Now, I know the food and catering business is a totally different ball game and I certainly don't expect the same miraculous profits that Nick and I achieved and so quickly. And I'm certainly not doing this out of some sort of sense of altruism. I can be a horror to work with, as well—ask Harriet—but I believe in you. I really think we might have something here.'

'Oh gosh, David, you make it all sound so easy.' I paused and then, excited at the prospect, asked, 'So where do we go from here?'

'Well, now I have you on my side—and you seem to be coming round to the idea—tomorrow my company will put in an offer on this place. I'm hoping I can negotiate directly with the solicitors and creditors before the estate agents actually take it on. So, first job is to actually get hold of the house before someone else does.'

'And then?'

'And then a lot of discussion about what exactly our USP will be.'

'Our USP...?'

'Unique selling point. We need to create something innovative that people will try to copy but won't succeed in being as good as the original.'

'A bit like Uggs you mean?'

'Exactly like Uggs: expensive, does the job, everyone wants the original...' David smiled at my allegory. 'People will boast that they've been here before their friends. They will have to book weeks ahead. So what do you think, Clem?'

'Me?'

'Yes, *you*, Clem. This place is going to revolve around you and your wonderful food.'

Excited now, I said, 'I've always loved the idea of an evening where twenty or so single people, who've never met before, gather around the kitchen unit to watch a cookery demonstration of romantic food—strawberries, champagne cocktails etc—and then they sit and eat it as they get to know each other. A sort of *Blind Date* meets *MasterChef*.'

'Brilliant. And we charge them a fortune to do it. Mums, desperate to get their single thirty-somethings married off, will buy gift vouchers for Christmas...'

'And then fabulous afternoon teas like at Betty's or The Ritz even.'

'Aim high, Clementine, aim high,' David grinned.

'And... and... cooking courses for high-flying executives who can run big businesses but can't boil an egg...'

'I'm first on that list.' David was laughing now. 'How about tiny, upmarket weddings? I know there isn't the space for hundreds of guests, but for those who just want a place to get married with ten, maybe twenty guests at the most?' He frowned. 'The orangery could seat four or five tables, do you think? And we could always put up a marquee.'

'There's the lodge house that some housekeeper of Peter's used to live in years ago. Ooh, and the summerhouse in the Secret Garden. They would be perfect for a romantic hideaway for a newly married couple or for any couple come to that. And this house and grounds would be *perfect* for a writers' retreat. There are actually bedrooms above the stables you know, where the grooms used to sleep. We could do something with those—kit them out with writing tables. What bliss for a writer trying to finish their novel: a beautiful en-suite bedroom with writing table; the tennis court when they need a break; fabulous meals to help their creative thought flow…'

'I think I might start writing a book,' David said seriously, and then smiled. 'Well, it's got you thinking anyway, Clementine. We would have to form a new limited company and employ staff. I can think of someone already who I think would love to be part of this.'

'Oh?'

'I mean, I might be totally wrong and I certainly haven't approached her yet. In fact, it's only just come to me…'

'Grace?'

David grinned. 'Exactly. She is so creative, she would be perfect being part of Clementine's.'

'Clementine's?' I actually felt my jaw drop.

'Of course, you daft thing. What else would your new enterprise be called?'

Much later, when I'd checked on the children, ensured all the doors were locked and tried, but failed, to sleep, I got out of bed and went back downstairs for hot milk and Patrick Gale. As I turned to go back up the stairs, the phone rang.

'Clementine?'

I didn't recognise the voice and stood there, frowning, thinking, *dear God, not Justin again.* 'Yes?'

'Clementine, my dear, I know it's rather late, but I happen to be in your area…'

'Yes?'

'I thought I could pop in and see you, m'dear… see if I can offer you some company for ten minutes. See how you're bearing up?'

'Who is this?' I sort of recognised the rather oily voice but still couldn't put a name to it.

'It's Neville, dear.'

'Neville…?'

'Neville Manning… *Oliver* to you.'

'Oh. Oliver. Oliver Cromwell?'

'Absolutely. Are you free for a little drink, dear? I can be with you in five minutes.'

I took a deep breath. 'Mr Cromwell, I think you'll find, like Christmas that you so happily cancelled, I too am cancelled: not available, off limits. Goodnight, Olly, and may your *Roundhead* wilt and perish!'

And with that, I carefully replaced the receiver, smiled at myself in the huge, sitting room mirror and went back to bed with Patrick Gale.

26

'You're doing what?' Sophie shouted, her face within inches of my own. 'You're turning dad's house—*my* house—into a... a café? Well, you can sodding well forget that right now. There's no way that I'm going to let you do that. This is mine and Max's house, not yours.'

'Look, Sophie—'

'No, *you* look. In fact, why don't *you* and...and little Austin... little Audi just fuck off back down to Emerald Street where you belong and leave us to it? I'm sixteen—old enough to look after myself. And Max too. He's my responsibility, not yours.'

'You're being ridiculous, Sophie.'

'*I'm* being ridiculous?' Sophie yelled. 'Me? It's not *me* that wants to turn our beautiful home into a stupid hotel.' She glared at me and then laughed nastily. 'And I suppose *you'll* be in charge of *extras*?'

I knew exactly where she was going with this one, but as calmly as I could—difficult when I wanted to slap her—looked her in the eye and asked, 'Extras, Sophie? As in?'

'As in once they've eaten, you'll take them upstairs for a… for a good seeing-to.'

'Erm, no, Sophie, extras won't be a part of Clementine's,' I said mildly. If the whole situation hadn't been so unpleasant I might have been tempted to laugh at her vernacular. 'It will be wonderful food, fine dining, upmarket cookery courses—as well as a hell of a lot of hard work.'

'You're not doing this, Clementine, you're *not*.'

I looked at Sophie's angry face, at her greasy blonde hair, her spots and fingernails bitten down almost to the quick and, despite the fury and disdain she was throwing out at me daily, felt a wave of pity for her. She was a little girl who'd lost her mum and dad and now her home was being turned upside down around her.

'Look, Sophie, I know you're missing your friends at your old school and don't want to be here—with me—at the moment. Shall I see if I can persuade your dad's solicitors to release any money there might be available from the estate which would let you go back to school there rather than starting sixth-form college—at least until the end of the academic year?'

'Oh, you'd like that, wouldn't you? Get me out of your way so you can take over Dad's house properly?'

'I was thinking of you, Sophie. What *you* would like.'

'And you seriously think that going back to that damned boarding school is what I would like? God, you have no idea. I *hated* the place. Hated the girls, all with their GHD-straightened long hair and their constant texting and their not eating…'

I was stunned; I thought she'd loved being away at school, couldn't wait to get back there. 'I'm sorry, Sophie. I thought school was the one place you were happy. And what do you mean "their not eating"?'

'What do you think I mean?' Sophie looked at me as if I were a halfwit. 'If you aren't a size four, and aiming for size zero, you're nothing there.' She pulled at the puppy fat around her middle. 'This—or rather the lack of this— is what you're judged on at school. If you're seen to be actually enjoying the scrambled eggs and toast at breakfast or the shepherd's pie at supper you're looked upon as some sort of food pervert.'

I actually laughed at that. 'A pervert? Oh, don't be silly, Sophie. Surely not…?'

She gave me such a look of contempt I immediately felt ashamed at my laughing at her. Here she was opening up to me—if only just a tiny bit—and I'd not taken her seriously. Had actually laughed at her.

'OK, well the place at Midhope sixth-form college is there for you, but you're going to actually have to start there this week or they'll withdraw the offer. They're over halfway into the new term now and we've been amazingly lucky to have been given a place at such a good college. If you don't turn up pretty soon you'll be too far behind with your work.'

Sophie looked up from where she was picking what was left of the black nail varnish from her chewed nails. 'I'm not going to *any* school. I'm sixteen; I don't have to go back. I'll get a job and a flat and Max and I can live there.'

'I think the law's changed, Sophie. I think you're supposed to be in some sort of education or training now until you're eighteen. Anyway, it's not what your mum or dad would have wanted.'

'And how do *you* know what *my* mum and dad would have wanted? You must have met my mum—what? Two or three times at the most? And been married to my dad for all of six weeks? You knew sod all about them... or about me.' She got up from the table, kicked the chair she'd been sitting on back into place and stalked to the hall door. Before she slammed it—with what must have been to her ears a most satisfactory crash—she turned back to me. 'You are not turning my house into a bloody hotel, Clementine. You are *not*.'

The next couple of days while David, the estate solicitors and I had meeting after meeting after meeting, I saw little of Sophie. Every morning I knocked on her bedroom door, tried to get her out of bed and to college and was met by a torrent of abuse, foul language and an absolute refusal to get out of her pit. Once I'd driven Max over to his little private school—I was working on Mrs Theobold for a place at Westenbury C of E for him from next September— and accompanied Allegra into her classroom, I'd try once more to reason with Sophie: to coax, to bribe and finally, in desperation, to manhandle her out of bed and into the shower and college but to no avail.

She wouldn't eat with us but, once we were all in bed, I'd hear her moving around in the kitchen opening the fridge and cupboards. On the couple of occasions I went down to her, to offer her a sandwich or the remains of supper, she said she wasn't hungry, but the next morning I'd notice food was gone.

My days were so full with plans for Clementine's I was unable to monitor exactly what she was up to. She didn't go out at all, not even into the garden with George for a breath of fresh air. She appeared to be losing weight, she slept a good deal and would make no decision about college despite my telling her their admin department had rung several times wanting to know if she was accepting the place they'd found for her.

And then she started throwing up. Because she had an en-suite I wasn't aware to begin with that she was being sick. It was only on one of my sojourns to her room—of which I was making at least four or five a day—to cajole her out, I saw that she wasn't there but was being violently sick in her bathroom.

'Sophie, let me help me you, sweetheart,' I pleaded, shocked at her wan appearance as she made her way back to bed and pulled the covers over her head.

'I'm fine. Go away. It's something I've eaten.'

'But you've not eaten anything for days.'

'Just sod off and leave me alone.'

Over the next twenty-four hours I hovered constantly outside her room, hearing her vomiting over and over again, or went in with glasses of water and dry toast only to be rebuffed and told to go away.

I rang Izzy.

'God, Clem, do you know what time it is? I was asleep. What's up?'

'It's Sophie. I'm so worried about her. She won't come

out of her room, she's not eating and she's been vomiting for the last couple of days.'

'Right, erm, let me think. OK, go into her room and smell her breath.'

'Her breath?'

'Yes.'

'What am I looking for?'

'You're not *looking* for anything. You're *sniffing*. I want to know if there's a smell of alcohol—could be she's drinking and can't handle it. Or pear drops.'

'Pear drops? As in Yorkshire Mixtures? You think she's been eating too many sweets?'

Izzy tutted down the phone. 'As in acetone smell. You know—nail varnish. If she's anorexic and deliberately throwing up, then her body has nothing to burn and will start eating away at itself. This gives off ketones which smell like acetone…'

'I'll ring you back.'

I went across the landing and back into her room. She was asleep on her side, breathing softly. I went across and had a good sniff. Nothing. God, this was ridiculous. I lay down on the bed beside her and took a deep breath at the same time as her eyes shot open and she jumped in terror at seeing my face right up against her own.

'Jesus, what are you doing? In my bed? Next to me? You weirdo…'

As she spoke, I was hit by a rush of breath so foul I immediately drew back.

'Sophie, I'm on the phone to Izzy. We're worried about you—we need to know what's wrong.'

Sophie looked at me for a couple of seconds before

rushing to the bathroom and vomiting once again. I held back her hair from her hot face as she retched and then ran a glass of water for her. She didn't push me away, but drank the water, wiped her mouth and then went back to bed.

I rang Izzy back. 'No nail varnish smell, no alcohol smell, but really bad breath...'

'Any possibility she's pregnant?'

'Pregnant? No, surely not...'

'OK, the bad breath could be a giveaway for...' I turned away from the phone as Sophie came into my bedroom.

'Clementine, it hurts, it hurts so bad. I can't bear it.' Sophie was doubled over, her face grey.

'Where's the pain, Clem? Ask her where it hurts.' Izzy was calm on the other end of the phone.

'Where, Sophie? Show me, darling. Izzy, it's her tummy and terrible pain in her right side.'

'OK, sounds like acute appendicitis. Foul breath is a typical symptom alongside the vomiting and pain in the right side. I'll get her an ambulance and then I'm on my way. I'll stay with Allegra and Max while you go to A&E with her.'

While Izzy set the ball rolling with regards to accurately diagnosing and getting Sophie into hospital, it was Mel who came over to relieve Izzy and stayed the night with Max and Allegra while I remained at the hospital with Sophie. Within an amazingly short time of her arrival, Sophie was having her appendix—on the point of bursting, according to the surgeon—removed, and by the early hours of the next morning she was back on the ward in a hospital issue gown, her face, leeched of any colour, chameleon-like on the starched white pillow.

While she slept I sat at her side and when she woke, knowing once again that her parents were dead and there was no mum or dad to hold her hand, she cried silently, huge tears rolling down her pale face and onto the bed's light blue coverlet. I realised I was crying too—for Peter and Max and now for Sophie—and I reached for her hand and held it firmly, hoping she'd realise without my telling her that I was there for her. And that I understood.

27

'My God, if everything else is going to be as good as this—' Izzy bit into the feather-light sponge, the thick cream shooting onto her chin '—then you will have customers knocking down the door to get in.'

Nodding in agreement, Grace reached for a beautifully starched snowy-white linen napkin to wipe the butter dripping from a miniature crumpet from her fingers but then thought better of it and, instead, found a tissue in her pocket. 'I don't want to spoil these napkins, Clem. A lot of work has gone into them.'

'Your work, Grace.' I smiled. 'They must have taken ages to starch and iron.'

'Totally worth it if I'm rewarded with afternoon tea like this.'

'What do you think so far?' I'd asked the four women over to give me their total and honest opinion about what I'd created and I stood there slightly nervous, holding my breath a bit like a child waiting for a teacher to tell them if their work was any good.

'*De-licious*,' Harriet sighed theatrically, looking round for the next taster.

It had taken over eight months' hard work to get to where we were now and, as the main chap from the local planning department had told me, if David Henderson hadn't been behind it, the whole project would have taken much, much longer, if it had been allowed to go ahead at all. The house had seen a continual procession of surveyors, architects, developers, conservation officers, tree people, joiners, decorators and men from the country lanes' department. 'There's actually a department for country lanes?' I'd asked in astonishment as the gang had descended with their clipboards and calculators, infuriating local commuters trying to manoeuvre their four-wheel-drives past them on their commute to Midhope train station, as well as local farmers trundling along in ancient, rusty tractors.

David had never let up for one minute, tearing strips off people who he thought tardy or incompetent, even exploding at one poor professional, 'Call yourself a surveyor, man? Good God, you couldn't survey the bloody *wondrous cross*,' which had made me giggle and sing Easter hymns for the rest of that morning. The whole project had, really frustratingly, come to a sudden standstill for several weeks when bats were discovered in the stable block and Batman had said they weren't to be disturbed, but had to be tempted out with their own personal bat boxes.

The week before Clementine's had its official opening, I'd asked Izzy, Grace, Harriet and Mel round to try out what I was going to give to the guests who had been invited.

David Henderson's business associates would mingle with the invited press, local dignitaries, wedding party planners and the owners and growers of locally sourced fruit and vegetables, and I knew everything had to be more than first rate. So, after feeding my critical judges six different canapés, I was now handing round plates of tiny, subtly flavoured pastel macaroons, finger sandwiches, delicate, crumbly scones oozing homemade blackberry jam and cream.

'Hope this jam wasn't made from Rafe Ahern's blackberries?' Mel asked, as she tasted the delicious preserve.

'It was, actually,' I admitted, laughing. 'The day I threw the bag of blackberries at him I was so cross with myself for wasting good fruit, I went straight back out with Max and Allegra and we picked loads more. The field over there—' I indicated with a nod of my head '—belongs to him and we just nipped out at dusk and helped ourselves. They'd only have gone to waste otherwise.'

'I've not met this Ahern chap,' Mel said, helping herself to a finger of shortbread. 'What's he like?'

'Well, you will, now that you're going to be working here.' I pulled a face, thinking of the occasions I'd had the pleasure of meeting my bad-tempered neighbour. 'He's not at all happy that we've turned this place into... let me think, what were his words, "a sodding circus, for people with more sense than money, in the middle of my land."'

'He's actually rather gorgeous,' Izzy said. 'In a Heathcliffe sort of way, I mean. If I wasn't a happily married woman I'd probably have a crack at him.'

'Well, you'd have to kick JoJo Kennedy out of bed first,' Grace smiled, and then started laughing at Izzy's crestfallen face.

'*The* JoJo Kennedy? Rafe Ahern is with JoJo Kennedy? Oh bloody hell, sod the diet then. Pass me one of those scones, Mel.'

'I didn't know that, Grace,' I said, really astonished. 'Are you sure? What on earth would a beautiful supermodel like JoJo Kennedy see in a bad-tempered bloke like Rafe Ahern?'

Grace laughed again. 'Absolutely sure. They've been together for six months at least. Apparently they met at some charity do for children caught up in the Middle East conflicts. Annabelle Ahern—you know she was a model herself back in the Sixties—told my mum all about it. Annabelle's delighted; she's hoping JoJo will persuade Rafe to go and live in London permanently and get him out of *her* hair. Mum says he's always nagging Annabelle about how much she spends and drinks and parties. Rafe ends up footing the bill for it all.'

'Annabelle's great fun, isn't she?' I said, remembering the afternoon I'd spent over at her place. 'When I'd murdered her hen, I actually went round to apologise. She just poured me a huge drink, told me not to worry and then gave me the lowdown on all the local gossip and showed me photographs of her and Mick Jagger and Jean Shrimpton in the Sixties. She was incredibly beautiful then.'

'She still is, don't you think? I'd heard M&S were after her to model their old-lady stuff.'

'I can't see her wanting to do that. When I went round she was wearing a mini dress and long white patent boots. Fab pair of pins on her still…'

'I'm really envious of Grace and Mel working here with you, Clem,' Harriet interrupted. 'Can't I have a job too?'

'Harriet, you have five children to look after,' Grace tutted. 'How the hell can you work as well?'

'Well, *you* have Jonty,' Harriet said. 'And I'm down to *four* kids now that Libby is away at university. *And* I have Lilian to help with the twins.'

'Harriet, I'm only doing two days,' Grace said.

'Suppose so.'

I suddenly felt a bit sorry for Harriet. 'I'm sure there'll be something for you here eventually, once we get going, if you really want a little job, Hat,' I said.

'Brilliant.' Harriet cheered up. 'I was just feeling a bit left out.'

'How fantastic is all this for me?' Mel asked, collecting up the dirty plates and napkins. 'To be honest, I wasn't really happy to come back up north after ten years in Essex. I know I said I was, but Julian and I always thought we'd end up with a B&B in the Cotswolds, not in Yorkshire. And I really didn't want to leave my job. Not having kids like you lot, I certainly didn't want to be at home all day twiddling my thumbs.'

'Mel immediately came to mind when David and I were initially discussing what staff we'd need,' I explained to the others as I offered a tray of minute pistachio triple-chocolate brownies. 'I knew she'd had to leave her job as a personal assistant and wasn't happy about it.' I smiled across at Mel. 'I can't tell you how good she's been at the paperwork, at organising all the work people so that I've been able to get on with planning menus and cooking and deciding the different type of events we're going to hold here.

'God, Clem, please don't bring out any more food,' Izzy said, frowning. 'If I'm now in competition with JoJo Kennedy, for heaven's sake, I'm going to have to start watching what I eat.' She eyed up a miniature cheesecake left on a slate serving plate. 'Is that lemon, Clem? Yes? Brilliant, lemons aren't fattening—and such a shame to leave it by itself.' She polished it off in one before looking at her watch. 'Going to have to make a move, girlies. Afternoon surgery starts at three, I'm afraid. Now, before I go, we did say, Clem, that once you'd sorted out this place we'd have a night out in Leeds. In the red-light area? See if we can persuade Lucy to make contact with you?'

'Izzy,' I said, frowning, 'this place is not exactly *sorted*, is it? This is only the beginning.'

'I know, I know. But I know *you* as well, Clem. I know you want to find out exactly where Lucy is. See if she's OK? We'll all come with you, make some enquiries on the streets, go back to the gay bar where she was dancing…'

I didn't want to talk about this. 'You're making it sound as if it's a girls' night out you're planning. You know, take a charabanc and go and stand in Chapeltown in our best going-out clothes; goggling the prossies, seeing how the other half live.'

'That's not fair, Clem,' Izzy said, offended. 'We want to help you find her; the last piece in the jigsaw as it were. She'd be able to stay here with you, get off the heroin, maybe work with you.'

'It really isn't as simple as all that. Jesus, who's that banging on the door?' I shot up from the table, scattering brownies as I went, happy to end that particular conversation.

'Who the hell's left that damned great car on the lane so that no one can get past?' Rafe Ahern nodded down the drive to where the roof of a rather battered green Range

Rover could just be seen poking through the hedge at the bottom of the drive.

'Ah, Mr Ahern.' Izzy smiled, extending a hand as she joined me on the doorstep. 'I've heard so much about you. Very pleased to meet you. How's JoJo? Still wooing the catwalk?'

'Is it yours?' Rafe snapped, ignoring Izzy's outstretched hand. 'What gives you the right to park there, blocking the road so no one can get past?'

'Oh, come on,' Izzy said, rebuffed. 'You'd have to be driving a damned great tractor not to be able to get past...'

He gave Izzy a particularly sardonic look before indicating, with a nod of his head, the ancient bright red tractor that was parked behind Izzy's car, its engine rumbling and spluttering like a bad tempered drunk. 'I knew this would happen, er...' Rafe Ahern was obviously racking his brains, trying to recall my name, if he'd ever known it in the first place. 'Er, once you started on this ridiculous project of yours.' And then, turning again to Izzy, asked, 'Why the hell can't you park in the drive?'

Izzy drew up her full five foot two inches, smiling patiently and sweetly. 'Mr Ahern, it may have escaped your notice but in the back window of my car there is a very large and very distinct card bearing the words DOCTOR ON CALL. I am that said doctor and I'm here on an official visit to tend to this good lady. Her... her bunions have become the size of... of *onions*.' Izzy nodded towards me as I stood, staring at her in astonishment. 'Now then, dear, I suggest lots of bed rest, cut out holes in your slippers to ease those swollen joints and absolutely no high heels.' And with that, she sailed down the drive singing, to a very familiar tune:

'Rafey, it's me, it's... Izzy...'

'Well, I think that was what can only be described as one hell of a huge success,' David Henderson grinned a week later, emptying the last drops of Moet into his glass. 'What do you reckon, Clementine?'

'I'm going to have to sit down,' I grinned back. 'I cannot believe the amount of press that were here. I know you said the local press would be here, but *The Yorkshire Post*...?'

The sheer number of people who had been invited and actually turned up to Clementine's official opening had bowled me over. It was so exciting, so wonderfully gratifying. The Orangery, that offered a private, fine—and exceptionally expensive—dining experience to a maximum of twelve at any one sitting, was already booked up three months ahead. Mel had been in charge of the diary and, throughout the three hours of this spring Saturday afternoon and early evening invitation, had calmly and professionally listened to what people wanted, assuring them they could discuss with me in the weeks before their booking what they would like to eat or, if they preferred, be served a menu of my choosing.

David had stood up and spoken to the gathered guests, introducing me as a former chef from La Toque Blanche in Leeds and telling them—while I blushed at the words—that they were witnessing the creation of a totally new and original venture that had his full backing and which, he was sure, would be copied, nationwide. Clementine's was now officially available for private parties, for retreats, for summer picnics in the grounds; for individual and group cookery tuition, for individual and group tennis lessons followed by Pimm's and whatever food they would like Clementine and her staff to cook for them. And for much, much more. He held up the glossy pamphlet which Mel, Grace, David and I had agonised and argued over for hours at a time, and was applauded heartily by foodies and David Henderson groupies alike, all eager to experience anything the Richard Branson of the north had put his name to.

High on the adrenalin of success, I just couldn't stop talking. 'And did you see Annabelle Ahern? Didn't she look wonderful? She was out in style with her Sixties mates, wasn't she? Not that I knew who any of them were,' I laughed. 'All before my time.'

'Well, for your information, Clem, in your sitting room today was Bobby Santano, Juliette Manning, Carol Fallon and Dave Clark...'

'Oh, I've heard of *him*. From the Dave Clark Five? I wondered who it was my mum kept trying to talk to. She always used to tell Lucy and me how she'd adored him when she was a teenager. She still had 'Bits and Pieces' on a 45 record when we were little girls, and if Lucy had been good she'd let us play her old music.'

David laughed. 'I thought your mum and dad were here to help look after Allegra and Max rather than get acquainted with past idols? Annabelle was obviously in her element, showing her old London mates how very forward-thinking we are *oop north*. I noticed she'd brought Selena Hamley-Smith and her cronies from Harrogate as well.'

'Who's she?'

'The Honourable Selena Sykes that was. She was here with her mother, Lady Anne Sykes—Anne and Annabelle were big mates in London in the Sixties and then both ended up here in the north. Gerald Sykes—Lord Sykes he is now—was a big mill-owner in Bradford and was very friendly with Mandy's parents. They were all at our wedding: the northern contingent en masse can be quite intimidating.'

David suddenly stopped talking, holding my gaze across the kitchen table and my heart began to race. He reached over, tucking a tendril of hair that had escaped from my ponytail back into place. His face was so near to mine, I could see the beginnings of dark stubble on his olive skin and caught the subtle citrus tang of some expensive aftershave. Unable to look away, I only knew I so very badly wanted to kiss him, the adrenalin coursing through my veins from the excitement of the evening needing some outlet. I felt high, reckless, suddenly not caring that he might see the naked want on my face. God, I wanted him to kiss me.

David moved his hand from my hair to my cheek, stroking my face with the backs of his fingers. 'Clem? Clemmie, I—'

'Mummy, where are you?' Allegra and Max could be heard galloping down the stairs towards the kitchen. 'Mummy, Auntie Mandy says can me and Max go over to her house for a little walk? She says we can look at the fish in the pond and they've got white birds like ours too.'

Allegra raced in as David sat back calmly in his chair. He was so unruffled I actually began to wonder if I'd imagined the gentle touch of his fingers on my burning cheeks.

'Ah, there you are, you two. You must be very proud, Clementine. What an amazingly successful afternoon.' Mandy Henderson walked quietly into the kitchen behind the two children. As usual she looked fabulous—coolly chic in an understated navy wool pencil-skirt and crisp white shirt. A navy cashmere sweater was slung around her neck and very high navy court shoes emphasised her stunning legs and height. 'Now, if that's OK with you, Clementine, I'll take these two across home with me. I think I have a couple of Easter eggs with their names on them.'

'Can we, Clem? Can we walk across with Mandy?' For the first time in months, since his parents' death, Max seemed animated.

'Yes, darling, of course you can.' I couldn't look at David, couldn't meet his eyes. Oh God, had I leaned into his hand, closing my eyes at his touch? Had I shown my hand? I had an awful feeling I had. Turning to the kids I said, too brightly, 'You'll need wellies, both of you, the fields are still very wet and muddy.'

'Come on, David, grab your jacket and let's go. I'll drop these two off in an hour or two before it gets dark, Clementine.'

'You can't walk in those, Mandy,' David said impatiently, nodding towards her red-soled Louboutins.

'I'm sure Clementine has a pair of something, somewhere, that I can borrow? Yes? Lovely, off we go then,' Mandy trilled. 'Oh, is the dog coming too? Come on then, George, you're welcome as well...'

There wasn't much tidying left to do—the three waiting staff Mel had hired on an ad hoc basis had quietly and efficiently cleared most of the dirty glasses, plates, napkins and bottles of champagne, stacking the clean stuff in the huge built-in cupboards expressly designed for that purpose.

I was shattered but restless. I walked through the French windows, whistling for George before remembering he'd gone with the others, and went to sit on the patio with the remains of my mug of tea.

'Are you all right?' Mel came out to join me, buttoning up her jacket against the cool evening air. 'Gosh, it's chilly out here, do you want your coat?'

'No, I'm fine. Mel, thank you so much for today—and for the last few months. I don't know what I'd have done without you.'

Mel smiled and came to sit beside me. 'I'm loving it, Clem, absolutely in my element. You and David are onto a winner here: this is just the start.'

When I didn't say anything Mel leaned over, unexpectedly taking my hand. 'Is it David?'

'Sorry?' Startled at the direct question, I felt my face redden and tried to hide it in my mug of tea.

'David?'

'Is it that obvious?'

'No. No not really. But working so closely with you both over the past few weeks once couldn't help but notice the frisson between the pair of you.'

'What am I going to do? I think I sort of fell in lust with him the minute he walked into Peter's kitchen on my very first visit here—gosh, exactly a year ago.'

'Oh, don't ask me, Clem. I wouldn't have a clue.' Mel paused and then said, 'OK, I suppose you can do one of three things...'

'Oh?'

'One: totally go all out for it if you think he feels the same. End up having an affair with him, wreck his marriage and claim him for yourself. Two: totally go all out for it, end up having an affair with him knowing he will never leave Mandy and become his mistress for as long as it lasts. Clementine's is probably most at risk with option two...'

'And three?'

'Three: you accept that David Henderson is not yours to have. He is married to the exceptionally ravishing Mandy, has been for the past however many years, and any affair with him can only lead to heartache... and I reckon you've had enough of that in the past few years, Clem.'

The next few weeks were a rollercoaster of emotions as Mel, Grace and I, together with new kitchen and serving staff, gardeners and cleaners charted new oceans in what appeared, at times, to be a particularly leaky and unreliable vessel. Suppliers let us down; I had to fire two kitchen staff on their first day for utter incompetence and a new gardener taken on to help Peter's old gardener, Eric, was caught mid-thrust, his trousers round his ankles, with one of the cleaners at the bottom of the garden just as, with what I hoped was a particularly beatific smile, I was serving Good Friday hot cross buns and afternoon tea on the lawn to the Bishops of Wakefield and York, together with a whole team of their overseas visiting dignitaries.

Word had spread about the fine dining in The Orangery, and I found I had to extend bookings to include Wednesdays and Thursdays instead of just at the weekend, in order to deal with the demand for tables. I took on more and more staff, Mel dealing proficiently with the applications, but insisting I interview prospective candidates myself for all positions, however lowly.

There was absolutely no let up from the hard work, but I

loved every minute of it, thriving on the challenge of turning Peter's house into the in-place to be seen at, but also a place for retreat from the modern world for those wealthy enough to be able to make it a temporary haven from whatever modern-day life and relationships had thrown at them.

Grace came up with the idea of a two-day retreat for abandoned wives—she said we could extend it to abandoned husbands if the idea took off—where these women would be free to do nothing but eat, (if they hadn't lost their appetite along with their beloved) drink, cry and talk, with a counsellor and divorce lawyer on hand to listen and advise. Izzy said she was ready to divorce Declan who was moaning and wanting attention because he had man flu, and asked if we had mates' rates and would the lemon cheesecake be a feature of the cathartic two days away?

'My aim,' I'd told the young reporter from *The Yorkshire Post*, feeding him a particularly delectable truffle risotto, 'is for Clementine's to be the most talked about venue, not just in Yorkshire but the whole of the north of England.'

'*Yorkshire is the new London,*' was the headline splashed across the cover of the *Yorkshire Post's Cultural Magazine* while inside, a six-page spread was given over to me looking very professional in my Clementine's black and orange apron as I worked in the kitchen. There was an interview with David and me and myriad photographs of the house and grounds showing it at its ravishing best. The phone never stopped ringing the week after its appearance on the newsstands in late May, both from other publications wanting to do features but, more importantly, from people wanting to book learner cookery courses, select, bijou christening and wedding receptions as well as the ever popular The Orangery at Clementine's. There was even a phone call from Yorkshire television who, eager to jump on the *Great British Bake Off* bandwagon, were making initial enquiries about our hosting a new competition called the 'Great Yorkshire Take Off'.

While Max and Sophie had initially wanted nothing at all to do with Clementine's, they began to realise and accept that without the business they would have been unable to stay in their much-loved house with all its comforting memories of their parents. Eventually, some of the excitement of their home being regularly featured in magazines and Sunday supplements was beginning to rub off on them until even Sophie, although she wouldn't openly admit it, appeared proud of how the place was turning out.

David was always on hand to help, coming over for at least a couple of hours each day but more often coming for breakfast and staying until he went home to Mandy for dinner. While he never again stroked my face or held my hand as he had the evening of our opening do, the air always appeared charged when we were together in a room and I loved the little glances across the room, the holding of each other's eye, which happened whenever he was over at the house.

One Monday, at the beginning of June, I had an evening off. I really needed it and had been looking forward to it all day. I'd prepared and served lunch to ten somewhat excitable elderly ladies in the shady part of the garden, their blue rinses bobbing in direct proportion to the amount of Pinot Grigio that was being quaffed as they celebrated yet another of their gang achieving her eightieth birthday.

'I don't suppose you've any of those Chippendale

chappies on tap to entertain us?' the birthday girl had asked as two of my waitresses and I cleared the pudding plates.

''Fraid not,' I'd laughed. 'You should have said, Celia— I'd have had them ready and raring to go for you.'

'Well, we may as well give it all we've got for as long as we've got it,' Celia cackled.

'Oh, darling Celia, mine upped and went years ago,' one of them sighed. 'I'm more than happy with Ryvita and Marmite and the parish magazine in bed these days. You might end up with crumbs in your nightie but at least you have the bed to yourself and no snoring to put up with.'

Max and Allegra were asleep, and Sophie was out with the lovely Sam whom she'd met in her first week at sixth-form college. Once she'd been well enough to pick up her AS level studies again she'd gone, on that first day, very hesitantly to the college and returned home full of it all, eyes bright, chattering about how lovely it was to be at a school with boys as well as incredibly friendly, welcoming girls. Her transformation from the terribly unhappy, quite obnoxious sixteen-year-old to the pretty, clear-skinned, shiny-haired almost-seventeen-year-old was nothing short of a miracle and I offered thanks on a daily basis both to Mel, who had been particularly patient with and friendly towards Sophie, but also to Sam who clearly adored her.

I had the house to myself. What utter bliss! I stretched, propping my bare feet up on the kitchen table and, ignoring the fact that a pedicure was long overdue, reached for my mug of tea and the crossword. *I'm happy*, I thought. *So, so happy*.

She came into the kitchen through the open French

windows so quietly it was several seconds before I realised I was no longer alone.

'Hello, Clem,' Lucy said, crossing the kitchen and joining me at the table. 'I want to see Allegra; I want to see my little girl.'

28

Lucy took a good look round at my beautiful kitchen, scrubbed, gleaming and ready for an early start in the morning and smiled, the little cat-like smile I recognised so well of old.

'Well, Clem, you've done OK for yourself, haven't you? But then you always did, didn't you? Always the one to come up smelling of roses while I continue to be covered in shit.'

'Lucy...' I got up from the table and went to hug her. 'Oh, Lucy...' She felt tiny, brittle almost, but her huge brown eyes were clear and her hair was clean.

'So, this is a bit of all right, Clem, isn't it? Read all about you in the paper.' She frowned. 'I could do with a drink/' She gazed around the kitchen once more 'I'm sure you've plenty on offer round here.'

My heart was still beating frighteningly in my chest and I had to take several deep breaths to try and stay calm. 'There's tea, coffee, water, juice. What would you like?'

'Oh come on, Clem, I haven't come all the way from Leeds for a cup of tea. You must have a bottle open somewhere?' She moved over to the huge industrial fridge that had been installed with the renovations and found a three-quarters-full bottle of white wine. 'No champers, Clem? In a posh place like this? You see, I have something to celebrate, so I could do with a glass of bubbly... but never mind, I'll just have a glass of this—if you don't mind?'

'Lucy, why are you here?'

'I told you. I want to see Allegra. You can't stop me seeing her, Clem. She *is* my daughter.'

'Lucy, you know you can't just have access to her like this. You know you have to apply through the courts.'

'Or social services, Clem. You know that.'

'No, Lucy, social services have absolutely no involvement anymore. Not for a couple of years now. They know I'm Allegra's legal guardian, that I am legally able to make all decisions about her welfare.'

'Yes but, Clem, I'm clean...' Lucy rolled up the sleeves of her thin sweatshirt and thrust both arms at me. 'Look. Look, Clem,' she said, angrily. 'I've been off H for six months now. I'm clean, I really am. Allegra's mine... she's mine.'

'Ssh, for God's sake, Lucy, be quiet...' I could feel pinpricks of sweat on my forehead and I wiped them away as I desperately thought what to do for the best. 'Look, you know you just can't come here at this time of night, just turn up and expect to see her. It's not fair on me and it most certainly is not fair on her.'

Lucy left her untouched glass of wine and started pacing the kitchen. 'Fair? Fair, Clem...? You talk about *fair* when you have all this—' she flung her arms round in anger and then came back to the table '—when you have all of this *and* my daughter.' She stalked right up to me and her face was white. 'I tell you what, Clem, I'll do you a swap; you walk the streets of Chapeltown and Midhope and see how fair you think that is then. Do you know the going rates?'

I glanced at the door leading to the hall and stairs, terrified Allegra or Max had woken and were creeping down to see what was going on. 'Shh, Lucy, please. For God's sake, lower your voice.'

'No? Well let me tell you, just so you'll know when we swap places, and you can then talk to me about what's fair and what isn't. Hand job? Cheap at the price: a tenner. Blow job? What do you reckon, Clem? What would *you* charge for some guy to stick his dick in your mouth round the back of the Sports Centre? Well, that's twenty quid—more if they can persuade you not to use a condom.'

'That is *enough*, Lucy,' I hissed. 'You need to go…'

'Enough? Oh, you've had *enough*? *Already*? Hang on, Clem, I've not got to the best bit. You'll need to know what to charge for full sex, especially with the Saturday afternoon punters who drop off their wives in town and, instead of going to Costa for a coffee and a custard slice like they've said, come straight down under the arches for a quickie…'

Lucy continued to pace the kitchen but seemed to have run out of steam. She folded her arms, leaned against the huge centre island and glared at me.

'And if I hadn't taken her, Lucy? What then?' I was angry now. 'We've been through all this so many times before. If I hadn't taken Allegra, agreed to give up my work, give up everything and moved back in with Mum and Dad with her in order to become her legal guardian, you know what would have happened. She'd have been given up for adoption like *we* were and then you would *never* have seen her.'

'But I… I *lent* her to you. It was always meant to be *temporary*, until I sorted myself out.' Lucy's eyes narrowed. 'But you've taken it one hell of a step further, haven't you? You've fucking well *stolen* her. You always thought you were better than me, didn't you? Always the goody-goody. Always sucking up to Mum and Dad and the teachers. God I can still hear it now, those bloody teachers.' Lucy adopted a high authoritative tone: '"Why can't you be more like Clementine, Lucy?" "How is it that you are identical twins and yet Clementine is an angel and *you* are a little devil, Lucy?"' She glared at me again and then suddenly moved over to the table, picked up her glass and downed the wine in one.

'Lucy…' I put my hand out to her. 'Lucy, you are my sister. I love you and I've always loved you, but we have to think about Allegra.'

'You came looking for me, didn't you? Sheena, down on Emerald Street, told me you'd been sniffing around, trying to find where I was.'

'Oh, she told you, did she? Good. I certainly wasn't *sniffing around*. I needed to know where you were, Lucy. I was desperately worried about what you were doing, who you were with, whether you were even alive. You made no attempt to keep in touch with me; you didn't even try to see Allegra. I moved us down into a little house at the bottom end of town, near Emerald House, so that you might realise where we were and keep in contact with us. But you disappeared, Lucy. For years, for God's sake.'

'Does she know about me?' Lucy asked, frowning. 'She does know you're not her real mother, doesn't she? That you're just her auntie…'

'Lucy…' I was frightened now. 'Lucy…'

'She doesn't, does she? She doesn't fucking know. She thinks you're her mother… Jesus, you've never told her.' Lucy slammed the glass down onto the kitchen unit. 'OK, where is she? Upstairs?'

'Lucy, please… not like this.' I put my hand out to stop her moving towards the door that led upstairs to the bedrooms and she brushed it aside.

Suddenly all the fight seemed to go out of her 'Clem, I just want to see her. Please? I promise I won't disturb her. But you have to let me see my little girl.'

I really didn't know what to do, but I was terrified that if I didn't let her see Allegra, she'd run upstairs anyway. 'Look, Lucy,' I said, trying to speak calmly. 'I'm going to take you up to Allegra's room, I'm going to go in there first and then I'm going to let you peep round the door. That's all. Now, do you *promise* me you won't try to do anything else?'

'I promise, Clem, I promise. Just let me see her…'

Together, we tiptoed up the stairs to the pink boudoir. Allegra's door was never closed—she liked to be able to slip into my bed in the next room in the middle of the night—and I went in and across to her bed. The curtains were closed against the summer evening sunshine, but the room was light, a soft breeze ruffling the rose-pink material as she slept. I kneeled beside her and glanced towards the bedroom door, knowing that Lucy would be able to take a peep at Allegra from her stance behind it.

Allegra stirred in her sleep and I prayed she wouldn't wake. Her breathing became deep and regular again and I tucked Hector elephant into her arms before standing up and walking to the door.

'Shh,' I whispered, as Lucy began to say something. 'Just wait until we get downstairs. I don't want Allegra or Max to wake.'

'Max?'

'My stepson.'

'Your stepson? So where's the father?' Lucy glanced at my ring finger as we began to tiptoe back downstairs. 'Where's your husband?'

'He's dead.' I paused. 'As is the children's mother. They were killed together in a car accident last October. I have parental responsibility for both him and his sister.'

'So you have *three* children?' Lucy stared at me as we got to the bottom of the stairs. 'But none of them are yours? So, if you have three and none of them are really yours, then you won't mind giving me back Allegra who really *is* mine.'

'Lucy,' I hissed, taking her arm and pushing her into the kitchen. 'Don't even think about it. I am Allegra's legal guardian, the only mother she has ever known and, I'm telling you right now, she stays with *me*.'

Lucy shook off my arm. 'You've done a good job; I can see that. She looks beautiful. I'm going ahead with this, Clem. I'm going to get her back.'

'What's going on?' Sophie walked into the kitchen with Sam. 'There's some guy in a car on the drive, Clem. When Sam asked him what he was doing he said he was waiting for someone inside... Oh my God, I don't have to ask who that someone is. Is this your sister, Clem?'

'I'm going, Clem.' Lucy looked Sophie up and down—at her long shiny blonde plait hanging over her shoulder, at her now-clear skin, at her white teeth held in place by the ubiquitous brace. 'I looked like you once, kid,' she said and, without a backward glance at me, strode from the kitchen.

I realised I was trembling and sat down heavily at the kitchen table.

'I'll get you some water,' Sam said, walking over to the sink.

'I think she needs gin,' Sophie said. 'Jesus, Clem, she didn't look too good, did she? She's so thin. And her teeth… they're all brown…'

'Heroin gives you a craving for sugary foods,' I said vaguely, my mind racing. 'And every time she manages to get off heroin, she'll be given a methadone prescription. It's still a drug, and opiates can attack the enamel. Methadone is taken orally as a syrup and the sugar doesn't help…' I trailed off, not knowing what else to say. Why the hell was I discussing oral hygiene like a dental lecturer when I was going to lose Allegra? I looked at the kitchen clock and was surprised to see it was only nine-thirty. A whole lifetime seemed to have passed in the twenty minutes that Lucy had been here. I needed to speak to someone who could help.

'Why was she here, Clem? What did she want?'

'Oh, just a social visit,' I lied. 'She saw one of the articles in the paper about Clementine's and was able to come and find me.'

'Yes, but what does she *want*, Clem? She didn't look all that sociable to me. She's not trying to blackmail you or anything is she?'

'Blackmail me? No, no, Sophie. She has nothing to

blackmail me about. You know that she's been heavily into drugs—you know all that. She seems to have been off them for a while now and feels that we can get together again. She deliberately kept out of my way when she was on the streets, on the drugs...' I trailed off again lamely, my head pounding. 'Look, you two, will you be all right to keep an eye on the kids and everything here? I'm going to take George for a walk. Get some fresh air...' And then, as an afterthought I said, 'Just keep the doors locked, won't you?'

Sophie stared at me. 'The doors locked? You never even keep them closed. You're frightening me now, Clem. *You're* frightened, I can see.'

'I'm fine,' I said, smiling. 'I'm just going to check on the children and then I'll take George out for ten minutes.'

'You go, Clem,' Sam said, flexing his gym-toned muscles. 'We'll be fine.'

I ran upstairs, popped my head around Max's door and then moved onto Allegra's room again. Oh, Jesus, I *should* have told Allegra. As soon as she was big enough to understand, I should have told her that I wasn't her real mummy. And I really, really had intended to do that. I'd become Allegra's legal guardian in order that the authorities didn't take her and put her with foster parents. I hadn't really wanted to take her on, didn't want to move back in with my parents and look after a tiny helpless baby. Hadn't wanted to give up my work at the La Toque Blanche where I'd just been promoted to sous-chef, actually being fully in charge when Gianni wasn't there. But Lucy had begged me, made me promise to take Allegra until she was off the drugs and was able to take care of her herself.

And I had.

We ran, George and I, running across the summer fields until we were exhausted. George who, because I'd been so ridiculously busy, hadn't been getting the exercise he needed, was obviously in his element, crashing through the cornfields, jumping the broken dry-stone walls, his pink tongue lolling comically as he ran. I knew I was running towards David, needing to tell someone I could trust about what was happening, someone who was a grownup and would know what to do.

Mandy was out in the garden, gloves on her beautifully manicured hands, striped-blue cotton cut-offs showing off her long brown legs and pert little behind. I hesitated, not really wanting to talk to her. While she'd always been unfailingly polite and friendly towards me, there was something about her that didn't lend itself to her being a Samaritan, to having a listening ear. Or maybe it was the simple fact that I was in love with her husband.

I made to retrace my steps back down the drive, back to the lane and the fields once more, but George had other ideas. With a joyous yelp, he raced across the lawn, partially demolished a bed of peonies and hollyhocks, lifted his leg dismissively against a blackcurrant bush and lay, tail wagging and a ridiculous grin on his hairy black face, at Mandy's feet.

Mandy jumped back, startled at the sudden appearance of a great hairy beast in her garden.

'Good God,' I heard her shout, before turning to see if there was anyone with George. Shielding her eyes against the setting sun, she spotted me at the edge of the lawn and raised her hand.

'Clementine, this is a nice surprise,' she called. 'Come and sit down. I don't seem to have seen you for ages.'

'Er, it's fine, really, Mandy. I was just out for a walk and George obviously decided to turn it into a social call.'

'But you were on your way *here*?' Mandy asked pleasantly, her tone indicating she was well aware there could have been no other plan.

'Er, well…'

'Was it David you were hoping to see?'

'I was just out for a walk, Mandy, that's all.'

'Because I'm afraid he's not here. He's in Milan with Nick.'

'Right, OK. Thank you. There *was* something I needed to talk to him about—just a little something about er… er insurance policies for Clementine's. But it really doesn't matter. Goodness, what wonderful… wonderful…' Shit, what were they called? '… Blue flower thingies you have.'

'Ceanothus?' Mandy asked, raising her immaculately threaded eyebrows.

Gosh, how did anyone get their eyebrows to behave so well? 'That's the one, Mandy. Right, George, come on, we don't want to come between a woman and her Ceanothus.' I knew I was rambling, but I really didn't want to talk to her. Didn't want to indulge in polite chitchat that might involve mention of the man I'd lusted after for well over a year. I knew if she started talking about him, I'd be unable to stop myself from blushing like a ridiculous lovesick adolescent.

'Actually, Clementine, there is something I'd like to have a quick word with you about?'

'Oh?'

'Yes. Now, how can I phrase this?' She smiled, but her amazingly navy eyes were not friendly. 'David, as I'm sure you realise, is an amazingly charismatic man...'

Even as I knew exactly where this conversation was heading, I couldn't believe that here was a woman calling her own husband 'amazingly charismatic.' 'Lovely' 'kind' 'a friend to all, man and beast' maybe, but 'amazingly charismatic'? Give over.

'People—men and women alike—adore him. Now, women particularly fall for him. Think they're in love with him. Indeed, think that he's in love with *them*—' she gave a little tinkle of laughter at the very thought '—and get terribly hurt when that, that *emotion* can never be reciprocated. Do you understand what I'm saying, Clementine? We really couldn't bear you to be under some misguided illusion, after what you have been through, you poor, poor girl, in the last year or so...'

Horribly embarrassed, I managed to muster as much dignity as I could, well, *muster*, and raised my own—desperately unthreaded—eyebrows in her direction. 'I'm really not sure what you're getting at here, Mandy, but let me assure you I have never assumed there to be *anything* other than a working relationship between myself and David.' I could feel my face flaming as well as my nose assume Pinocchio proportions. 'Please assure David, if you are in contact with him, I will sort out the insurance issue myself—it really isn't a problem.'

I smiled in what I hoped was a gracious manner and made to take a swift exit, head held high. Which, had George not decided to take advantage of the beautifully soft, velvet-green grass and taken a protracted and obviously highly satisfactory dump in the middle of Mandy's lawn, I would have done.

I walked as far as the bottom of the Hendersons' drive before I allowed the tears to fall and once I started crying I couldn't stop. Huge fat tears splashed wetly down my face and, unchecked, fell down on to my white shirt. I made my way blindly across the fields, falling over a couple of times which made me howl more. I didn't think I'd cried like this for years. I'd lost my sister, I was about to lose Allegra and I'd stupidly thought I might have a chance with David Henderson. *You stupid, stupid bitch*, I berated myself as I walked, head down, not really looking where I was going. Why hadn't I told Allegra from day one that I wasn't her real mother? How in God's name was I going to break it to her, now that she was almost six years old?

'Would you like porridge for breakfast, Allegra? Have you read your reading book today? Oh, and by the way, would you like to meet your real mother, darling? Yes, she does look a bit like me, doesn't she?'

Unconcerned, George ran ahead, sniffing badger trails, chasing rabbits, lifting his leg delightedly against bushes and trees as he went. He stopped suddenly, mid-sniff, and, without warning, retraced his steps before racing off at a tangent in quite the opposite direction to home.

I whistled—the best way one can whistle when one is sobbing and snotty—but George was deaf or daft—possibly both—to my call. Bloody dog. I needed to get home. I didn't know what time Sam had to leave and I didn't like the idea of the children being by themselves.

'George…' I set off after him but he disappeared over yet another dry-stone wall. I really was going to have to get some obedience classes sorted for him. 'George!'

A strange moaning sound, steady and repetitive, was coming from behind the next wall and I stopped in my tracks, every sense alert trying to make out what the noise was. It was getting dark and I began to feel anxious. To my left and down the valley I could see Peter's house—my house, I berated myself—lit up and welcoming, waiting for me to get home so that Sam could drive the five miles or so back to his parents'. The noise stopped abruptly and, in the still quiet, I whistled once more for George who'd not reappeared. 'I'm going without you, George,' I called at the top of my voice. 'If you don't get here this minute, you daft dog, that's it—you're on your own…'

Still no sign of him. Bugger. It really was quite dark over by the wall and, as the grunting began again, shadows from a couple of young saplings, in full leaf now that we were approaching mid-June, moved slightly in the cool night air. I inched forward towards the broken stile and, nervous of what was on the other side, shouted again, for George.

The dark figure of a man suddenly loomed out of the shadow and I gave an involuntary squeak of fear.

'For heaven's sake, stop making all that bloody racket, will you? It's bad enough your damned dog dancing around like a demented loon at a party, without you joining in.'

29

I looked at Rafe Ahern in terror, my heart hammering from the shock of his sudden spectre-like manifestation from the other side of the dry-stone wall. His looming appearance from out of the shadows wouldn't have been out of place in an ancient black and white horror film.

'Jesus wept, what on earth are you doing making me jump like that?' I finally spluttered. 'And me "*making all that bloody racket*"? *Me?*' I had a sudden awful thought that maybe Rafe had been on the job, taking advantage of the warm June evening for a bit of alfresco rumpy pumpy before being disturbed by an overenthusiastic George. He was a bloody noisy lover if that was the case. All that moaning and groaning? Not my cup of tea at all.

As Rafe stood there glaring at me, occasionally turning his head to berate an invisible, but obviously overexcited, George to 'shut it,' the moaning, interspersed by a slight wheezing accompaniment, began once more. Well, if JoJo Kennedy was behind the wall with him, she was an obvious asthmatic and shouldn't be getting her kit off in a damp field, supermodel or no.

'Can you come and get this damned dog of yours? He's frightening Twiggy.'

Twiggy? Twiggy was behind the wall with him? Crikey, if that was the case, Rafe Ahern must have dumped JoJo for an earlier model—in every sense of the word.

'Hang on, I'm coming over.' I climbed over the stile, not seeing the fresh cowpat until it was too late. Great stuff. Here I was, about to meet a Sixties icon, eyes puffy from crying, legs scratched from the particularly pernicious nettles I'd landed in when I fell earlier and now stinking of cowshit.

'Oh... what's the matter with him? Is he all right?'

'He is a *she* and, if the damned vet doesn't get here soon, *she* will be no more...'

'The poor thing. What on earth is wrong with *her*?' I asked as the grunting started anew.

Rafe Ahern gave me such a withering look, I actually felt myself wither. 'What the hell do you *think* is wrong with her? Her waters broke half an hour ago but she can't get the foal out.' He glanced at his watch once more. 'Vet should have been here an hour ago.'

'Shouldn't she be in a nice warm stable somewhere?' I asked, rubbing my eyes and feeling a scratchy tickle start at the back of my throat 'You know, if you knew she was about to give birth why did you leave her out in the field?'

'Well, yes of course, if I'd *known* she was going to go into labour three weeks early, I'd have brought her in. Luckily, a couple of walkers spotted her and called in on Ted Jarvis who rang me.'

I sneezed. 'Ted Jarvis?'

'Farmer. Puts his cows on my fields occasionally. Lives across the valley.' He looked at his watch again. 'Shit, I should have been at Manchester airport by now.'

'Oh, anywhere nice?' I asked, trying to be pleasant through my sniffing, sneezing and the surreptitious wiping of my nose on my sleeve. 'I always like Greece at this time of year… you know, before it gets too hot? Or the South of France?'

'Syria,' he said shortly and then turned from Twiggy to look at me properly for the first time that evening. 'Have you got a cold? Do you need a hanky?'

'Allergic to horses,' I sniffed. 'Anyway, I'd better be off…'

Rafe pulled a clean white handkerchief from his jeans' back pocket. 'Here, have a good blow on that, and then you're going to have to help me.'

'Help you? Me? God, I don't know anything about horses, pregnant or otherwise.' No way was I going to tell this bossy boots I was actually frightened of the damned great brutes. Having said that, poor old Twiggy was so frightened herself she didn't appear at all dangerous.

'Normally, I wouldn't interfere with a mare when she's foaling—best to just stand back and let her get on with it, but she's been straining for nearly two hours now…'

I had a sudden vision of Lucy in Midhope General, shouting and swearing as Mum and I tried to calm her, hold her hand, help any way we could as she struggled to push out Allegra.

'Oh, hang on.' Rafe suddenly got down on his knees right beside the mare. Under the horse's tail, a whitish, glistening bubble about the size of a grapefruit had begun to protrude. 'Her membranes are out.'

Twiggy lifted her head a couple of times trying see along her flank, but she appeared exhausted and soon sank back onto the ground. Rafe said nothing, but looked constantly at his watch.

'Shit,' he hissed again, hitting buttons on his mobile. 'Graham, Rafe Ahern again. I need you here, right now, or this mare won't survive.'

I looked at my own watch. Sophie would be wondering where the hell I was, especially after coming home to find Lucy standing in the kitchen earlier. While Rafe left his message, I hastily rang the home number.

'Sophie, can you get Sam to stay with you a bit longer?'

'What's happened? Where are you? Are you all right? We were just considering ringing the police…'

'No, no, I'm fine. Honest. I'm helping Rafe Ahern with a horse that's gone into labour in one of the fields. I don't know how long I'll be, but don't worry. Is Sam OK to stay with you?'

Rafe flung his mobile onto his jacket and went to the mare's head, crooning and stroking her with such tenderness I couldn't believe this was the same man who'd shouted at me for murdering his chicken, and at Izzy for parking in the lane. 'Don't know where he is,' he muttered. 'Probably in the pub in the village.'

'Do you want me to run down? See if I can find him?'

'No, there's not the time.' He moved back down to the mare's rear end and looked at his watch once more. 'You see, the foal itself isn't visible. Dangerous, very dangerous if the foal can't be seen in the membranes after ten minutes.' Rafe stood up, paced a bit, fondled George's ears absentmindedly a couple of times and then obviously made a decision.

'Right, I need to get her up.'

'Up? Are you sure? Isn't it best to be lying down to give birth…?'

Back came the withering look. 'You mean in a labour ward with clean white sheets and a nice bit of gas and air? Believe me, we need to get her up.' Rafe moved over to the wall and picked up a halter. 'OK, there's obviously some obstruction. By getting her on her feet the foal will move back into the expanded uterus for a second and hopefully the obstruction might shift.' He managed to get the halter over the mare's head although she obviously wasn't happy about it. 'Right, pull on the halter and I'll try to get her on her feet.' Rafe took the riding crop he'd picked up with the halter and hit the mare hard on her behind shouting, 'Up, up, up,' as he did so.

'Stop it,' I shouted. 'Stop it. What the hell are you doing? You can't hit a poor pregnant woman like that.'

'It's a bloody *horse*, Clementine, not a woman,' he said savagely and hit her again.

Enraged, Twiggy managed to get her forelegs off the damp grass before deciding she wasn't up to it, settling back, grunting once again, on to her side.

Rafe hit her once again and this time she bared her huge yellow teeth at me. I jumped back in terror, letting go of the halter. 'Grab the sodding halter,' Rafe roared at me, hitting Twiggy once again with the crop. This time she managed to heave herself up onto all four feet and Rafe shouted, 'Pull her, Clementine. Get her walking.'

He ran up to me, grabbed the halter from my hand and pulled, walking the mare as she stumbled but stayed upright. 'Believe me, Clementine,' he breathed as he pulled on the halter, 'I hate doing this to her, but it's either this or she'll die, as will her foal.'

Twiggy suddenly dropped back down to her knees and, grunting, turned onto her side. Rafe moved down to her tail end. 'Oh, shit. Still nothing. OK, let's try again. You get her walking and then I'm going to have to help her.' He cracked the whip on her flanks twice and bellowed in her ear as he did so. She got onto her feet once again, and as I pulled on the halter she stumbled unsteadily after me. Immediately, Rafe plunged one hand into the mare's vulva, gently keeping it there as she slowly ambled after me.

'Oh my God, I feel like I'm on the set of a James Who-is-it drama,' I panted, desperately trying to keep the mare from falling back down.

'Herriot,' Rafe panted back at me. 'James Herriot. Right, when she has a contraction next I'm going to apply some traction...'

Rafe didn't say anything else, but I could hear his steady breathing and occasional muttered curses. The mare's legs suddenly folded like an ironing board, and she went down.

'Right, OK. Something's happening here. I can see the foal now but its legs are stuck back, rather than protruding. I need a cloth.' Rafe looked round and grabbed his jacket but, as it was made of a coarse thick material, threw it to the ground in a temper.

'Give me your shirt,' he shouted.

'My shirt?'

'Yes, your bloody shirt. Get it off and throw it over.'

Hastily, I let go of the halter and, as the mare's head sank onto the ground, unbuttoned my white, now dirty, cotton shirt and threw it to Rafe. Quickly, but very carefully, he reached into the mare once again, wrapping the material round the foal's hooves and gave a slight twist. 'Needed to do that so the hooves wouldn't cut her insides as I twisted... Right, OK, we appear to be in business.'

I moved down to Twiggy's tail end, just as a pair of hooves, followed by legs and then a head, slithered wetly onto the grass. The mare raised her head and grunted and sighed as the rest of the foal followed.

'Oh, a baby,' I said, and was surprised to find I had tears running down my cheeks. 'A little baby. Get out the way, George,' I added as I pushed the dog away and sneezed, trying to see the new foal in the dark. 'Look, it's a little boy.'

'That,' Rafe said, giving me another of his looks, 'is part of the umbilical cord. As far as I can see, she's a little filly.' He was just about to say something else when a hearty voice called out from a distance. 'Are you there, Rafe? Ahern?'

'Over here,' Rafe called. 'About bloody time, too, Graham,' he added as an old jeep bumped towards us down the field, its driver hanging out of the open window.

'What *have* you been up to?' Graham asked lasciviously as his eyes came to a halt on my breasts, covered only by a fairly scanty bra.

Rafe took his jacket and placed it around my shoulders. 'Don't want that pervert looking at your tits,' he muttered.

'Do you mind if I borrow this to walk home?' I asked, suddenly feeling shy at standing semi-naked in front of the two men.

'Just hang on ten minutes and I'll walk down with you,' Rafe said. 'It's dark across those fields. Right, Graham, seeing you're the vet and I'm paying you, I'm going to leave both of them with you now.'

The vet was already unloading a huge arc light and medical equipment from his jeep. 'You can certainly leave the one in the bra with me,' he shouted over his shoulder. 'I'll check her over and give her a lift home…'

'Just concentrate on *my* two girls, Graham,' Rafe said mildly.

'Well, from what I can see, you've done a pretty good job between you.' The vet nodded towards the beautiful black foal that was already up on shaky legs looking for her mother's teat. 'If you don't hear from me tomorrow, Rafe, assume you don't need to put either of them in the stable; they'll be fine out here.'

We walked almost in silence the half-mile across the fields towards home. 'Why Twiggy?' I asked. 'Why call a horse Twiggy?'

'That's my mother for you. She was a model in the Sixties, and so every mare we've had has always been named for one of them. Over the years we've had Chrissie, Shrimp, Cheryl, Yasmin, Naomi, Linda etc. etc. My mother thinks it hugely funny to think of her competitors munching grass and being put out to stud. Twiggy is actually the second Twiggy we've owned. We thought she was past it—basically put her out to grass for her retirement.' He laughed. 'Never thought, when we let her out with Keith—yes, after Keith Richards—the pair of them would be up to no good. But then, that's Keith Richards for you.'

'Where *are* all these horses?'

'Oh, the ones that are being trained are over in Ireland— my father's side of the family have always kept racehorses. The four that are in the stables are basically my mother's responsibility. She still likes to ride them.'

'Right, we're here. Thank you so much for walking me back...'

The events of the evening—Lucy's unexpected turning up, my being well and truly put in my place by Mandy Henderson and then this last hour acting as midwife had me charged with a nervous energy and I knew I was a long way from being able to sleep. I turned to Rafe. 'Would you like to come in? Have a coffee or something?' I felt shy again, but suddenly didn't want him to go.

'Thank you. I could murder a beer.' Rafe looked down at himself, at his filthy stained white T-shirt and then across at me. 'Actually, I'm going to have to get off—I'm in desperate need of a shower.' He smiled down at me. 'As are you.'

'You're welcome to have one here,' I heard myself saying. 'I can stick your jeans on a quick wash and dry them while you have a shower and a beer...'

He hesitated. 'I really don't want to put you out. I'm sure you have enough on with this place...'

'It really is no bother—and to be honest I could do with the company.'

'Oh?'

'Long story.'

I led Rafe into the kitchen where Sophie and Sam were making some sort of stir-fry.

'Oh, I'm really glad you're still here, Sam,' I said. 'Thanks very much for hanging on until I got back. This is Rafe Ahern, our neighbour. We've been acting as midwife to his horse up in one of the fields.'

'I couldn't leave Sophie alone here with the kids after your visitor earlier,' Sam said, stirring the pan with a flourish.

Rafe raised his eyebrows but said nothing.

'He's here because he's starving,' Sophie snorted dismissively. 'Honestly, you just can't feed him enough. He's already finished off what we had for supper.' And then, turning to me said, 'God, you look a mess, Clem. What's wrong with your eyes? Have you been crying…? 'Phew,' she curled her nose in disgust. 'What is that smell? Is it the dog?'

'All of us, I'm afraid,' Rafe said. 'I think we've all picked up our fair share of cowshit…'

'Right, come on,' I said hastily, 'let's get showers going.'

After I'd shown Rafe where he could shower and handed him the huge navy bath towel in which to wrap himself afterwards, I looked in on the kids and then went to my own bathroom. Blimey O'Reilly, I looked a fright. Any makeup I'd been wearing earlier had long since gone as a result of my sobbing, sneezing and sniffing. My eyes were puffy and red, as was my nose, and my hands were filthy from hanging onto Twiggy's halter.

I peeled off my filthy jeans, pants and bra, kicking them into the corner of the bathroom before stepping under the shower where I let the needles of scalding water and Jo Malone do their work. If only I could cleanse my mind of the fear brought about by Lucy's visit as easily.

I washed my hair, scrubbed my filthy fingernails and, once out, rubbed Hermes' Kelly Caleche—a last present from Peter before he died—into my skin in an effort to erase the smell of cowshit and sweating horse that still seemed to be in my nostrils. I pulled on a clean pair of jeans and sweater, scrunched my hair as best I could, applied a slick of lipstick and bronzer and went to find Rafe.

He was already in the laundry room, the navy towel wrapped around his waist, drinking from a bottle of Peroni that Sophie had found for him, obviously trying to work out how the washing machine worked.

'I can stick all this lot on a quick wash,' I said. 'You'll probably have to give them a second wash when you get home, but at least I can get them dry enough to actually *get* you home. Can I get you something to eat?' I asked, suddenly embarrassed at my close proximity to this tall, powerfully built man whose lower body was covered only in a towel. His bare chest was tanned and smooth apart from one small mat of black hair and, while I could imagine Rafe Ahern having little patience for the demands and narcissism of the gym, his upper arms and torso were taut and well-muscled.

He frowned and looked at his watch. 'I'm trying to work out the best way forward. I should have left the country for the Middle East by now. I think I'm probably going to have to drive down to London in the early hours of the morning rather than try and get another flight from Manchester...'

'I could scramble you some eggs?' I said. 'If you're going to spend several hours on the motorway after playing vet to Twiggy, you should eat.'

'Thanks, I won't say no to that. I'll just go and make a couple of phone calls first.' He took his mobile, wallet and keys from the jeans' pockets and, taking a business card from the wallet, picked up his mobile, leaving the other things on the work surface. 'Where's the best place to get a signal?'

After I told him, I cracked and scrambled eggs, toasted a couple of slices from a loaf of granary bread I'd made that morning and found some smoked salmon I was using for a canapé do in a couple of days. I snipped chives, filled a cafetière with good strong coffee and made myself a huge mug of tea. Rafe was still on the phone, so I found cutlery and a napkin and then, leaving the plate of food to keep warm, went to gather his wallet and keys from the laundry room so that he wouldn't forget them once his clothes were dry.

His wallet was open where he'd left it and, as I picked it up with the keys, I couldn't help but see the instantly recognisable, very beautiful face of JoJo Kennedy pouting up at me from the photo window of the wallet. And, for some very strange reason I couldn't quite grasp, I felt a lurch of something in the pit of my stomach as I remembered this was Rafe Ahern's girlfriend.

'This is seriously good,' Rafe smiled as he tucked into the eggs. 'I'd never have thought to put chives in with scrambled eggs.'

'I'm surprised you know what they are—Peter certainly never did.' I smiled back, ridiculously pleased that not only was this usually irritable man wolfing down my food with obvious pleasure, but he knew something about herbs too.

'I actually love cooking—when I get the time, which, at the moment is very rare.' He paused and put down his knife and fork. 'I'm sorry about Peter. It was very rude of me not to send my condolences; he *was* my neighbour after all. You must have had a tough time of it.'

'Yes, but more so for his children. It's been a particularly bad time for them, losing both their parents. I have to keep a constant eye on Max who seems outwardly OK, but is, I know, hiding a lot of his hurt inside still.'

'And the daughter?'

I smiled. 'A totally different story. Sophie, being a typical teenager, hated me from day one for daring to marry her father and then, after his death, I became her punchbag for all the anger and distress at losing her mum and dad as well as the usual teenage angst she was having to cope with.'

'She seemed OK this evening?'

'She is, she really is. I can't tell you the change in her over the last few months. She's actually a very bright girl and is loving being at the local sixth-form college rather than being away at school. Once she realised I was on her side and that we didn't have to move out of here she started to come round a bit. And then she fell in love… which always helps. Sam is just brilliant.'

Rafe finished his plate of food. 'And you have a little boy of your own too?'

'A little girl, Allegra. She's just six…' My heart did a little flip as I spoke. Allegra *wasn't* my little girl and Lucy was absolutely right; by deliberately keeping from Allegra the fact that I was her auntie and not her mother, I *had* actually stolen her.

'Are you all right?'

'Sorry?'

'You've gone very quiet and a bit pale suddenly?'

'No, I'm fine.' I smiled, pushing all thoughts of Lucy, for this evening at least, to the back of my mind. 'Would you like some apple tart?'

As I found cream to go with the tart and poured Rafe a

coffee, he excused himself once again to make more phone calls.

'As soon as those jeans are anything like dry I'm going to have to dash.' He frowned, sitting back down at the kitchen table and pouring a puddle of cream onto his pudding.

'Syria, you said? That must be horribly dangerous as well as distressing?'

'Well, it's not a bed of roses…' He paused to eat. 'Bloody hell, this tart is good too. No wonder this place is doing well.' He glanced around at the kitchen taking in its industrial sized hobs, cookers, steel sinks and fridge.

'It's terribly early days,' I said. 'I think we're just about breaking even so far. A lot of its success is obviously due to it all being owned by David…'

'Yes, Henderson is certainly a shrewd one. Knows what he wants and goes out to get it.' Rafe looked directly at me, holding my gaze for a few seconds and I could feel myself redden.

'So, Syria?' I asked, changing the subject. I had an awful feeling Rafe knew all about my thing for David Henderson and it suddenly all seemed a bit silly, a bit adolescent.

Rafe wiped his mouth on his napkin and reached for the cafetière. 'Syria…?' He sighed. 'Syria is a bloody awful mess. Syria is full of remarkable, horrific, inspiring, frightening stories.'

'But aren't you terrified going there? I'm actually amazed they let you in to report? I mean, I thought they'd arrest you as soon as you set foot in there?'

'It is getting harder and harder. When I said I was off to Manchester airport to fly to Syria, I was being flippant. I think I had my arm up a horse's rear end at the time.'

I laughed. 'So where *were* you off?'

'Beirut, in Lebanon.'

'Hell, I thought that would be just as dangerous?'

'Almost. Probably not quite. Once—*if*—you manage to get a visa from the Syrian embassy in Beirut, you are then driven up the road to Damascus. It's about an hour to the border and another hour or so actually to the capital. You are then searched and searched and searched again by the Syrian Security Services.'

'I feel frightened just talking about it,' I said, gazing in awe at this man. Strange to think that just a few hours ago he was acting as midwife to a horse, now he was sitting eating my apple pie and, I supposed, in a few days' time I would see him on TV, reporting from the rubble and dust that was now Syria.

'The other way in is without a visa. You can try and get in over *any* of Syria's borders, but most of the media and aid workers without a visa try to get in via Turkey. Just as the poor bloody refugees are leaving, heading in one direction out of Syria and into Turkey, reporters are going the other way, to try and report what's happening in their country.' Rafe looked at his watch. 'And now, I really must be off.'

While Rafe dressed in still very damp jeans, I made sure the house was secure, ran up to her room to tell a half-asleep Sophie I was driving Rafe home and grabbed the Mini's keys.

As he unfolded his long, damp-jeaned legs from the depths of the Mini passenger seat, Rafe reached over and kissed my cheek. He held my gaze for a couple of seconds with his blue eyes and said, 'Thank you, Clementine. I'll be in touch.'

I drove the two miles home, touching my cheek where'd he'd kissed it, my head so full of the events of the evening I literally thought it might burst.

30

'Oh, Clem, why the hell have you kept all this to yourself?' Izzy paced the patio, coffee in one hand, large slab of millionaires' shortbread in the other. 'You have to tell Allegra. As soon as possible. This afternoon when she gets home from school.'

I nodded miserably. 'I know, I know. You're absolutely right...'

'I mean, what if Lucy comes back in the next few days— finds Allegra in the garden or something when you're not actually with her? What if *she* tells her that you're not her mother? That she is?'

'Izzy's right, you know, Clem,' Mel said, pouring herself more juice before coming to sit down. Mel and Grace had both been at work at Clementine's that morning—Mel since six-thirty—and we'd had a full on few hours cooking and serving a traditional English breakfast to twenty American tourists. They'd been booked in to eat by their upmarket travel company—en route from their hotel to Howarth and

Brontë country. The mainly women tourists seemed to be under the impression the house was David Henderson's own home and, as such, were determined to have a photograph with David, wandering into the kitchen and even upstairs and generally getting under our feet in order to try and catch him *en famille*.

We'd finally managed to wave them off around eleven-thirty and the four of us were now sitting with our feet up enjoying an hour's break in the warmth of a beautiful June day. Eric was out mowing the lawns and the heady scent of cut grass mingled with the sweet scents of alyssum, wisteria and jasmine, while the insistently spirited chatter of a couple of sparrows was in competition with the more gentle muted call from a family of wood pigeons. God, I adored this place. I was determined, even as we sat, to make sure Clementine's was going to go from strength to strength, to make it the success that David Henderson had envisaged.

'Look, Mel, I know you're right, I should have told Allegra from day one that I wasn't her real mother, but as time went by I'd sort of convinced myself that I was. I've thought of myself as her mother now for years. I *am* her mother. Does that make sense?'

'But surely you must have known Lucy would want to have Allegra once she was able to take care of her, herself?'

I could feel myself struggling not to cry as the others looked at me expectantly. 'What is it with you lot, I always end up confessing my life story?' I sniffed.

'It's because we're your women friends and women friends have to know everything about each other. That's what it's all about,' Izzy said, comfortably. 'So, come on, what other bits have you missed telling us? *Apart* from the fact that you aren't Allegra's mother after all?'

'That's a bit harsh, Izzy.' Mel interrupted. 'We all have private things we might not want people to know.'

'*I* don't,' Izzy said. '*I* tell everybody everything…'

'OK, OK, I'll talk,' I said, holding up my hands in mock surrender. 'When I left sixth-form college I wasn't quite sure what I wanted to do. I knew I wanted to go to university at some stage and my parents certainly wanted me to do that. But I'd done art at A level and really got into it so was toying with art college rather than the law degree my father had wanted me to do.'

'That's strange,' Grace interrupted. 'My father, who actually was a solicitor in Midhope, was expecting me to do law and go into the family firm, but I chose teaching instead…'

'Fathers do have this thing about law, don't they? So, anyway, I did a foundation year at Leeds Art College but then decided it wasn't quite what I wanted. What I *really* wanted to do was go travelling. My mum and dad weren't happy that I decided against doing a degree, but I told them I could always do one later and I set off. I did a couple of years au-pairing in Italy and Monaco and then came home before setting off for Israel. I worked on several kibbutzim and absolutely adored it…'

'Israel? Wasn't that dangerous?' Mel frowned. 'I didn't think you could go and volunteer to work there anymore with all the unrest in that area?'

'As long as you went through a volunteer agency and were sensible about security, it was fine. It really was. Both my kibbutzim were well away from the main problem areas and I just loved it all. After I'd picked pears and mangoes and worked with the hens, I said I wanted to work in the kitchens and, because most of the volunteers preferred to be outside, the kibbutzniks were happy to let me work preparing food. It was there I really began to love to cook—wasn't fazed by cooking for huge amounts of people.'

'I'm surprised you came back. To wet, miserable Midhope I mean,' Izzy said, putting the final bit of cake into her mouth. 'Did you learn to make this delicious stuff there?'

'I fell in love…'

'Ah, I knew there'd be a man in there somewhere,' Grace laughed. 'There always is.'

I smiled too. 'I met him on a trip up to Haifa, in one of the cafés, just as he was planning on leaving Israel to move to London to work in one of the hotels there. He was a chef—his uncle had a very upmarket restaurant in Haifa—but he wanted experience of working in England. When he left for London I went with him, but I really hated living in London and was missing Lucy so, after just a couple of months, he agreed to move up to Leeds as long as he could get a job in a top restaurant there. That's how we both ended up in La Toque Blanche—him as chef and me as general dogsbody to begin with. I was given more and more responsibility, until I was cooking like the rest of the chefs. It was a wonderful time.'

'And where was Lucy all this time? What was *she* doing?' Grace asked.

'Lucy didn't do sixth form—in fact, messed about so much in the fifth form she came out with virtually nothing. She was driving Mum and Dad mad, staying out, drinking, smoking dope…'

'You really are quite different, aren't you?' Izzy mused.

'Anyway, when she was only seventeen, Lucy met some guy down in town and went off with him. I only met him a couple of times—I reckon he was a dealer—and really didn't like him, but Lucy was totally under his spell. Weird really because Lucy had never done anything anyone had told her to do and here she was, doing anything and everything Samir asked her. They went to live in Sheffield while I was at art college, but we tried to see each other as often as I could. Problem was, every time we met up he'd come too. He was terribly controlling, but she was obsessed with him.'

'What about your parents?' Izzy asked. 'Didn't they see much of her?'

'Not really. She basically kept out of their way except when she and Samir fell out. I reckon he used to hit her but she never would admit to it. On three occasions she went back home and she really did try to be good and live under Mum and Dad's rules and try to find work. She actually worked in the Co-op in our village for a while, but I wasn't at home anymore—this is when I was au-pairing in Italy— and she would have found it really hard without me. And then Samir would contact her and she'd be off with him again.'

'So this Samir is Allegra's father?' Mel asked.

'No, no,' I frowned. 'All this with Samir was before she was even twenty. And then I went off to Israel and when I'd been there six months Mum and Dad paid for her to come out and join me.'

'That must have been really good for you both then?' Grace asked hopefully.

I closed my eyes as I remembered how awful it had been.

'From day one Lucy thought she'd come to a holiday camp. Working on a kibbutz is bloody hard work. You're up at four in the morning before it gets too hot and it's hard, physical graft doing some pretty monotonous jobs. She wouldn't get up in the morning, did as little as she possibly could and spent most evenings drinking.'

'Ew, not good for you then?' Mel sympathised.

'No, it was awful because I felt responsible for her, and embarrassing as the kibbutz community got really fed up with her. They're really hard-working, all the Israelis who have decided to make their home on a kibbutz, and just don't suffer fools gladly. Lucy and I ended up arguing and she changed her ticket after only six weeks and flew home. That's when I moved to my second kibbutz.'

'Blimey, you could write a book about this,' Grace said. 'So what then?'

'By the time Ariav and I had moved up to Leeds, Lucy was on heroin and was working the streets of Midhope. Ariav would come with me down to Emerald Street and we'd find her, give her some money, take her for something to eat but we just couldn't get through to her. She wouldn't let us try to help her to get off the drugs.' I looked round at these lovely women who were my friends, at their sympathetic faces but they really had no idea what life was like for the girls who regularly sold themselves in order to get drugs.

'Ariav and I had always hoped to go travelling again— we both had itchy feet—but I hated the idea of leaving Lucy, and I kept making excuses not to set off.' I took a deep breath. 'And then... and then I found I was pregnant and basically Ariav didn't want to know. Said I'd have to get rid of it. But I *wanted* the baby—wanted Ariav's baby. I told him I was going to keep it. I was convinced he loved me enough to stay with me and our baby—but, boy, did I get that wrong.'

'Oh no, you poor thing,' Mel said, frowning. 'What happened?'

'He buggered off, basically. Upped and left. To this day, I've no idea where he went or where he is now…'

'And the baby?'

'I had the abortion Ariav wanted me to have.'

I've always reckoned there is no class barrier to those who go ahead with terminations; one can be from the lowest echelons of society or right at the top, but if a baby's not wanted, or the pregnancy can't go ahead for any reason, it's totally irrelevant who or what your background is. There was no look of horror on these women's faces, no condemnation of my actions, just sympathy.

'I've never forgiven myself for ending the life of my own unborn child and find it a bit difficult to talk about…' I said, swallowing hard so as not to cry.

'More coffee, Clem, and one of these brownies,' Izzy urged, patting my arm, and making me smile.

'Is that your answer to everything?' I sniffed, leaning back as Izzy filled my mug.

'Pretty much,' Izzy said. 'Or gin. Or having pornographic thoughts about Tom Hardy… So, go on, what then?'

'I carried on living in Leeds and working at La Toque Blanche, working like a maniac to try and forget both Ariav and the baby I'd got rid of. But it just wasn't the same without him and I was seriously considering setting off again—I fancied South America this time. And then Lucy turned up out of the blue at my flat. Said *she* was pregnant and where should she go for a termination?'

'Gosh,' Grace said. 'Isn't it amazing how quickly women get pregnant when they don't want to? And when you're desperate… I mean, that's the main reason Dan and I split up, because I *couldn't* get pregnant.'

'Lucy was a good five months pregnant with Allegra before she realised she actually was pregnant.'

'You see, I just don't understand that,' Izzy frowned. 'I knew from day one with all my three that I was pregnant with them…'

'Yes, but you're a doctor and not a drug addict, Izzy,' I said. 'Lucy was so thin, wasn't menstruating every month and was in a world of her own a lot of the time. By the time she realised she was pregnant it was almost too late for a termination. To be honest, I assumed she'd miscarry naturally what with the drugs and the mess her body was in.'

'But she didn't,' Mel smiled.

I smiled back. 'No, thank goodness, or Allegra wouldn't be here today.'

'But I don't understand how a heroin addict can produce a healthy baby?' Grace asked. 'And surely social services would be involved?'

'Lucy suddenly decided she really wanted this baby. I think she saw it as something of her own to love; that our real mother had given *her* away, and she wasn't about to do the same. Typical Lucy, she just didn't think any of it through as to how she was going to look after it. Once I got Lucy to come with me to my GP, all hell let loose. Social services were in there from the start doing pre-birth assessments as to what should happen to the baby once it was born. I persuaded her to come and live with me in my flat in Leeds—I was lonely living by myself after Ariav disappeared—and funnily enough, those final months of her pregnancy were good. She behaved herself, drank the gallons of milk and fruit and vitamins I bought, slept a lot and watched TV. It was a bit like being little girls again when we did everything together.'

'So who's Allegra's father?' Grace asked.

I hesitated. 'Well, in the words of Lucy, "No bloody idea".'

'What a mess.' Mel frowned. 'So, do you think part of you was looking after this unborn baby because you'd regretted terminating your own, Clem?'

'You don't need to be a damned psychologist to work that one out,' Izzy snorted. 'I bet that's how you felt, Clem, wasn't it?'

'Yes, I'm sure it was,' I sighed. 'Everything wasn't going too badly at all. Even Mum, excited I suppose at the thought of being a grandmother, was back there for her.' I laughed. 'We used to go round to Mum and Dad's for tea, and then Dad would drive us down to the station and we'd get the train back to Leeds. Social services backed off a bit and Mum and I assumed they'd help Lucy get her own accommodation once the baby was born…'

'And? Did they?'

I sighed. 'Lucy went off one afternoon when I was at work and didn't come back. She took the train to Midhope and went down to Emerald Street to see her old druggy mates. She started using again…'

Mel was horrified. 'What, even when she was pregnant?'

'Yep. I think she thought she'd been good, and just one bit wouldn't harm her, especially so late in the pregnancy. She didn't stick at one hit and a couple of weeks later went into premature labour. Her mates were sensible enough to ring for an ambulance and got her to hospital. Social services were swarming like flies; they got in touch with me, and Mum and I went to be with her.'

'And was the baby... I mean, was Allegra OK?' Grace asked.

'Allegra was born a heroin addict.'

'Shit!'

'OK, that does sound very dramatic, but she was born heroin-dependent and had to go through withdrawal.'

'I've seen it,' Izzy said, frowning. 'Not at all nice for a baby. They can have terrible diarrhoea, sweating and tremors that they have to go through in order to withdraw.'

'It was the high-pitched screaming that got to me when I first picked her up,' I said, remembering the awful noise Allegra made for the first few days of her life. 'But I guess because Lucy and I are identical twins, she looked like me. She had my features and I loved her straight away.'

'Did social services take her away to foster parents?'

'They wanted to. Mum and I spent a week persuading, arguing, pleading even, that we were the best people to look after Allegra. Eventually they agreed to an interim care order.'

'What does that mean?' Mel asked.

'It confers enhanced parental responsibility on family members for a short time. Lucy and Allegra came back to Mum and Dad's with us, but she couldn't cope with it all. Allegra was still a colicky, irritable baby and cried constantly. She wouldn't breastfeed, she slept only for half an hour at a time. After six weeks of absolute hell when, to be honest, I was on the point of giving Allegra up too, Lucy upped and went again…' I looked at my watch. We'd been talking for over an hour and I was now way behind with food preparation for the eight people that were booked in for an afternoon cookery lesson on Yorkshire Fayre. I stood up and made to clear our mugs and plates.

'So? What then?' Grace demanded.

'I knew I couldn't give another little baby up. So, after three months of looking after Allegra, I applied for and was granted a Special Guardianship Order which basically means I'm Allegra's legal guardian.'

'For how long? Are social services still involved?' Izzy asked. 'I thought they would be, but you've never mentioned them. Mind you, you've never mentioned *any* of this, have you…?'

'Social services have no involvement whatsoever with us now apart from some ongoing financial support that I was able to apply for. An SGO—a Special Guardianship Order—provides a legal permanence but also preserves the basic link between a child and her real mother. Six years on and Lucy has never wanted to do anything about that link until now. I'm Allegra's legal guardian until she's eighteen, unless…'

'Unless?'

'Unless Lucy makes an application to have her back. She can demand this through the courts at any time.' I looked round at Grace, Izzy and Mel who were watching me carefully. 'The law says that every child has a right to a meaningful relationship with its real birth parent…'

'Well, then the law is a fucking ass,' Izzy snapped, but then her voice softened. 'You've been incredibly lucky, Clem. In how well Allegra's turned out, I mean. I've seen children, born to heroin-addicted mothers, who have permanent congenital anomalies. Although, to be fair, that's not the norm. What you do often see is some intellectual impairment both with verbal and performance skills by the time these children reach Allegra's age.'

'Well, that's why I was so over the moon when Mrs Theobold, Allegra's headteacher, stopped me in the playground to tell me what a bright, advanced little thing she is. I can't tell you what a relief it was.'

Izzy smiled but then frowned. 'But what I don't understand, Clem, is why you moved Allegra out of your mum's place? Why down to the Emerald Street vicinity where you could bump into Lucy at any time?'

'I really couldn't take much more of living with my mum, her coasters, "serviettes" and the *Daily Express*. She means well, I know she does, and she's been through a hell of a lot with Lucy, but I was twenty-eight, and living at home when you're that age is not good. I'd started my degree course, so I wanted to be down near the centre of town anyway to save money on transport. But really, I moved down there because... because I loved—love—Allegra so much I had to make this guardianship permanent. I've spent the last six years *dreading* Lucy just turning up out of the blue, demanding to have her back. I needed to find Lucy myself. I've spent the last couple of years looking for her, so that I could persuade her to make this all permanent. I want... I *need* to adopt Allegra. She's my daughter, but I have to make her *legally* mine before it's too late.'

*

'Phone, Clem.' Betty, one of my kitchen staff, had arrived for her afternoon shift just as the phone started ringing in the kitchen.

'Mrs Broadbent? It's Mrs Theobold at Westenbury C of E. Could you come straight down to school? There's a woman been hanging around, asking the children in the playground which is Allegra.'

31

'I'm assuming this woman is your sister, Mrs Broadbent?' the Fear-Bold asked as she led me into her office and indicated that I should sit down.

'It will be,' I said. 'When I spoke to you the other morning about her visiting me, I didn't think she'd be hanging around so soon.'

I don't know why the hell I'd thought that. When Lucy wanted something she wanted it immediately, whether it be nicking a tenner from Mum and Dad to buy the latest *Power Rangers* figurines to compete with Toby O'Neill— our neighbour at the time—when she was nine, or using my untouched new Rimmel lipstick before I did even though she knew I was saving it for its first outing on Friday night at Youth Club.

I'd thought it best to inform this martinet of a woman the circumstances behind Allegra's birth when I'd first enrolled her in her school. I'd done the same at her nursery and the community school down on Beaumont Street. When I'd dropped Allegra off in the playground the morning after Lucy's visit, I'd managed to have a word with Mrs Theobold about Lucy's sudden appearance and to reiterate that under no circumstances was Allegra to be allowed to leave school with anyone but me or my mother—even if she looked just like me.

'I suggest you take Allegra home with you now, Mrs Broadbent,' Mrs Theobold said, unexpectedly kindly. 'It's almost home time anyway. While we do have as much security in the school as possible, if you are concerned that Allegra's mother might attempt to take her, it might be a good idea to have a word with the police.'

I looked at the headmistress, realising what she'd just said, and was struck, perhaps for the first time in years, with the enormity of what I'd pushed to the back of my mind and refused to acknowledge: that Lucy was Allegra's mum and I wasn't.

She led me in silence down a corridor illustrated with a giant Goldilocks, the Three Bears and myriad bowls of porridge, each decorated with stripes, dots and stars in every colour found in the standard pack of thick, wax crayons I remembered so well from my own school days.

Mrs Theobold went into the classroom—'Good afternooooon, Mississ Theoboooooold'—and bent to speak to a couple of tots before moving to have a word with Miss Fisher, Allegra's teacher. I took the opportunity to scan the classroom for Allegra, and found her holding court with five other little girls, the navy ribbon on one of her plaits hanging by a whisker as she nodded and jiggled in time to some music her group was improvising with the help of a set of percussion instruments. She was so beautiful, with her dark hair and bright eyes; with her perfect little white teeth that she now showed to the world as she flung back her head and giggled delightedly at the rude farty noise made by another group's trumpet. I almost wept with pride and love, as well as the awful churning fear that I might lose her.

One of the little girls in Allegra's group spotted me in the doorway and nudged Allegra before pointing towards me.

'Mummy,' Allegra shouted, abandoning her mates and flinging herself at me. 'Why are *you* here?'

'Oh, I was just passing so thought I'd call in and see if I could take you home a bit earlier than usual. I thought we could sit in the garden and eat ice cream. What do you reckon?'

'I'm going home early,' Allegra announced to her merry band of musicians. 'To eat my Mummy's homemade ice cream in the garden.'

'Allegra, sweetie, there's something I need to talk to you about…'

She looked up from her bowl of chocolate and vanilla ice cream but didn't say anything.

'Allegra, come and sit with me because this is important.' She got up from the wicker garden table and came to sit on my lap in the shade. 'Allegra, I have a sister that you've never met.'

Allegra's head came up in surprise. 'A sister? Like Sophie is Max's sister?'

'Yes, although my sister is a bit different because, not only is she my sister, she is my twin.'

'You mean like Molly and Tilly?'

'Yes. Just like Molly and Tilly in Mrs Marshall's class.'

'Where is she?' Allegra gazed around the garden as if expecting my clone to suddenly manifest itself.

'Allegra…' Oh, Jesus, how the hell did I say this? I took a deep breath and held her sticky ice-cream hand. 'Allegra, my twin is called Lucy and… and she had a baby. And… and she wasn't very well so she asked me to look after her baby for her. You see, darling, that baby was *you*. And although I'm your mummy, Lucy, my twin sister is your first mummy. You were in her tummy before you were born and before I *became* your mummy…' Shit, I was making a total rat's arse of this. I felt a trickle of sweat run between my breasts.

Allegra gazed up at me wide-eyed. 'So aren't you my mummy anymore?'

'Yes, yes, of course I am, darling.'

'So I don't have to go and live with this other mummy?' Allegra's face clouded and I saw real fear in her eyes.

'No, no absolutely *not*. You're staying *here* with me and Max and Sophie and George,' I said with more confidence than I actually felt.

Allegra popped her thumb in her mouth and said, 'Well, that's all right then,' before snuggling into me and reaching for the remains of her ice cream.

At bedtime, once I'd tucked Max in and promised I'd be at his cricket match on the Saturday—how the hell I was going to manage it with a full house at Clementine's, I wasn't really sure, but I couldn't let him down especially as he'd been promoted to play for the Under 10s—I returned to Allegra's pink boudoir to check she was asleep. She wasn't.

'Mummy?'

'Yes?'

'Have I got Mummy Lucy and Mummy Clementine now like Katy?'

'Katy?'

'Katy Who Has Two Mummies, in my class.'

'Oh right, yes.' I remembered The Fear-Bold proudly telling me, as she showed me round on my first visit to the school, that she had 'all manner of families' in her establishment including—and she'd held them up almost as a trophy— 'two *lovely* lesbians and their daughter—conceived with the help of a *turkey baster*, no less.' Maybe this was the way forward with Lucy: sharing Allegra between us. Oh, but I didn't want to share her. She was *mine*.

'Allegra, you do have two mummies but you live here with me and if Mummy Lucy comes to school or into the garden to take you out for... for sweeties or... to see a kitten...'

'A kitten?' Allegra's head came up off the pillow.

Jesus, I realised I was suddenly investing poor Lucy with dangerous paedophile tendencies rather than portraying her as Allegra's real mother.

I stayed with Allegra, stroking her hair until she slept and then, feeling depressed, went downstairs. *If in doubt, bake*, I'd always told myself and, with Sophie's seventeenth birthday due in a couple of days, decided I'd make her a knockout cake. She was up in her room revising for the AS level exams she was in the middle of so, once I'd done an hour's prepping for the following evening, I went into the pantry to find a large enough tin in which to bake a cake.

When I came back into the kitchen after a good five

minutes rummaging at the back of the pantry, David Henderson was standing at the huge island, arms folded.

'God, David, you made me jump.'

'Clem, I...' He hesitated. 'Mandy tells me you came over a couple of nights ago?'

Had it only been that long? It seemed a whole lifetime had passed since Lucy's visit, since my being told exactly where I stood with regards to *Mr* Henderson by *Mrs* Henderson— and since I'd fallen head over heels in love with Rafe Ahern despite his hand being stuck up a sweating horse's fanjo.

Head over heels? In love? With the miserable, bad-tempered, not wildly attractive Rafe Ahern? Give me a break.

I stared at David, taking in his handsome tanned face, his obviously expensive black pinstriped suit, his immaculate white shirt, his general aura of wealth and competence and my heart didn't do the usual gymnastics it had been conditioned to do ever since I'd first met this man over a year ago.

'Clem, Mandy told me what she said to you. She had absolutely no right...' David suddenly walked over to me, took my shoulders and held me tightly at arm's length so that he could look directly into my face. 'Clem, I... oh God... oh, just don't say a word,' he sighed and, bending his face to mine, kissed me long and hard.

Come on, heart, I urged, *get going. This is the bloody Olympics: your big chance. Go for it...*

Nothing. Nothing at all. The old heart was sulking in the corner, refusing even to don its leotard for an initial warm up. How long had I waited for this moment? To be kissed by David Henderson?

David pulled me to him, wrapping his arms round me so that my head rested on his tiepin where it dug painfully into the side of my head. 'Look, Clem, Mandy doesn't know I'm here. I got back from Milan an hour ago and knew I just had to come over to see you. I can't offer you anything at the moment, I just don't know how things are going to work out…'

Things? I pulled myself out of David's embrace and went over to fill the kettle to give myself time to think. I realised I hadn't said a word apart from '*God, David, you made me jump*' as I came out of the pantry. I really, really didn't know what to say. What was it that David thought he might eventually be able to offer that he couldn't quite offer at the moment? A life without Mandy? The position of mistress? Or a quick tumble over the eggs, flour (supreme self-raising) and sugar I'd assembled on the island for Sophie's birthday cake?

And what was it about *me* that I never seemed to have anything that really *belonged* to me? My parents weren't really mine; my daughter wasn't really mine; Ariav, who had stipulated he'd stay only if I got rid of my child, hadn't really been mine; Max and Sophie weren't mine. And I knew, if David had come along, even a week ago, with this offer of 'not quite sure what it is, but I'm offering it anyway,' I'd have been ripping his shirt off and cracking eggs with gay abandon, even with the almost certain knowledge that he'd never leave Mandy and could never really belong to me.

Before I could try and explain to David how I felt, the phone rang at the same moment that Max came into the kitchen clutching his framed photo of Vanessa and weeping.

'Clem?' Max sobbed. 'I want my mummy, Clem. I want her.'

'Clementine?' Mandy Henderson barked down the phone as I simultaneously picked up the phone and a distraught Max. 'If my husband is there, would you tell him supper is ready and going cold? Many thanks.' She put the phone down on me before I could say a word and I was left beginning to wonder if anyone would ever allow me to speak again.

Once I'd found Max some clean pyjamas and stripped and remade his wet bed, Sophie sat with him until he slept again and then she joined me in the kitchen.

'Sorry, Sophie, this was going to be your surprise birthday cake. No surprise now,' I said ruefully.

'I think I've had enough surprises this year, don't you?' She paused. 'And actually could I have a vanilla buttercream filling rather than chocolate, and strawberry jam rather than raspberry? And…' She tried to hide her blushes in the fridge as she searched for the butter. 'And erm, how old were you when you first did it?'

'Did it? Did what? Made a cake?' I smiled as, still red-faced, she started beating the butter and sugar in a large glass bowl with a wooden spoon. 'Use the electric beaters, Sophie. Don't make work for yourself. How old was I when I first had sex, is that what you're asking?'

'Er, yes. I suppose with you having Lucy for a sister, you were both at it much younger than me?'

At it? What a marvellous turn of phrase, I thought, at the same time as giving thanks to whatever deity might be listening that I hadn't been tempted to ravage David Henderson on the granite. How truly dreadful to have been caught 'at it' by this seventeen-year-old who seemed to think because my twin was a sex worker I must too have had my fair share.

While Sophie continued to beat the butter and sugar, I cracked eggs—without Mr H's help—and sifted flour. 'I was nearly nineteen, Sophie, when I first had sex, so I was older than you. And since then, I've probably been in very few relationships—a lot fewer than you'd think.'

'So, do you think I should do it with Sam?'

'Sophie, my darling, do you *want* to "do it" with Sam?'

'I dunno, really—I'm worried our braces will get in the way. I mean, how awful if we were magnetically attached to each other.' She glanced at me over the mixing bowl and we both started laughing.

'All I will say, Sophie, is never do anything you don't want to do. Never be pressurised and give in because you feel you ought, or it seems to be the easier option. Oh, and if you are going to "do it" make sure you use a condom.'

'I could never have had this conversation with Mum, you know,' Sophie said sadly. 'She never listened to anything *I* wanted to talk about. It was all about *Justin*, or what new *car* she was having or where she could go off on *holiday* once I was out of the way and back at school.'

'That's because you were an 'orrible adolescent,' I said, trying to be diplomatic. 'You think everyone is against you when you're fifteen and sixteen. Right, that cake looks to be shaping up well. How do you fancy earning some money once your exams are through? We've got a really busy couple of months ahead and I'm going to have to take on some temporary staff. Mel, Grace and I need help in the kitchen and waiting on.'

'Can Sam have a job too?'

'Absolutely. I've already had a word with Harriet—you know, Harriet Westmoreland?—who says her son, Kit, needs to start earning his keep over the long holiday. And Izzy's daughter, Emily, fancies working some hours too.'

'Oh, that sounds really good.' She turned to look at me. 'Do you think Max is going to be OK, Clem?'

'I think it will take time, a lot of time. It's a terrible thing to happen to an eight-year-old. To lose both your parents.'

'I've never known him wet the bed before,' Sophie went on, embarrassed for him. 'Why's he started doing that now, do you think?'

'Anxiety, stress, unhappiness. Not only has he lost his parents, but his home has been turned into a restaurant around him as well.'

'Thank goodness we didn't end up in one of those awful little houses we went to look at.' Sophie placed the cake tin in the waiting oven. 'What are you going to do about Lucy? Have you told Allegra about her yet?'

'Yes. I had to go and see the head this afternoon. Lucy was outside the playground gates, asking the other kids which one she was. I told Allegra about her when we got home.'

Sophie whistled. 'Blimey.'

'Blimey, indeed. I'm going to have to let Lucy see her. If I don't, she'll just turn up anyway, here or at school.'

'Suppose.' She paused, suddenly shy. 'Thanks, Clem...'

'For what?'

'For being here and looking after Max. And me.'

I kissed her cheek and gave her a hug, the first she'd ever allowed me to give. 'My pleasure, Sophie. Really.'

I didn't kid even myself that the reason I was switching on the late evening news was simply to catch an updated weather forecast so I'd know if the next day's booked-in tennis and lunch for six could be served in the garden. I wanted to see Rafe; I wanted to see him in action, wanted to know if he was there, in Syria, and surviving.

I'd switched on the TV in the little snug that, now the huge, formal sitting room had been made over to a guest dining room as well as conference room, sufficed as our main family room. I loved this room. I loved its open aspect onto the garden, its book-lined walls and piano that I kept promising myself I would learn to play once I had more time. It was still incredibly light outside—I glanced at one of the daily papers that were bought in for the guests, but which I filched for my own use at the end of each day and saw it was June twenty-first: mid-summer's day.

I sat on the edge of the sofa telling myself, as I had previous two nights, that Rafe probably hadn't even got through security yet; that there would be other reporters, perhaps more senior, who would actually appear in front of the cameras. There were various news stories: a huge financial loss by one American bank; a missing sixteen-year-old, political infighting among the ranks of the Conservatives.

And then he was there, on my screen, explaining how a US-led coalition aircraft was providing significant support to Kurdish militia fighters seeking to defend three autonomous enclaves in the country's north from attacks by IS, but that a programme to train and arm five thousand Syrian rebels to take the fight to IS on the ground had suffered setbacks...

I hadn't really taken in before what a beautiful voice he had. It was commanding and clear, belonging to an obviously educated man. There was no doubting the northern accent, and yet I could also ascertain an occasional slight Southern Irish intonation.

He looked tired but sublime.

Clementine Broadbent, you silly bitch, sublime with a commanding voice he may be but, just like David Henderson, he belongs to someone else. He belongs to JoJo Kennedy.

I switched off the television and went to bed.

32

I need to talk to you, David.

The morning after David had come round and kissed me in the kitchen I sent a simple text. I'd spent one of those awful sleepless nights when you fall asleep because you're so shattered, but wake up a couple of hours later and know that you're going to be spending the rest of the night flinging the sheets off because you're too hot, and bashing the pillow into submission as you try to send worries over the waterfall. This was a trick Izzy had sworn by to stop one's mind going over and over problems: every time a worrying thought came into your head you had to blithely command it 'off you go—over the waterfall, bugger off you horrid problem…' Unfortunately, every time I found myself dropping off to sleep, it was *me* going over the waterfall and I woke, heart pounding, swimming upstream. At five o'clock I'd had enough, had a shower and went into the dew-soaked garden with George and a strong cup of coffee.

It was the start of another incredibly beautiful day, and George was in his element chasing the early-morning bunnies that Eric the gardener was forever muttering about. Shit, what was I going to do about David? Here was a man I'd spent a year having increased-pulse-rate fantasies about and, let's be honest in all this, thoroughly enjoying the lingering looks, the brushing of his arm against mine, the delicious feelings that came about by the very fact of *having* a fantasy love object. Because, at the end of the day, that's what David Henderson was: stardust, fairyland, pure fantasy. Now that there was a chance this fantasy might be coming to fruition, I was running scared. Scared, I also now realised, that my backing off from his advances might lead to his pulling out of Clementine's. And that was something I couldn't bear to happen.

My phone beeped as George and I walked in the Secret Garden that was, even at this early hour, suffused with the extravagant calls and song of birds and insects.

I'll be over at midday.'

I glanced at my watch as we walked. It wasn't quite six o'clock. David Henderson was obviously another Margaret Thatcher—ruling their world on too few hours' sleep.

I made sure not to drop Allegra off in the playground as was my usual wont, but walked down to the village a little later with her and accompanied her into school, delivering her right to the classroom and Miss Fisher's care.

As I began my walk back up the hill out of the village towards home, a black BMW sidled up beside me, following in my footsteps until I turned and saw Lucy at the open window of the car's passenger side.

'Clem, we need to talk.'

Hadn't I sent a similar text to David Henderson only a couple of hours earlier? 'Yes,' I said, knowing she was right.

'I thought I'd see you at the school gate but we obviously just missed you…'

'We?' I peered into the car and saw a youngish Asian man in a black T-shirt and jeans, shades hiding his eyes.

Lucy didn't bother introducing us, and after a somewhat disinterested glance he looked away. 'Get in,' Lucy ordered, 'and we'll drive you up.'

'It's OK,' I said. 'I need the exercise. The gates at the bottom of the drive are on a code so you'll have to wait until I get there.'

I needed the five minutes or so walk up the hill to try and dispel the fear that was mounting at Lucy's—not totally unexpected—reappearance, and to think about what I was going to say to her. The gates were very rarely locked, particularly now with so many staff and customers needing entry at different times of the day and evening, but after Lucy's initial visit, I'd started to lock them whenever practicable, making sure Mel, Grace and Betty knew the code to let themselves in.

Betty had obviously forgotten it. She was sitting on the grass verge on the lane, pressing numbers on her mobile while the black BMW was parked up, like an indolent black cat, at the side of her.

'I'm glad *you're* here, Clem,' Betty said, indicating with

a nod of her head the BMW. 'I'm sorry, love, I've forgotten the code. And I suppose that's your sister? Probably a good job I couldn't remember it—I wouldn't have known if to let them in or not.'

'Don't worry, it's fine.' I smiled, sounding more confident than I felt. I keyed in the code, the wooden gates to the drive slowly opened and Betty and I walked up to the house as the BMW went full throttle past us, scattering Peter's doves in its wake.

'Do you want me to stay with you?' Betty asked, obviously dying to know what was going on. 'Rather than getting on with the veg, I mean...'

'No. Honestly, Betty. She's my *sister*, after all. There's nothing to be worried about.'

'Hmm. Well, I don't like the look of the chap she's with. I'd keep an eye on the silver if I were you...'

I wondered if Betty would have felt differently if the man had been white, no sunglasses and driving a white Ford, but wasn't about to question her obvious pigeon-holing of Lucy's friend.

I suggested we sit in the garden—I didn't want Lucy and the man wandering around the house—and asked Betty to bring us out some coffee.

Lucy pulled a face. 'Ooh, get you, ordering people about to wait on you. You *have* got it made, haven't you?'

'Lucy, I don't *own* any of this. I work here, just like the other staff do...'

'So, it's David Henderson is it who owns all this gaff?' The man spoke for the first time, gazing round at the beautifully manicured lawns, at the trees and flowers in full summer bloom and at the mellow walls of the house where a couple of swallows, oblivious to the human activity below, were systematically swooping in and out of its ancient eaves.

'Lucy, do you think we can talk without—sorry, I don't know your name…?'

'Adam,' the man said, sitting down and putting his feet up on the chair opposite.

'…without Adam being here? I think this is between you and me, Lucy, don't you?'

'Oh, it's fine, Clem. Adam's my boyfriend—my partner— and once I get Allegra back to live with me, he'll be a *big* part of her life. We have a stable relationship which is what the courts will be looking for.'

I felt sick. 'I am her legal guardian, Lucy. You know that. *You* disappeared. *You* didn't want to have anything to do with her, years without any contact. There's no *way* any court will let you have her…' The sick feeling was suddenly replaced by a blind fury. 'I will fight you *every* step of the way, Lucy. You may be my sister, and God knows I've sided with you, fought for you, *loved* you all my life, but you are not having your own damned way over this. You are *not* having *my* daughter.' I was trembling and stood up to try and control myself.

'But, Clem,' Lucy spoke slowly, the little cat-like smile that I knew of old which used to have Mum wanting to slap her, playing on her lips, 'she's *not* your daughter, is she? And there's no reason for me not to have my own daughter: Adam and I have a flat, we are in a stable relationship, I am clean and out of trouble.'

Adam snorted. 'Apart from the shoplifting last week, Luce.'

Lucy glared at Adam and then turned back to me. 'As I told the magistrates, "Not Guilty".'

Adam guffawed, and there was real humour in his laugh. 'I think your answer was "Half Guilty," as I recall.'

'It was Buy One, Get One Free. How could I be *fully* guilty if one of the bottles was free?'

I stared at Lucy, my anger beginning to subside. Adam, surely, had just given me my 'get out of jail' card? No court would hand a little girl back to a mother she'd not seen for years, a mother who'd abandoned her at a few weeks old and who'd just been caught committing a crime the previous week.

'What was it?' I asked Adam conversationally. 'Perfume?'

'Vodka...'

Lucy shot him such a look of fury he shut up and leaned back in his chair, closing his eyes against the morning sunshine.

'I'm telling you now, Lucy,' I said, refusing to sit down again, 'Allegra stays with me. I've spent the last couple of years looking for you to let you know I intended applying to adopt her. Now that you're back in touch, I'm giving you official notice that that's what I'm going to do. I have an appointment with my solicitor in the morning and I shall do everything in my power to not only to keep her with me as her guardian, but to set in motion all I will have to do to legally adopt her.'

'You'll have a fight on your hands, Clem.' Lucy was about to turn nasty—I recognised the signs of old. 'I have an appointment with *my* solicitor too.' She got up from the table, kicking Adam who appeared to be dropping off.

'And don't think about hanging round the school again, Lucy, or... or I'll have the police onto you,' I shouted after her as she and Adam climbed into the BMW.

'Oh, don't worry, I won't,' she called. 'I know how to play the game; from now on I'll be a model parent, going through all the correct channels to get my own little girl back.' She suddenly jumped back out of the car and headed towards me. 'And don't you *ever* think you're better than me,' she spat. 'I might have walked the streets—a common prostitute—but don't kid yourself you didn't marry this Peter Broadbent chap for his money and this house. Yes,' she sneered, 'I read all about him in *The Yorkshire Post*. And if that isn't prostitution then I don't know what is.' She paused for a couple of seconds. 'What was the line in that Richard Gere film Granny Douglas used to watch over and over again? When that rich chap is trying to set the prostitute up in a place of her own? And he says, "It will get you off the streets." And she says, "That's just geography." Well, there you go, Clem...' Lucy laughed in my face. 'It's just fucking *geography*.' And with that, she turned on her heel and was gone.

'Clementine, what is it? Are you OK?' David seemed to appear from nowhere and came and stood behind me as I worked at the kitchen. Betty was laying up tables in The Orangery and Mel was in the office. He closed the kitchen door leading to the rest of the house, took my hand and led me back outside where, an hour earlier, I'd faced Lucy. He took my hand and I let it stay in his. 'I'm sorry, I'm a lot earlier than I intended, but I had to see you...'

'David, when I came over the other evening, when

Mandy told me to back off—and she did, and I don't blame her a bit—I needed a friend to talk to.' I took a deep breath. 'Allegra's real mother had just come to the house.'

'Sorry?' David stared at me.

'I'm Allegra's aunt, I'm not her actual mother. My sister, Lucy, is her biological mother. I've been her legal guardian since she was born. Now Lucy wants her back…'

'Oh God, you poor, poor thing.' David stroked my hair and I knew this was my opportunity to speak. To tell him this thing between us was going no further.

'And David, I have spent the last year, as I'm sure you are fully aware, dreaming of kissing you, fantasising about… about *being* with you.' Not really knowing if last night he'd been offering me a place in his bed, to be his mistress or to be the new Mrs Henderson, I didn't quite know how to actually phrase it. 'But I suddenly realised last night that this has to stop. That I'm not going to be the one to break up your marriage.' I felt amazingly calm as I went on. 'The only thing that is important to me at the moment is Allegra and my keeping her with me.'

David said nothing but stopped stroking my hair and sat down at the table.

'I'm really, really sorry, David,' I went on, speaking in a rush. 'You belong to Mandy, and I'm *so* fed up of being with people who don't really belong to me…' I tailed off, not really knowing what else to say, frightened that Grace, who was already late for work, might suddenly appear and see us together and put two and two together. David still said nothing for a while but just looked at me.

'I thought… I thought it was what you wanted, Clementine. I feel a fool now. I apologise,' he said stiffly.

'Oh but it *was*, David. It was. God, if you'd have kissed me even… even two weeks ago.'

'Is there someone else?'

'No. No.' God, what is it about the male ego that men think a rejection must mean there is someone else involved? I took a deep breath. 'David, this has been a really strange year and a half. I've gone from being single, to being married, to being a widow, to being the mother of three children and, thanks to you, to being in charge of this wonderful place. And now my sister is trying to take my little girl from me. Allegra is the only one that matters to me at the moment. If I've led you on—and I know I have—then I'm truly sorry and can only apologise.'

David smiled wryly. 'Do not adultery commit; advantage rarely comes of it. Who said that, Clem?'

'I've really no idea, David.' Jesus, all I needed was a 'starter for ten' at eleven o'clock on a Thursday morning when my mind was racing over the possibility of losing Allegra as well as suddenly remembering the four malevolent-looking lobsters that were awaiting my attention in one of the kitchen's deep steel sinks.

'David,' I took his hand. 'You have every right to, but please, please, I beg of you, don't give up on Clementine's… especially now as I will have to prove I have a stable home for Allegra.'

David looked at me in astonishment. 'Clementine, I may have lost my head over *you* but, let me assure you, I never lose my head where business is concerned. Why on earth would I give up on this place? Just as it is beginning to really take off…?'

'And is it?'

'Taking off?' He smiled. 'You've obviously not read the latest reviews on Clementine's. There were two last weekend: one in *Yorkshire's Best* and one in *Out of London*. Both were gratifyingly sycophantic. Oh, and my bank manager took me out for lunch to celebrate too, so it must be true.' David was still smiling but there was real sadness in his eyes. 'You are a very beautiful girl, Clementine—inside and out. I only wish I'd acted earlier …'

'David, I need you to be my friend.'

'And I am, Clementine, I am.' He got up as we heard a car on the drive, bent over and kissed me chastely on the cheek. 'Even if the very thought of you drives me to distraction.'

'I'm so sorry about Lucy wanting to have Allegra back, Clementine.' The week after Lucy's second visit, Harriet had brought her son Kit and his girlfriend Poppy round for an informal chat re their working at Clementine's over the summer school holiday. Sophie and Sam had taken them, as well as Emily, Izzy's daughter, for a conducted tour of the house and grounds and they were now drinking coke and, by the sound of the music and laughter emanating from the Secret Garden, having a great time getting to know each other.

'Thanks, Harriet, it's all pretty horrid,' I sighed, handing her a coffee.

'How much does Allegra know of it all?'

'Well, she knows Lucy is her real mother, but I certainly haven't told her Lucy wants her back. I just can't tell her, Hat, I can't.'

'God, I'm not surprised. So, what's happening at the moment?'

'She's at Mum and Dad's at the moment for the day. Now that school's over for the summer they like to take her out occasionally.' I smiled. 'One day is usually enough, and to be honest I don't like to let her out of my sight at the moment. I keep thinking there might be a time when I don't have her at all...'

'Surely not? No court in their right mind would take her away from you after six years. Especially when Lucy went back on the heroin before she was born and then abandoned her to go back on the streets?'

'Although my solicitor tries to be upbeat about it, he's worried that I didn't tell Allegra that I wasn't her real mother. He tells me if a real mother is off drugs and wants to resume care of the child she has to make an application to court—which we're still waiting to hear if Lucy has done—and then her situation will have to be assessed. The thing is, I should have let Lucy see Allegra, let her get to know her when she came round. And now I can't because I don't know where she is. Lucy is very crafty—she'll tell the courts I wouldn't let her see Allegra.'

'But that's understandable...'

'Probably not in the eyes of a court. I *should* have arranged for Lucy to come round and meet Allegra.'

'Well, I wouldn't have let her,' Harriet said stoutly.

'Apparently, some professionals have a view that a drug user is not necessarily a bad parent.'

'And being a prostitute?' Harriet raised her eyebrows.

'Hat, it's a profession. There are plenty of street workers who are loving, caring mothers just like any other. Kit's a good-looking boy,' I said, changing the subject. 'The afternoon-tea ladies will love having him waiting on them.'

Harriet laughed. 'Well, they'll have to get past Poppy first. She and Kit have become quite an item over the last year.'

'Where's she from? Does she live near you?'

'No, not at all. She lives near Harrogate—a vicar's daughter, no less. When Kit goes over there, he crosses himself, as much as from being on hallowed ground as to protect himself from the vicar. Bit of a bad-tempered old git, according to Kit. If Poppy is going to work for you, I think it can only be at the weekends. She can stay overnight with us then, but getting her back to Harrogate at other times might be difficult. It also means I get some sleep...'

'Oh?'

'I spend the nights when she's staying with us listening for every creak and footstep that might mean Kit is up to no good. I tell you, it's knackering. It's bad enough losing sleep when your kids are babies; no one said you have to go through it all again when they're eighteen.'

I laughed at Harriet's gloomy face. 'And Nick doesn't help. He just says let them get on with it, and then snores the night away. I suppose it's because she's a vicar's daughter I feel particularly responsible.'

'Well, there's five of them, including Emily, who all want to do some work. There's some basic food preparation—Betty is always twittering she needs help—but the rest is waiting on. It might be that they just get to work a day—two at the most—every week. And I know they're all going off on family holidays at different times—Sam's parents have asked Sophie to go to Italy with them for a week—so there *is* work for all of them, albeit not full-time.' I looked at my watch. 'And I'm interviewing a new chef in an hour. I'm a bit excited because he's—hopefully—about to jump ship from The Ash House in Wetherby.'

'Wow.' Harriet was impressed. 'I love that place—Nick took me there for my last birthday—I think he's still paying back the bank…'

'David says if we can get him, hire him. We are so busy I just can't do it all on my own even with the sous chef and the other kitchen staff we now employ.'

'Oh, Clementine, you have done so well. I'm so pleased for you.' Harriet beamed, draining her cup. 'Right, must dash. Anything I can do for you?'

'Tell you what, leave the kids with me—the silver needs cleaning and shelves need wiping down. In fact, there are loads of little jobs that need sorting.' I looked at my watch again. 'Shit, where does the time go? You wouldn't drop Max off up in Netherdene would you? He has holiday cricket sessions all this week.'

'No problem. Oh, and Poppy's mum, Sarah, will pick her and Kit up. Apparently Sarah's mother is friendly with Annabelle Ahern, so Sarah's going to bring her over for a drive out, drop her off for half an hour or so and then come and pick the kids up.'

33

'Clementine?'

'Yes?'

'Rafe Ahern.'

My perfidious heart that, only the previous week, had refused to open even one eye at David Henderson's kiss, leapt out of its slumber and was immediately doing a back somersault.

'Clementine? Are you there?'

'Yes,' I squeaked.

'Right. OK. Listen, I feel I owe you thanks for the other night with Twiggy and...'

'Yes?'

'... and the scrambled eggs.'

'Really, really no problem at all,' I gushed. 'More drama there than on *The Archers*, ha ha...'

'Right. OK. So, do you have time in your busy schedule to let me take you out for dinner?'

I stuck the phone under my chin and plunged both wrists

into the nearby sink of icy water full of blanched asparagus. Anything in order to slow my pulse and return to speaking as a sensible grownup, rather than a helium-imbibing teenager.

'Shit...' I could hear Rafe speaking as, panicked, I delved among the asparagus to retrieve my dropped mobile.

'Sorry, Clementine? You've gone a bit faint and woozy?'

'Sorry, Rafe, just dropped the phone in the asparagus'

'Right. I can hardly hear you, Clementine. Monday night any good? I know restaurants tend not to be too busy on Mondays?'

'Thank you, Rafe. That would be *very* pleasant,' I said, speaking slowly and an octave lower in an effort to sound relaxed and in control but sounding, instead, like Margaret Thatcher on the *Today* programme. I didn't even bother looking at my diary. It would have to be OK.

'What's up with you?' Izzy asked as, ten minutes later, she walked into the kitchen with Sid. 'You've got a right soppy look on your face.'

'Rafe Ahern is taking me out for dinner.'

'Heathcliffe?'

'Yes.'

'I thought you didn't like him? You said he's really bad-tempered...'

'He is.'

'And arrogant...'

'He is.'

'And when I said *I* fancied him, you said I must be blind...'

'I believe I did.'

'And, is he, erm, still with the gorgeous JoJo Kennedy?'

'Shit.'

'Hmm. I take it that means yes? I saw him on TV the other night. He's a bloody good reporter. Is he back from Syria then?'

I frowned. 'He must be, unless he was ringing me from London. He's not taking me out until next Monday.'

'So what sort of dinner is it?'

'What sort? Oh, only a thank you dinner,' I said, coming back to earth with a bump at the mere mention of JoJo Kennedy, and realising that that *was* all it was. 'You know, to say thanks for helping to get Twiggy back on the catwalk as it were…'

'Catwalk?'

'Well, horse walk, then. Now, your daughter has done a sterling job with the silver and I've given her some idea, and a bit of practice, of what I expect from her as a waitress. She's outside with the others having pizza if you want to take her home in ten minutes.'

'Have you time for ten minutes yourself? I want to know what's happening with Allegra. Where is she?' Izzy glanced out of the window.

'Sorry, Sid,' I said, handing him a biscuit. 'She's at my parents.'

'Go and play outside, Sid, so Clem and I can have a chat…'

'Hellooo?' A tall, attractive woman with a mass of dark cloudy hair who I guessed to be in her late forties, knocked on the open French window before stepping through and into the kitchen where Betty, Jim—my sous chef—and I were in full swing with preparations for tonight's menu in The Orangery, as well as baking numerous cakes for another private tennis party and picnic the following day.

I couldn't think who she was and looked at her, trying to work out if I'd met her before.

'Hi, I'm Sarah, Poppy's mum. I've come to pick up Poppy and Kit…? Oh what a heavenly place, what a wonderful kitchen. Gosh…'

Of course. This must be the grumpy old vicar's wife from Harrogate. 'Hi, Sarah, do come in. The kids are just finishing off skinning broad beans for me outside. It's such a tedious job, I told them to sit in the garden with some music.'

'Oh, what utter heaven,' Sarah repeated, gazing round in wonder at the fully equipped kitchen that, although extremely functional, had managed to retain some aspects of its former life as a bespoke country house kitchen. 'What are you making? May I see?'

Betty glanced over at me, making a face behind Sarah's back at her effusive enthusiasm, but I fully understood the magnetic pull, the almost sexed-up feelings Sarah was obviously experiencing.

'I've read all about this place, of course,' Sarah said as she walked round, looking at everything, sniffing the pots of herbs and the tiny, wonderfully sweet home-grown tomatoes Eric had just brought in; stroking the metallic fridges and worktops almost with reverence. Oh well, she was a vicar's wife, I supposed, but weren't these religious types supposed not to worship any false idols?

'Do you cook?' I asked, smiling at her wide-eyed demeanour.

'Oh God, yes. I adore anything to do with food. Baking's the thing I really love, but I've been experimenting with a lot of Middle Eastern and vegetarian stuff at the moment. I was *so* envious when Poppy said you might have some work for her, that I bundled my poor old mother into the car and said I was bringing her to see Annabelle Ahern—do you know Annabelle?' Sarah laughed. 'She and my mother were great pals in London in the Sixties. Anyway, I hope you don't mind but I used my mother and Annabelle as an excuse to pick Poppy up and have a good look round.'

'I don't mind at all.' I smiled. 'I'm always happy to have people here who love food and cooking as much as I do.' I raised my eyes pointedly at Betty who tutted into the cream she was over-whipping.

'That is so kind. My sister said this was an amazing place...'

'Your sister?'

'Selena Hamley-Smith. She brought Mummy over to your opening day...?'

'Oh of course, they were both with Annabelle. I remember now. Golly, do I curtsey to you? David Henderson said Selena was an "Honourable"—so I guess you are too?'

Sarah laughed and Betty banged her bowl on the steel worktop and revved up the mixer to high. 'Well, yes, I am—well I *was* the Honourable Sarah Sykes.' She frowned. 'It all seems to have gone a bit downhill since those days.'

'For God's sake, Betty...' I took Sarah's elbow and motioned her outside. 'She's like a woman obsessed with that mixer. Come on, let's find Poppy...'

My life over the next week or so was, it seemed, spent split three ways. Physically, I was in the kitchen: cooking, preparing food, watching Paul, the new chef we'd purloined from The Ash House at Wetherby, meeting guests, running the first of a ten-week advanced cookery course and sorting problems, as well as in meetings with David, Mel and Grace. Emotionally, I was either in a state of nervous anxiety as I waited every morning for the official letter from court telling me I must present myself to a judge or bench of family magistrates or, still in a state of nervous anxiety, planning what to wear and practising little things I might say on my forthcoming dinner date with Rafe Ahern.

You've probably totally blown up your feelings for this man anyway, I scolded myself as I bashed bread dough into submission. *When you see him, you'll probably laugh, 'Ha ha' at the ridiculous notion you thought the bad-tempered tractor driver in any way attractive.*

'You're talking and laughing to yourself again, Clem,' Betty would sniff. 'You'll have them men in white coats after you if you don't watch it…'

With regards to Allegra, my solicitor had outlined what course of events he thought might happen but, as it was rare for Special Guardianship Orders to be revoked anyway, and because his firm had never had to handle such a revocation, he couldn't really be sure, he said, how it might pan out, or what timescale we were looking at.

On the Monday morning of my dinner date with Rafe, Izzy

rang to say she was coming over to pick up both Max and Allegra so that I could go and buy myself something lovely to wear for my 'hot date'.

'Are you sure?' I asked, loving the idea of some time to myself in the shops.

'Absolutely,' Izzy said firmly. 'You've not had a day off in months. I'm assuming Top Cat can hold the fort for the day?'

'Top Cat?'

'Oh, I mean Top *Chef* don't I? Your whizz kid?'

I giggled. 'Top Cat will do actually; he reminds me of a self-satisfied cat that's got the cream. God, he's full of himself but, yes, he's really excellent and will be more than happy to try and get the better of batty Betty...'

'Well, I hope he can *do* it better than you can *say* it,' Izzy laughed. 'Right, Sid and I will be over in half an hour, so get your flat shoes on in readiness for pounding those pavements.'

Just over an hour later I was at Piccadilly Station in an exceptionally hot and humid Manchester, running for the free bus that would take me down to the shops of St Anne's Square and King Street. I felt ridiculously excited at the thought of buying new things not only for me, but for Sophie, Max and Allegra too. Once Peter's solicitors had dropped the bombshell that we were hugely in debt, the kids had had nothing new at all, apart from inexpensive gifts for birthdays and Christmas.

The heatwave of the past few weeks had been threatening to break in a thunderstorm all day and, as I came out of

Karen Millen into the mid-afternoon sticky city heat, the heavens opened with a vengeance. Desperate to protect my totally over-the-top amount of newly acquired purchases, I dashed once more for the free bus that would take me up to Piccadilly and the train home. Everyone else, unfortunately, had the same idea and bus after bus went by full of very wet passengers fleeing the downpour. By the time I managed to board a bus I was soaked through and it was standing room only. Clutching my carrier bags, rather than any means of keeping myself upright, I endeavoured to keep my balance but it was like being a domino; as the bus lurched so did I, knocking into people who, glaring at me, found themselves falling too. After a second woman shouted, 'For God's sake,' at me, a middle-aged, balding man took obvious pity on me and, standing, offered his seat.

'No, no,' I shouted, lurching once more into the people standing in the aisle. 'Thank you so much, but I'm sure the pregnant lady there—' I nodded towards a large, sweating woman, '—would like to sit down before me.'

'Who are you calling pregnant?' she shouted back. 'I'm not fucking *pregnant*.'

Scarlet with mortification but, despite myself, emitting little uncontrollable snorts of hysterical giggling, I managed to keep myself upright until the bus came to a standstill. My phone beeped as I excused my way to the exit.

Rafe.

Betty Boop informs me you're out shopping. Is seven-thirty all right for tonight?

I texted back, my heart hammering at the thought of seeing him later that evening.

Lovely, I'm hot, wet and ready to come

Shit! I looked in horror at my phone. Entangled with shopping, I'd hit the *send* button before writing 'home.'

Home, that should have ended with home.

I desperately hit the buttons and sent the message. Jesus, I was a damned liability. I go awol for one day and cause mayhem. And Rafe Ahern would think I was *just* as silly as I'm sure he'd always thought.

All the way home on the train I kept waiting for a message to come back from Rafe.

Nothing at all.

'Blimey, Clem, you look gorgeous.' I'd decided at the last minute to wear the beautiful black dress Peter had bought me for the 'big proposal' and Sophie, who'd never seen it before, had me twirling round to get a better look. Most of the stuff I'd bought in Manchester was for the kids, but I'd treated myself to a ravishing pair of red strappy sandals. 'Hang on,' she said and disappeared upstairs, returning five minutes later with a tiny red Mulberry clutch. 'Dad bought me this,' she said, handing it to me. 'It's not really my thing, but it goes fantastically with those shoes.'

And it did.

'I'm a bit nervous,' I admitted to Sophie and Sam who were babysitting Max and Allegra for the evening.

'Why?' Sophie asked, mystified. 'It's only old Rafe Ahern taking you out to thank you for being assistant midwife.'

Sam grinned. 'Oh, for heaven's sake, Sophie…'

'What…? Oh, my God, she doesn't *fancy* him, does she?' She turned to me. 'You don't *fancy* him, do you? But you've always said Rafe Ahern is a bad-tempered, miserable old sod with no sense of—'

'Shh,' I warned, blushing furiously as Rafe appeared at the kitchen door. My heart went into overdrive, as much at seeing him—tall, dark, blue-eyed and utterly sublime—standing in the kitchen and looking at me with raised eyebrows, as what he might have just overheard.

'Shall we go, Rafe?' I asked, smiling sweetly, before turning to Sophie with a cut-throat action that sent her into peals of laughter which, in turn, made me giggle.

I was half expecting the rusting red tractor to be parked at the bottom of the drive but, instead, there sat a sleek classic Aston Martin.

'Lovely car,' I said.

'Lovely dress,' he replied, grinning.

He said nothing for a while, concentrating on the bends in the road which were being hidden by the late-July evening sunshine. 'Could you pass me those sunglasses in there?' He indicated the car's glove compartment with a large, tanned, very masculine hand and I wanted to take hold of it, just to feel his hand in mine.

'Where are we going?'

'I've booked a table at The Box Tree in Ilkley. I hope that's OK?'

'Oh gosh, I've always wanted to go there. How wonderful. You can 'Call the Midwife' anytime you like if I get to be rewarded with The Box Tree every time.'

Rafe grinned. 'So how was Manchester?'

'Well,' I said, 'It was hot, wet…' I felt myself going scarlet.

'And you were ready to come? Home that is?' He burst out laughing.

'You could have texted me back to say you'd got my second text. How mean is that…?'

'The whole thing made me laugh so much, I had to show it one of the guys at the TV studio.'

'Oh, you're joking. I'm so embarrassed.'

'Don't be. It was wonderful. It was you…' Rafe turned to look at me with those beautiful blue Irish eyes and I was lost.

'So tell me about your little girl? I've met Peter's children but not your own daughter.' The waiter poured wine as Rafe passed me the plate of four tiny canapés that had been brought to our table in the bar. It was a bit like relaxing in one's own sitting room at home and, not for the first time, I mentally applauded David Henderson's foresight in his plans to maintain the ambience of Clementine's as a family home. I bit into the tiny pink peppercorn macaroon stuffed with a chive and cream cheese filling and swallowed.

'Allegra is not my little girl.'

'Oh?' Rafe frowned. 'Sorry, I thought she was your daughter.'

'Allegra is my ward. My twin sister is her real mother…'

'Oh.' Rafe chewed on his own macaroon.

I really didn't want to go into the whole story of mine and Lucy's birth and the huge mess I was in with Lucy and Allegra just at that moment. I didn't want to see the shock, the sympathy, even the disdain that I'd seen on so many faces in the past when I'd opened up about my birth and heritage as well as Lucy's profession.

'Lucy, my twin, was unable to look after Allegra when she was born so Mum and I took Allegra on and then, when she was three months old, I became her official legal guardian.'

I paused, wanting to get off the subject, wanting to have Rafe continue to look at me as he had been doing as he passed the canapés. 'Do you have children?' I asked, desperately trying to get off the subject of Lucy.

'Yes.'

This wasn't the answer I'd expected. 'Oh?'

'I have a six-year-old son.'

'Where is he?'

'He's with my ex-wife in London.'

'Oh. Right. And do you get to see him? Does he come up to Yorkshire?'

Rafe smiled wryly. 'When I can get my wife—my ex-wife—to agree to it, but it's a constant battle. I'm afraid she doesn't like me very much.'

'Why on earth not?' I asked indignantly, forgetting that, until just over a couple of weeks ago, had I met her, I'd have been in total agreement with her, commiserating hugely about her choice of husband now sitting opposite me.

'I was away more than I was with her, I'm afraid. As a foreign correspondent one has to have one's bag packed and be ready to leave at five minutes' notice.' Rafe tapped his jacket top pocket. 'My passport is always to hand and a bag packed ready in the boot of the car.'

'Well, surely she realised that when she married you?'

'She thought she could change me; thought that by her getting pregnant I'd be more likely to stay in London at a desk job rather than spend half my time up in Yorkshire and the other half in the middle of yet another war.'

'Didn't she want to come and live up here? I couldn't imagine anyone not loving the hills and moors round here?' I trailed off as I realised I was beginning to sound like Cathy in *Wuthering Heights*. And Izzy was right. Rafe Ahern, with his brooding, dark good looks was Heathcliffe to a T.

'Unfortunately not. And, totally my fault, I met someone else.'

My heart plummeted and I reached for my glass taking a too big gulp of the wine. 'JoJo Kennedy?'

Rafe raised his eyebrows. 'Ah, you read the papers.' It was a statement rather than a question.

'Don't really have the time,' I muttered. 'Grace told me.'

'Grace?'

'Grace works part-time for us at Clementine's. I think her mother is friendly with your mother? Grace is mum to Jonty who is David Henderson's grandson.'

'Ah, David Henderson...' Rafe raised his eyebrows once more and was about to say something, but our waiter came over and took us upstairs to the dining room.

'God, this is divine,' I said, relishing every mouthful of the *amuse bouche* of broccoli and blue cheese foam that had been placed in front of me.

'Is this the sort of thing you rustle up at your place?' Rafe was obviously amused by my look of reverence.

'Rustle up? Blimey, if only it was so simple. But yes, this is the sort of thing we serve in The Orangery. You'll have to come over one evening,' I added shyly.

'Is that an invitation to dine with you?' he asked softly.

Our eyes met. 'Yes, I'd really like that,' I said and, smiling, he stroked the back of my hand with a feather-light touch. God, who would have thought one's knuckles were an erogenous zone? I felt my nether regions turn to liquid.

'Your pupils have just got very large.' Rafe took my hand in his large one. It was tanned from his week in Syria and I was having great difficulty not imagining the touch of that hand on the rest of me.

'It's the amuse bouche,' I squeaked. 'Broccoli is amazingly good for the eyes…'

Rafe laughed and poured more wine as I willed my traitorous pupils to calm down and compose themselves. 'So, I assume JoJo is more understanding about your time away then?' I asked.

Rafe snorted in derision. 'As long as JoJo is getting what JoJo *wants* she's exceptionally understanding.' He hesitated. 'And at the moment what JoJo wants is the lead singer from Perplexed.'

'Ted Mallabourne? Wow, *he's* gorgeous… Not that you aren't, I mean…' I went scarlet, and reached for my glass once more. Where was a sink of blanching asparagus when a girl needed one?

'Ah well, enough about me,' Rafe said. 'Tell me more about your niece. It can't have been easy these last few years?'

'My niece?' For a moment I couldn't think who he was talking about. 'Sorry, as far as I'm concerned Allegra is my daughter.' I put down my knife and fork. 'But I may well have to get used to her being my niece; my sister Lucy is determined to get her back.' All the excitement of being out on a date at The Box Tree with Rafe Ahern began to drain out of me as the reality of possibly losing Allegra hit me, once again, head on.

Rafe took my hand once more. 'I'm so sorry, Clementine. Come on, tell me all about it...'

Over the most divine sea bass and roast Jerusalem artichoke, I found myself telling Rafe everything. He was obviously good at his job as an investigative reporter and asked questions, drawing me out, letting me talk. The bottle of white burgundy that, after finishing his one glass, Rafe seemed to feel was my responsibility to finish, obviously helped loosen my tongue and I told him about my violent, drug smuggling, jailbird mother and Lucy's use of heroin as well as her work to feed that habit.

'I actually need Lucy to get in touch again,' I told Rafe as we were drinking coffee. 'Now that Allegra knows of her existence, I think it's only right that they should meet; that I should be as upfront and honest as possible with both of them. Surely that will stand me in good stead when it comes to my being hauled in front of a judge? And despite everything, Lucy *is* my sister. I still love her, want to have a relationship with her again. But...'

'But...?'

'But on the other hand, the last thing I want is for Allegra to decide she likes her real mummy better than me, that she wants to live with Lucy. And not with me.'

The drive home was lovely. Rafe didn't say much, but plugged in a Bach sonata and let me ramble on, occasionally asking questions but generally just listening as I talked.

'One of your mother's friend's granddaughter is coming to work for me, part-time,' I was saying conversationally as Rafe finally pulled up outside the house.

'My mother's friend's granddaughter?' Rafe laughed. 'You've lost me…'

'Your mother's friend—Lady Anne Sykes? Lives in Harrogate?'

'Yes, I know her well.'

'Her daughter, Sarah. She has a daughter called Poppy…'

Rafe didn't say anything for a good thirty seconds, but then looked at me, frowning.

'This Poppy's mother, Sarah… She's Selena Hamley-Smith's sister?'

'Yes, that's right. Selena came with your mother and Lady Anne…' I laughed. 'Hallowed company, indeed, for Clementine's on its open day.'

'She's married to a vicar?'

'Who? Selena Hamley-Smith?'

'No. Her sister, Sarah. This Poppy girl's mother…?'

'Oh yes. That's *right*, she is. Do you know her?'

Rafe took my hand and my heart began to limber up. He looked into my eyes and I didn't care about JoJo Kennedy. Didn't care that he was probably still in love with her. This was *my* night and he was going to kiss *me*. To hell with tomorrow...

'Clementine, my lovely,' Rafe said seriously, 'I think there's possibly something you need to know...'

34

Refusing to say anything more, Rafe came round to my side of the car, helped me out of the low bucket seat and indicated we go into the house.

'What on earth is it?' I asked, stopping on the path that led round to the back of the house and the kitchen and turning to him. 'You're worrying me.'

'Let's just go inside. I might be totally and utterly wrong about all this.'

'About all what, for heaven's sake? Oh, God, it's nothing to do with Allegra is it? You don't know something? Heard anything? About the family courts and Lucy?'

'Let's just go in, Clementine.'

'Hi, did you have a good time?' Sophie was on the point of going upstairs to bed and leaned over the banister as we walked through the hall.

'Where's Sam?' I asked, as Rafe went through to the little snug.

'Went ten minutes ago. He's doing a job for his dad in

the morning. Are you all right?' She peered at me, frowning. 'You seem anxious…? The kids have been fine. Honestly.'

'No, everything's good. Thanks, darling. I'll be up to check them both in a few minutes.'

She grinned and whispered theatrically down at me. 'Just behave yourself. Don't believe him if he asks if you want to see his cockerel…'

'Behave yourself, *yourself*.' I grinned, despite myself. 'Anyway, they're all hens…'

'That's what they all say,' she said sagely, disappearing up the stairs.

'I've poured us a brandy,' Rafe shouted from the little snug. 'Is that OK?'

'Of course. I've had enough to drink,' I said, 'but you go ahead.' I went to sit down on the sofa and looked at him. What *was* wrong with him?

'Right, Clem, as I said I might have got this totally wrong…'

'What? What is it?'

'Well, there's always been some scandal concerning Gerald and Anne Sykes's family. Mum would never tell us what it was about—Anne had sworn her to secrecy, which was a bit daft really because it must have all been in the local paper at the time. But anyway, Mum had a bit of a fall out with Anne a couple of years ago and she said something about The Lady Anne always thinking she was better than her when really she had absolutely nothing to be uppity about as her daughter had been in prison for bringing heroin into the country…' Rafe drained his glass and looked at me.

'Right. OK…' I frowned, looking at Rafe's unsmiling face. 'I know where you're heading here, but there must be *loads* of women who've been imprisoned for drug smuggling. Mind you, I'm amazed what you're saying about Sarah. She's absolutely lovely. Can't imagine *her* drug smuggling…'

'The family scandal *continued*, according to my mother. And of course, this bit never got in the paper.'

'What bit?'

'While she was in prison, Sarah Sykes gave birth to a daughter.'

There was a rushing sound in my ears, the room seemed to shift fractionally and I could see two of everything on the table in front of me.

'Clementine? Oh shit, you're not going to faint on me, are you? Here, have some of the brandy.'

I shook his hand away impatiently, and then shook my head to try and stop the ringing in my ears. 'No, I'm OK. I've never fainted in my life. It's too much of a coincidence all this, Rafe. And you said child—that Sarah had a child while she was in prison. There are two of us: me *and* Lucy. And there's absolutely no reason why our real mother was even in prison in this area or from this area. People get adopted from all over the country, you know that.'

'I'm amazed you've never tried to find out who she was,' Rafe said. 'Were you not curious? Didn't you want to *know*?'

'At one point, yes, I did. When you're eighteen you're allowed to find out, but Lucy got really cross whenever I mentioned it and at the end of the day finding out could have been opening one hell of a can of worms. My mother was a dreadful, violent woman who gave both her babies away. Would *you* want to find a mother like that?'

'So you think what I've just said about Sarah Sykes is nonsense?'

'Yes, I do actually. Sarah is really lovely. I liked her instantly.' I laughed. 'And I can't really see me, or Lucy, being the granddaughter of Lord somebody or other. As if! Mum always said our real mother, if she was still alive, was probably a drug addict, possibly on the streets somewhere. You only have to look at Lucy's problems to see what our real mother was like. Our real father, whoever he was, must have been OK—I mean, *I've* not turned out too badly.'

Rafe smiled at me. 'I think you've turned out really well. I'm sorry I got carried away with thinking Sarah was your mother. If she comes over again don't say anything will you? I'm sure it's something she's tried to forget over the years.'

'I wouldn't dream of it—nothing to do with me.'

'Just tell me your birthday, Clementine, before I go.' Rafe stood up, looking at his watch and I felt a huge pang of disappointment that he was making a move to be off. 'I'm sorry, I've a load of really important phone calls to make— I'm probably going to be off again in the morning...'

'My birthday?'

'Yes.' He looked slightly embarrassed. 'This is my feminine side coming out—I'm big into astrology, you see...'

'Astrology?'

'Yes. In fact, when I'm abroad, particularly somewhere like Syria where the sky at night is absolutely incredible, I lie there, just looking at the stars...'

'Isn't that astronomy?'

'You can't have one without the other.'

'Can't you? Well, I'm Aries—born March twenty-first. I've always loved that Lucy and I were born on the first day of spring. So what are you?'

'Sorry?'

'Your birth sign?

'Mine? Oh I'm a Leo.' Rafe looked down at me. 'Look, Clementine…'

'Does that mean…?' I began. We both started speaking at once.

'Go on…' Again we spoke at the same time.

Oh, this was ridiculous. I reached up on tiptoe and kissed this tall, gorgeous man on the lips and then, as I stood back, slightly embarrassed that I'd made the first move, his hands were in my hair and he was pulling me towards him, kissing me with such expertise I thought I might pass out with the sheer joy of it.

'All I could think of while I was away was you, down to your bra in that muddy field with Twiggy…' Rafe whispered into my ear, kissing my neck and throat.

'Even with a runny nose?' I asked, kissing him back.

'Even with a runny nose.' Rafe smiled. 'Anyway, it wasn't your nose I was looking at…' Rafe pulled away. 'Much as I can't bear the thought of going and leaving you all alone, I'm already an hour late making those calls and the numbers are in my office at home. Are you around in the morning?'

'Yes,' I said, grinning like a half-wit at Rafe. Not only had he kissed me with such abandon, he was wanting to see me again. And as soon as the next morning.

'We've a party of twelve in for someone's golden wedding anniversary lunch,' I said, 'so I'll be up early.'

Rafe kissed me softly on my forehead. 'You've got under my skin, Clementine…' he said. He picked up his jacket from the sofa and left.

After Rafe had gone, I let George have a quick run outside in the garden, locked up and went to see Allegra and Max. I loved them both; there was no way I was going to let anyone but me look after either of them. But, once in bed, as my mind whirled and jumped from too much alcohol, Rafe's heavenly kisses, and the strange revelation about Poppy's mum, Sarah, the ever-present terror of losing Allegra began its insidious nightly visit, worming its way into my head until all other thoughts, desires and even worries were gloatingly squeezed into submission by its pervasive serpentine coils.

'Sarah Sykes *is* your real mother, Clementine. There's no doubt about it.' Rafe handed me a whole load of photocopied cuttings from a couple of 1984 editions of *The Yorkshire Post*. Sarah's—much younger—tear-stained face stared back at me from beneath the front cover heading '*Not so Honourable now!*'

'Poor Sarah,' I said, glancing at the kitchen clock. It wasn't quite 7 a.m. and Rafe's knocking had woken me from what seemed only a couple of minutes' sleep. Embarrassed at being caught in my ancient *My Little Pony* nightie, I tugged it down over my backside and tried to act like a grownup. 'But I don't know why you think this proves anything. It's no more than what you told me last night. Where've you got all this from?'

'I've a good mate at *The Yorkshire Post* and he was more than happy to dig these out from their archives for me last night and fax them over.'

'It still doesn't prove anything, Rafe. Do you want coffee?'

Rafe shook his head and passed me another two photocopied sheets of paper. I felt the blood drain from my face as I read the words on the two birth certificates. Both recorded the births of little girls born to Sarah Sykes on March 21st 1984—mine and Lucy's birth dates—in Styal, Manchester. No mention was made of any prison or institution, but the area of Styal is synonymous with the Manchester women's prison.

'Coffee,' Rafe said. 'You need coffee.' He went over to the coffee machine and started feeding it pods of the strongest espresso.

'Daisy and Rosie…' I looked up, stricken. 'Rafe, I don't know who I am. Am I Daisy… or am I Rosie? Which am I? Who am I?'

Rafe abandoned the coffee, came over to where I was standing in shock and wrapped his big arms around me, enveloping me in his chest. It felt so safe—so good.

'But Clem, this is good. Don't you see? You've met Sarah. You like her. You said she was lovely…'

'Oh, Rafe…' I said. 'Oh God… her hair is like mine. Why didn't I see that the other day? Oh God, she loves cooking… she said so. She was sniffing my herbs just like I do. Shit, Rafe, Sarah's my mother. She's my mum.' I sat down, hand to my mouth, reading the words again and again. *Daisy and Rosie*. Which one was me?

'Yes,' Rafe said, going back to the coffee machine. 'I just couldn't believe Sarah wasn't your mother, last night, but you wouldn't have it. I knew it would be pretty easy through all my contacts to come up with your birth certificates.'

'Oh, so you're not into astrology…?

'Astrology? Load of bollocks! Don't believe a word of it.' He grinned, handing me a coffee so strong I could have stood a spoon up in it. 'I didn't want to tell you what I was up to because you might have stopped me and, ethically, if you'd forbidden me to nosey around, I wouldn't really have been able to go ahead.'

I wasn't really listening. I was staring at the column on the certificate that gave the child's father's name: *John Lipton*. I had a father—a real one. With a name too.

'Do you think Sarah knows who I am? Do you think that's why she came round the other day?'

'I've no idea—I've never actually met her. I know Selena quite well—bit of a snob actually—but although I knew she had this sister who wasn't often talked about, I don't think she's ever been over here before. How did she seem with you? Nervous?'

'No, not at all.'

'I mean, did she look you up and down trying to work out if there was any resemblance? Did she ask if you had a twin?'

'No, nothing like that. She was here to pick Poppy up— she's Harriet Westmoreland's son's girlfriend and I was showing them both what they'd have to do if they came to work for me.'

'Oh, shit, Clementine, I'm going to have to get off. I'm getting the shuttle from Manchester to London at ten—got a big meeting with my news team.'

'Right, OK.' I was still in such a state of shock, I didn't seem to be able to take in any more information.

Rafe came over and stood in front of me. I realised he was dressed in chinos and a navy shirt that matched his eyes— ready for the off, in fact—and felt at a distinct disadvantage in my nightie. I hastily rubbed sleep from my eyes. God, I hadn't even brushed my teeth...

'You can't imagine the self-control I had to exercise last night in order to drag myself away from you.' He smiled, taking a lock of my hair and winding it slowly round his fingers. 'But I really *did* have phone calls to make and… I wanted to sort this out for you before I left today.'

I smiled wryly. 'I think this is only the beginning of sorting all this out…'

'Would you rather I hadn't, Clem? Would you rather you hadn't found out about Sarah?'

'No, no. Not at all. I've spent all my life being told that my real mother was a nasty piece of work, violent and into hard drugs. Now this… are you sure there's no mistake?'

'No, Clem, there can't be, can there?' He bent to kiss my head. 'What are you going to do?'

'Do? Erm, well, go and have a shower, start thinking about the lunch party…'

Rafe tutted. 'You know exactly what I mean. What are you going to do about Sarah? Hell, I really am going to have to go. Sort it, Clem. Go and tell her.'

'Harriet?'

'Yes?'

'It's Clementine.'

'Hi, sweetheart, how are you?'

'Do you have Poppy's address?'

'Her address? She's actually here. Shall I put her on?'

I panicked. 'No, no, I don't want to talk to her.'

'Are you all right?'

I hesitated. I'd spent the last nine hours—after Rafe had brought me the evidence of who Lucy and I probably were—on autopilot. I'd chopped, sliced, mixed, cooked, smiled and served and, if you were to ask me what, I'm not sure I could have answered. My emotions veered from laughable disbelief that Sarah could be my mother, to euphoria that she was and back to utter despair if she *wasn't*. Betty, Mel and I had finally cleared up after the lunch party and Paul, the new chef, was now jack-booting about, giving orders to a couple of frightened minions, as he revved up the kitchen once more for the evening's guests.

I made a quick decision. 'Do you fancy a drink tonight?' I asked Harriet.

'Tonight? Yes, OK. Where do you fancy?'

'Oh, just come here. Paul's in charge of The Orangery this evening and I was actually out last night so don't really want to ask Sophie to babysit again… is that OK? I'll make us some food?'

'Sounds wonderful. Are you sure you're all right?'

'Yes, I'm fine. But, erm, I could do with chatting to you about something…'

'Right.' Harriet laughed. 'Sounds interesting. Look forward to it.'

After I'd put the phone down and rounded up Max and Allegra, whom I'd promised to take to the late afternoon showing of some must-see cartoon and then pizza, it suddenly occurred to me that Sarah probably wouldn't want *anyone* to know about her past, but especially her daughter's boyfriend's mother. Shit, why hadn't I thought about that before ringing Harriet?

Before I set off with the kids to Midhope and the cinema, I rang my solicitor, as I did almost daily, to find if he'd heard anything about Lucy starting proceedings to reverse the Special Guardianship Order.

'Mrs Broadbent,' Duncan Black, my solicitor sighed, 'I keep telling you. *You'll* be the first to hear anything, not me. Your sister won't even know I'm your solicitor—why should she?'

'I know, I know, I'm sorry,' I said. 'It's just I keep thinking you might have heard something from other solicitors in town—you know when you're out for a drink or something...?' I paused, feeling silly, as I always did.

'It really doesn't work like that.' I could almost see him raise his eyes in despair at my harassment of him and his practice. 'Just sit tight. If your sister is going ahead you will have a letter from the courts and then... *then* you come to me.'

In the end I decided I might as well ask Grace, Mel and Izzy for a drink as well as Harriet. Izzy was driving over anyway to drop Emily off to work for me and, while I obviously saw Grace and Mel on a fairly regular basis, we were usually too busy to actually chat about anything other than Clementine's.

'So, how was the "thank you dinner" with Heathcliffe?' Izzy asked as soon as she sat down outside in the garden.

'Oh, just that,' I said, not really wanting to go into any great detail with Izzy. I didn't want her thinking that the meal out with Rafe had been anything but a thank-you, or she'd be wanting a total post-mortem of all that had gone on.

She was rummaging in her oversized bag and pulled out

a copy of *Hello* magazine, sliding it across to me as I sat down to join her.

'I wasn't going to show you this,' Izzy said seriously. 'I mean, I don't know how far you've gone down your little meander with the dark, brooding one... But, before you get too involved, I'd take a look at this.'

Taking up two full double pages of the magazine were photograph after photograph of JoJo Kennedy. JoJo wearing evening dress for some award; JoJo at this year's Glastonbury festival dressed in green Hunters and the tiniest of denim shorts; JoJo at home, reclining on a leopard-skin sofa, two overweight pugs in her arms...

I glanced up at Izzy who was looking at me sympathetically. 'Next page...' She nodded briefly at the magazine, open on the wooden patio table. I turned the page, a huge photograph of JoJo wrapped around Rafe, with the caption *'JoJo Kennedy at the London home she shares with the BBC's Middle Eastern correspondent, Rafe Ahern'* staring smugly up at me.

35

'Oh God,' Izzy said, staring at my face. 'I knew it. You've fallen in love with him, haven't you? You've slept with him, haven't you? I bet he didn't tell you anything about *living* with bloody JoJo Kennedy, did he?'

I felt winded, cheated, bereft almost. I'd not thought for one minute that Rafe had ever actually lived with the impossibly ravishing JoJo Kennedy, let alone be living with her still. I closed the magazine, saw, with sinking heart, that it was the current edition and, handing it back to Izzy, forced a smile. 'OK, what'll anyone have to drink?'

By the time I'd checked on the kids in the snug, been reassured by a somewhat disdainful Paul that everything was *more* than on schedule in the kitchen, as well as given confidence-boosting pep talks to Sophie and Izzy's daughter, Emily, who were both waiting on diners in The Orangery for the first time that evening, there was laughter coming from the garden. Collecting wine, glasses and nibbles, I plastered a bright smile on my face and went back outside.

'Sorry it's a bit of a busman's holiday coming back here instead of going out,' I apologised to Mel and Grace, 'but no babysitter, I'm afraid.'

'No problem.' Mel smiled. 'Julian is away for a couple of days and I'm more than happy to leave the decorators and renovations to come and sit in this wonderful garden with you lot.'

Harriet caught my eye. I knew she didn't want to ask me what I wanted to talk about, in front of the others, if what it was concerned only her.

I took a deep breath, pushed the image of Rafe's blue eyes gazing in seeming adoration at JoJo out of my mind and said, 'Something really, really weird has happened…' The four women stopped their chat and looked at me. 'I know this sounds stupid, and it really is absolutely wonderful… but by telling you, I might really be giving away someone else's secret… but I have to tell someone before I burst.'

Izzy's head came up and she looked at me pointedly. I knew she was thinking I was going to tell them all I'd been having a thing with Rafe Ahern, but that he was living with JoJo Kennedy and what should I do?

'The thing is, I know who mine and Lucy's real mother is…'

'Gosh, Clem, that's the last thing I thought you were going to say.' Izzy looked apologetic.

'Who is it? How've you found out?' Grace and Mel spoke as one.

I turned to Harriet. 'Sarah, Poppy's mum, is also my mum. And Lucy's of course.'

'Sorry?' Harriet stared at me. 'Kit's Poppy? Sarah Rabbitt?'

'Yes.'

'How do you know? Did she tell you the other day?'

I shook my head. 'I honestly don't think she has any idea. Hang on.' I went inside, returning with the two birth certificates. 'Here, look…'

Mel, Grace and Izzy craned their heads, leaning over Harriet to get a good view. 'OK,' Harriet said, frowning, 'but what makes you think Sarah Rabbitt is this Sarah Sykes? I mean she's a vicar's wife, Clem. And she's absolutely lovely. I can't see her being the violent drug runner you said your real mum was.'

'Here…' I handed her the *Yorkshire Post* cuttings and, again, the others leaned over to see what the cuttings were.

'Shit. It is… That's Sarah, isn't it? There's no mistaking her. And look, she really does have a look of you.' Harriet stared at me.

'The thing is, Harriet, what if the vicar doesn't know about her past life? What if he doesn't know she's been in prison, had two babies that she gave up for adoption? I can't just turn up on her doorstep in Harrogate and say, "Excuse me, Reverend Rabbitt"—bloody hell, he's not really called Reverend Rabbitt, is he?—"is your wife in? Because, actually, she's my mum, she gave birth to me and my sister when she was in Styal prison."'

Harriet gave a nervous giggle. 'Worse, Clem, the poor man is actually called Roger.'

'What? My mum is married to Roger Rabbit?' I began to giggle myself and Izzy joined in.

'You have to tell her, Clem.' Mel leaned forward and patted my arm. It reminded me of only a month or so previously when Mel had said exactly the same about my telling Allegra about Lucy.

'Well, you certainly live life on the edge, Clem,' Grace said, pulling a face. 'Your stress levels must be way over the top. In just over a year you've finished your degree, married Peter—' she counted on her fingers '—moved here, *buried* Peter, become stepmother and guardian to two more children, set up Clementine's, found Lucy—who seems to be playing a cat and mouse game with you—and now found your real mother ...' Grace helped herself to a tiny mushroom pastry. 'Anyone else would be talking gibberish on a psychiatrist's couch by now.'

You've not included lusting after and rejecting David Henderson or falling madly in love with Rafe Ahern, I mentally added to Grace's list. *Oh, and now just finding out he lives with another woman as well. Jesus, never mind the shrink, just bring on the men in white coats and take me away...*

'Clem?'

'Sorry?'

'You were miles away,' Grace said. 'Now, what can we do to help?'

'I don't think there is anything, Grace. I just need Harriet to find Sarah's phone number for me—I have Poppy's but I obviously don't want to go through her—and then...'

'And then?'

'And then I will ring Sarah and make some excuse to get her over here.'

'Sarah?'

'Yes?'

'It's Clementine Broadbent. From Clementine's? We met the other day?'

I looked out of the kitchen window where the rain was trying its best to beat a patch of gangly gladioli into submission and suddenly felt very tired. Maybe it was best all round if I let sleeping dogs lie; leave the unopened can of worms unopened… I couldn't think of any more metaphors and leaned my heavy head against the cool windowpane.

'Oh hi, Clementine. Do you want Poppy? I'll just get her.'

'No, no, Sarah, it's, erm… you I wanted to talk to…'

'Me?'

'The thing is, when you were here the other week, you seemed so interested in Clementine's and you said… erm…' I quickly parroted the words I'd been rehearsing for days. 'You said you were into Middle Eastern food. I know absolutely nothing about this,' I lied. 'I, erm, wondered if you fancied coming over and sharing your expertise with me?'

'Me?' Sarah said again. 'Gosh, Clementine, I really am no expert… just have an interest really…'

'Right.' I didn't quite know what else to say.

'But I'd *love* to come over again, anyway. I was fascinated by what I saw the other day.' She hesitated. 'And I *could* bring over the recipes I've concocted,' she went on shyly, 'if you think they might be worth looking at?'

'That would be great, Sarah. Is late tomorrow afternoon any good? I'm up to my ears the rest of today and tomorrow lunch, but Paul, the chef, will be in charge after that...'

I spent the rest of the day working flat out in the kitchen interspersed with taking Max to a sleepover with a school friend and keeping an eye on Allegra and her little mate Martha who was over for the afternoon. I bribed Sophie, with a tenner and the promise of Chicken Caesar salad for supper, to take the girls and George out for a walk over to the nearby farm where there was a public gallery to watch the milking, and then into the little farm shop that sold homemade ice cream.

The lunch party was for David Henderson and a load of Russians and I always felt nervous cooking for David. The evening dinner, although only for six, included the food critic from *Yorkshire And The North*, and the menus they'd asked for were challenging. Pushing all thoughts of Rafe, Sarah and Lucy from my mind, I concentrated on what I was good at, haranguing Betty as well as chivvying Sam and Emily to work faster in the process.

'Bloody hell, Clem, will you slow down a bit?' Betty complained. 'I've not had me break yet and these new potatoes are covered in mud.' She held up dirty hands, dripping water from one of the huge sinks.

'No time for a break, Betty. Grab yourself a coffee, and I need those potatoes five minutes ago.'

'Bloody Hitler,' she swore under her breath. 'They'll be taking on new staff at Marks and Sparks for Christmas soon...'

'Fine, Betty,' I snapped. 'Just sort the damned potatoes

and then you're free to bugger off to M&S to sell Rudolph knickers and snowmen jumpers.'

'Hey, you're getting like that Geoffrey Ramsden,' Betty sniffed, swishing potatoes in the sink at a furious rate. 'You'll be f-ing and blinding next.'

'It's Gordon Ramsay,' I laughed, 'and I fucking won't!'

By four o'clock the next afternoon, I was physically drained but mentally buzzing. It felt as if someone had dropped me a couple of tablets of speed as the thoughts in my head careered and tumbled like an overenthusiastic spin dryer. Mel, who'd been working all day, knew Sarah was on her way over and offered to take Allegra home with her.

'Can I Mummy, can I go with Auntie Mel?'

'Yes, if that's all right, Mel? Are you sure?'

'I'd love this gorgeous little girl to keep me company.' Mel smiled her lovely smile at Allegra. 'Shall we have chips for tea?'

Allegra's eyes widened. 'Chips? And can I stay the night?'

'Allegra…' I shook my head at her.

'There's a bed made up, Clem. I'd honestly love to have her.'

Allegra was off upstairs to get her pyjamas before I could say another word. If I ever got the chance to have Allegra christened, I thought, Mel would be first on my list for godmother.

'Are you OK, Clem? Nervous?' Mel studied my face as I reminded myself that I might be gaining a mother, but my possible losing of Allegra meant any chance of my adopting and actually christening Allegra was, at the moment, pie in the sky.

'I can't tell you how glad I am you and Julian moved up here.' I sniffed, giving her a hug. 'Now, if I'm to give Sarah the shock of her life, the least I can do is not to be smelling of roast lamb and garlic while I do so.' I stripped off my black and orange apron and hat, hugged Allegra, went back in for a second hug with Mel and headed for the shower.

'Sarah, I've actually got you here on false pretences,' I said, taking a deep breath as Sarah delved into her rain-spattered bag, bringing out handwritten recipes on lined A4 paper which she shyly offered to me.

'Oh.' Sarah looked at me, embarrassed, taking back the sheet of paper before I could touch them.

'Come and sit down, will you? I'm sorry we can't sit in the garden, but we can talk in here.' I led the way into the snug and we sat next to each other on the sofa where Sarah looked at me expectantly. 'Look, Sarah, there's absolutely no easy way of saying this...' I handed her the photocopies of the cuttings from *The Yorkshire Post*.

Sarah visibly paled and her hand flew to her mouth as she realised what the cuttings were. 'Look, this was years ago,' she said, her hand shaking as she handed them back to me. 'It's got absolutely nothing to do with Poppy.'

'Poppy?'

'Well, I'm assuming that's why you've brought me over here...?' She looked at me defiantly. 'To tell me this is why you're not going to let Poppy work for you after all?'

'No, no! Oh, Sarah...' I felt my own hands tremble as I handed her the copies of the two birth certificates. 'I'm doing this all wrong. Shit.' I swallowed. 'Sarah, this is my birth certificate. And my twin sister Lucy's...'

Sarah was so deathly white I jumped up and poured us both a brandy as Rafe had done a few evenings previously. I was never quite sure if it was the best thing for shock, but it seemed to do the trick. The colour seeped back into her cheeks as she took the glass from me and sipped the alcohol.

'The thing is, Sarah, am I Daisy or Rosie...?'

Sarah looked at me, her large brown eyes amazingly like Lucy's, Allegra's and my own. 'Daisy was born first,' she said, her mouth trembling. 'Rosie fifteen minutes later...' She looked dazed. 'Does that help?'

'No, I'm afraid it doesn't. But really, it doesn't matter, does it?' I smiled, realising it truly didn't.

'Clementine, you need to know...' Sarah seemed unable to speak. 'You need to know that all this in the paper about me attacking the police and smuggling drugs is largely untrue.'

'Sarah, I'm not here to judge you.'

'No, listen, Clementine, let me tell you how it *really* was. Let me tell you the whole dreadful story...'

I sat and listened for the next hour, letting Sarah speak and weep as she told the story of the battle of Orgreave and the ill-fated trip to Amsterdam where she'd been set up by the man she loved. I tried not to interrupt, but became increasingly angry at the miscarriage of justice that had ended not only in her being locked up for almost three years, but in her being forced to give up Lucy and me.

'Why didn't you just have us fostered and then come and claim us back when you were out?' I asked.

Sarah swallowed, trying, but not succeeding, to stem the flow of tears. 'Oh Clementine, God knows, I wish I'd been stronger… wish I'd have insisted that the babies were looked after until I could care for them myself. But my family—oh God, my bloody family—said if I kept them they'd have nothing more to do with me. I had no money, no job and no home. How could I have looked after two two-year-olds—who didn't even know me—once I was released?'

'So, this John Lipton…? My father?'

'Johnny? I adored him.' Sarah looked at me. 'You have a lot of his looks, Clementine. If I tell you he was the most beautiful…'Again, Sarah was unable to continue.

'Rogue? Actually rogue isn't a strong enough handle for what he did to you. Bastard…?'

'*Bastard* will do, Clementine. Unfortunately it took me ages to accept he knew all about the drugs—that he'd just used me to get them into the country. I was convinced he'd come and find me and tell the truth.'

'So where is he now? Any idea?'

'He's dead. Oh gosh, Clementine, this is your father and I've just glibly told you he's dead. I'm so sorry.' Sarah's face was stricken. 'He was rotten right through to the core—John Lipton wasn't even his real name. He told me he'd been an art student, but he never was. Basically, Joseph Lennon was a liar through and through. He *was* from London, that bit was true, but a warrant was out for him for drug dealing in Kensington and Chelsea, so he nipped up the motorway to Leeds and just carried on doing what he'd always done: lying, cheating, dealing, conning people out of money… you name it, he did it.'

'How do you know he's dead?' I asked.

'He was on TV.'

'TV?'

Sarah smiled wryly. '*Crimewatch*. About twenty years ago. He was murdered in some gangland drug war. Joseph Lennon was just a petty drug dealer and smuggler, but he stepped on the toes of some big boys in Birmingham. And they came after him and finished him off.'

'Oh Sarah, I'm so sorry… You loved him.' I was shocked at her words.

She smiled again. 'Amazing, isn't it? Even after all he did to me, even after I was married with my children, the knowledge that Johnny was dead filled me with such depression I actually was quite ill for a while.'

'But you're happy now? You have Jennifer, Jamie and Poppy? Gosh, they're my brothers and sisters.' I looked at Sarah in delight. 'Wow I have a family, a real, big family… and Roger? You're happy with Roger?'

Sarah looked at me, and the tears rolled down her face and onto her hands as she wept, unable to stop.

Much later, after I'd cooked spaghetti for Sophie and Max and invited Sarah to eat with us, Sarah and I took George for a walk across the wet fields. The August storms that had been with us for the past couple of days had finally abated and the air smelt fresh and clean. As we walked, we continued to talk, thirty years of our lives condensed into several hours of conversation. Sarah wanted to meet my mother, she said, to thank her and my dad for adopting us and was determined to tell Poppy and Jamie everything about her past. Roger had always told her there was absolutely no need for their children to be told of her 'past misdemeanours'. God, he knew, had forgiven her and taken her into his heart. As such, the children's lives must remain unburdened by her past. Or so he'd told her.

And together, Sarah said, we would look for Lucy and tell her how much she was loved. As well as making her see that Allegra must surely stay with me—the only mother she'd ever known.

36

'So, where do we start looking? I really don't know Midhope like I know Leeds and Harrogate.' Determined, desperate even, to find her other long-lost baby now that she'd found me, Sarah was back at Clementine's two days later before seven-thirty in the morning, waiting impatiently while I did a couple of jobs in the kitchen before handing over to Paul for the day.

I passed Sarah a coffee and a homemade ginger and dark chocolate muffin, ignoring the three missed calls that showed up on my mobile from Rafe. 'Come on, have this. I bet you've not had breakfast, have you?'

'Clem, I don't think I've eaten *anything* much for two days,' she said, her eyes bright, her whole demeanour alive and excited. 'Or slept much,' she added.

'What've you told your husband and children?' I asked, finally managing to get Sarah to sit down and eat.

'The truth,' she said, defiantly. 'Roger obviously knows

the whole story... and has held it over me as a sort of blackmail for the past twenty-five years.'

'Blackmail?'

'Oh, you know—do this or I'll tell the kids; do that or they'll know what sort of mother you really are...'

'You're joking? I thought he was a vicar—a man of God?'

'Yes, well, there are vicars and there are vicars,' Sarah said, devouring the muffin. 'Heavens, this is scrummy.'

I smiled, suddenly seeing the leggy, enthusiastic boarding-school pupil she must once have been.

'Anyway, I sat Poppy down and told her absolutely *everything*. I didn't miss out *one* sordid detail. Roger was hopping about like a demented rabbit.' Sarah giggled into her coffee. 'Oops, that's funny, isn't it; bloody stupid name for a vicar, anyway. So, Roger Rabbitt...' She chuckled again and her laugh was so infectious, I joined in. 'He was hopping about, shaking his head at me not to tell everything, to perhaps give Poppy a watered-down version of events...'

'And? How did she take it?'

'Brilliantly. Thought it was "cool" what I'd been through and obviously couldn't believe that her boss here is her *sister*. I tell you, Clementine, I wish I'd told the kids years ago. I wouldn't have had to kowtow to Roger so much if he felt he had nothing on me.'

'I know you're not happy with your husband, Sarah,' I probed gently.

'Happy?' Sarah's face clouded momentarily and then she smiled. 'With him? No. With Jennifer and Poppy and Jamie? Yes. But... oh, we need to find Lucy.'

'Mummy?' Allegra came into the kitchen, barefoot and

in her pyjamas, suddenly shy at seeing a stranger sitting at the table so early in the morning.

'Oh... oh is this Allegra?' Sarah breathed, getting up from the table. 'You weren't here the other day, darling. Mummy's told me all about you...'

Unfortunately I hadn't told Allegra all about Sarah.

'Allegra, you know that Lucy is your real mummy...?'

Allegra nodded, staring at Sarah who was trying not to cry as she devoured Allegra with her eyes. 'Well, Granny Douglas isn't *my* real mummy.' Jesus, this was complicated. '...arah is my and Lucy's *real* mummy and your *real* granny.' I suddenly felt guiltily sorry for my mum and dad; after all, they were *real* to me and Allegra.

'So does *everyone* have two mummies then?'

'No, darling.' Sarah smiled, taking Allegra's hand. 'Just like Mummy Lucy wasn't well enough to look after you when you were born, I couldn't look after your Mummy Lucy or Mummy Clementine when *they* were born...'

'So, now I have two grannies *and* two mummies?'

'Yes, darling,' Sarah said, 'and we all love you lots, but Mummy *here*...' Sarah took my hand in her free one. 'This Mummy here is your special one.'

Leaving Betty and Sophie in charge of Max, the three of us drove over to Mum and Dad who'd agreed to have Allegra for the day. While Sarah was eager to see where Lucy and I had spent our formative years, she suddenly panicked, overcome by nerves, and didn't want to come into the house to meet my parents.

'Later,' she frowned. 'Another time, I think, don't you...?'

And I understood.

Once back in the car, I pointed the Mini in the direction of the town centre. We drove past the university and along the ring road towards Emerald Street.

'I'm almost certain she won't be anywhere round here,' I said to Sarah as we drove past row upon row of mean terraced streets. 'She's moved on, said she has a lovely flat with this Adam guy. She's clean, off the heroin, just biding her time until she can claim Allegra back.'

'Right, OK,' Sarah said, 'but you never know. How about we park up and just wander round and ask anyone if they know her, and perhaps can get her and this Adam's address in Leeds?'

'I used to do that on a regular basis,' I said. 'It never got me anywhere because, unbeknown to me, Lucy had already moved to Leeds when I lived round here. Look.' I pointed to the terraced house I had rented for almost two years. 'That's where Allegra and I used to live.'

I couldn't believe so much had happened since we'd moved out. I gave an involuntary shiver—where would Allegra and I have been now if Peter hadn't come along and taken us on board?

You're a strong, capable woman, I reminded myself. *You would have found work and you'd be renting somewhere, probably near Izzy, and you and Allegra would be fine...But then you wouldn't have met Rafe Ahern...* My heart did a little flip as I thought of Rafe... kissing me, his hands in my hair... telling me I'd got under his skin. *But that would have been a good thing*, I told myself angrily, *because Rafe Ahern belongs to JoJo Kennedy...*

'Do you think...? Clem?'

'Sorry, sorry, Sarah. What did you say?' I wrested my thoughts away from the traitorous one and concentrated on what Sarah was saying as we walked the streets. It was almost eleven o'clock and the sun, beaming down on the cracked dirty pavements, was hot.

'I was just thinking, didn't you say you'd been to see some woman when you were looking for Lucy a year ago? Maybe we could go and knock on her door again? Does she live round here?'

'Erm… Sheena. That's it, Sheena.' I couldn't remember her name for a moment. We were just passing Emerald House, and I remembered she didn't live too far past the tower block. 'OK, but she didn't know where Lucy was last time. And, I really do think Lucy's totally moved on now. Here…' I recognised the brightly painted red door that Yusuf and Musa had brought me to over a year ago in our search for Lucy and nodded towards it.

'Come on,' Sarah said, impatiently, leading the way.

Sheena's door was open and, as we walked down the alleyway to her garden, I could see her on her knees, doing something with trowel and pots. She looked up as we neared and I could see her wondering who we were.

'Oh, it's er…?' Sheena frowned.

'Clementine,' I smiled.

'I remember. You were looking for your twin sister?'

'Yes, that's right.'

'You found her then, I suppose?'

'Well, sort of…'

'Now she's back…'

'Back where?'

'Emerald House. I thought you must know. Thought you must be on your way there...?'

'No, I'm looking for her again. I really didn't think she'd be down here now but Sarah...' I pointed towards Sarah who was staring intently at Sheena, taking in everything she was saying. 'Sorry, Sheena, this is Sarah... Sarah wanted to come down. I did see Lucy several weeks ago and she said she was living with someone called Adam.'

Sheena snorted. 'Yes, well, I reckon Adam has lived with *most* of the girls down here.' She stood up, rubbing her knees as she did so. 'Arthritis... reckon it's all that getting down on me knees to give the johns a good seeing to.' She cackled lewdly. 'Occupational hazard, love.' Sheena laughed again before glancing both at me and then at Sarah. 'Emerald House—your sister's back there...' She paused. 'But she's not in a good way...'

In the three or four weeks since I'd last seen her, Lucy appeared to have shrunk. She lay under the grubby pink and yellow candy-striped flannelette sheet, one thin arm flung out to the warm, stuffy room as she slept. As we stood by the bed, unsure what to do next, Lucy scratched constantly at the tell-tale tracks on her arm. There was an overpowering smell of cigarette smoke and perfume in the foetidly close space, as well as an underlying odour of dirt—of unwashed body.

Lucy moaned in her sleep and then, as if realising she was no longer alone, slowly opened her eyes. Her pupils were mere pinpricks in her huge brown eyes, made larger by her gaunt pale face. She frowned, scratching again at the marks on her pale arms, looking from me to Sarah and back once again to me.

'What do you want, Clem?' Her words were slurred, almost incoherent.

'Lucy…' I was so shocked by her appearance I could hardly speak. 'Lucy, I'm here for you. I want to help…'

Lucy closed her eyes. 'Too late, Clem, too late.' She opened her eyes again. 'Who the fuck is this? Some social worker you've brought? Some solicitor you've paraded down here to prove I can't have Allegra back?' A tear rolled down her cheek and on to the stained, unsheathed pillow.

'Lucy, I'm Sarah. I'm your mother…'

'My mother?' Lucy stared at Sarah. 'Like hell you are. That bitch up at home with her petty rules, with her middle-class… blue-loo down the bog… with her shoes off at the door… with her sodding *serviettes*… that's my mother.'

'Lucy, this is Sarah, our *real* mother.' I knelt down by the bed, stroking my sister's hair. Despite the heat of the day, her forehead felt clammy and cold. 'I've found her…'

Lucy suddenly sat up, struggling within the twisted sheets to move over to the right-hand side of the bed before retching and then vomiting into the bucket on the floor.

'She needs an ambulance.' The pretty young black girl, who couldn't have been more than Sophie's age and who had initially shown us up to Lucy's room, reappeared at the open door. 'I'm telling you, she's frightening me. I don't want her in my flat like this. She needs help.'

After Sarah and I had driven the ten minutes or so to

Midhope General, following the ambulance with Lucy in it, we'd waited for what seemed like hours while Lucy was assessed for a possible heroin overdose. Eventually, we were allowed to see her on the ward where she lay attached to an IV drip that, the nurse explained, contained a drug to block her body from absorbing any additional heroin that might still be in her system. Another drip was putting fluids back into her body as Lucy was severely dehydrated. The nurse, a jolly Irish woman, assured us she'd be fine, that if there was such a thing as a *small overdose*, then this was one. This wasn't the first time Lucy had been brought in, she said and it probably wouldn't be the last. Just as Sarah and I were debating what to do—Sarah was determined she was going to stay the night with Lucy and then take her back home with her to Harrogate to recuperate—Adam sauntered onto the ward.

'Babes, how're you doing?'

'I think you'll see,' I said furiously, 'if you *can* see anything with those damned great sunglasses on, that my sister is in a pretty bad way.'

'Oh, don't give me all that sister shit,' Adam sneered, sitting on the bed. 'You've not been around for her before. This isn't the first time she's ended up here.'

'I think the important thing, rather than blaming anyone, is to decide what's going to happen tomorrow when Lucy can leave,' Sarah said, holding Lucy's hand.

'And you are? Not seen *you* before.' Adam didn't appear overly curious as to who this stranger was holding his girlfriend's hand.

'This is Sarah, Lucy's real mother,' I said.

'Ah, the jailbird? The drug runner?' Adam gave a short

445

bark of laughter. 'Well, you *are* all coming out of the woodwork.' Adam turned to Lucy, who was now awake and gazing at Adam with such devotion that I immediately knew there was no way she was going to leave the hospital with anyone but him. I recognised that look on her face of old; it was the same mixture of relief, fear and love that would be on her face when she was living with Samir in Sheffield.

I felt depressed. Do we ever learn from our mistakes? Are we somehow hardwired to constantly repeat our involvement in these toxic relationships?

'I want to come home, Adam, back home to the flat with you.' Lucy smiled almost shyly at him. 'I'm sorry for the other week… it won't happen again…'

I glanced across at Sarah who was still holding Lucy's hand, probably realising as I did that there was nothing more she could do to help Lucy for the moment. I was convinced the unexpected appearance of her real mother meant nowhere near as much to Lucy as Adam being back by her side, ready to take her back to his place in Leeds.

I needed to keep this man on my side for Lucy's sake. 'Adam, I really appreciate you coming to be with Lucy and taking her home tomorrow. Would you let us have your address and Lucy's phone number so at least we know where she is? Sarah and I really don't want to lose contact with her again…'

Adam looked doubtful. 'I don't like giving out my personal details.' He frowned. 'What do you think, Luce, do you want these two to know where you are?'

'Up to you, babes, whatever you think.'

The depression I'd been feeling was suddenly replaced

by a burning anger. Where was the strong feisty girl that was Lucy? I knew she was still there somewhere, hidden underneath all this pathetic deferring to the wishes of this man. What I didn't know was why, since the age of seventeen, my twin had seemed unable to function without the need for such a controlling man?

'Who knows?' Sarah had smiled sadly across at me when I put the same question to her as we drove back home. 'Why did *I* feel alive only when I was with Johnny? I think perhaps these relationships are as much a drug as the stuff Lucy has been addicted to over the years. Lucy probably sees Adam as the one constant in her chaotic life—she feels safe and loved with him.'

'But that's ridiculous,' I said angrily. 'I always loved Lucy, was there for her—as were Mum and Dad. She had just the same upbringing as me.'

'But you were the *good* girl,' Sarah said gently. 'Look, I'm no psychologist, but when Lucy saw you getting all the attention because you did well at school, when you were the teachers' favourite, your mum and dad's favourite...' Sarah paused, not saying anything for a couple of seconds. 'And then your mum tells her she was the daughter of a violent jailbird—Lucy would have seen a reason for her behaviour. She would have had a peg to fit it on to. She would have thought there was no help for her because she was born that way.'

'A self-fulfilling prophecy, you mean?'

Sarah smiled that sad little smile again. 'Or, what I've just said is a load of psychological claptrap and you only have to look at Joseph Lennon's genes to see where Lucy's problems lie.'

'I have his genes too, Sarah.'

Sarah shrugged. 'Then I give up… I don't know.'

We didn't speak for a couple of minutes, both of us deep in our own thoughts. And then Sarah said, 'At least you know you will be keeping Allegra. There is no way any court would allow her back with Lucy.'

'I knew that, Sarah, as soon as we saw Lucy in that bed in Emerald House,' I said quietly. I looked across at her. 'And this is the awful, awful person coming out in me…' I could hardly get the words out but needed to say them, needed to confess. 'Even while my twin was lying there in that awful state… I knew I'd won… that Allegra was mine.'

I pulled into the drive of Clementine's and burst into tears.

37

'That Ralph chap called round while you were out.'
Betty gave me a knowing look as she topped and
tailed green beans.

'Rafe.'

'Sorry?'

'His name's Rafe, and you're taking too much of the bean
off. Chop right at the end, Betty, for heaven's sake.'

'Good-looking chap, isn't he?' she said, trying to gauge
my reaction and, in doing so, almost losing the end of her
thumb.

'Is he? I hadn't noticed. For God's sake, give me those
beans, Betty and start the washing up, would you?'

'Anyway, he wanted to see you. Said to ask you to give
him a call.'

'Right.'

'Number's on the pad over there.'

'Right.'

'So are you going to?'

'Betty...'

'Because he said it was important.'

'*Betty*...'

'And now it's too late to see him because he said he was leaving at four and wouldn't be back until tomorrow evening.'

'I...'

'And it's now well after five.'

'So it is...'

'And you've missed him.'

'So I have...'

'And he did say it was important.'

'So is the bloody washing up.'

Betty held up her hands. 'Right, I've passed on the message,' she said self-righteously. 'I've said my piece. On your head be it.'

I fetched the six lobsters I had cooked earlier, pulling off claws and cracking them with such ferocity the succulent white meat shot into the air.

'...only he did say he wanted to see you...'

'Enough, Betty, for the love of God, enough. One more word about Rafe sodding Ahern and I will shove these lobsters where the sun don't shine...'

Now it was late afternoon, and way behind with preparations for a party of eight arriving in just a few hours, I couldn't believe so much had happened with Lucy in such a small space of time. So many emotions were flitting, nonstop, through my head: relief that, for tonight at least, Lucy was safe in hospital; sheer delight and utter relief that Allegra *had* to be staying with me for the foreseeable future; guilt that Allegra definitely being mine once again had come about because Lucy was in a bad state. But underlying all *those* emotions was an almost overpowering longing to see Rafe, to have him here, standing in the kitchen with me; to carry on where we'd left off only a couple of days previously. But Izzy's shoving of *Hello* magazine—with its cosy, loved-up pictures of Rafe with JoJo Kennedy—under my nose, had scuppered any dreams I'd had of Rafe being a free agent. How dare he take me out, tell me I was under his skin, make out that JoJo was off with Ted Mallabourne from Perplexed?

I knew once back from the hospital, I would have returned Rafe's calls hoping, against all the odds, that Rafe was going to tell me the magazine had got it wrong—it was out of date, that he and JoJo were no longer together. And I would have listened, taken it all in, simply because I *wanted* to believe that was the truth.

It was Mel, just about to leave for home after her shift in the office, who drew my attention to a booking for the following evening.

'You look knackered, you poor old thing,' she sympathised, once I'd told her about spending the afternoon at the hospital with Lucy. 'But once you get this evening's do over and done with, you can have a rest tomorrow. There's nothing booked in all day apart from that dinner for two I was telling you about the other day. Do you remember, the woman rang to say she wanted no expense spared, wanted to know what champagnes we have in the cellar? Said it was a surprise dinner for her boyfriend, and that if *he* didn't propose she was going to do it for him…'

'Oh gosh, is that tomorrow? I was thinking it was *next* week. Not a problem; I've already planned what I'm going to cook, and Emily is down to waitress. It's no big deal, a dinner for two. I just need to check what champagne we have in. With all that's been going on with Sarah and Lucy—' not to mention Rafe '—I don't know if I'm coming or going…'

'I'm not surprised,' Mel said, giving me a quick hug.

'I tell you, Mel, I'm going to stay in bed in the morning, and then spend the day with Max and Allegra.'

'You do right—you deserve some time off,' she said. 'And I'm so pleased that Allegra won't be going anywhere at the moment. I know it's hard for you seeing Lucy as you saw her today, but I'm assuming it means Allegra will stay here with you…?'

Once she'd gone, I put meatballs in the oven for the kids' tea and started to wrap the present I'd bought for my dad's birthday the following day. Unable to find the Sellotape, I tried the office and found it underneath the huge bookings ledger that had pride of place on the leather-topped desk.

I glanced across at the open ledger where the one name booked in for the following evening immediately jumped out at me: 'Josephine Kennedy/dinner for two'.

'Paul, I know you're not supposed to be working tomorrow evening, but I wondered if I could do a swap with you—I'll do the lunch party if you do my evening shift?'

'No can do, Clem.'

Oh God, why couldn't the man speak standard English? There was no way I was cooking dinner for Rafe Ahern and his soon-to-be fiancée.

'Look, Paul,' I said desperately, 'I just can't do tomorrow evening.'

'*Moi non plus...*'

'Sorry?'

'Me neither.'

'*Why* can't you? What's so special about tomorrow night?'

'I'm up for an award: Yorkshire Chef of the Year.'

'Are you? Well, you kept that one quiet.' I was disgruntled now as well as desperate. Why had no one nominated *me*?

'Right,' I said, thinking on my feet. 'So, I don't suppose you'd consider missing it in order to cook dinner for a world-famous model...?'

'Clem, I wouldn't consider missing it if the said famous model was lying naked with her legs akimbo on a bed of black silk.'

'There's no need for vulgarity, Paul,' I snapped. So, I take it that's a no?'

'Got it in one.'

Bastard.

You are a professional, Clementine, I told myself the next morning after yet another sleepless night thinking about and longing for Rafe. *You can do this. You simply go ahead and cook and keep out of the way of the pair of them.* Sophie had left for Italy with Sam and his family the previous morning, and both Kit and Poppy were off at some pop festival. Luckily Emily, Izzy's daughter, was booked in for waitressing duty that evening. She'd only done a couple of shifts for me, but she was already shaping up nicely and I'd had several compliments plus some very generous tips to pass on to her.

As soon as I'd got out of bed—eschewing the promised lie-in—I'd rung the hospital to see how Lucy was, and been informed by a rather irritable nurse that she'd discharged herself around midnight and gone home with Adam. At least she was with Adam, in his flat, and not alone in that dreadful room in Emerald House.

Thinking Rafe might suddenly appear in the kitchen to explain, to let me down gently, to tell me he was going to marry JoJo, I showered and washed my hair and put on full makeup. If he was on his way round to do the dirty deed, I could at least show him I didn't care. But I *did* care. I was so, so in love with Rafe Ahern and there was an end to it. Stifling a sob because Allegra had come into my bedroom and was giving me a worried look, I plastered a smile on my face, Rosy Skies on my lips and, swinging her up on my back, carried her down for breakfast.

It was only as I was poaching eggs for Max that I remembered Betty saying that Rafe was leaving after four yesterday and wouldn't be back until this evening. Just in time for his romantic dinner with JoJo, I thought sourly, suddenly feeling silly at having on my tightest jeans and brightest lipstick.

'You look *lovely* this morning,' Max said through a mouthful of toast.

I dropped a kiss on his fair head. 'Thanks, darling.' At least one man thought I was his number one.

Before I knew the true recipients of this romantic dinner for two, I'd spent a good hour enjoying the challenge of planning a menu to reflect true love, but I now sat at the table, furiously kicking the chair opposite as I perused the menu I'd lovingly and proudly come up with:

An amuse bouche of East Coast Oyster
Beef carpaccio
Gratinated lobster with truffle gnocchi and escargot fricassee
Champagne sorbet
Star anise mango with almond tuile and vanilla cream

I was just wondering if I dare sabotage the whole shebang and serve the *loved-up* couple (*Hello* magazine speak) Irish stew and dumplings followed by Spotted Dick and tinned custard—it might at least render *Rafe's* dick out of action for the night—when the phone rang. If it was Rafe ringing to explain, I wasn't going to answer it.

Shaking my head at Max and mouthing '*I'm not here*,' I watched as Max picked up the phone and said, 'She's just here,' handing me the phone before going back to his breakfast.

'Clem, it's Izzy. Really sorry, darling, Emily can't work tonight…'

My heart sank. 'Why, what's the matter?'

'Poor love has twisted her ankle badly. I was showing her how to do Bumps—do you remember doing Bumps with a skipping rope when you were a kid? Great fun—and anyway, she fell over the rope and her ankle is the size of a melon. I said I'd give you a ring early so you can get Sophie or one of the others to work instead.'

'Izzy, there are no *others* tonight. I really needed Emily…'

'What about Betty?'

'I need her in the kitchen with me.'

'Mel?'

'She's not a *waitress*. Anyway, she and Julian are off to London for a couple of days. It was Julian's daughter, Penelope's, birthday a couple of weeks ago and this is the first chance they've had to go down to see her.'

'Right. Is it a big do?'

'Just one couple.'

'One couple? Two people? God, it's not worth putting your pinny on for that. Cancel it and come to the pictures with us instead.'

'Don't be ridiculous,' I snapped, although more than a part of me was already wondering if I should.

'OK then.'

'OK what…?'

'*I'll* come over to wait on them.'

'You?'

'And Hat and Grace.'

'Izzy, I don't need three sodding waitresses—who're *not* waitresses—to serve one couple.'

'Well, we *were* off to see *The Escort*. Listen: "Desperate for a good story, a sex-addicted journalist throws himself into the world of high-class escorts when he starts following a Stanford-educated prostitute." I actually reckon we'd rather come and play at being waitresses.'

'No, Izzy, absolutely not. No way. Not a chance in hell…'

'So, show us the waitress outfits,' Izzy beamed. 'Are they like little French maids' costumes?'

'You know perfectly well the kids wear black T-shirts and orange and black aprons,' I said, seeing Harriet's and Grace's raised eyebrows. 'Oh good, you're wearing black trousers.'

'As instructed by our boss here,' Harriet laughed. 'I've always wanted to be a waitress.'

'Right, you three, seeing you're all here—but honestly I only need one of you to be waiting on this couple.'

'We can take it in turns,' Grace laughed. 'Bagsy the pudding course.'

'Seeing you're all here,' I interrupted, 'you need to know who it is you're waiting on...'

'Jeremy Corbyn and his wife?' Izzy volunteered.

'Has he got a wife? I thought he had a thing going with Diane Abbott...?'

'Get with it, that's ancient gossip,' Izzy tutted.

'Wills and Kate? Gosh, was never sure how to curtsy properly. And is it ma'am to rhyme with arm or jam...?' Harriet looked slightly worried.

'Have you lot been drinking?' I asked crossly.

'Absolutely not...'

'We called for a quick one at the Rose and Crown...' Izzy and Harriet both started speaking at the same time.

'JoJo Kennedy and Rafe Ahern?'

'Yes.'

'Sorry?' All three looked at me in surprise and then Izzy said, 'Oh dear, oh deary, deary me.'

'JoJo Kennedy, the model?' Harriet asked. 'Oh, she's *lovely*. Of course, Rafe's having a bit of a thing with her, isn't he?'

'Bit more than a *bit of a thing*,' Izzy said grimly. 'They were plastered all over last week's edition of *Hello*.'

'What's the matter, Clem? What is it?' Grace had taken one look at my face—as Harriet continued to extol the virtues of the supermodel—and was no longer laughing.

'Bloody Rafe Ahern,' Izzy snapped. 'He allows Clem to murder his mother's ridiculous chicken, ropes her in to act as midwife for his damned donkey or whatever it was— where he nicks her shirt, leaving her in just a bra for every passing pervert to goggle at—*then* makes up for it by taking her to The Box Tree, then spends all night finding her real mother for her and then… then kisses her passionately in the kitchen…'

'I didn't tell you he'd kissed me…'

'You didn't have to, Clem. I'm a doctor—I *know* these things…'

'And then he has the nerve to flaunt his—let's face it— *ravishing* lover on *your* doorstep… in your own restaurant?' Grace was really cross now.

'Worse, I'm afraid,' I said, trying not to cry.

'Go on…'

'It's a surprise engagement do. If Rafe doesn't propose to JoJo, she's going to propose to him.' I blew my nose, the sound trumpeting round the cavernous kitchen like some out of control elephant.

'How on earth do you know that, you daft thing?' Harriet asked, smiling indulgently while patting my hand.

'JoJo told Mel on the phone. And, and I've fallen so in

love with him. And I know I shouldn't, because he belongs to someone else...'

'JoJo Kennedy...No contest.' Izzy shook her head.

'Izzy!' Both Harriet and Grace glared at Izzy who threw up her hands in the manner of a Jewish mama.

'Look, I need to mothball my lust for Rafe Ahern.'

'You can't *mothball* lust...'

'I need to forget my feelings for him and do a professional job here. This is *my* restaurant and David Henderson would have a fit if he knew we were standing around acting like a bunch of schoolgirls. Besides, JoJo Kennedy has no idea I've fallen in love with her fiancé-to-be. It's not her fault, after all.'

'OK,' Harriet said. 'You cook and keep out of the way and we'll wait on.'

'And see what we can hear as they're eating...' Izzy said.

I gave her a warning glance and she threw up her hands once more, muttering 'all right, already' under her breath.

'Is everything ready in The Orangery?' Grace asked.

'They're not eating in there. Mel offered her the summerhouse in The Secret Garden—Betty's laying the table down there now.'

'So we have to totter all the way down the garden with the food? Won't it go cold before we get there?' Izzy pulled a face.

'Not at all. We place the hot dishes inside thermal containers.' I frowned as I suddenly remembered how big the thermal serving dishes were. 'Actually, I probably would have two waiting staff out there even for one table. Betty would have had to help Emily this evening. So, I do need two of you out there and someone front of house to meet and greet. I don't trust *you*, Izzy...' I lowered my voice as Betty came in from the garden. 'And Betty would spend all evening gawping at JoJo. Would you do that, Grace? You've met Rafe?'

Izzy and Harriet had a good three-quarters of an hour to practise and hone their waiting skills down in the summerhouse while Grace and Betty helped me put the final touches to the food. It had been raining for the past few days and I'd thought we might have to abandon the idea of al fresco dining, but the day had segued into a perfectly mellow August evening. The night-scented stocks and honeysuckle were already breathing out their heady scent and the newly mown lawns and footpath down to the summerhouse were dry. The lights in the summerhouse twinkled in the warm dusk of the evening: the perfect ambiance for a romantic tryst.

The crunch of tyres on the gravel set my heart pounding and I buried my head in the fridge for a good few seconds before bringing out the bottle of Bollinger JoJo Kennedy had specified, with trembling hands. What if he came into the kitchen? I had a horrid feeling I might punch him hard before begging him not to marry JoJo.

'Right, front door is open,' Grace said, sensing my nervousness. 'I'll go and do my front of house act and take their orders for drinks in the garden.'

'Rafe,' she said gaily as she set off down to the open front door. 'How lovely to see you. Do come into the garden and take a seat. It's far too nice to be inside, don't you think...?'

'Well, there's no *woman* with him,' Grace said, a few minutes later as she bounced back into the kitchen before heading to the bar to find whisky. 'No JoJo Kennedy that I can see. Are you sure you've got this right, Clem?'

'Really? He's by himself?'

'Yes, absolutely. He asked for a whisky and soda and I took him down to the summer house. He's in there all alone.'

'Well, did he say anything?'

'No,' Grace said, shaking her head. 'He seemed surprised when I took him down to the garden, but—'

She was interrupted by the sound of another crunch of wheels on the drive and we all looked at each other.

'Here she is,' I said, my heart descending to somewhere around my knees as I turned back to the beef carpaccio I was fiddling with. 'Front of house again please, Grace.'

'Is she gorgeous?' I asked Izzy and Hat as they returned with plates and waited for me to assemble the lobster.

'Of course she's gorgeous,' Betty piped up from the other end of the kitchen. 'She's a supermodel—what do you expect?'

'No wonder she's so thin,' Izzy said indignantly. 'She's eaten the oysters but just picked at the carpaccio. Do you mind if I…?'

'Help yourself, Izzy. Pointless it going to waste. Anyway, she's probably too nervous to eat, waiting for Rafe to get down on his knees.'

'I have to say, Clem, they don't look to be a couple in love. His body language is all wrong.' Harriet wiped down the granite surface with a cloth. 'I'm going to have a good listen when I go out there again. See what they're saying.'

'Really?' My head came up, just as I saw George racing past the kitchen door. 'Oh, shit. I forgot all about George. I usually put him in his kennel in the kitchen garden when guests are around…' I popped my head out of the kitchen door, shading my eyes against the darkness which seemed to have descended in the last ten minutes. I stepped into the garden, whistling quietly for him to come back to me but could see no sign of him, his blackness completely camouflaged by the inky darkness.

There was no way I was going anywhere near the summerhouse, but it looked as if George had no scruples about doing just that. I was about to retrace my steps and send one of the others after him when a beautiful, tall blonde woman walked up the path towards the house. Dressed in the shortest and slinkiest of midnight-blue dresses, she was instantly recognisable as JoJo Kennedy.

'Hi, you must be Clementine. I've heard all about you.'

Had she? Why?

I smiled, embarrassed, and muttered something about looking for a dog.

'Right,' she said, looking straight at me, taking in every aspect of me. 'I'm looking for the loo.'

I pointed JoJo in the right direction, and she was about to pass me and head for the front door and the Ladies; when she turned and said, smiling, 'It must be very difficult for you, Clementine. I am *so* sorry.'

'What must? What's difficult for me?'

'If I'd known *you* were the woman that's been hanging round Rafe, I certainly wouldn't have booked our special meal here. Rafe is a bit concerned you might have taken his friendship rather too seriously, if you know what I mean. He's feeling very guilty, really quite embarrassed about the whole thing, especially after all you've gone through with the death of your husband...'

Not to mention the death of his chicken?

'Rafe's just been telling me all about it over dinner—delicious food, by the way. I suppose his finding your real mother for you can't have helped with how you feel about him...? You're probably emotionally dependent on him at the moment?'

George came crashing through the hedge of the secret garden, raced over to JoJo and stuck his nose up her crotch.

'Christ! What is it with you northerners and your animals? You shouldn't have dogs in a restaurant. Get off, you damned thing!' JoJo tried to push him away but George was in love. With eyes only for his new friend, he continued to sniff and follow her, gazing up in adoration with his black eyes.

'Heel, George,' I shouted and then, nodding towards the front of the house, said, 'the loo's that way.' I grabbed George's collar, turned on my own heel and, like Cinderella, slunk back to the kitchen where I belonged.

38

'Clem, Clem, *Clem*.' Harriet skidded to a halt on the kitchen floor, flinging the thermal containers onto the centre island. 'He's just told JoJo it's all over. He's in love with you.'

'With me?'

'Yes, his exact words, and he *knew* I was hovering, listening. He said, "I'm sorry, JoJo, but this just isn't going to work. I told you in London that I didn't want to carry this on. I've fallen in love with Clementine..." He looked *right* at me as he said it.' Harriet was almost jumping up and down in her excitement.

'What? That Ralph chap has dumped JoJo Kennedy for *you*...? Betty stopped scraping plates and stared. 'Well, there's nowt so queer as folk.'

'Gosh, this is just like being back at school when you passed messages to your best friend that so and so fancied them. Now, any message back? Shall I go back down there and pass him a *note*...?'

'Just pass me the *wine*, Harriet, I need a drink.' I felt utterly dazed. 'Just tell me again what he said.'

'I'll act it out,' Harriet said, laughing. 'Right, Betty, You're JoJo...'

'I wish,' Betty snorted.

'And I'm Rafe. OK? "I don't want to carry on with *you*, Betty, sorry, JoJo...' Harriet said, affecting a deep, masculine voice. '"I'm in love with *Clementine*...".'

'Erm, would you mind awfully if I tell Clementine that myself?'

We all turned, horrified, to the open kitchen door where Rafe was standing, eyebrows raised.

Harriet went scarlet and, after what was probably only a second's silence, but which seemed to go on forever, Grace poured her a glass of wine. 'Nice one, Hat...'

'Right,' Izzy, said, walking into the kitchen carrying plates of untouched food. 'The party appears to be over... Lobster, anyone?'

'But I feel so sorry for her,' I said as Rafe and I sat in the garden. The inky blackness was lit only by the fairy lights in the huge cedar tree behind us. 'She's driven all this way from London to surprise you and then you turn her down...'

'Clem, I'd already turned her down two weeks ago. I told her I was in love with someone else. I told her all about you.'

For a split-second Rafe seemed unsure of himself—or was it of *me*? He took my hand, looking into my face for confirmation I felt the same way.

'But, why come all this way up here to see you? Why tell

465

Mel in the office it was a special dinner and she was hoping you'd propose? I don't get it.'

Rafe sighed. 'Clem, I honestly knew nothing about what she'd planned. Do you think I'd have come round here, tonight, if I'd known JoJo would suddenly show up?'

'All right then, if you didn't know she'd be here, why *did* you turn up?'

Rafe seemed embarrassed. 'I thought the flowers were from *you*...'

'What flowers?' I stared at Rafe.

'The huge bunch of red roses that arrived at the house a couple of days ago—my poor mother was convinced she had a secret admirer—with a note telling me dinner for two would be served at Clementine's this evening...' Rafe trailed off and then added, 'You did sort of issue an invitation when we were at The Box Tree.'

'But if you told JoJo it was all over a couple of weeks ago, what was she doing up here? I thought she'd gone off with Ted Mallabourne, anyway?'

'JoJo likes the chase; she wouldn't believe anyone capable of kicking her into touch. She'd have been convinced the only reason I told her about you was to get back at her for having a fling with Ted Mallabourne.'

'She *is* utterly ravishing,' I said, gazing down at my black and orange pinny.

'Ferrari body, Mini mind, I'm afraid.' He smiled, stroking my face with the back of his hand. 'She had absolutely no interest in my work—what I'd seen in the Middle East... I don't think she even knows where Syria is, let alone the horror of what's going on there.'

'Well, what about *Hello* magazine?' I asked, still not convinced.

Rafe frowned. 'What about *Hello* magazine? I'm afraid I don't read it.'

'This week's edition. JoJo is in it... and you. You're wrapped round each other—the magazine says you share her flat...?'

'*Her* flat? It's mine.'

'Oh, it's your flat?' I said, surprised. '*Hello* magazine made out it was hers.'

'I told her it was all over between us a couple of weeks ago, that I knew what she'd been up to with Ted Mallabourne. That's when I knew it was over—I didn't care a damn *what* she'd been up to. Anyway, she said would it be OK to use the flat for some photo shoot while I was away—it is a rather lovely flat—and I said OK, as long as she was gone by the time I got back.' Rafe frowned. 'I bet I know the photo you mean—it was taken by a friend of hers, six months ago, just after we met. JoJo does *not* like her own company. Once she realised her fling with Ted Mallabourne was going nowhere, she must have organised this little reunion dinner, assuming I would be won over with her charms once more and—how did she put it?—I'd realise I didn't fancy *the cook* after all...'

'And?'

'And what?'

'*Do* you fancy the cook?'

'That is such a *revolting* expression.' He grinned. '*Fancy* her...? Clem, I'm so in love with her I can't think straight. I can't sleep, I can't eat, I just want to have her up against that cedar tree and…' He smiled again. 'You wouldn't happen to know where this cook is, would you?'

Rafe took my hand and pulled me towards the tree and, with the late summer evening scent of stocks and jasmine assailing my senses, leaned me gently against the cedar, cushioning my head with his arm.

My knees almost buckling from the sheer joy of being kissed so expertly by this beautiful man, I leaned into his neck, breathing in the faint tang of sandalwood.

You're off to the 2016 Olympics, I told my heart and, looking into his blue eyes that were so full of love for me, I kissed him back.

39

The Secret Garden couldn't have looked more ravishing, the gossamer mist already relinquishing its early-morning embrace of the summerhouse to the promising warmth of a glorious June day.

Sarah turned and smiled as George and I made our way across the dew-shot lawn towards her. She was wearing a plain yellow cotton dress but had nothing on her feet while her cloud of still-dark hair framed her pretty face. It was obvious from the state of play in the actual summerhouse that Sarah had been up since the crack of dawn, and I smiled back at her, picturing her leaving the lodge house at the bottom of the garden where she—and also Poppy, now that she'd finished school and was off to Newcastle University in the autumn—had made her home, tripping barefoot through the early morning garden to get ahead with the forthcoming events of the day.

'Are those for in here?' she asked, looking round for a suitable spot to place the large jug of celandine, buttercups, campion and ox-eye daisies I'd gathered from the wild-flower meadow the children and I had created the previous spring.

'No, these are for Peter,' I said. 'I'm going to put the jug down by the bench where the children go when they want to just sit and remember their father.' I kissed Sarah's cheek and continued down, across the Secret Garden, to where the bench stood in a patch of now fading bluebells.

'These are for you, Peter. Thank you for loving me and changing my life.' I placed the jug of flowers at the foot of the bench and, sitting down on the already warm wood, closed my eyes and remembered.

It was a simple ceremony led by Ben Carey, the new curate of Westenbury Church who, still in love with Sarah, had moved heaven—literally—and earth to be given the post on the death of the previous incumbent and so be near the woman he adored. I suspect there was a more physical influence on the interviewing board in the guise of David Henderson than any spiritual intervention, but had kept that little conjecture to myself these past few months.

Not long after Sarah and I had been reunited, Sarah made the huge decision to leave Roger and move out of the rectory into a little cottage near Poppy's school. Both she and Poppy had spent their weekends and holidays with us at Clementine's and Roger Rabbitt, once he'd got over the shock of Sarah daring to leave him, had apparently found much solace in one of his parishioner's arms as well as in, allegedly, her nifty way with beef and Yorkshire pudding.

As we walked up through the fields back to the house

Allegra, in white dress and shoes, ran ahead, racing with Max and Sophie to be first in the Secret Garden to scatter rose petals on the guests as they came through the wooden gate. Betty, in charge of the four young waitresses from the village, was already waiting, a rose behind each ear and, I suspect, already a couple of glasses down, to hand out the first celebratory champagne and canapés.

As we sat down to the meal that Sarah, Jamie—now working for Clementine's after chef Paul's timely defection back to The Ash House—and I had prepared over the past few days, I looked down the table at all the guests who we'd managed to accommodate around the one huge circular table in the summer house.

Sitting together, and laughing loudly at something Sophie had just shouted across at them, were Izzy and Declan, Mel and Julian, Harriet and Nick as well as Grace and her husband, Dan. Down the other end were my parents, the Hendersons, Annabelle Ahern and the Honourable Lady Anne—my mother obviously over the moon to be in such hallowed company as my natural grandmother as well as Yorkshire's top businessman and his wife. Sitting across from me were my half-siblings—Jennifer, Jamie and Poppy—along with their mother—my beloved Sarah—and her partner, Ben Carey.

Sophie rose from her seat and calmly helped mop spilled orange juice from Allegra's new white dress as my daughter surreptitiously buried her stockinged toes into an uninvited guest's black fur under the starched, snow-white tablecloth. Allegra grinned up at her stepsister, pointing to George's just visible black nose, before Sophie returned to her own seat next to Max.

The man to my right stood and, clinking a spoon against his glass, asked that the guests join him in a toast. He looked around the summerhouse, his glance resting first on Theo, his seven-year-old son, and then on Lucy sitting between Sarah and Allegra. Looking down at me with love in his eyes, he raised his glass. 'To Clementine, the one true love of my life.'

I looked back at Rafe, at his dark hair and blue eyes, at his face so full of love for me and knew my cup of happiness ranneth over.

About the Author

Julie Houston is the author of *The One Saving Grace*, *Goodness Grace and Me* and *A Village Affair*, a Kindle top 4 bestseller. She is married, with two grown-up children and a mad cockerpoo and, like her heroine, lives in a West Yorkshire village. She is also a teacher and a magistrate.

Hello from Aria

We hope you enjoyed this book! If you did let us know,
we'd love to hear from you.

We are Aria, a dynamic digital-first fiction imprint from
award-winning independent publishers Head of Zeus.
At heart, we're committed to publishing fantastic
commercial fiction – from romance and sagas to crime,
thrillers and historical fiction. Visit us online and discover
a community of like-minded fiction fans!

We're also on the look out for tomorrow's superstar
authors. So, if you're a budding writer looking for
a publisher, we'd love to hear from you.
You can submit your book online at ariafiction.com/
we-want-read-your-book

You can find us at:
Email: aria@headofzeus.com
Website: www.ariafiction.com
Submissions: www.ariafiction.com/
we-want-read-your-book

- 🄵 @ariafiction
- 🄵 @Aria_Fiction
- 🄾 @ariafiction

Printed in Great Britain
by Amazon

57475190R00286